THE CALL

Derald W. Hamilton

D HAMILTON BOOKS

The Call

Copyright © 2010 Derald W. Hamilton
All Rights Reserved

Editing by Kimberley Rufer-Bach, Sonia Schell; Mary
Linn Roby, Michelle Pollace, Amy Surdacki, Olga Perez,
Lynne Thomas Adler, Todd Rothbard and Jo Sarti
(www.ggservice.com)

Book and cover design by Rebecca Hayes
www.rebeccahayes.us

Published in the United States by
D Hamilton Books
Campbell, CA
www.dhamiltonbooks.com

ISBN-10: 0-9846192-0-8
ISBN-13: 978-0-9846192-0-7

This book is dedicated to the loving memory of my dog, the only recollection of unconditional love I can recall. In a world filled with conditions, demands and expectations, thank you for being the source of that love. Know that you are greatly missed.

Acknowledgements

There are many people who, without their help, cooperation, and encouragement, this book might never have been written. It is to these folks I would like to express my gratitude and heartfelt thanks.

To Mary Burke who helped me realize my writing was better than ordinary; Todd Rothbard who provided me with low rent housing while I was in the throes of bringing Ishmael O'Donnell to life; to Kimberly Ruferbach, Amy Surdacki, Michelle Pollace, Sonia Schell, Mary Linn Roby, Jo Sarti, Anita Johnson, Lynne Thomas Adler, Todd Rothbard and Olga Perez for their help in editing.

Special thanks to: Jo Sarti for my first publishing opportunity, Sonia Schell for providing me with a musical outlet, and to Amy Surdacki for providing me with spiritual parameters.

To Kathy Schmidt, Alexander Clerk, and Barbara Grover for helping keep my psychological balance.

To Becky Hayes for assisting me in the publishing of this novel.

To Dr. Lynne Thomas Adler and Kory Trebbin for their help with the computer.

To Cathleen Broer for her assistance, encouragement, and affirmation of this endeavor.

And finally, thanks to me, because I really worked my @#$% off to bring this novel to fruition.

The Call

Prologue

Last night I dreamed I was back at Parkins Theological Seminary. Once more I found myself standing on the icy cobblestone walkway that extended from the two-story red brick student center to the portentous neoclassical cathedral that stood at the focal point of the campus. It was winter, sometime in the mid 1970s, and snow enveloped the landscape. But with the imperviousness of a dreamer, I did not feel the cold. As I drew nearer to the cathedral, I could see its doors open wide, beckoning me inside its cloistered halls (where the wisdom of the divine awaited to be imparted). Clearly I was one of those whom the Almighty had singled out to do His service.

Stepping inside, I found myself on the stage of an arena that could have seated an audience of thousands. To my right an orchestra pit was filled with giant-sized statues of Jesus and the Greek god Dionysus. I was no sooner able to take in the panoramic view before a dozen or more stagehands ushered me backstage with such words as, "You're late. The show's about to start. You're not even in costume! We've got to get you ready. Do you know your cues? Have you got your lines memorized? And, for God's sake, don't forget your mask! All eyes will be on you. So, go out there and break a leg!"

Less than a heartbeat later, I was on stage before an audience of thousands. I felt my throat constrict, and my mind began to fog over. When I glanced down, I discovered that I was naked, except for the mask.

That's when I woke up, my forehead covered with perspiration and my heart throbbing rapidly in my chest with the impact of a sledgehammer. Only when I realized that I had returned to reality did my panic subside. But the memory of that dream has continued to dog my waking moments, and I have kept the memory to myself for fear of being mocked.

But my time of silence has passed, and my story will not go untold. Just as I, the dreamer, dared to venture inside that cathedral, you will now come with me inside the cloistered halls and meet, as I did, the people who deemed themselves obligated and worthy to pay heed to a curious phenomenon known as a *call*.

I

In The Beginning

The Call

Call me Ishmael. No, I'm not the same Ishmael who went to sea with a nutty captain looking for a big fish. Yet, just as he started out on a quest, I guess I can make a similar claim.

The literal meaning of my name is "God hears." The name also denotes the tribal outcast—a person linked to a group by title, yet set apart in some way as someone not desired in the mainstream of the social order—a pariah, or reject of sorts. In the Bible's Genesis account, Ishmael was the illegitimate son of Abraham and his wife's handmaiden, Hagar, a "necessary" alliance since Abraham was destined to be the father of all the Middle Eastern tribes, and Sarah, his wife, was ninety years old, way past her childbearing years. Abraham's very name means "Father," but he didn't have any kids, a fact that may have caused him a good deal of embarrassment. But because it was his destiny, it was only right that he give the Lord a hand in its fulfillment. And since he even had his dutiful wife's go-ahead, he got to have a little fun in the process. Out of that union with Hagar, Ishmael was born.

According to Biblical accounts, when Ishmael turned thirteen, God rejuvenated Sarah's womb, and brother Isaac was born. Sibling rivalry ensued, and Sarah, angered by Ishmael's mockery of his half-brother, ordered Abraham to get rid of both Ishmael and his mother. God told Abraham to do as his wife commanded and assured him that He would make a nation out of Ishmael as well as out of Isaac's people, although Isaac's people would be God's chosen ones. The two brothers were not destined to see each other again until the time of Abraham's death, decades later.

As I mentioned earlier, Ishmael was the name I was given by my mother, Sarah Elizabeth Olafstotter, a Christian who was always reading the Bible, having hailed from a 1930s Iowa farm family, as did my father, Abe O'Donnell. Measuring six feet, three inches with jet-black hair and striking brown eyes, Abe was quick to gain notoriety as the veritable blight of Jefferson County, and the personification of a rural Studs Lonigan. However, unlike old Studs, that hapless, ill-fated, Irish American, South Chicago youth whose fatal and irreversible ruination paralleled America's stock market crash of 1929, Abe O'Donnell had the good fortune to be born later and was thereby able to partake of the benefits of a nebulous salvation in the form of a world conflict which was to transpire just a few years hence.

Nobody could ever conceive of Abe and Sarah as a couple. Abe stood over a foot taller than Sarah, and while Sarah was meek and soft-spoken, Abe was loud, brash, and insufferable. Then, too, Sarah had graduated second in her high school class and attained a degree in accounting at the local community college while Abe received Ds and Fs in practically every course, excelling only in sports. By the time he had reached the eleventh grade, even his interest in sports began to wane, and he dropped out of high school that same year, thus further reinforcing the notion among the town's folks that Abe O'Donnell was a lost soul destined to walk a short road to perdition.

Unlikely as it seemed, Abe came calling on Sarah, persuaded her to go out with him, and despite his reputation, he conducted himself like a perfect gentleman. He held the car door for Sarah as she entered and exited his car. He made no improper moves and was polite in his conduct and use of language. This was their first outing; there would be many more to follow, much to the astonishment and chagrin of her family and the community-at-large. Sarah's father repeatedly warned her about Abe, but his words fell on deaf ears. Love had blossomed, and the only entity that stood any chance at all of driving a wedge between the two of them was the up-and-coming World War II. Abe was working on his grandfather's farm when he received his draft notice; it arrived in the mail shortly after the attack on Pearl Harbor.

Army life agreed with Abe. He exuded enthusiasm for everything it threw his way, from K.P. to close order drill. It was said he displayed a greater love for war than General George Patton and looked forward to the experience of combat like a child looks forward to visiting a candy store.

During the Battle of Africa, young Abe was accorded a battlefield commission. He also distinguished himself with a Bronze and Silver Star and five purple hearts. In practically every aspect tangible to Abe at the time, the war and Army life provided him the opportunity to flourish. In fact, he liked it so much he decided to make a career of it.

This came as somewhat of a shock to his bride-to-be back home, but Abe was firm on the matter and would countenance no opposition.

After World War II, Abe and Sarah were married at the Lutheran Church in their hometown of Cooper. It was a festive event that all the locals attended. Sarah wore the traditional white gown. Abe was garbed in his military attire.

At the reception in the church social hall, the minister pulled Abe to one side and said, "Look Abe, I know you've been all over the world and have probably seen a lot of things, but your bride's never journeyed much beyond Jefferson County. You're going to need to be gentle, because this move you're getting set to make is going to be rough on her."

Abe laughed and said, "Don't worry about it. I know just how to handle her."

The minister pushed his glasses up on his nose and said, "I hope for both your sakes that's true. And also, the honeymoon's going to be a shock for her. I've known your bride since she was a little girl and she's very sensitive and might be a bit scared of the transition married life holds—and I believe you know what I'm referring to."

Abe grinned, "Yeah," he said.

"Now Abe, are you going to be a man and maybe wait for the second night, or are you going to be a mouse

The Call

and demand it right then on the first night?"

Abe smiled and said, "Well sir, I'm what you call a rat. I got it the night before."

A few years later my mother found herself pregnant with twins. Naturally, she wanted to give her children biblical names. However, in spite of all her reading of the scriptures, her knowledge of the Bible failed to evolve beyond a superficial understanding. She never could fathom the implications of names, or what nefarious themes they might carry with them. My identical twin's name, Isaac, means "laughter," an unlikely irony since any laughter to be connected with him would come to represent bitterness and anger, as a result of a singular occurrence in which, at the moment of his death, his life's essence became one with mine. Isaac died from the measles just prior to his third birthday. I also had the measles; our temperatures exceeded 105 degrees, but I survived. My earliest childhood recollection was the death of my twin brother, when I was lying in my bed in our room as my brother breathed his last. At the exact moment of his death, I could feel his spirit flow into me and merge with my own.

Being so young I didn't comprehend what was happening, but as I grew older I found the words to describe what were to become an indelible memory that, to this day, I can recall as readily as if it happened yesterday. An overpowering, sweeping sensation that seemed to come at me from the outside, and like a well-focused whirlwind, it penetrated the innermost core of my being, leaving me beset with chills and inward convulsions as if two souls were vying for control. The intensity of these feelings lasted for many minutes. I may have screamed, but no one responded. The room seemed to spin while shapes appeared contorted, and a loud cacophony of sounds thundered in my brain. Then all was still and quiet; the sensations dissipated as quickly as they arrived. From that point onward I often felt strange, conflicting sensations quavering within me, and seizures would take hold, which grew more intense as I approached maturity.

My mother, now Sarah Elizabeth O'Donnell, deeply mourned my brother's death. It was a difficult and lengthy mourning. Often she would take me to my brother's gravesite, where she would stand, holding my hand, and weep for extended periods. Then she would say to me, "Your brother was such a good boy. You two would have been so happy going through life together. I just know you would. But now he's gone, and that never can be."

My legs would grow tired from our prolonged interludes of standing by Isaac's grave, but my mother's words left a strong impact on my young, impressionable mind, and as time passed, began to plague me. But even as a child, I wondered what my mother's response would be if she knew that the child standing beside her at Isaac's gravesite was actually the two of us.

Living with Isaac's soul was something I dared not share with my parents or any friends I made during our short stays at military posts, but it caused external conflicts all the same due to my inclination to withdraw into myself. In the fifth grade, for example, I was called on the carpet for my attitude. When report card time

The Call

came, the teacher, a gruff, aging spinster, summoned me to her desk and told me that I seemed to have very little interest in what was going on in class. I saw little reason to contest the teacher's observations. All the moving about we did while my father was in the service of our country had kept me from establishing roots, not to mention the fact that Isaac's constant badgering had caused me to turn more and more inward. Father, being the martinet that he was, gave me further cause for retreat.

I dismissed the teacher's words shortly after our talk. However, my mother was as quick to express her disappointment upon viewing the unsatisfactory mark on my report card, as my father was to become enraged and indignant, towering over me and pointing his finger in my face. "Look, you little bastard!" he said, "You're going to start showing a little more enthusiasm for school and for life in general, or I'm gonna drop-kick you in the fucking balls!"

Mother, who frequently defended me, was silent this time, a reminder that ultimately I would have to defend myself against him alone. But as yet I did not know how.

Throughout my formative years, we moved around a lot, as military families do, enjoying what my mother referred to as a nomadic existence, one tour being very much like another. But, during my thirteenth year, there was one tour of duty I remember that seemed to mark a turning point in my life. It was right after my father had finished a hardship tour in Korea and we had accordingly endured a thirteen-month period of separation. A letter arrived three months prior to the completion of his

Korean tour, stating that we were to be stationed at an Army post in Virginia.

It was typical of the many posts I had seen, a base comprised of modest wooden buildings, with the exception, of course, of the general's quarters with its meticulously manicured hedges and grass mowed as short as a G.I. haircut.

Base housing, too, bore great similarities to that we had lived in before, comprised chiefly of tract homes, which, with the exception of the general's home, were one story with three bedrooms and one-and-a-half baths. The powers that be deemed it best to segregate the housing of the officers' families from those of enlisted men's, which meant that, among other things, officers' housing came with lawns already installed while enlisted men were required to install their own, frequently with little success.

Upon our arrival, certain adjustments needed to be made. Mother and I needed to acclimate to Father acting as the head of the house again, and one of the things that he insisted on was that we start attending church together. I found this turn of events to be a bit strange and somewhat inconsistent with Father's character, particularly since his interest in matters of a religious or spiritual nature up to this point had always been very marginal.

One evening, as we were clearing the table of dirty dishes, I asked Father what brought about this change. The only answer I could get was "It's just a good habit to get into."

Somehow I instinctively knew the conversation would not go much further, but youthful impulse prodded me to inquire some more, "But, Dad," I said, "I don't get why this is suddenly so important."

Again he replied, "Because, it's just a good habit to get into." This forced closure to the conversation. After all, it was not my place to question my elders, and as he put it, "There are some things you just do! You don't go asking 'why' all the time!"

The base chapel was, outwardly, just another renovated, white building with tinted glass in its windows, a steeple, and a sign at the front denoting its function. When we started taking part in services at the base chapel it became very apparent why my father was now so gung-ho about church attendance, the base general and his wife being devout churchgoers, setting an example for the other officers and their families.

The first sporadically attended service we took part in was presided over by a junior chaplain by the name of Captain Thomas Sutton, a short man with a paunch and light brown hair shorn to a flattop who, thanks to his lack of charisma, was forced to depend on the spirited content of his sermons and his ability to move inductively in its presentation. In the congregation were his wife and four daughters, whom I later came to know as Becky, Paulette, Mindy, and Cindy. Almost instantly my eyes were fixed upon the eldest—Becky, a pert, clear-faced girl with dark brown hair.

Right after the sermon, when it came time for the congregation to partake in Communion, I started to go to the altar, but Mother grabbed my arm and told me that I couldn't participate in this particular ritual.

"Why not?" I asked.

"Because you've never been baptized! You've never professed to believe in God!"

"I don't. So why do you drag me to church?"

"Let him come," my father said.

"But Abe," she protested, "he's never ..."

"It's okay. Let him come."

"Abe, this is wrong."

"*Let him come*," Father insisted.

Mother looked angry. Up to this point she had been the one who told me that Communion was a ritual reserved only for those who believed. But now that Father had assumed the lead in matters of a religious nature, it was suddenly all right for me, a nonbeliever, to take part in this ritual. Why, I wondered, had the rules suddenly changed? I wanted answers, but all I had was my father's go-ahead, which, in matter of fact, fell only inches short of a direct order. I backed away and assumed my position in the pews. I couldn't put my finger on it, but something did not seem quite right about my father giving his permission. I was later to find out why.

After dismissal from the worship service, when the three of us were out of earshot of fellow parishioners, I received a brief but stern reprimand from my father to the effect that, when I was told by him to do something I was expected to do it. "You don't wait around for us to explain our reasons," he added.

After chapel services, coffee and donuts were served in the social hall, another wooden, white building positioned directly in back of the chapel. It was there that Becky walked up and introduced herself to me. "Hi," she said, "my name's Rebecca Sutton, but everybody calls me Becky. What's yours?"

The Call 15

She looked at me with smiling eyes, and I felt drawn, as though a part of me was one with her. Oblivious to the drone of the people around us, I could think of no one but her. And yet there was a conflicting sensation, discordant echoes of reproach from my dual self, telling me, "No! She's not yours! How dare you! She's mine!" a voice which, with substantial effort, I was able to ignore.

Becky and I became friends quickly. It helped that our families became close, since, as a consequence, Becky and I were accorded more time together. On occasion we would take in a movie, and although I wanted to hold her hand, I could never muster enough courage. Our folks also took us on frequent car trips where, in the back seat, we indulged in intense conversations, oblivious to our surroundings, often looking deeply into each other's eyes.

At home I sought to share with Mother my concerns and curiosity about our budding relationship. Yet, it seemed that each time I approached the topic, my father, who always seemed to be within earshot, would intercede with a warning that if I kept on worrying like that, I'd get ulcers. He repeated this somber admonition on several occasions, each time with increasing fervency. I often wondered why he harbored such an obsession with ulcers and why he was so insistent that I was going to get them.

While we were stationed in Virginia, the Cuban Missile Crisis developed. As the situation intensified, it was announced that President Kennedy was to address the nation. In response, the base general issued an order stating that all military personnel and their families were to watch the broadcast. This insured that I made a point of not doing so.

After Kennedy's speech, base activity revved into high gear. My father increasingly found himself confined to the base, sometimes putting in fourteen to sixteen hour workdays. This lasted for several weeks and was incredibly stressful. Thanks to orders direct from Washington, constant alert status was maintained.

After several weeks of accommodating these accelerated demands, my father collapsed under the strain and was rushed to the base infirmary. Dr. Harold Steiner, a tall, overbearing, imposing man with a full head of jet-black hair and a stern expression, met mother and me in the waiting room to tell us that my father had developed a severe case of peptic ulcers.

I covered my mouth with my hand, trying to conceal my laughter. I found the irony of this set of circumstances extremely amusing, given Father's near constant admonition that I'd be the one getting ulcers.

"Yep," Dr. Steiner replied. "I'm ordering him hospitalized. He'll be placed on a bland diet, and priority will be given to the coating of that ulcer."

My father was hospitalized on post for approximately three months. During that time he was placed on a bland diet, regularly medicated, and closely monitored, and every half-hour he was made to drink a half-a-glass of half 'n' half for purposes of coating the ulcer. He could only be released on Sundays to attend church with his family.

Even though my mother was continually emphasizing to me the seriousness of the situation, a part of me had to laugh, and I would frequently go off in

The Call

private to do so. Life is full of ironies, and I found this one to be hilarious.

Father's ulcer created another problem, namely flatulence, an item Dr. Steiner insisted he should not attempt to control. The next Sunday this became a real issue. The chaplain in charge was Colonel William Fleetwood, a short, heavy-set man who must have swallowed a megaphone as a youth. Furthermore, what he lacked in physical stature, he more than made up for by his own brand of charisma and presence in the pulpit. His sermon that morning sizzled with hellfire as he called upon all of us wayward sinners to bow down in repentance. He spoke with such force and conviction that I could almost feel the devil's pitchfork piercing my flesh, prior to my being enveloped in eternal flames, a certain consequence were I not to turn away from my wicked ways. "There are none righteous, not one," he declared fervently, "and all man's righteousness is as filthy rags." Understandably, given my status as a nonbeliever, I began to feel certain uneasiness. As for my father, he began feeling something different. At the sermon's climax, he began to experience severe gas pains. Remembering what the doctor had told him, he wasted no time in releasing the flatulence in the form of a loud blast that reverberated throughout the chapel. The sound was bad enough but the smell was even worse.

Everyone was staring at us with shock and indignation. In the front pew, Becky was holding her hand over her mouth to keep from laughing.

The conclusion of the service made things worse instead of better. My father, never one to suffer embarrassment gracefully, was quick to place the blame on me. The general's wife, a dowdy woman nearing sixty with bluish gray hair, spoke her mind: "Young man, I thought that was the most disgraceful display of disrespect and misconduct ever to come into God's house! I hope your father has some fitting punishment in store for you!"

"Don't worry!" my father assured her. "He knows he's being punished when we get home!"

"But I didn't do it!" I protested. "He did!"

"If you were mine," an old man blustered, shaking a finger in my face, "I swear you wouldn't be able to sit down for a week!"

"Blaming a good man like your father for what you know you did!" the young wife of an enlisted man cried. "That's disgraceful."

"I think you ought to apologize to your father right now, young man!" the general's wife exclaimed.

I met with Becky later on during the social hall gathering. "You really let one fly during services today," she said, smiling slyly.

"I didn't do it!" I protested. "But why should you believe me? Nobody else does."

"I believe you." She assured me, which, had it not been for Isaac's voice, would have reassured me.

After the social hall gathering, Mother and I drove Father back to the base infirmary and accompanied him to his quarters in utter silence.

After Father had gotten situated in his room, Mother turned to me and suggested that I go into the waiting room and watch TV. "There's something I need to discuss with your father in private," she added.

"Okay." I walked over to the TV area, but nothing could drown out my parents' voices as my mother defended me, and my father insisted that, in shifting the blame, he had done nothing to really hurt me. When my mother accused him of not giving a damn about his family's well-being, he continued to protest, but when she turned on the big guns and told him that she knew he had been making inquiries about my being baptized without even consulting me, it was clear that he had been bested. Luckily for Father, the doctor chose that moment to interrupt, and when Mother told him what had happened in church, he collapsed in laughter. It was, in its own way, a comedy of manners that I was almost glad I had not missed.

But a somber tone was soon to follow as a nurse appeared just then to demand to know what was going on. "I've been receiving complaints about the noise level." Then she looked at the doctor desperately clutching his sides. "Doctor?" The nurse stood there, her eyes fixed upon the doctor, her face rendering a look of amazement and concern.

"I'd better call the paramedics,." the nurse said, then turned and rushed to the intercom. The paramedics came and carted Dr. Steiner over to emergency.

An hour later, the head of the base hospital unit, Lt Colonel William Williams, entered Abe's room. He was a tall, husky-looking individual in his late fifties. He stood before my mother and father rendering a look void of expression and said, "Major O'Donnell, we just lost your attending physician to a case of ruptured appendicitis. A new doctor will be assigned to you in due course.

Meantime, a full report detailing the cause of his demise is being compiled. Due to the sensitive nature of the report's content, the staff here at the hospital has deemed it best to render the contents classified. This means that no one with knowledge of the incidents leading up to our physician's demise is to render this information public. To do so would be cause for breach of confidence."

"Meaning?" my mother asked.

"Meaning," replied Colonel Williams, "that neither of you are to reveal the fact that your husband was the one who expelled gas in church. We cannot have you compromising the dignity and decorum we bestow upon our officers. We are called to lead by example. The revelation of such a foible would make this task exceedingly difficult for both the major here and for his fellow officers, and it could serve to undermine the state of efficiency we need to maintain here on this base, which is of a vital nature now given the state of emergency brought about by the Cuban Missile Crisis."

I could almost feel myself losing my morning meal as I listened to the colonel's pronouncement.

"I see," I heard my mother say. "So my son needs to continue to bear the brunt of the ridicule that rightly should go to his father?"

"Exactly, Mrs. O'Donnell."

"I understand! You're all a bunch of bastards!" My mother quipped, then turned abruptly.

Colonel Williams halted her progress. "Mrs. O'Donnell," he said, "this is the Army. Certain things must take precedent. In this instance, the concerns of national security far outweigh your son's dignity."

My mother glared angrily at Colonel Williams and

said, "You are a bastard! Then she shifted her glare to my father and said, "And you, Major Abe O'Donnell ... don't think you'll always have a war to hide behind!" She turned and hurriedly walked out.

"It's not my fault I got sick!" my father shouted.

My mother and I left the hospital around three that afternoon. As she drove, I noted the tear stains on her face. I found my voice halfway through the trip. "Mother, I didn't let that fart."

Mom smiled and said, "I know you didn't, Ishmael dear. There's something I need to discuss with you when we get home."

"What is it, Mom?"

"Please, Ishmael. I need time to gather my thoughts. This isn't an easy thing for me to talk about, and it's probably going to be even less easy for you to hear."

My curiosity was quickened by my mother's words while uneasiness gripped at the lining in my stomach. If I wasn't to receive a scolding for my alleged folly in God's house, then what else could my mother have to say to me? The rest of the trip left me in a most anxious state of mind.

At home, once in the living room, Mother said, "Sit down Ishmael, please."

By now my curiosity was killing me. Whenever Mom put a "please" at the end of a sentence, it always signaled something bad that was coming.

"Ishmael," she said, clearly agonizing over her choice of words, "I might as well confess this to you. I'm a lousy parent. I've tried the best I know how, but try as I might I just can't seem to cut it."

"What makes you say that?" I asked. There was something about the way she was looking at me that awakened within me a sense of pity.

"I don't know how you're going to take what I have to tell you, but if I keep this from you, I'm afraid it's going to eat me alive. After your brother died I was sick a lot. Some might say it was from the grief brought on by losing Isaac, I don't know. He was such a sweet, loving little boy. Even today I can feel his arms tugging about my neck."

I was becoming increasingly uneasy. It was difficult enough for me to cope with the fact that Isaac had taken up residence inside me. I certainly did not want to be reminded how much my mother had loved him.

"After I'd been hospitalized numerous times, your father finally got fed up and said to me 'I'm sick of putting up with all your illnesses! You don't care whether you get better or not. And if you don't care, then neither do I. Good-bye and to hell with you. I'm going home to Dad.' Those were his exact words." It was becoming clear to me that I was going to have to grit my teeth and listen to this, although I hated hearing about such an interaction. Somehow it awakened within me an enhanced sense of what a shaky, clay-like foundation my life was seemingly built upon. "When I told my doctor what your father had said to me he said, 'Mrs. O'Donnell, you have two boys. One's just a toddler. The other will be a boy the rest of his life. As long as you stay married to Abe, you will always have at least one boy.'"

When I asked her why she hadn't left him, she sighed. "Because I'm a Christian," she explained, "and I

The Call

believe very strongly in the sanctity of marriage ... for richer, for poorer, for better, for worse, in sickness and in health, until death do us part. Besides, in my day they taught us that once you make your bed, you lie in it. And if you want to know the truth, I knew that if I were to divorce him, I wouldn't get a dime of spousal or child support from him."

It took her a few minutes to regain her composure. Then she looked squarely at me and said, "Your father is a man with very fixed priorities. His first priority is the Army, his second is himself, and if there's anything left over, it's for us. That's the way it is and that's the way it always will be. I can't right the wrong he did you, and I hope you can forgive me."

"What's to forgive? Father's the one who should be here crawling on his knees begging forgiveness."

"He won't; you'll never get an apology out of him. To his mind he did what was necessary, and we need to respect his reasoning. We're extensions of him and we have a duty to act in accordance with that role. It's part of the game."

"Like in Oscar Wilde's book *A Portrait of Dorian Grey*. He's the one who sins, and we're the portrait that bears the imprint of his evil deeds ..."

"Since when have you read Oscar Wilde?" Mom asked, intrigued.

"For a book report in English class."

"I'm not sure I approve of you reading Oscar Wilde at your age, but yes, that's how the game is played."

"Well," I said, "I don't want to play anymore."

Once having stated my position I kept it, not only

refusing to attend services, but staying strictly away from the hospital. For once, I didn't care about the consequences.

As the weeks passed, new chaplains came pouring onto the base. One junior chaplain by the name of Lieutenant Festus Moran, a slender man in his thirties who wore wire-rimmed glasses, and whose light brown hair was thinning noticeably in the front, was intent on starting up a children's Sunday school program. And what better way to guarantee himself an audience than to visit all the families and make sure that they would see to it that their offspring became his captive audience. He even visited my father in the hospital to enlist his assistance, assuring him that I would be a welcome addition to his Sunday school program.

Coming across my name on the roster, he took note of my conspicuous absenteeism, and one Sunday afternoon, after services, he visited my convalescing father at the base infirmary.

"I'm trying to put together a Sunday school program," he said, "and I note that you have a son … Ishmael I believe is his name."

"Yep," my father said with a sigh, "he's my son."

"I also note that he hasn't been in church attendance for the past several weeks," the lieutenant continued.

"I've been trying to figure that out myself. All my wife will tell me is that he didn't feel like coming, and she didn't feel like arguing with him. That's another reason why I want to get out of here. I'm absent from the house for just a few weeks, and the whole family goes to hell. Like I always say, a boy needs a father's good strong

The Call

arm for guidance."

"I'm glad you feel that way, Sir, because I'm sure your son would make a welcome addition to our Sunday school program."

And that was how our next confrontation began.

I received a phone call that Sunday evening from Becky who had called to voice her concern regarding my absenteeism. "Are you okay?" she asked.

"That depends on how you define the word." I replied. "I'm all right physically. But otherwise, I'm not so sure."

"Well, I also called you to say I miss you," she said, suddenly sounding shy.

I suggested an after-school rendezvous, and for the next several days we met at the playground and played as if we were little kids, swinging on the swings, teeter-tottering, crossing the parallel bars, and rolling in the grass. One day, as we lay gazing up at the sky, Becky asked me if I believed in God, and when I told her that I didn't, she asked me why.

"Well, to believe in something means you have to have faith in it, right? I see nothing to have faith in. All I see is hypocrisy and insanity."

"You're still mad about what happened a few weeks ago." She said with a note of shrewdness in her voice.

"Wouldn't you be?" I retorted.

Becky shrugged and said, "I don't know. I've never been put in that type of situation. What's it like?"

I looked up at the sky trying to gather my thoughts. "It's like I'm not seen as *me*. I'm always viewed as something else, and that something else is always what somebody over me says I am. It's like standing in a shadow and never being able to step out and reveal who you really are."

Becky smiled. "That's interesting. I've always wondered who I was, too, and how others see me."

"No kidding?"

"Yes. Ishmael?" Becky then gave me a coy look.

"What?"

"Do you think I'm pretty?"

And when I told her I did, she leaned over and kissed me. It was a long kiss, and afterward, before I could stop her, she ran away, leaving me with my head reeling.

Father was released from the infirmary on Friday of that week. Mother drove down to pick him up, but I refused to go. He asked for me as soon as he stepped in the house. When Mother told him about Becky, adding that she thought she'd been good for me because my grades had been improving, and I had actually been reading something as challenging as Oscar Wilde, my father fell into a rage, demanding to know why she hadn't insisted I attend chapel services and visit him in the hospital. My mother, as usual, tried to make a point of the fact that I was my own person, but by the time I came home, my father had whipped himself into full fury.

"When he gets in, we're going to have a little talk," my father said.

Unfortunately, I chose that moment to walk in from outside. Father turned abruptly and faced me. He pointed to a chair. "Sit down! I wanna talk to you!" he said in a loud, commanding tone. "You haven't been attending church services with your mother, and you also haven't been visiting me. And I'd like to know why."

"Well, Dad," I said as I looked at him with my self-styled shit-eating grin, "who'd welcome a boy who farts in church?"

"You keep mouthing off like that and you're gonna be finding out something. How do you think it makes your mother and I look when our son doesn't show up on Sundays?"

"About as bad as it makes me look when people think I farted in church."

"That's beside the point. Look, I have a peptic ulcer, and I've been told by my doctor that I'm supposed to avoid stress as much as possible. So beginning this Sunday, we are going to start attending church again, as a family."

"Oh come on," I spat out the words. "It's so obvious you're just doing this to suck up to the chaplains and that holier-than-thou-general."

My father bellowed, whipping off his belt, "You've been asking for this for a long time!"

My mother lunged between us. "Don't you lay a hand on that boy!"

"Get out of my way! He's my son, and he needs to be disciplined!"

"He's *our* son, and you need me to agree to a drastic step like this."

"I need what?"

"Put down that belt, Soldier! That's an order!"

I stood there transfixed by my two embattled

parents, each vying desperately for control of the situation. Endless moments elapsed. Father relinquished his hold on the belt. Then, crumpling over and grasping his sides, he headed for the bedroom. "Ohhh, the pain," he cried. "My ulcer is killing me."

"Take your medication, Abe," Mother told him "You'll live." She added, She then turned toward me and said, "Look, go to church with us this Sunday, okay? Please? Do it for me."

The following Sunday the three of us arrived at the chapel. Before we could enter the building, Lt. Moran approached us. "Good morning, Sir." He said, extending his hand. Glad you could be with us today. And this must be the young man I've been hearing so much about."

I grinned half-heartedly.

"Well," he continued, "we just started our Sunday school program and we'd sure like to have you with us."

"Thank you," I said, "but I'm afraid I'm not …"

"He'll be there," my father said in a grim, authoritative tone.

"It's over at the chapel annex. I'll show you." And Lt. Moran, placing his hand firmly on my shoulder, escorted me to the chapel annex. When I looked back at Mother, she smiled and waved.

The annex was a small building filled with Sunday school paraphernalia. Bibles and picture books expounded on biblical themes, plus toys and board games abounded on the shelves and on the floor. On the walls were several pictures of Jesus. One picture portrayed him kneeling in the Garden of Gethsemane, another showed him dancing around in a circle with children, another was of him on the cross fully clothed, and another was a full-faced portrait of Jesus. Children of various age levels were sectioned off by way of partitions. What must have been a preschool class was singing *Jesus Loves Me*, and at other tables, grouped according to age, children were busy coloring pictures, or constructing cathedrals out of Styrofoam.

Lt. Moran escorted me over and introduced me to the class as well as the teacher, who happened to be his wife. She was a perky lady with an effervescent personality, coupled with a condescending attitude toward the children in her care. Being with her was like being enrolled in Miss Nancy's Romper Room School. We were all her charges, and much as she wanted us to love her, she wanted even more to make sure we respected her. "Okay children," she began as I took one of the chairs, which were arranged, in a circle around her, "we're in class now, and we're here to learn what God has to teach us."

I was relieved to see that Becky was one of the group, but not so pleased to find myself sitting beside Colonel Fleetwood's son, Eugene. He was a capacious, sandy-haired boy about a half-a-head shorter than me, yet clearly outweighing me by at least seventy-five pounds. In every way he appeared to be a younger version of his father, replete with the megaphone mouth and a face that seemed fixed in a pugnacious snarl. "Well," he said in a loud voice, "if it isn't the old fart blaster himself!"

Everyone tittered and even Becky grinned.

"Eugene!" Mrs. Moran snapped. "That was uncalled for!"

"That's okay, Ma'am," I responded. "If you really

want to smell a stink, move a little closer to Eugene. His bad breath and body odor would rival a stock yard."

The class morphed to gales of laughter, which dissolved into a wary silence when Eugene, clearly enraged, threw himself at me and knocked me to the floor where, in a desperate attempt to regain my freedom, I lifted up my right knee and caught him in the crotch, an impact that sent him reeling, clutching at his testicles. This gave me the opportunity to punch him full in the face. I'm not sure what would have happened if I hadn't been restrained by one of the attendants.

"Hold on, son," he said. "That's no way for Christian brothers to act."

"I'm nobody's brother!" I retorted. "Let go of my arm!"

"Now everyone settle down!" Mrs. Moran cried. "This is no way to act in God's house."

"I thought this was just the annex," Becky said.

Once again everyone laughed. .

"That's enough!" Mrs. Moran shouted. "I will not tolerate this conduct, nor will I accept disparaging comments about a place of worship! You should all be deeply ashamed of yourselves! We're here to learn about how to be God's servants, and God does not like it when we behave this way toward one another!" After five minutes of what Mrs. Moran called a "time out," she resumed the class.

Mrs. Moran then began to talk about the squalid conditions the people in Hong Kong lived under, after which she instructed us to pray for these people. Pray? I thought. I never prayed in my life.

That afternoon, after we had returned home and had

The Call   31

lunch, we received a call from Colonel Fleetwood. Eugene had reported the Sunday school incident to his father, and Mrs. Moran had backed up his claim. My father said he'd have a talk with me.

"Ishmael," he demanded, "did you knee Eugene in the crotch?"

"He was on top of me," I retorted, "What was I supposed to do, die from lack of air?"

"Now look!" he shouted. "I've had just about enough of you and your sarcasm! Get in the car!"

"Why? Where are we going?"

"Don't give me a hard time," he commanded.

"But where are we going?"

"You're going to apologize to Eugene for what you did."

"Why should I apologize when I'm not the least bit sorry?"

My father was just reaching for his belt when my mother came into the room. Giving him a withering look, she listened to my account of what had happened with Eugene and then said that she needed to talk to my father in private.

Next week I accompanied my parents to church but did not attend the Sunday school class. Once again there was a gathering of parishioners in the social hall in back of the chapel where coffee and pastries were served. I was off by myself munching on some fruitcake, when Lt. Moran appeared and after a few desultory remarks about my not attending Sunday school, mentioned that he had heard that I was thinking of being baptized.

"Look," I replied, "I don't know who told you that,

but that's not true. I have no intentions of getting baptized. I only go to church because my folks tell me to. It's not like I want to be here or anything."

And excusing myself, I walked away. Lt. Moran impressed me as a poor man's Wally Cox, and I definitely didn't like being around him.

But the spirited young lieutenant was not one to take my no for an answer. Following our latest encounter he appeared in my father's office almost on a daily basis and relentlessly badgered him about why I didn't attend Sunday school. My father, who would bring the matter to my attention, and, in turn, would unremittingly hassle me, made me aware of this interaction. One day, as I was in the driveway, standing by the car, Father approached me glaring down at me with a strong paternal stare. "Ishmael," he said. "why won't you go to Sunday school?"

I looked up at him and replied, "Because I don't like Sunday school."

"Well, I have to do things I don't like to do. Maybe I don't like going to church."

"I don't either. But I go."

"Now look, Ishmael! There are some things we just do. We don't ask why. We don't discuss and debate. We just do them because they have to be done."

"Yeah. I've run into a lot of things like that since we've been living here," I said going into the house and heading for my room only to be intercepted by my mother who asked me what was wrong.

"It's Dad," I replied. "We had another 'talk' about Sunday school."

"I've been meaning to talk to you about that, too."

The Call

"Ah Mom …"

"I don't mean like that. I just had a question for you. I know you don't like Eugene Fleetwood, but I can't help but think there's something more about Sunday school besides Eugene that's turning you off to the notion of going."

"It's the teacher." I admitted.

"What's wrong with the teacher?"

"She talks down to us. She tells us to do things I can't do."

"Like?"

"Pray."

"That's right … I never taught you about praying. I'm sorry."

"It's not something I really want to do, anyway."

"All praying is, is talking to God. He's open to hearing whatever you have to say."

"But she tells us what to talk to Him about," I protested.

"Well, Ishmael, you've got a mind. I believe you can decide for yourself what you think is worth talking to Him about."

"Never really had anything to say."

"Well, when you do, I'm sure He'd be more than happy to listen," she suggested.

Later that evening, after supper, as I was doing my homework, I heard my mother talking to my father in the kitchen, "Look, Abe," she said, "knock it off with the Sunday school stuff. He's already had one bad experience and he most likely doesn't want another."

"Ahhh, it ain't gonna hurt him," my father replied.

"And it's not going to help him, either. Do you ever hear a word of what I tell you? He goes to church now. That's more than he was doing when you were hospitalized. And he's content to do so, as long as he doesn't have to sit with you. Now I regard that as positive. He's even asking me questions about God, and I can tell him about what a loving Heavenly Father we have, one capable of forgiving us all our transgressions. So back off, or you'll ruin what little headway I've been able to make."

Ironically, not only did my father back off, he actually stopped going to Sunday service except when Colonel Fleetwood or Captain Sutton was preaching. Before this, he had not been so bold. But the post had recently changed generals, and the current general in charge really didn't care about whether or not the men under his command attended chapel services.

As for my mom and me, we continued to attend services. She attended because she was part of the choir. I attended to get away from Dad.

While we were still stationed in Virginia, President Kennedy was assassinated, an event that stunned the entire nation. Everyone I came in contact with rendered an outward appearance of mourning, for to do otherwise bordered on sheer blasphemy. My father was no exception; registering his outrage by destroying my Vaughn Meter *First Family* album, wherein the president was lampooned and satirized.

The entire base flocked to both the chapel and the parade grounds for memorial and commemorative services to pay tribute to a man who inspired so much

The Call

pride and affection. People openly shed tears during chapel service. At the parade grounds, there was a full uniformed assembly that marched in tribute while at varying intervals "Hail *To the Chief*" was played, during which time we were all called upon to stand.

Becky sat at my side for most of the services. During the course of these ceremonies, particularly the one at the parade grounds, she held my hand and wept. At fourteen, I was at a loss to comprehend why there was so much emotional solemnity surrounding the event, but it sure felt great holding Becky's hand, and for this reason I discreetly withheld my apathy over the platitudes rendered on behalf of the late president and turned my attention to the welcome task of being Becky's comforter.

The bond between Becky and me grew stronger. We were constantly in each other's company, romping about the playground, rolling in the grass, and taking long walks during which time we carried on earnest discussions about life. As the months passed, I came to believe, at long last, I could silence the voice inside me that told me what I had with Becky wasn't truly mine. Yet, while that voice remained silent, reality spoke with a thundering resonance. Both our fathers received orders from Washington, D.C., calling for their transfers to Korea.

It was on a Wednesday that both our parents met us after school to tell us where they were being sent and when. In both instances, we were only given five weeks to pack up our lives in Virginia and prepare ourselves to make another move. Becky and her family would return to their home in Kentucky, while my mother and I would return to California.

On our last night together, Becky and I met and talked for hours on her porch. To my surprise her folks allowed us to be alone. I can still recall the grief I felt at losing the closest friend I had ever had. We lingered until her parents began flickering the porch lights off and on, and after a last embrace, swore that we'd keep in touch and meet again someday. I desperately wanted to believe that to be true. Yet, having been brought up as part of a military family gave me good reason to be less than optimistic about the prospects. That same evening at home, sensing my sadness, my father approached me and said, "Look, I know it's hard leaving your friends like this, but you need to start looking forward to making new friends."

"Why?" I said. "They'll just be dead to me in the end. And the leaving hurts too much."

"That's a loser's attitude," he told me, "Feeling sorry for yourself doesn't do anyone a damn bit of good." He turned and went back to the den and started leafing through his papers.

Great, I thought, once again my life's being turned upside down, and I can't even be allowed the luxury of a little self-pity. I'll bet if Mother died, he'd only allow me ten minutes to cry.

Mother was upset too, and, as I learned later, with good reason. It seemed, on numerous occasions such as this when geographic separation was inevitable, my father had taken a mistress. But my mother had been well trained over the years, keeping her feelings to herself, and saying nothing. Little did I suspect that such a practice would inexorably cut short her life by many years.

The Call

A year passed. My father completed his tour of Korea just as I completed the ninth grade. It had been a pleasant tour for him—so much fun, in fact, that he had actually considered requesting an extension for another six months. But in the end, for reasons neither my mother nor I were privy to, he decided against it. Instead, just before his homecoming he announced to us that he was being assigned to a three-year tour of Germany. Once again it was time for us to pack up our lives and head out to new surroundings.

Once we arrived in Germany, I soon learned that the move was an all-too-transient one. Five weeks into our stay, my father called the family into the living room for a conference.

"Okay," he began in his usual authoritarian manner, "I want you both to listen up and listen hard. My assignment here isn't what I anticipated it to be. I'm with an engineering unit that might be gearing up for Vietnam. This means that we can anticipate a move at any time. We need to prepare ourselves accordingly."

"Hey, wait a minute!" I said. "We just got here! Why are we talking about leaving already?"

"Because, Ishmael, that's the way it is!"

It was the ultimate, final decree, leaving no room for debate. As usual, I withdrew from the conversation at this point, suppressing, as I had done so often before, my feelings of anger and resentment.

As the stress of preparing for Vietnam mounted, my father found himself paying frequent visits to the base infirmary. He complained about pains in his legs and problems with his ulcers. As time passed, he acquired a dependence on a number of prescription drugs. Some were intended for his ulcers, others for his leg pains, and others simply for his nerves. One drug allegedly contained cobra venom, or so he privately claimed.

At times he would report to the infirmary at noon and be sent home for the remainder of the day. During this time off, he would slip into a drug-induced sleep that would render him incapable of slumber during the standard nocturnal hours. Deprived of the capacity to sleep, he would prowl around the apartment most of the night, seeking any source of distraction available. Armed forces radio and television went off the air around two in the morning, making it necessary for him to pursue more creative forms of diversion. Sometimes he would play solitaire. Other times he would sit on the toilet and read while he smoked his cigarette.

My mother found her husband's unusual nocturnal habits, and the attitudes and moods accompanying them, increasingly harder to accept. She observed him becoming increasingly more irritable, withdrawn, opinionated, and judgmental. Civil conversation became more and more a rarity as his demands on us became greater and greater. As her anger increased, the more petulant her husband became, and friction between family members, intense as it was even at the best of times, mounted.

It wasn't just family friction we needed to address. It seemed as though Lyndon Johnson's face filled the screen on armed forces television every hour on the hour. "Why are we in Vietnam?" he would ask in his Texas drawl. And on and on he would go with one justification after another. As far as my father was concerned, to dispute his rationale would be akin to subversion stopping just short of treason, making this still another form of familial stress.

To add to all this, the armed forces newspaper *The Stars and Stripes* blatantly censored the news, validating U.S. policy, justifying our Southeast Asia armed intervention, and never giving any other side to the story.

The U.S. Army run high school I was attending on base was, of course, rah-rah U.S. policy. Scrawled across the gym in bold white spray paint were written the words, "We support U.S. policy in Vietnam." No attempt on the part of the school administration was made to remove the graffiti or to levy charges of vandalism for the act.

School spirit ran high, particularly when it came to sports, football and track figuring most prominently. A week before any big sporting event, a leading athlete, situated in the front central part of the cafeteria, would take it upon himself to demonstrate the school's esprit de corps by yelling at the top of his lungs, "What's the good word?"

To which the students assembled would all yell, "Beat Wiesbaden!"

All this did not make for the most tranquil of dining atmospheres, but then again, tranquility did not rank high on the school's list of priorities.

I would often come home exhausted and demoralized at the end of a school day and seek the seclusion of my room to unwind from the bedlam of academia, and perhaps do a little homework. Such behavior proved unsettling to my father, and he would continually berate me for it, confronting me in my room or calling me to the living room where he would address his concerns. A typical conversation went as follows:

"I think it's high time you came to the realization that you are almost a man," he would say, "I also think it's high time you started acting like a man."

"Okay," I said, willing to concede this point if it would put an end to the exchange.

"Well, you need to start doing more than just saying 'okay.' You need to quit shutting yourself off from life. Quit retreating into your own little world. Get out there! Get involved with life! Get involved with people! Girls! It's about time you started showing more interest in girls! Show more school spirit! Get involved with extracurricular activities! And quit feeling sorry for yourself!"

Ultimately, I took him up on his advice if for no other reason than to get him off my back. I joined the school photo club and did some freelance photography for the school newspaper and the yearbook, ultimately becoming so absorbed in this pursuit that I often forgot to do my homework, and my grades began to suffer. As a consequence, it came as no surprise to me when my father, one night, while sitting in his favorite green chair in the living room smoking a cigarette, caught a glimpse of my report card laying on the coffee table.

"Ishmael!" he yelled. "Get out here! I wanna talk to you! Now! Your grades are dropping, and I think you know what that means."

"But I …"

"No 'buts'! You've been slacking off on your studies, devoting too much time to extracurricular activities. It's time you got your nose back to the grindstone. You'll never get into college with grades like these."

But this time, I found his stern warnings and admonitions to be wearing thin. Something inside me no longer cowered in the face of his wrath, and it occurred to me that towing the line under these given circumstances was tantamount to an exercise in absurdity. Through my usual sense of suppressed anger, I could feel laughter fighting its way to the surface. Some of it was Isaac's, but a portion of it was my own.

Religion was not the big issue at this post as it had been at the post in Virginia, but there was a sophomore track star by the name of Glenn Turner whose athletic prowess and evangelical presence tended to spearhead an athletic faith movement of sorts. He was a slender, blond-haired, blue-eyed, handsome youth whose height exceeded six feet. He was frequently called upon to speak at the Catholic youth rallies, during which he was fond of quoting two biblical passages from Second Timothy 2:5: — "And in the case of an athlete, no one is crowned without competing according to the rule,"— and Second Timothy 4:7 — "I have fought the good fight, I have finished the race, I have kept the faith." The quotes seemed quite apropos as they applied to both himself as a runner and an athlete, *and* they were great crowd-pleasers.

Soon after I arrived, his mettle was put to the test in a contest with the yet-to-be-defeated Wiesbaden Warriors. Both the football game and the track meet took place simultaneously, and the spectators were given the chance to cheer on the members of the track team as they came into the home stretch by the football stadium.

The Warriors were wiping the field with members of our football team, leading with a score of 87 to 22. It was the bottom of the third quarter, with little chance of victory for our side. Then, as we all glanced to the left, the two opposing track teams were seen speeding toward the finish line by the outer perimeter of the football field. From a distance none of our boys could be seen, and it appeared that Wiesbaden would claim a second victory over us that afternoon.

Then, out of nowhere, from the faceless pack, Glenn Turner shot forward in a brilliant show of celerity, passing the Wiesbaden runners as if they were motionless, quickly gaining in line to the first-place position. The crowd stood, rendering a thunderous ovation as this youthful competitor drew near the finish line.

Realizing that this was an opportunity for a prize photo, I grabbed my camera, scurried down from the bleachers, and headed toward the finish line, determined to get a shot of Glenn crossing over. My mission was met with success, my shot timed to perfection. Then the unexpected took place as Glenn Turner, upon crossing, fell to his knees, convulsed, and desperately gasped for air. The thunderous ovation died and someone cried, "Call an ambulance!"

I continued to take shots until the paramedics finally arrived, placed Glenn on a stretcher, and carted him off to the base infirmary, at which point some people began to boo at me and toss various objects such as pop bottles and empty food wrappers in my direction.

The Call

Glenn died that day of respiratory failure. In the days that followed, the base flag was lowered to half-mast and an athletic scholarship fund was set up in his name. A school talent show took place later on that week in the school auditorium. Before it started we were all made to observe a moment of silence in memory of Glenn Turner.

His funeral was to be held that Friday. When my father asked me if I was going to attend, I said that I hadn't planned on it, and added that I hadn't really known the guy.

"Ishmael," he said in a grim tenor, "I strongly suggest you attend."

"Why?"

"I believe you know 'why,'" he added, throwing the base newspaper down in front of me.

It came as no surprise to me that there was a front-page layout of Glenn Turner. I recognized the pictures. They were mine. "Hummph," I said. "Those are my pictures, but they gave me no byline."

"Yes!" Father retorted. "And thank God for that! What you did was disgraceful ... reprehensible beyond measure! Using that boy's death as a photo shoot. I swear, sometimes I don't even want to know you! And when you were clicking away at that camera of yours, did you give any thought to the grief you may have caused that boy's family? Did you? His poor family is going to have to live with losing a son," he added as he rammed his fist against the article, "and now they have to contend with this!"

"Well, if it's that bad, why'd they print my pictures?" I asked.

"That's beside the point!" he barked. "This pictorial

display caused me a great deal of embarrassment and shame! I just thank God the paper had the decency to omit your name. If they hadn't, everyone I associate with on the base would know my son had taken them! My son ... a ghoul! So you're going to that funeral, if for nothing else than to pay your last respects to that boy ... to show there's still some decency left in you ... maybe even to say you're sorry!"

I attended the funeral and took my trusty camera along. After all, if proper respect was to be rendered to Glenn, it seemed only fitting that his story be given proper closure.

And once again, although the school paper, the yearbook and the base tabloid used the photos, I was given no byline. A tinge of indignation shot through me at having been denied a byline, but I also felt like laughing a bit at the irony of the situation. My pictures were good enough for public usage, but my deed was too shameful to gain me any notoriety for taking them.

The following Monday, during physical education, we were all gathered together by our coach just outside the gym in a field near the fence. Our coach was a tall, slender, balding man who constantly wore a scowl, and had a habit of addressing us as though he were a sergeant addressing recruits. "All right, you bastards!" he shouted, "We're gonna do something out of the ordinary today! One of your own is no longer with us! He died giving his all for this school! He understood what it meant to run the good race! He knew what it meant to fight the good fight! Now we're gonna see how much he taught you guys! This period we're all gonna take part in a commemorative run of two laps around the school's perimeter in memory of

The Call 45

our fallen comrade! So I want you bastards to get out there and give it your all for Glenn Turner!"

Lighting out with a collective cheer, over one hundred students attired in gym shorts and T-shirts took off running, filled with the fires of inspiration and a supreme sense of esprit de corps.

I modestly assumed my position of last place amid the runners, walking when I felt the need to do so. Glenn Turner died from giving his all. If I were to give my all for something, I deemed it only fitting that it would be something of my own choosing.

As talk and rumors about Vietnam continued, I became affected with feelings of anxiety and helplessness. Having heard that some of the troops who had families were being issued twenty-four hour notices to report to Vietnam, I lived with the constant fear that this could happen to us, particularly since post regulations expressly stated that all base privileges for dependents would be rendered void within one week after the departure of the main breadwinner. My classmates disappeared with such rapidity, that I soon found myself in classes with strangers. Lyndon Johnson's *Why Are We in Vietnam* speech was played on armed forces television every two hours and on armed forces radio every hour.

Even at home I found myself bombarded with militaristic rhetoric whenever my father came upon me reading *Mad Magazine*. With a quick sweep he would snatch the magazine from my hands.

"I think it's high time you started taking life more seriously, and quit retreating into what you call irony," he would say. "I don't know how many times I have to tell you, you're getting to an age now where one day the prospect of getting drafted will be staring you squarely in the face. And with all that's happening with Vietnam, you're going to be greatly affected. So I'd be seriously thinking about cleaning up my act if I were you. Start reading articles in *The Stars and Stripes*. Get *Newsweek* or *Time*. Straighten up your room. Take more pride in your appearance. Get your hair cut. Shine your shoes. Quit dressing like a slob. Shave more regularly. And start behaving like someone with dignity. Life's not the joke you seem to think it is. Life is serious business."

One day I came home from school to find Father sitting at the kitchen table smoking a cigarette. "I have an article I want you to read," he said, handing me *The Stars and Stripes*.

"What's it about?" I asked.

"Just read and absorb it!"

As might have been expected, the article in question extolled the virtues of conformity in outward appearance, and pride in self, while at the same time condemning the vices of eccentricity, taking life too lightly, and being too individualistic.

"That's what I've been trying to get through that thick head of yours," Father said when I had finished skimming it. "The way you're always reading those damn comic books, showing absolutely no respect for rules ..."

From the corner of my eye, I saw Mother fix on my father with a venomous stare.

"I'm not sure I know what you're talking about," I countered.

"I'm talking about the embarrassment you caused

your mother and me when you took those damn pictures of that dying athlete, how you disregarded his family's grief at his funeral, how you wouldn't even pay proper tribute by giving a good run during gym class."

I was shocked. My face must have given me away because my father told me that he had ways of finding out about such things. "And what I found out about you just sickens me! Here I am, known for being the most straight-laced officer on the base, with my uniform pressed more neatly and my shoes outshining anyone else's, and damn it, you're my son! You're supposed to be an extension of me. But you run around with uncombed hair and your face looking like you haven't shaved for a week, not to mention those pimples."

"Abe," my mother interjected, "he's only fifteen and just started shaving this year, and all teenagers get acne."

"You stay out of this!" my father shouted and then, turning back to me, continued his scolding, "You're sloppy, you've got no sense of self-pride, you do stupid things, you show no regard for order and discipline, you have no sense of propriety, and I swear most of the time, I'm ashamed to be around you!"

"Well, don't think always being around you is a ball either!" I said, my voice brimming over with anger. His words stung beyond my ability to describe.

"I've had just about enough of you!" He shouted. "Go to your room!"

Next morning at breakfast, after father had left for work, Mother said, "We have to be patient with your father. All those pills he takes causes him see things in funny ways."

"I hardly think it's funny, Mom." And so, once again, she let him play fast and loose with me. Once she had tried to defend me, but now it was clear that I would have to fend for myself.

Six weeks later my father's unit was scheduled to ship out for Vietnam, after having been given an eight-week notice, enough time to get their dependents situated stateside and clear up any other essential matters. Once again it was time for us to begin packing up our lives and heading elsewhere.

That evening, just before dinner, Father called us to a meeting at the kitchen table. "Okay." he said in his usual brusque and authoritative tone, "arrangements have been made to fly us to Maguire Air Force Base in three and a half weeks. Meantime, we have to coordinate with the movers, sell the Volvo, and arrange for shipment of the station wagon so it will be waiting for us when we get stateside. I'm counting on you to organize things around here and dispose of things that are not necessary, which includes your comic book collection, Ishmael. I also thought it might be good if during the course of our drive back to California we stop for a week in Iowa to visit family." He went on. "It would do all of us good, and it would give us a chance to rest a bit. Then, after we arrive in California, we can allow ourselves time to make some necessary renovations on the house. My guess is it probably needs it by now."

"As for you, Ishmael, you have three weeks to finish up six weeks of school. You're going to have to go to the office and get the necessary paperwork clearing you for this accelerated program."

The Call 49

"Then I have to get it signed by all my teachers," I told him. "You have to have a C average in all your classes to be able to do that."

"Which is really no problem, right?"

"I have it in all my classes except biology. I got a C- in that class."

"But you can bring it up to a C!"

"I don't know. Biology's a hard class for me."

"I said you can bring it up to a C!"

"I can try."

"You're going to do more than just try!" he warned me.

Given his intonation, I knew my options were limited. As a consequence, I went to have a talk with my biology teacher the next day. Mr. Cogan was a robust, towering man with light brown hair cut short, and steely blue eyes. Unlike my father, Mr. Cogan was moderately approachable. After I had explained my situation, he looked over his grade book and said, "Well, I'd like to help you. You've made significant progress since last quarter. You brought your grade up from a D-. I know that took quite a bit of effort on your part. But I'm not sure I can justify giving you a full C."

"Is their some extra project I could do?" I asked.

"Well, you could always do that," he said in a tentative tenor, "but I don't think it would be enough to up your grade."

"And what happens if, by the end of the three weeks, I can't make a C?"

"Then I would have to issue you a C- along with an incomplete for the course. That would mean you'd either have to make it up in summer school or next year."

"I'd still like to try."

"Okay, Ishmael. You hand in the project, and I'll look it over."

The following Saturday morning I was heading out the door toward the base library, having stayed up late the night before making sure my assignments for my other classes were in order, which hadn't been easy since practically every half hour Father stuck his head into my room to tell me to turn off the light and go to sleep.

The next morning, fuzzy headed from lack of sleep, I was about to leave for the library when my father demanded to know where I was going.

"To the library."

"What about your school work?"

"I'm tending to it."

"What about biology?"

"I'm tending to that, too."

"Did you turn the paperwork into the office."

"Not yet."

"Why not?"

"Well, …"

"Look!" Father shouted, "I told you what needed to be done before we leave, and you're going around with that paperwork in your pocket …"

Just then Mother walked into the living room. "Look Abe," she said, "he's doing the best he can and …"

"Then he'd better start doing better! There is only so much time …"

"And that's the reason I'm going to the library," I interrupted.

"Then I suggest you get moving," Mother said,

The Call

showing a rare exhibit of defiance.

I spent the entire day at the library pouring over material pertinent to the subject matter we were going over in biology class. My notes were copious and organized to the best of my ability. By the end of the afternoon, the only thing that remained for me to do was to hit the typewriter. That task consumed the remainder of the weekend and was made even more difficult by my father's constant monitoring of my progress, until, finally, exasperated, I yelled, "You think all this harassing is going to make me go any faster?"

"Watch your tone, boy!" he replied, "I can still take you over my knee and paddle you!"

Monday morning I approached Mr. Cogan in his classroom with the completed project in hand. He looked it over and said, "Hmmmm. Good report. It definitely scores you some points. Unfortunately, it's still not enough to bring the grade up to a C. I'm sorry."

"Me, too." I replied. I turned to leave. The knot in my stomach grew tighter. I knew I was going to receive hell that evening, as if I hadn't received enough over the past few days.

I completed all my classes on schedule except for biology with its C- that doomed me to making up the class. My father was disgusted and showed it, and although I tried to tell myself I didn't care, I was, I found, so tired of his disapproval. I also knew that soon I would have to do whatever it took to get away from him.

The trip was fraught with every pitfall imaginable. The flights to McGuire Air Force Base in New Jersey were booked solid. Family accommodations for the delayed departures were practically nil. The only sleeping facility available for us was a room with a double bed and a crib. "Wow!" I said upon seeing my sleeping accommodations, "Where's my rattle and pacifier?"

"I've just about had all I'm gonna take from you! Just shut up!" My father hollered.

Mother leaned over and whispered, "Don't antagonize your father. He's under a great deal of stress."

"Really?" I said. "And here I thought he was just being his usual, lovable old self. Look, next time we have to move, why don't you guys just put me in a foster home. I can't take much more of this."

The flight lasted approximately fifteen hours, during which time we were served one meal. A very attractive stewardess with an extremely surly attitude served it to us. The food tasted terrible as well.

After what seemed like an eternity in the air with communication between the three of us becoming increasingly strained, we finally landed at Maguire Air Force Base in New Jersey. .

After reclaiming our luggage and locating the car, Father assumed the wheel and we began a twelve-hour drive along the Pennsylvania Turnpike, which was interrupted at one point by a highway patrol car that signaled Father to pull over.

"You were going close to eighty." The patrolman said. "That's well over the posted speed limit. I'm going to have to issue you a ticket."

Father told him to have it sent to his APO address over in Vietnam.

"Yeah," said the officer, "I know how you guys

operate. You'll just send a document back to us that says, 'Try and collect it.'"

Father said nothing. He knew what the patrolman said was true.

We arrived in California with three weeks left before Father had to take off to Vietnam. But these circumstances were to change quickly. We hadn't been in our house in Folsom for more than a couple of days when Father received a communiqué from the Department of the Army stating that there would be an additional four-week delay in his departure time. "Typical army," he said, uncharacteristically compliant. "Hurry up and wait."

"Well," Mother replied, "let's make the most of that time. We can do additional renovations on the house, and I really think we should have the place carpeted."

"Okay," Father replied. "But I'm going out to the base tomorrow. I want to find out as much as I can about what's going on. And let's get junior here enrolled in summer school. He messed up back in Germany. Now it's time to pay the price."

The next day, while Father was out at the base, Mom drove me to the high school to enroll me in the summer school program. The six-week summer class went by swiftly, and required so little effort on my part that I assumed that standards must have been lower at that school than they were overseas. At the end of the session I actually received an A in biology. For that effort I received no paternal applause—only the impression that this was what I was expected to do. To celebrate this moment of affirmation, I hopped on my bike and pedaled furiously from my home to a vacant field by the American River, where I screamed myself hoarse and called him names, none of which were vile enough to sum up the stark hatred I felt for him.

Several minutes elapsed. Then I rolled over on my back and looked upward through the amorphous willow, walnut, eucalyptus, and oak trees into the deep blue, beholding a fathomless sky. I drew in deeply the many smells of the natural surroundings that were overtaken by the odors emitted by a nearby sewage treatment plant. The temperature was hot, with just enough humidity to drench my clothing with the perspiration that poured from me while in the throes of physical and emotional exertion.

As I stared up into the clouds, I reflected back over the years—the pain of leaving so many places, the public denigration by my father, the loss of friends, the pummeling into submission at every turn. Then I remembered my sporadic religious orientation and Mother's faith in a loving Heavenly Father. God? Love? Father? I thought. The terms did not equate. Not only did I feel alone, it seemed my existence had no value.

Walking to the edge of the cliff overlooking the river, I struggled with the impulse to throw myself into the surging water. But something held me back, and I collapsed to my knees, exhausted. Only then was I aware of a sense of peace and renewed resolve. "You're here. Make your life count," I heard a voice within me say. What voice was that? I had never heard this voice before. Unlike the coarse and abrasive voice of Isaac, this voice was warm, loving, caring, and affirming.

A week later, after my mother and I had seen my father off to Vietnam, I heard the same voice again. "We

The Call 55

have things to do," it said with in a firm but loving tone. "Now is when we begin."

Whose voice was it? I wondered. One thing alone was certain. It wasn't Isaac.

The peace and freedom I experienced once my father was gone was exhilarating. Now I could absorb myself in my studies without the prospect of constant interruptions. Evenings would find me hitting the books until the early morning hours and oftentimes falling asleep at the desk.

In contrast to the more militaristic setting of the base high school, the teachers at this high school were far more lenient and affirming, especially the ones in the social sciences and humanities departments. When report cards were to be issued, I received As in everything except for Cs in both Math and PE. These grades remained consistent throughout my junior year.

As for my social life, an old issue soon emerged. There was a Campus Life Club at the high school I was attending, the influence of which spread like a cancer. A Jacob McPherson, whom everybody referred to as "The Preacher," spearheaded the club. Ironically he bore a striking resemblance to the late Glenn Turner. And, like Glenn Turner, Jacob, too, was a member of the high school track team. He came up to me one day during lunch period on the quad, introduced himself and startled me by asking if I knew Jesus.

"I have had a few Hispanic friends in the past," I admitted, "but none of them went by that name."

"No, I mean Jesus. Jesus Christ, The Lord of

Creation," he said in an earnest tone. "The Jesus Christ who wants to be your Lord and Savior." Handing me a tract entitled *The Four Spiritual Laws*, he then extended an invitation for me to attend the next Campus Life meeting. It was a club, I was soon to learn, that was affiliated with the larger institute known as The Christian Youth Association, an organization that met once a month at one of the churches in the uptown area of Carmichael.

For lack of anything better to do during an extended lunch break, I took Jacob up on his invitation. While in attendance, I became drawn to a certain individual who gave me incentive to continue partaking in these meetings. It was one member who stood out for me—Laurie Rogers, a slender, sensuous young woman with long black hair flowing down her back and a smile that triggered my emerging adolescent hormones.

However, as much as I enjoyed being near Laurie Rogers, I hated the Campus Life Club meetings, in part because the students gathered there came across as the dorkiest group of misfits I had ever known. The games they played were inane, including, as they did, one that involved a specially wired chair that gave whoever was sitting in it a jolt of electricity when someone was operating the remote control. For example, it was during an election year and one of the students was called upon to recite the alphabet in the same way Richard Nixon would deliver a campaign speech. As for the songs, one clearly stands out in my mind to this day. It was called the laughing song and went something like this: 'Ho ho ho Hossanah, Ha ha Hallelujah, He he he he saved me, Now I got the joy of the Lord.'

I endured a good deal in order to be near Laurie, and

eventually it paid off. But, despite out growing friendship, there was friction. Of course, given my background, I was no stranger to friction, but I always liked a little variety with my friction *and* Laurie and I always wound up having the same argument about why I wasn't a Christian.

"Don't believe in it, actually," I would reply.

"But Jesus died for you! Doesn't that mean anything to you?"

"It makes very little sense. We didn't even live in the same era."

"No! No! You don't understand!" Sometimes, at this point, she became so impatient that she stamped her feet.

"Look, do we have to do this? I really don't want to argue the matter with you."

"I just don't want to see you burning in Hell!" Once she regained her composure, she would go on to give her testimony. "I've had a very troubled family life. I've got epilepsy and my mother doesn't like to deal with it. I haven't seen my real father in years."

"You're lucky," I said.

"Why do you say that?" she asked.

"I see mine more often than I'd like to."

"And my stepfather at one time tried to molest me. If I didn't know Jesus, I'd never have made it this far."

I became almost nauseous at this part of her testimony. For me it fell under the heading of *too much information.*

When we weren't engrossed in arguments of this nature, we could be seen walking about the campus or the rustic streets of Folsom holding hands, even though every time we did, we were on the receiving end of catcalls.

It was the morning before our first class when she met me in front of the office and confronted me on the matter. "Ishmael," she began, "is there something going on that you're not telling me?"

"Like what?" I responded.

"Are you telling them things about us?" Laurie asked. "Remember, God is watching and listening and He knows if you lie."

"I've said nothing."

"Then why haven't you done anything to stop them … to uphold my honor?"

"You expect me to fight half the male student body?"

"That's part of what it means to be a man, Ishmael! That's what the Lord expects a man to do … to be the woman's protector! But I don't suppose you've ever read that in the Bible!"

"Never read the Bible, actually."

"You know, Ishmael, some of my friends in my Sunday school class have been talking to me. They're saying I've been dating a non-Christian!"

"What do you want me to say?"

"Will you be attending the Campus Life Conference meeting next week?"

"If you want to go." I felt like something of a phony agreeing to attend that kind of function. I didn't enjoy it. But I put up with a lot of discomfort and misery already for the sake of being with Laurie who was, after all, one foxy lady, even if her God talk had a way of neutralizing my hormones.

One week later, in the evening, a group of us attended the youth evangelical program held at the

The Call

Memorial Auditorium. It started off with a comedy folk group followed by the main speaker, a hellfire preacher who put Chaplain Colonel Fleetwood in the shade. For more than an hour and a half this man spoke fervently about the fate of the unsaved, the fires of hell, and our only hope of salvation through the cleansing blood of Jesus Christ. Hell was portrayed particularly vividly. Certainly, by the time he had finished what he had to say, I knew I didn't want to go there.

It was this very threat of Hell that scared me into salvation that evening. Much to the delight of Laurie and Jacob, I joined the group going to the alter crying, "Oh, God, save me! I don't want to go to Hell! Help me Jesus! Help me! Help me!"

The preacher was a chubby man-boy who, even though in his mid to late twenties, still appeared to sport traces of baby fat. He was quick to receive all of us coming forward, saying, "Hallelujah! All heaven is now rejoicing for these sinners who have returned to the fold!" Then he stretched out his hands and prayed for a few minutes, before announcing that since we'd all made our first step on the path of righteousness, we needed to be baptized.

"This is what the Lord has commanded for us, and this is what you must do as an act of submission and obedience," he said, "And like this profession, your baptism needs to be made public. Remember what the Lord says in scripture: 'Acknowledge me before men and I will acknowledge you before the Father. Deny me before men and I, in turn, will deny you before the Father.'" After that, he gave us some literature to read, and the service would have come to an end if a scuffy-looking man with a full-face beard had not appeared beside him.

"Hey, you're not really gonna swallow all his bullshit are ya?" he demanded. "Let me tell you what's really happening!" But before he could continue his tirade, two uniformed attendants escorted him outside.

"That's another thing I need to tell you," The preacher said. "The closer you get to the Lord, the harder the devil works on you."

Laurie and Jacob had their hands full during the drive home. It took all the tenacity both of them could muster to help me regain my composure.

I was baptized the next week in the church where Laurie was a member. Of course, by that time the effects of the preacher's sermon had worn off and I found that the everyday life as I was now supposed to live had certain drawbacks. At the Christian Youth Association meetings they continually preached and admonished us to respect and obey parents, give up the "in crowd," pray constantly, and surrender all our individuality. I did not find any of these stipulations very palatable. But, for the sake of being near Laurie, I endured.

Two weeks later, on the night of the District Christian Youth Association meeting that took place at the Bethel Temple, Laurie passed out in the reception area from a petit mal seizure. A few of my classmates were passing through the foyer at the time of the incident. One of them boldly stepped over to where I was standing and said, "Ishmael, what have you done to that girl?" Then he turned walked away, snickering as did the rest of the guys in the group.

The Call

I watched as the church ushers tended to Laurie. As I stood frozen, my eyes fixed on her small body lying motionless on the ground, I heard Isaac's laughter thunder in my brain, and a chill ran down my spine.

When she fainted again the next day in her third-period class, rumors began flying about the school that I had made her pregnant. Certain classmates would yell out such witticisms as "Hey poppa, where's my cigar?" or "Ishmael's going to be a pappy!" I felt embarrassed. Laurie and I had never advanced beyond hand-holding and already I was being made out to be the number one stud on campus. I found myself again retreating inward. Such notoriety was impossible for me to endure. Laurie's fainting spells eventually subsided, but the damage had already been done.

One Wednesday afternoon she confronted me regarding what she had heard transpire on campus during the week.

"Why haven't you tried to squelch these rumors about me being pregnant? She demanded. "Have you told these people it's just not true?"

"You think the rumors would stop if I did?"

"And you call yourself a Christian!" She exclaimed. "It's my reputation that's at stake here! You're the man! You're supposed to be the one who protects me!"

"Regardless of what label you put on me, I'm still me," I told her. "And just how am I supposed to go about protecting you? The more I deny it, the more they're going to believe what they're saying. People are going to believe what they want to believe. What I tell them isn't going to mean squat."

"What kind of man are you?" she said with anger in her voice.

"A piss-poor one, I guess." I replied in a tone of resignation.

Feeling a profound sense of shame and defeat, I turned and walked away, all the while wishing the earth would swallow me whole. I could hear the muffled rumblings of laughter in my brain. Isaac was at it again.

It was near the end of my junior year that Mother and I received a letter from my father in which he announced that his tour of Vietnam had been extended to eighteen months. He also announced that he had been promoted to the rank of Lt. Colonel, had received a bronze star, a distinguished service cross, and a purple heart for his role in the Tet Offensive. Later that evening I heard Mother crying in her room. My assumption was that she was upset over the news of Father's extension, as it was, but only in part. The worst blow was when she found out via the military grapevine that while over in Vietnam he had fathered a son by a Vietnamese woman.

As I read the letter I felt an overwhelming sense of disgust which did not equate with one of the Campus Life admonitions, "Respect and be obedient to your parents, for such is right in the eyes of the Lord."

Respect toward parents, I thought. This is going to be very difficult.

I received mostly As and Bs throughout my senior year. Yet, because of my mediocre performance during my freshman and sophomore years, when it came time to apply for college my only options were the local community colleges, even though many of my fellow graduates whose overall academic records were worse than mine, had no problem being accepted by four-year institutions.

Father was granted leave and made it home for my graduation, after which we dined out. After listening to me on the subject of this apparent inequality, my father asked me, "How would you like to go to West Point? I have connections," he assured me. "Just finish your two years at the community college and I guarantee you'll get in."

"But I'd have to start all over again as a freshman," I said, aware that West Point was one of those ultra-exclusive institutions that only recognized its own academic accreditation. "I'd be twenty-five by the time I graduated."

"And that's the ideal time to begin a military career."

Military career? I thought. That was an idea I hadn't even remotely entertained.

"I'll have to think about it," I told him

"Think about it real hard, okay?"

Clearly nothing would have pleased my father more than if I were to follow in his footsteps, and West Point was where he fixed his hopes. But since I did not share his affinity for military mission, I was understandably ambivalent about the kind of future he undoubtedly had in mind for me. When I actually saw the school's catalogue, I knew at once that, not only was West Point not the place for me, but that I had no intention of exchanging my father's heavy hand for that of the military. Having lived under the same roof with my dear old dad for the past eighteen years was all the military service I cared to indulge in. As for whatever future prospects I might entertain, I was determined that they be my own.

A few weeks later Abe assumed his station at an obscure post in Missouri. Mother and I did not join him. So, once again, Father was left alone, and he was never able to keep to the straight and narrow when left alone. He managed to involve himself with a local woman by the name of Tamara, who worked as a short-order cook in a diner not far from the base, a woman to whom he actually became engaged after assuring her that he was divorced.

Before the actual date set for the wedding, he was scheduled to report to Korea, which he did, stopping on the way to see my mother and me. It was at this point, however, that the girl's father managed to trace his whereabouts, and he received a call from the girl, a call that my mother, unfortunately overheard. What went on between them subsequently, I don't know, but I was aware that the girl's father called to inform my mother that she was pregnant, and demanded that she make arrangements for child support.

Mother was outraged by the prospect, yet it was a familiar outrage she had harbored throughout the course of the marriage, and it was a culmination of something she always held inward, and in doing so, I could see it ultimately breaking her spirits. and I feared the same fate for myself.

It was about this time, as fate would have it, that my mother was diagnosed with severe rheumatoid arthritis,

The Call

which the doctors all estimated would get significantly worse over time. That same afternoon she was given more troubling news; when Tamara's father called complaining about the "runaround" he was receiving from the military bureaucracy, and that even the District Attorney's office had run up against a stone wall, all of which came, as she explained to him, as no surprise to her.

"The military operates that way," she told him, "If nothing else, it's a bureaucracy and it does look after its own."

"Well, what am I supposed to do about it?" He replied. "I have a daughter who's scheduled to give birth any day now. What am I supposed to tell her? And what am I supposed to tell the child when he or she gets older?"

"Look, I'd like to help you, but there's only so much I can do. When your daughter gives birth, you could forward the picture of the baby to him and hope he has enough of a conscience to respond. Of course even that's a gamble. I'm sorry, but I don't know what I can do for you. I'd send you some money for support, but I have to make do with what he sends me, and that just barely gets me by. He keeps a lot for himself."

"Well," he said, "it's not your fault. But I'm gonna get him! He's gonna be hurtin' when I do! And I'm sorry for you!"

Almost immediately after Tamara's father terminated the conversation, my mother received a call from Father. Father cut right to the chase. He didn't bother to ask her how she was before he was off and away on the topic of getting a visa for a Korean woman, who, he said, could provide my mother with live-in help. As she explained to me, he made no effort to disguise his interest in the woman. I felt like throwing up at hearing her disclosure. Isaac too had a bit of a laugh over the matter.

Mother's anger gripped her again while her arthritis pain shot through her body like a surge of electricity through a powerhouse.

After I completed my stint at the community college, I was able to transfer my credits to the University of California at Davis, a campus not far from home, where I signed up to major in American Studies, with minors in American History and English. The flurry of college life was almost too much for me. Students flocked about protesting the war and seeking support for their chosen political candidate. Outside agitators and speakers canvassed the campus in ever-increasing numbers, and a new breed of collegiate humanity known as the "Jesus freaks" stormed the university grounds, fervently advocating a return to Christian fundamentalism. Some garbed themselves as hippies, while others were decked out as super straights and hailed from such organizations as Campus Crusade for Christ and the Navigators.

The months passed quickly. I knew my father's tour was rapidly drawing to a close. I also knew that it was all too likely that he would bring his Asian mistress home with him. It was a scene I did not care to be a part of. Yet, if I wanted to continue my education and maintain my draft deferment, it appeared I had no other choice. And then, after weeks of worry, I was notified that I had been placed in the draft lottery pool for a year, so my current eligibility rating had been changed to a 1H. This meant the people at the draft board would have to exhaust all the 1As before they could get to me. I was incredibly relieved when I learned that the tyrant dictates of military conscription no longer ruled me. I was now free to change my course of action. All I needed to do was complete the current spring quarter, seek out full-time employment during the summer months, and, if I were to choose to continue my educational pursuits, I could do so on a part-time basis.

I could also move out of the house. A sense of liberty overwhelmed me. Maybe God was on my side after all!

Early June marked the end of my junior year at the university. I took a series of civil service exams, and by August had landed a clerical position with the State of California. I would work the graveyard shift, which was fine by me because it offered the highest pay and I needed all the money I could get. Next up, when it came time for me to enroll for the fall quarter, I limited myself to only two classes.

Everything was set. Father would not be home for at least another four months which would afford me plenty of time to sort out my finances, gather together my belongings, and seek residence outside the confines of my familial dwelling. I was ready now for my mother and father to address their domestic matters without my having to be present to watch.

My father put in for and was granted another

extension of his tour of duty in Korea. The Korean Consulate and the U.S. Immigration Bureau had proved to be quite formidable adversaries and were not all that eager to grant Su Lin her visa. My father knew that, after this tour, he would be assigned a desk job at the Presidio in San Francisco, where he would rewrite military regulations until his retirement papers could be officially processed, a procedure that would probably take only a few months. Subsequently, he would undergo the military's official parting inspection, thus ending his life with military mission. Knowing him as I did, he could see the future looming in the distance: The grim edifice of death stared him down and drew him ever nearer to the intransigent and inevitable confrontation with his own mortality. For my father, Su Lin was a part of the integral life force associated with the military mission, something he needed to hold onto—something he craved desperately and yearned to possess in the days when the coming night would draw its ominous shade upon him.

Thus, Lt. Colonel Abe O'Donnell was awarded a medal by the Korean government for his part in the facilitation of benevolence and goodwill on the part of the armed forces. The *Stars and Stripes* actually ran a picture of him being awarded the medal by a prominent Korean official. His picture also appeared in one of the Korean tabloids. We received an 8" X 10" glossy photo of the event, along with the medal. Once again, Mom added both to the drawer that contained the rest of his memorabilia. We also received word he would be arriving home in the latter part of August which was, as far as I was concerned, perfect timing since it gave me enough time to finish up classes for the spring quarter and begin apartment hunting.

I managed to find a place I liked with two bedrooms, and one-and-a-half baths in downtown Sacramento in the latter part of July. It was located close to my place of employment. The carpeting needed to be replaced but it was clean and well lighted. I was able to coax a friend of mine from high school to join me in the venture. Together we managed to furnish the place in "early cheap" via the purchasing of furniture and other needed supplies from Good Will and various other thrift stores. It was Spartan compared to home accommodations, but well worth the trade when it came to feeling free at last.

A few more weeks passed. I enrolled in the fall quarter figuring on taking only a few classes and allowing myself some extra time to lay the groundwork for my senior project. It was important, the department heads insisted, how the project was drawn up and presented in order to proceed on to graduate study.

Meanwhile, my father, the soon-to-be Lt. Colonel Emeritus Abe O'Donnell, was at the Presidio, waiting on his retirement. The duties were limited and his hours were flexible, so he had plenty of time to devote to his pet project. He had enlisted the aid of an attorney who advised him to have somebody sign on as Su Lin's fiancé. The individual in question would need to appear before a notary and sign a document attesting to the fact that he was indeed her fiancé and that he would be the source of her support. This, of course, was designed to assure the Bureau of Immigration and the Korean Consulate that once Su Lin had entered the United States she would not become a ward of the state. Abe desperately went through a list of people he thought might serve as viable alternatives for the task at hand. Finally, only one name remained.

The fall quarter on campus once again drew to a close. Seasonal demands necessitated my tending to the exigencies and tyrant dictates of the Christmas holidays. Although the season was named for the one whose faith I now embraced, it was still a time for gritting my teeth and wishing it would pass by as quickly as possible, without leaving any irreparable damage in its wake. It was a time when I needed to dip into what appeared to be my already-overextended budget for the buying of gifts, and a time that necessitated my paying homage to home and family, be they ever so dysfunctional. I had managed to avoid any prolonged visits with my father for the past few months since his return stateside, although he persisted in trying to arrange contact with me. Now, the period of avoidance would end.

It was Christmas day when I showed up at my parents' house bearing gifts and libations. For the first time in many years, we were celebrating a Christmas together.

A turkey was in the oven and a white tablecloth graced the dining room table, complete with the good china. pumpkin pie, yams, string beans, dressing, mashed potatoes, and gravy. All made their appearance on the table. We had a tree, embellished from top to bottom with decorations. Shocked by a house that looked like something out of Charles Dickens' *Christmas Carol,* I asked my mother how so much had been accomplished,

The Call

especially since her rheumatoid arthritis had shown no signs of remission. She informed me that some neighbors had been helping her out since my departure and that my father had helped out with the cooking. It was this information that made me feel guilty. "Your father has been obsessed with the Su Lin issue, so don't be surprised if he brings it up today," my mother told me as I helped her take the turkey out of the oven.

"This is precisely what I wanted to avoid," I told her.

"I realize that, dear," she replied, "But you know as well as I do that when your father wants something he'll go to any lengths to get it. And right now you figure into his strategy."

Shortly thereafter, father emerged from the den and we exchanged stilted familial greetings. At first conversation was general, and then, knowing that father wanted attention focused on him at all times, I feigned interest in his activities, asking about his Presidio assignment.

He, in turn, spoke at length on the exercise in futility that had been thrust upon him. His final task, as they processed his paperwork, was to write and rewrite certain military regulations. He lit up when he went on to talk about the desperate conditions in which the Koreans lived and how glad he had been to be able to help.

"You have no idea of the conditions these people live under," he said. "It's poverty like you can't even imagine. But I was there to facilitate goodwill on the part of the Army and if I could have just made a small difference … you know what they called me? Papa San."

Apparently growing tired of father's recounting of his military adventures, my mother tried to redirect the conversation over to me, "So how's the job going?" she asked.

"Oh fine," I replied, pouring gravy on my mashed potatoes. "Pretty much routine. A lot of boring work that needs to be done. You know, keep the wheels of bureaucracy turning."

"But don't you find graveyard a terrible shift?" she asked.

"You get used to it. Besides, it keeps the money coming in."

"I can't believe you'd settle for something like that!" Father chimed in. "So routine, so dull! Now my career, I'm proud to say, had adventure to it! I really think you ought to reconsider …"

"What about school?" Mother interrupted. "What's going on there?"

"Well, I've about completed all the necessary requirements for my two minors. What needs doing now is my senior project."

"What's that going to be about?"

"Religious thoughts and attitudes in America. It's going to be a bit tricky. Professor McRae is a real stickler when it comes to culture and its definition, so I have to keep it within those boundaries. It's a lot like walking a tightrope." I tried to change the subject by congratulating my mother on the meal.

"Know who taught me how to prepare food this way?" Father replied.

"No, who?" I asked.

"Su Lin. That woman can cook … she taught me

how to use soy sauce in ways you couldn't imagine. And talk about cleaning. My quarters were the most spotless of any officer's in the Army. And ..."

"I don't get it about your senior project," Mother said, trying desperately to change the subject, "How does religion have anything to do with culture?"

"Oh, it has everything to do with culture," I replied. "People exercise their faith and beliefs totally within the context of their surroundings ... you know, the folkways and the mores they've grown accustomed to. The way we practice our faith in twentieth century America is totally different from how the first-century Christians practiced their faith because the culture is different." At this point I could see my father's eyes glazing over, as I was determined to continue.

"Back in first-century Israel, a boy didn't really toy with the idea of what he was going to be when he grew up," I said, "He pretty much knew what he was going to be doing based on what his father did for a living."

"I can see merit to that," Father chimed in.

"The custom of dating and the selection of your own mate was also pretty much a moot issue, and the period of engagement was unheard of back then. The parents selected your mate for you and you became betrothed by the time you were between seven and ten years of age. And you and your bride didn't move into your own house. You were expected to add on to your father's house."

"You know," Father said, getting up from the table, "speaking of that, I've got something to show you." Taking a picture from a box in the living room, he handed it to me. It was a photo of a fifteen-year-old Korean girl holding a trumpet. "That's a picture of Lin Chow," he said. "She was one of the orphans who played in a musical group known as the Mice Band. I recorded some of their stuff. I'll play it for you guys later. I was considering adopting her, and bringing her home so you could have a girlfriend. She'd be twenty-one now. Old enough to be your wife."

He was, I thought, even more outrageous than usual. "Thanks," I said, "but I believe I prefer the twentieth-century way of choosing my own mate. Pass me a little more of those green beans, please."

"So when are you going to do so?" he blurted out. "I haven't seen you do much for yourself so far along those lines! Matter of fact it seems to me you're wasting your life, working at a nowhere job, being lackadaisical about your education …"

"Oh, leave the boy alone!" Mother interrupted. "He's doing fine. Better than most of his peers, I'd say."

"Fine, my ass!" my father shouted, slamming his fist on the table. "When we were his age we were one year away from getting married. I had served in the military! You were working an accounting job! We had our path already drawn up for us."

"Things were different back then," my mother reminded him. "We had the war and …"

"We got a war now in case no one has noticed!" Father shouted.

"And I suppose you'd like nothing better," I broke in, "than for me to don a uniform and go fight it."

"And why not?" he replied, peering at me wild eyed. "I was proud to wear the uniform of my country. I was proud to serve beside my countrymen."

"I'm not you, Dad," I countered. "I like my life just as it is."

Father sighed, sank back down in his chair, and waved his arm in dismissal. "Never mind," he said. "Forget it. You're going to do what you want to do."

"There's no sin in that. And I'm not hurting anybody."

"That's a matter of opinion."

"Why don't we change the subject?" Mother suggested.

"Good idea," he said. "I've also got some pictures of Su Lin I've been meaning to show you two. They're right here in the box. Look at her. I never met someone who worked harder and gave so much of herself, yet still managed to retain so flawless a physical appearance. I tell you, I know you guys are just going to love her!"

As my father continued to extol his praises on Su Lin, I noted my mother's face getting redder with each passing minute, perhaps from embarrassment, perhaps from anger, or maybe a little bit of both. She bore a striking resemblance to a volcano on the verge of eruption.

When dinner finally ended, I helped rinse off the dishes and placed them in the dishwasher, after which we retired to the living room to open our presents. "You and Su Lin are going to get along just fine," my father said when I assumed a lotus position on the floor beside the tree. "You know she sits just like you're sitting right now."

"Dad," I said, "I really don't want to hear anymore

about Su Lin."

Father was shocked into silence. He was not used to being addressed in such a fashion.

For my father I had bought four dress shirts, four ties, and a $50 gift certificate from Sears. For my mother I had bought a body towel, since her arthritis had advanced to the stage where it was becoming harder and harder for her to shower and dry off, along with a half a dozen bright colored scarves, the sort she liked best. "Thank you, Ishmael!" She cried, kissing me on the cheek.

Her gift to me was something I had been meaning to get myself for some time, Elton John's album *Tumbleweed Connection*. "I couldn't find that album at the base exchange," she said, "so I had to get it at a civilian record store."

"Good," I replied. "I'm glad to see you sometimes venture beyond the base in your shopping."

My father didn't even pretend to listen to us.

"I have a few items I want to show you guys," he said.

"More memorabilia from Korea?" My mother asked.

"Yep," he replied, "I think you'll find these things mighty interesting. I ran across this one guy who was one of the civilian workers in the mess hall. He was also a painter. I gave him a picture of you and from it he painted your portrait."

I glanced at the portrait. It was a somewhat younger version of me, and I was Korean. I turned it aside feeling a mounting stream of disquietude building up inside me. It was a sensation I was no stranger to, yet I tried my hardest not to let it show.

The Call

It must have been clear that I was not impressed because my father began to rant at me. "This is the work of a very talented man," he told me in a tone of reproach. "You should feel privileged he took the time and effort to paint this portrait of you!"

All this happened so many times before. Nobody truly knew the real me—only my father's distorted concept of who he wanted me to be. "Well," I said, "if you believe he deserves that much respect, you might want to place the portrait on the wall in your bedroom."

"No!" Mother cried, clearly upset. "I believe we need to discuss it later, Abe."

Next, father pulled out his old Army fatigue jacket and actually told me that now it was mine because he believed I was big enough to fill it. As I took the jacket in hand I couldn't help but think I had missed something along the way—as if there was some sort of connection I could not truly fathom, or didn't really want to comprehend. I looked it over. There was plenty of pocket room and it came complete with a hood, a great commodity in case of inclement weather. "Thanks," I said. "I'll just remove the U.S. Army insignia. Otherwise it would be an illegal jacket."

"Don't do that," my father told me in a firm, resolute tone. "Leave it on."

I had no intention of doing that, but I said nothing more. Everything was just as it always had been. I was simply an extension of him. Clearly, as far as he was concerned, I did not exist.

When evening came, I felt it was a good time to dismiss myself from the festivities. Instead, however, my father said that he needed to talk to me in private.

Dad's den was definitely his room—sort of a combination office and military trophy room. On the walls were numerous eight-by-ten glossy photos he had taken of the various military bases where he had been stationed, coupled with medals and insignias he had acquired during his thirty-year stint in the armed forces. He also had numerous pictures on his desk. A few were of mother and me, but there were about a dozen of Su Lin and a couple of the Mice Band. The bookcase was filled with books on Asian culture and World War II history, topics that had become his passion.

"Have a seat," he said.

I sat in the chair adjacent the couch.

"Your mother tells me you decided to go half-time on your studies."

"That's right. No draft. No hurry."

"When do you anticipate finishing your bachelor's degree?"

"Two years."

"Are you sure you need to take that long? You know we'd like for you to move back home. You can cut your workload back to part time, and devote full time to your studies."

"No thanks," I told him. "I prefer to do things this way."

"Just as you like, I suppose," he said. "But there's something else I need to talk to you about. It concerns Su Lin."

"Dad," I said, rising from the chair, "I thought I made it clear earlier this evening that I didn't want to talk about her. Now if this is what you dragged me in here to

The Call

talk about then the conversation is over and I'm going home."

"Now just hold on, Ishmael! This is important!"

"To you, perhaps."

"No, this is something that concerns all of us, as a family."

"Then why isn't Mom in here with us?"

"I'll get to that. But first I want to tell you about Su Lin!"

"Like I said earlier, I've already heard more about Su Lin than I want to hear."

"I just want you to know I've never met a person who gave so much of herself."

"Yeah, I heard about her giving."

"Son, this is serious. She's had a very hard life and I want to see that she has a shot at something better. Now, she's got a sister who lives in Dallas, but she's agreed to, once she gets over here, stay with us and help your mother out with the house work. Now, we know your mother's health is not getting any better, and having Su Lin here will be an enormous help."

"Why not just hire a maid to come in a few days a week?"

"That is not an option!" he snapped.

"And why isn't it?"

"Because it just isn't! Now don't argue with me! I've been trying to get Su Lin a visa to come to the United States, but before she can come I have to present proof that she will not become a ward of the state. I've been in contact with an attorney and together we've explored all the possible options and have come to this conclusion:

The most viable option is for us to present notarized documentation stating that she will be married to someone upon her arrival. That's what's needed to address the issue of support. I've done an extensive search for possible candidates and only one option remains open to me."

"As long as it doesn't concern me," I said, starting for the door, "I don't care what you do."

"It *does* concern you. I want you to sign on as Su Lin's fiancé."

"Are you insane?" I demanded. I had known him to be outrageous before, but never like this.

"No," he said, revealing his ultimate authoritative appearance. "I've never been more serious. It's the only chance we have of getting her to the States."

I felt a chill go through me and watched solemnity enshroud my father's countenance. Once again I felt like a powerless child going up against the wrath of a vengeful and angry god determined to have his way with me. Words stuck in my throat. My body started to tremble helplessly.

"We'll talk about it later," I heard myself say. All that I wanted to do was to get out of that house before intimidation set in.

My father called to me, "Wait! How do I get in touch with you?"

Trying in desperation to hold back the tears that were yearning to flow like an angry river, I continued my mad rush to the front door. "I'll be in touch!"

"Don't you want to have dessert with us?" I heard my mother say.

Saying goodbye to my mother, I rushed out the front

The Call

door to my car. I turned on the ignition and drove off into the night, overwhelmed by pangs of anger, loneliness, and dread. Once again I was in a double bind: I was damned if I did and damned if I didn't. If I signed the notarized paperwork I'd be guilty of signing a fraudulent document, facilitating an immoral living arrangement, and hurting my mother in the process. I'd also once again be relegated to my father's shadow, a cog in his machine. If I did not do what he'd asked me to do, I'd be committing the sin of selfishness and condemning somebody halfway around the world to a continued existence of poverty, disease, and starvation. It was a terrible position for me to be in, and Father was quite adept, as usual, at being responsible for my problem. As always, I found myself lacking in the emotional resources needed to contend with him. And that was not all. Isaac was at it again. His laughter resounded louder than ever. Isaac, please!" I cried. "For once in your death, shut up!"

A couple of months passed. I was into the winter quarter at the university and still working the graveyard shift at my state government job. One evening, while I was tending to matters in the central filing room, I received a call over the intercom, something that never happened on the graveyard shift. The call was from my father, who had somehow tracked me down, something he had a talent for doing. "Dad," I said, "I can't talk here. My boss is very strict about us taking personal calls at work." That, of course, was a lie. Nobody really cared.

"This is important," he insisted. "It's about Su Lin." When do you get off work? I need for you to meet me at the notary's office. I had the papers drawn up and I need your power of attorney."

"I really don't want to talk about this," I told him.

"Just do it, okay? I'm counting on you. I mean it! This is very important to me!"

I felt myself begin to shake.

My boss, a paunchy man of about fifty, who was sitting at the desk where I had taken the call, asked me if something was wrong.

"More than I can say," I replied.

"Care to talk about it?" My boss was quite caring and understanding when it came to personal matters with his employees. But I was very leery of taking anyone into my confidence.

"If I started doing that I wouldn't get any work done," I replied.

"Your father?"

"Yes."

"Thought so. I had one of those. Judging from your age I'd say your father is right on the verge of having a midlife crisis."

"What makes you say that?" I asked.

Carl gave me an embarrassed look and said, "Because I'm having one myself. Fortunately I'm single and if I'm smart I'll stay that way. Only problem is, I never was that smart."

The shift drew to a close. As for me, dutiful son that I was cursed to be, I wound up appearing at the notary's office at the hour my father had specified. Both my folks were at the front door awaiting my arrival. Father was all decked out in his military apparel with shoes spit polished. His uniform had been freshly pressed with all the insignias in place, including the medals that he had been awarded over the span of thirty-one years in the Army. He stood erect, at attention, a figure in sharp contrast to me, unkempt as I was. I felt dwarfed by his presence. We proceeded inside the notary's office. Father stood behind me projecting an aura of command.

The notary pointed out to me where I needed to sign, her face expressionless. It made me feel sick to realize what she must be thinking, given the contents of the document I was signing. Afterwards I went home and took a long shower, trying to wash off the disgrace I felt for what I had done.

One week later Father called me again at work, and said that we needed to talk.

"No," I retorted, "you need to talk. I need to get back to work. Please don't call here again."

"Carl," I said, hanging up, "I've got a problem. I'm afraid he's going to keep calling me here and I need you to run interference. I need to focus on what I'm doing."

"Wrong!" Carl said, laughing. "Around here you focus on something interesting like sex or playing mind games with yourself so you can keep awake and keep working. You focus on what you're doing around here and it'll put you right to sleep. I ought to know. I've been working this shift for the past five years."

"If you feel that way, why do you keep working it?"

"For the money! Do you think I do it because I enjoy it so much? For some reason the Department of Motor Vehicles feels it's necessary to maintain and expand its document control division and to do so requires a graveyard shift. And for reasons that are beyond my ability to fathom, the tasks we perform here at this ungodly hour the department thinks are necessary."

"Whatever," I replied. "But look, if my father calls could you tell him that policy dictates no personal calls or that I'm not available?"

"No problem. Consider me your interference runner."

So, as Carl valiantly tried to hold my parental adversary at bay, both the Korean Consulate and the U.S. Bureau of Immigration denied my father's petition for Su Lin's visa, a refusal he regarded as a direct slap in the face. There was in no way he was prepared to accept it as a final answer. Together, he and his attorney formulated another strategy, one that would once again require my appearance before the notary.

This time, however, I went to the house and confronted him directly

"Father," I said, this time facing him dry-eyed and with no quiver in my voice, "to paraphrase an old saying, use me once, shame on you. Use me twice, shame on me. I don't want to be a part of this. I think it's sick. I think it's disgusting. And I think you're giving Mother the royal shaft pursuing this matter like you're doing." I then got in my car and drove away. Strangely enough, although all this should have been said a long time ago, I felt, as I drove away, like a boy who had just lost his father.

My father's retirement papers finally came through. On a crisp morning in early February of the following year the troops were lined up in front of the Presidio headquarters for final inspection, one that would mark the end of Lt. Colonel Abe O'Donnell's illustrious career in the military. Unfortunately the matter of Su Lin had still not been resolved, nor was he prepared to go down in defeat on the issue. Cashing in on a privilege accorded retired military men, he began hopping on board military flights to Korea on a space-available basis. It was there he could enjoy the company of Su Lin and arrange face-to-face confrontations with the Korean Consulate. These confrontations did not give him too much leeway, but he kept on pushing the issue.

At the same time, the father of the girl in Missouri sent a process server to the house, and although my mother turned him away, it was clear that she was badly shaken. I tried to distance myself from the drama but couldn't help but be disturbed by the notion of what might happen next. After all, given my limited perspective, the entire scenario appeared ripe with potential for severe domestic upheaval.

Meanwhile my father's obsession with the Su Lin issue continued to fester, even though each time he returned from Korea with nothing to show for his trouble. Then, on one journey he took ill and was hospitalized on the base. During his stay at the hospital, his attending physician informed him that he had emphysema. Perhaps it was the shock of hearing this news, or perhaps it was due to weakened resolve—I never knew the actual reason—but shortly after that, he quit hopping military flights and gave up on trying to gain a visa for Su Lin.

After he had been home for a few weeks he called me at work asking to speak with me. When I arrived at my parents' house the following Saturday, I found my father, still in his pajamas and robe, his hair disheveled, his face unshaven, at the kitchen table smoking a cigarette, sipping on a cup of coffee, obviously trying to collect his thoughts.

"So what's my status?" I asked, sitting down opposite him. "Am I still your son or have I been officially disowned?"

"You're my son and I love you," he said unexpectedly. "Nothing is going to change that. I just need to know a few things."

"And they might be?"

"When are you looking to graduate?"

"This June."

"And after that? What are your plans?"

"I really don't know. I have my job. The way things are with the economy right now, I guess I should count myself lucky just to stay where I am."

"We're O'Donnells, Son. We never content ourselves to just stay where we are. You ought to know that with all the moves we made while you were growing up. What I'm trying to say is that the time is coming for you to focus on what it is you're going to do with your life. Your mother and I are not always going to be around. You know that I have emphysema."

"I note you're still smoking," I said.

"It's too late for me. I can't quit."

"Who was it who told me as a child the word 'can't' is not in the O'Donnell's dictionary?"

Father grinned and said. "That old fool. He smoked then too. I don't think my nerves could stand it if I tried to quit."

The Call 87

It was a strange feeling. For a moment we were not at odds with one another. He was actually reaching out to me, man to man. He was, in fact, almost amiable. I glanced at my father as he exuded words and gestures reflective of humility and contrition, and hard as it was for me to accept, I felt a begrudging compassion for the man I had often held in contempt and disdain. A part of me wanted to say, "Well, what do you know, you're human."

"I see," I replied. "Well then, all I can say about what my plans are is that I've really been too busy to think about them. I know I'll still have my job. Oh yes, state policy dictates I'll be getting a raise in June. I haven't the money for graduate school. If that's a goal, I'll have to start saving for it."

"That's a start. But what about West Point? What about your military career?"

"Dad, I could never be a soldier. You ought to know that by now."

Father then leaned forward, clenched his fist, shook it at me, and raised his voice, "Son, all men, deep inside them, have it in them to be warriors. If they haven't, then they can't truly call themselves men. It's the nature of our makeup. It's the goal of our existence. It's how the nature of men balances with the nature of women." Even though he spoke deliberately and with authority, the words were those of a madman, in my opinion. How could he justify the glory of dying in battle for an ideology he did not necessarily believe in?

"To die in battle for a cause is perhaps the most noble way in which to face your maker," he went on, "a privilege beyond reckoning … and a privilege I'll never have. Mine's the straw death, son. It's too late for me. But it's not too late for you."

I stood up. "Dad," I said, "even though I'm not sure what I want to do after graduation, I know that the so-called privilege you're talking about isn't going to be it. I need to excuse myself. I have homework I need to do and my apartment needs cleaning."

Outside, the sun was shining, a flock of birds were flying in from the south. Taking in the natural beauty surrounding me, my thoughts reflected back on my father's words. "How glorious to die in battle," I mumbled. "Thank you, no. I prefer to die of old age like a sane human."

I finished my senior project in time for June graduation. It was a one hundred page, double-spaced, typewritten dissertation on religion and the American culture. The theme of the paper was simple—it attested that within the confines of the American culture, we have recreated God in our own image. The professorial staff liked it. They awarded my efforts with an A, which accorded me with half-time honors. However, others within the program called me a heretic, a blasphemer, and even questioned how I could call myself a Christian. My graduation ceremony was finally at hand. It took place at the campus stadium where, to a background of "Pomp and Circumstance" played on a miniature organ, the capped and gowned students took their places at the front. The speaker droned on for approximately forty-five minutes and at the conclusion, we lined up in accordance with our degrees and majors.

The Call

Because I was only a part-time student who worked full time, I was pretty much cut off socially. Only Mom and Dad, along with my Aunt Myrtle and Uncle Philip, were there to see me graduate. After the ceremony the five of us commemorated my achievement by going out to lunch.

"Now that you've got your degree, what do you plan on doing with the rest of your life?" My father was quick to ask once we were settled in a booth.

"Tell you what I'd be doing if I was your age," my Uncle Philip, a portly, balding man with a gray complexion, interjected, "I'd be goin' into plastics! That's where the money is!"

"Oh pshaw, Phil," replied Aunt Myrtle, a raven-haired matron in her late sixties, "the boy's not even educated along those lines." Then she turned to me. "It's computers you should look into. That's where the future is."

"Remember our talk about a military career?" My father asked. "I can still get you into West Point."

"Okay," I said, "you're all so concerned about my future, so here it is." Everybody leaned forward in anticipation of what my plans were. "In a little less than forty-eight hours, I'm going to work."

Everybody leaned back with a groan.

"Work?!" my father said. "What work? You have some serious decisions to make about your future."

"Oh stop it, Abe." My mother said. "He's got a job. He's not starving. And he certainly hasn't been living off of us for some time now. Just be happy for his success and enjoy the moment." My father remained silent throughout the rest of the festivities.

Although I was grateful for my mother's intervention a part of me knew, deep down, that Dad was not altogether wrong in his counsel. I would need to make some move toward a future. But it was too soon for me to do anything about it now.

A couple more years passed. I transferred from the Department of Motor Vehicles to the Department of Education with the hope of acquiring a promotion. I took a few business courses at the community college and received a promotion to secretary, again with the Department of Motor Vehicles. This time it was a day shift job. But life was proving itself to be emptier and emptier the longer I maintained my status quo, and I still felt guilty about the part I had played in the Su Lin affair, and my father continued to dog me with calls at work.

Other changes transpired. My roommate left the apartment to marry an old high school flame. I advertised in the newspaper and through my old alma mater for a new roommate, but my next roommate and I were not compatible. He liked to party until the morning's wee hours and many times he came up short on his share of the rent and the utilities. There were also instances when the cops paid us a visit late at night because he was playing his music too loud. Housework was also not one of his strong suits, and it wasn't long before the apartment resembled a dump.

After a few months of living in this chaos, I decided to take the path of least resistance and move into a vacant apartment near my church, an American Baptist church situated in downtown Sacramento. In the years that followed, I became more and more enmeshed in various church activities, teaching children's Sunday school classes, working in the kitchen preparing food for various functions, serving sporadically as night watchman for the church grounds, and even helping out in the church office typing memos, filing, and doing other chores. The ministerial staff always appeared to be a bit standoffish whenever I tried to initiate conversations with them and I never could figure out why; two fellow church members, Sol Pickering and Mary McMillan, were continually socializing with the ministerial staff and getting along with them quite famously.

Sol Pickering was a well-groomed young man in his early twenties. His family had been with the church for generations, so he had acquired an inherited prominent standing among both the members and the clergy. Whenever he dropped by, the staff, the clergy, and the members would all flock around him, exchanging greetings and offering up small talk. Sol's effervescent smile and bright, sanguine demeanor were always winning favorites of all he came into contact with. He was also a favorite among the college girls.

Mary McMillan, a slender red head, also came from a multigenerational church family. But unlike Sol, Mary was more reserved. Yet she was still popular, not only with boys, but with the older members of the church. Although only twenty-four, she had already turned down a multitude of marriage proposals.

When both Sol and Mary announced that they had received the Lord's leading into the ministry, the ministerial staff and a large portion of the church members reveled at the news, set aside scholastic funding for them, and prayed for them during the course of a church service with a laying on of hands.

I too had experienced what I felt to be something similar. It happened one night while I was walking alone at a park by the Sacramento River. As I wandered about the park, I lifted my voice up in prayer, asking the Lord how I could cleanse myself of the awful guilt I felt for my part in the Su Lin matter, the terrible feelings of emptiness and loneliness that always seemed to dog my footsteps in spite of my professed faith in Christ. Where could I go? What could I do? What proactive measures could I take to feel whole again? When the answer came, it brought with it a sense of peace. It was not a road to Damascus experience, but I knew it to be possessed of divine inspiration because I never entertained such a thought before: the thought was to go into the ministry. I was stunned by this call and asked God, "Is this what you are really saying to me?"

"What's stopping you?" I heard an inner voice say. "You have the intelligence. You have the sensitivity. You have the compassion. You're certainly no stranger to pain. You have the mind of a scholar and the heart of a child. Need I say more? The call is yours. You have but to claim it."

Never in my life had I experienced so much affirmation. I felt a sense of cleanliness, wholeness, and clarity. My heart was light. My spirit danced inside me.

I allowed a few weeks to pass to give myself enough time to assimilate the message. Finally, unable to keep the experience to myself any longer, I made an appointment with the senior pastor, Reverend Jonah

The Call

Michaels, a gaunt, grim man in his late fifties. In spite of the contributions I had made to the church over the years, Reverend Michaels had chosen to distance himself from me and I was always at a loss to figure out why.

At the outset of the meeting in his office, I told Reverend Michaels that I believed I had experienced the Lord's call to ministry. To my surprise, he responded by asking me if I were certain it had not been Satan who had called me. And when I registered surprise, he told me that it said right in Scripture that even the Lord of Darkness could disguise himself as an angel of light.

I was beginning to get angry. How dare he? Who was he to tell me I had encountered Satan?

"So, why do you reserve that question for me, yet you give affirmation to Sol and Mary?" I asked angrily.

"I know you, but I know them much better," he replied. "One of my gifts is that of discernment. It is a gift the Lord has bestowed upon me and it's proven itself to be quite reliable over the years. So I have no reason to question it now. I truly believe that Sol and Mary have received the Lord's calling."

"And me?"

"To be honest," he said, "I don't believe the Lord reserves a calling of that nature for someone like you."

I felt like I had been kicked in the gut. "And you can be certain of that?" I demanded

"As certain as I am of the sun rising in the east and setting in the west," he told me. "I know you. I've known you for the past four or five years. I've watched you meander around the church like a stray sheep over the years, and I can only guess what your background is. I've never met your folks. I don't know anything about your family. As I said, you're like a stray sheep and although I believe the Lord takes in strays, I do not believe he calls upon them to be shepherds, especially not someone as introverted, undemonstrative, and highly guarded as you. And having read your senior paper, I find it hard to even accept you as a true believer."

A bolt of rage coursed through me as I listened to his words. It was by far the most disdainfully sanctimonious lecture I ever had the displeasure of hearing, and there I was, on the receiving end of it. Every part of me wanted to lash out at the man. Yet, I exercised restraint and withheld my natural impulse.

Reverend Michaels then shook his head reticently and said, "It's not for you, Ishmael. Purge the thought from your mind. I'll even pray for you to have the strength to do so."

Bowing his head, he began to pray, "Oh Lord, we beseech thee to guide us in your path of righteousness, and in so doing, banish all Satanic influences from us. Help young Ishmael to find his right path and not trod in ways you have not blessed for him. We ask this Heavenly Father, in the name of Jesus, Amen. Now go, Ishmael, and may God go with you."

All this left me stunned. I felt like the devil's spawn and a black sheep rolled into one. Just outside the office I ran into Sol. "Hey, Ish!" he said grinning. "What's happening? You're lookin' a bit down! What gives?"

"It's a long story, Sol," I replied.

"Well, it just so happens I'm free for the next hour," he said, "so why don't we go somewhere and talk about it?"

The Call

There was a coffee shop within walking distance of the church. Upon our arrival I proceeded to tell him of my call and what happened when I shared all this with Reverend Michaels. Sol grinned, gave a wave of dismissal and said, "Ah, don't pay any attention to that old fart. If you really want to find out if it was from God or Satan you've got to be like Peter and test the waters!"

"Could you be a little more specific?" I asked him.

"Well, your first step would be to write to some of the seminaries," he suggested. "Then, after you've narrowed down your choices, apply for admission and see if they'll accept you. If they do, you can bet the call has God's seal of approval. If they don't, then Satan never truly got to first base, did he?"

"And finances?"

"That's also part of God's package deal."

"Okay then, if that's all there is to it, why did the staff affirm you and Mary and give me the cold shoulder?"

"Okay Ishmael, I'll give it to you straight," Sol replied, sipping his coffee. "Mary and I come from long-established families of this church. But, like the man told you, you're a stray ... someone who shows up out of nowhere with no known roots. Don't you see? It's politics, all politics! There might be an element of the spiritual, but most of it is about who you know, and what you bring to the table. I've known most of the families in this church since I was born. I even know most of the established families in the other congregations within fifty miles of here because I grew up going to youth group events with their kids. I even stayed in their homes and dated their daughters."

"Look," he went on. "I want to make this very clear. My affirmation and Mary's stem chiefly from who our families are. You know, our pedigrees. We can back up the spiritual end of the spectrum by tossing out some God talk. It's the type of language we've been around most of our lives. Connections, that's the ticket. You'll have to get by principally on the spirituality you bring to the table and eventually, as you pick up on the old ecumenical savvy, the connections will develop."

"But what about my being undemonstrative, introverted, and guarded?"

"Of course you're undemonstrative, introverted, and guarded. That's because your level of comfort around the church isn't as high as mine. But I wouldn't let that stop me. Look in the Bible. Moses didn't start out as any kind of showman. And for that matter, look at Jesus. I never heard anyone describe him as being charismatic. So don't let Reverend Michaels's words get you down. I love the man to pieces, but he's an old fart and I've told him that to his face. Oh, and by the way, I liked your senior project. Very scholarly, and believable, too. Listen, I've got to go now. Keep me posted on your progress, okay?" Sol's explanation made it easier to accept Reverend Michael's rejection, and although I still had a sense of being outside some sort of inner circle, I followed his advice.

One seminary in particular, located in Oklahoma right on the Cherokee Strip, seemed to stand out for me. I sent them transcripts of my college work and received a very encouraging letter from the seminary's dean, one Archibald Shyster, who seemed very cordial and receptive to my attempts at gaining admission. He even stated that because of my high degree of academic excellence, I might qualify for a scholarship. I was quite enthused about this prospect, although a bit bewildered. I had maintained academic honors during my junior and senior years of college, but my lower division work tallied out to something just below a B average. But it was all there in black and white—proof of my admission and my endorsement from the Almighty.

Shortly after Archibald Shyster sent the letter endorsing me as a possible candidate for a scholarship, he sent me another letter informing me that God had seen fit to call him into a pastorate at the First Christian Church of Big Springs, Texas, thereby requiring that he resign his post as dean of the seminary. Assuming the position of dean for the interim would be Professor Rupert Babcock.

Shortly after receiving confirmation of my admission to seminary, I stopped by the church in the middle of the week and shared the information with the church staff. Again I received no affirmation, just solemn stares, stiff congratulations, and looks of condescension. Reverend Michaels shook his head and with a look of sorrow on his face and said, "God help you, boy. God help the church," a sentiment the rest of staff seemed to echo.

Mary McMillan, however, came to my defense. "I think it's disgraceful the way you're all disparaging Ishmael's good fortune!" she exclaimed. "Obviously he wouldn't have been admitted into seminary if he didn't have the Lord's endorsement! I think we all need to rally behind him and be supportive! After all, aren't we all family here?"

"See here, young lady," Reverend Michaels began.

"No," Mary told him, "*you* see here! Just because you've been in the ministry for the past one hundred years, don't think you have a monopoly on who it is that God deems worthy of His calling!"

"Maybe so," Reverend Michaels's replied, "but pardon me if I still harbor strong reservations."

Although Mary and Sol's affirmation carried weight, in the end it was Reverend Michaels's position that won out. I only received a marginal endorsement from the congregation at large, and I would be accorded no laying on of hands.

Three more months passed before it was time for me to begin gathering things together for my journey to Oklahoma. During the last week before my departure I stayed at my parent's house. My folks were elated with my decision, particularly with regards to the seminary I had chosen. To my astonishment it was the same seminary that Chaplain Thomas Sutton had attended and graduated from before he entered the Army. Mother went on to inform me that she had received a card from Mrs. Sutton wherein she stated that Becky had just graduated with a liberal arts degree from Parkins University; a goal she had achieved in only three years. She was married to someone by the name of Sam Baker, a fellow graduate, and was residing in the university town of Idle, Oklahoma. Mother went on to state that Paulette, the second eldest of the Sutton girls, was still in the process of completing her undergraduate degree at the same university.

Mother then placed the letter on the dining room

table and exclaimed, "Wouldn't that be great? Paulette could claim real status having you, a seminary student, for a boyfriend and I just know the two of you will be so good for each other!"

I looked at Mom, sighed, and said, "Mom, this is reality. You know things don't work that way."

"You could look her up," she said hopefully.

"Do you want to marry me off?" I asked. "It's been over fifteen years since we were stationed in Virginia. My interest in the Sutton girls is water under the bridge."

"You know what your problem is, Ishmael?" my father said. "You're a pessimist."

"I'm a realist," I countered. "And if reality is at times less than optimistic, I can only plead guilty as charged."

"That's a hell of an attitude for a preacher to have!" he grumbled.

Despite his stern tone, Father was quite pleased in my choice of career paths, more so than I think he had been of anything I had ever undertaken. I was pleased at his positive reaction, but suspicious at the same time. He never gave me his approval without there being some hidden agenda, but I was not to find out what that agenda entailed until later.

Then there were the dreams that would plague me until my time of departure—dreams I could not fully comprehend; yet they were brutally consistent, blunt, and mounting in intensity night after night, always featuring my dual soul, Isaac, laughing at me, mocking me. What did it mean? I had to go to seminary to find out.

II

Parkins University - Seminary

"I can't believe this!" Professor Rupert Babcock shouted. It was late August and the semester was to begin in another week. "Dean Shyster left this place in such a mess, it's going to take a miracle to sort it all out! These accounts are in shambles, there's no order to the academic records, admission standards are nonexistent … I am outraged! And he left me holding the bag! God called him to Big Springs! Horse manure!"

His secretary, Ms. Adams recoiled in the face of his fury. "Must you be so coarse?" She asked.

"Coarse?" Babcock protested. "I'll tell you what's coarse! The mess my predecessor left me, that's what's coarse! Of all the backstabbing, deceptive, dirty dealing … and he has the audacity to say God called him to a church! That guy has all the principles of a polecat, and the ethics of a weasel!"

Rupert Babcock's assessment of the situation was virulent, but accurate. As he looked around the office he could see stacks of misplaced files, overdue accounts, mismanaged financial statements, assorted transcripts of prospective students, and contract disputes. "Bad record keeping and faulty accounting is one issue, but while he was here he robbed us of our credibility, our integrity, and our academic standards!" Babcock went on. "We're nothing without those things! Nothing! Look at the people he admitted! Look at this file … Markem McClusky, alligator wrestler. This guy doesn't have any more than a tenth-grade education! How's he supposed to contend with the academic rigors of a graduate seminary program?"

This was, he knew, a college that had been well known for its strict academic standards, while demanding of its students only the most exemplary form of Christian conduct. Its faculty and staff were held to even stricter measures of honesty and integrity. Such had once been the Parkins legacy.

"Let's see," Babcock went on, calmer now, but still clearly distressed, "we also have a number of alumni entering the seminary. Naturally their churches are funding much of their education. I don't know. I've always been a bit leery of students entering the seminary right after their undergraduate studies. I always believed they should be out in the world for a while before embarking on an endeavor such as ministry. But my predecessor seems to disagree. I guess he felt the wolf breathing at the door and was desperate for bodies. And what do we have here … Sharon McMillan, the class valedictorian … that isn't too bad. Although with her looks I picture her more as a model or a show-business figure. I can just see her pastoring a church, giving a Sunday morning sermon. She'd have an attentive congregation, but I guarantee it wouldn't be her sermons they'd be paying attention to!"

"Mr. Babcock! Get that lecherous grin off your face this instant! A married man of your age! You should be ashamed of yourself!"

"But I ain't dead." He shot her a quick, sly glance.

"Let's see what else we have … Wanda Epperson,

she's okay, a bit on the shallow side. Frumpy too."

"Now isn't that being a bit judgmental?"

"Not really. I've known her since she started here as a freshman and she's always maintained that she is one to whom the Lord commends. She's also after her MRS degree, you know. And she's already got the sucker who's going to give it to her picked out. The poor bastard'll never know what hit him."

Babcock continued perusing the files. "Let's see, Lewis Coppel, PE major, Religion minor. He's okay. All right, here's one of Shyster's little bloopers, Rufus Pelmonte. I've known that boy since the day he was born. Cheated by the Lord and dumb as an ass! It's been said that to survive as a minister you have to have three distinct attributes: one, the heart of a child, two, the mind of a scholar, and three, the hide of a rhinoceros. This guy is definitely lacking in one of these attributes. Only problem is, he's too dumb to know it. Now I know all Shyster wanted was warm bodies! And here's another. Hiram Southey. Straight Cs! And he is practically void of any social graces! He's brash, belligerent, argumentative, obnoxious, and just because his father's a minister doesn't mean he automatically gets a ticket to instant admission. And then there's Kathleen McKensie. Talk about something being wrong!"

What indeed was wrong with Kathleen McKensie? Professor Babcock knew the answer to that question all too well. "Kathleen's from all over the place, lively, sensitive, but damaged. Her father's an army chaplain. He may be exemplary in his field, but he remains clueless in matters pertaining to his family, or he just doesn't care to acknowledge Kathleen's problem. How she made it through college, I don't know, but whether or not she's up to seminary work, I can't be sure. She had a severe case of dyslexia coming into Parkins, and I'm not sure to what extent she's overcome the problem since she's been here."

"But she *did* make it through college," Ms. Adams replied, "and her grades weren't all that bad."

"Yep. Major in music, minor in religion. But based on what I heard, she had the consistent help of both Sharon McMillan and Laurie Parson, two of the smartest students to ever attend Parkins." Rupert shook his head in dismay and said, "I hope she's up to it, but I seriously have my doubts."

"She'll do just fine," Ms. Adams assured him. "And besides, you know what the politics are like around here. You know good and well that we are answerable to the churches in our fellowship. They fund this seminary and you know that many of our alumni students are sons and daughters of ministers serving those churches, and those churches are funding the education of these sons and daughters. That's what keeps us afloat. Many of them are here to uphold a family tradition, and who are we to break the chain? We have to find a way to get them through! The same holds true for the Methodist students. The Methodist denomination is the second most populous denomination represented here, and a lot of our funding comes from them as well. So, if you're wise, you'll respect the politics. This isn't the past anymore, Mr. Babcock. We have got to learn to move with the times and the changing climate."

"What about doing the right thing?" Professor

Babcock grumbled.

"As long as it doesn't conflict with the politics."

"Look, if I play favorites, it's bound to show."

"Be subtle. Don't let it show."

"But I am not a politician. I'm a teacher."

"Not anymore," she told him, "If you expect to survive an interim as acting dean, you'd better become a politician. Archibald Shyster was as incompetent as they come as an administrator, an academician, and a theologian, and you might not think too highly of him as a man, but boy, how he could play politics! It was the only way he survived this post for so long. So play the game, just for a little while. You know it has to be done. Save the morality and integrity for the classroom. While occupying the post of acting dean, you're a politician. Here. Drink this coffee. And remember that you have one week to put the seminary retreat together."

"Okay, let's carry on," Babcock said. There was weariness in his voice. "Did you say we have Laurie Parson as one of our in-coming seminarians?"

"Yes. She spent a year working as a secretary, then was able to secure a government loan for her graduate work."

"Wonderful. She was an excellent student. Finished her undergraduate work here in just three years."

"We also have her brother, Benjamin."

"Not so wonderful."

"He's married now to Jana Wentworth."

"Isn't marriage a grand institution?" Babcock said dryly. "I swear, if I didn't laugh, I'd cry. Ben and Jana's marriage was shotgun enforced because Ben's preacher father found out the couple was having sex. He made his son marry her, yet ol' Shyster just admitted Ben anyway!"

"But Jana's a preacher's daughter." Ms. Adams protested.

"You think that always makes a hill of bean's worth of difference? Believe me, I've known the Wentworth family for going on thirty years and I've watched Jana grow up. Her association with the church has always been nominal at best. And now she's the wife of an aspiring minister! I don't know about you, but back in my day when a man answered the call, his entire family was there to uphold and support his decision. I certainly don't see that feature present with today's applicants, and I sure as hell don't see it when the ministerial candidate is bound by a shotgun marriage!"

"But what about the other candidates?"

"I don't see it much with them, either." Babcock grabbed a handful of files from his desk. "Leonard DeWilde, former engineer and CEO of an automobile manufacturing firm, now aspiring ministerial candidate. From what I gather, his wife is not very happy with his decision. Here's another. Jack Logan, stock broker, appliance salesman, and businessman."

"Sort of a Jack of all trades, eh?" she said laughing.

"I'm trying to ignore that, Ms. Adams. Anyway, he's currently working as a janitor at the Parkins University Place Church. Professor Wilson got him the job. Jack's got three kids with one on the way, and needless to say his wife is none too happy about him dragging her and the kids away from their comfortable lifestyle just so he could answer his calling. And finally, there's Jerry and Linda Cantrell. They were both psychiatric social workers. Now they're aspiring to be a husband and wife ministerial team. And they're Presbyterians, too. We don't get too many of those. I don't anticipate too much trouble from them."

"So, is that it?"

"No, there's more, but they're mostly single. There's Jason Tyler, former insurance salesman. There's Norman Decantor, graduate of Michigan State University, major in Voice, who spent the past twenty-five years as an opera singer. And finally, there's Samuel Church, fresh from a small college up north. Shyster would let someone like him with less than a 2.0 grade point average into this place. Then we have the Methodist students. Lawrence Viscount. He's okay, although a bit on the obnoxious side. Randal Von Krumpke. Hmmm, graduate of Oral Roberts University. Wonder why he'd choose us? Jessica Bently. Licensed to preach at twelve. Ordained at twenty. And Samuel Hill, plumber. Another one of Shyster's follies. No degree."

"Uh, Shyster was making allowances for students over forty."

"Yeah, I can see him doing something like that. But I didn't think the Methodist convention was lowering their standards for candidates as well. And here's Reginald Dexter's file, a sixty-five years old, retired college psychology professor! Unitarian, too. Now we've never had one of those!"

"Dr. Shyster figured he'd make a welcome addition."

"But we're Trinitarian! Unitarian is something totally outside the sphere of our influence!"

"Now, Shyster felt that he could perhaps teach us a

The Call 109

few things."

"I'll bet he could. It might be even more than we can handle. And look at these credentials!"

"Sort of balances out the Markem McClusky admission, doesn't it?"

"It sure does. But neither should be here," Professor Babcock snapped, and then, seeing the look on Ms Adams' face, wished he hadn't. It would be to his advantage to keep on this woman's good side, and he knew it. Given the mess the former dean had left everything in, he was going to need all the help he could get.

Reginald Dexter, his hair just touched with gray, pulled into the parking lot of the dorm to which he had been assigned and sighed. He didn't want to live here, even if it were for only three days a week, not just because it meant living with kids years younger than he, but because it meant being separated from his wife Eleanor with whom he had just spent a delightful summer, parachuting from planes, bungee jumping, hang gliding, dirt biking, wind surfing, and taking in theme parks, all the while experiencing a greater enhancement of the bond that already existed between them. The sex was better too, and lately Reginald's mind was fixed as heavily on that aspect of their renewed relationship as on anything else. One thing Reginald learned over the course of the past summer was that nothing seemed to stimulate the libido more than participation in extreme activity.

However, now was the time for his concentration to shift over to the reinvention of his professional self. At sixty-five he could no longer call himself Reginald Dexter, psychology professor. The University of Oklahoma Board of Regents had seen to that, tagging him with an emeritus after his name, which meant that he had to have new credentials, and a new career. Retirement was not meant for a man as vigorous as he.

Shouldering his luggage, he grabbed his favorite desk lamp from the back seat, and was greeted at the reception window by Benjamin and Jana Parsons, the dorm parents.

"Reginald Dexter's the name," he told them. "I'm one of the new seminarians and I'm seeking the guest quarters. I was informed that those quarters would be the most practical accommodations seeing as I'm only going to be sleeping over three nights a week."

"That's correct," Benjamin, a tall, slender youth told him. "You'll be sharing the guest quarters this week with Charlie Donahue, second-year seminarian. I'm Benjamin and this is my wife Jana. I'm also a new seminarian and durin' your stay here at the dorm, Jana and I will be your mom and dad."

"Interesting familial arrangement, especially since you two were probably still in diapers when I was attaining professorial status," Reginald said dryly. "By the way, any chance of my getting a single room?"

"Only if you want to pay the seven-day-a-week rates. Besides, the guest quarters are the only rooms we have that are carpeted. The other rooms are real shit pits. They don't even have drapes on the windows. You'll like Charlie. He's a real trip. Why don't I show you to your room? Need any help with your baggage?"

"I'm not quite that old and feeble. Although you

could carry this lamp for me."

On the way to the guest room, Reginald tried not to notice the ceiling dotted with chipped plaster and the bare tiled floor.

Once alone, Reginald unpacked his bags, plugged in his lamp, made up his bed, hung his clothes in the closet, and began his tai chi exercises. Just as he entered the "crouching tiger" pose, a man burst into the room, one hand outstretched and introduced himself as Charlie Donahue, a second year seminarian.

"Well you sure picked quite a time to start," Charlie said. "One foot in the grave, the other on a banana peel. Why now?"

"Well, how else would a youthful and exuberant person like myself spend his time? I got tired of the bar scene and disco is dying out."

"Ha ha. By the way, what's that you're doing?"

"Tai chi. It's a series of ancient oriental exercises used for meditative practices. It energizes the system and clears one's thoughts. It's amazing what decrepit old muscles like mine can do when you push them."

"Oh man! You need to start meditating on Jesus!"

"I'm Unitarian. That makes me a bit more eclectic regarding my spiritual focus."

"It also makes you a candidate for Hell!" Charlie snapped, his air of good will momentarily vanishing. "If you're a Unitarian, what're you doing going to a Trinitarian seminary?"

"Berkeley's too far to travel," Reginald said, resuming his tai chi moves. "Besides, the former dean seemed to think I'd make a pretty valuable contribution to the place."

"Archibald Shyster?" Charlie laughed as he sat down on his yet unmade bed. "That old fart? Why, that SOB nearly drove this place to the brink of bankruptcy. If it weren't for the fact that he took in so many students and ignored so many academic standards, we wouldn't be here having this conversation! And you know something? I don't think our chances are very good of seeing graduation unless the current administration can pull a rabbit or two out of the hat. This place is becoming so liberal now I think they'd even admit someone with horns and a tail."

"I could tell the man was a raving con artist the day I met him." Reginald agreed.

"Guy's got no business in the clergy, but, what can you do? There're probably all sorts of people in this business that don't belong, present company excepted. You stick by me during the retreat. I'll teach you how to spot them!"

Reginald laughed, "Okay, you do that!"

Charlie went on to confess that until the previous year he had rarely set foot beyond a fifty-mile radius of Neoshe, Missouri where he received a fundamental and parochial education from grade school up through his collegiate studies at the Ozark Bible College. After college he followed in his father's footsteps, pastoring at the church where his father had served for close to twenty years. He went on to state that his religious roots had been entrenched in the Pentecostal Holiness tradition, and a lot of what had been revealed to him during the past year proved to be quite unsettling.

Reginald could see that Charlie was also startled

The Call

when he indicated his own faith, but it was clear that his roommate was a man who could absorb a lot of surprises. Besides, the fact that he was not rooming with a younger man was a big plus, and he was convinced that the two of them could, after a fashion, make this relationship work.

I arrived on campus a couple of days later. After a quick glance at living quarter options, I found the men's dormitory to be the one most accessible in both cost and availability. I went to the reception window just behind two other prospective residents. One of them, the tallest, biggest, and muscular hulk of a man I'd ever seen, was wearing faded blue Levis overalls, and weighing what I estimated to be close to four-hundred pounds, while the other, long haired, bearded one, was carrying a guitar in a canvas case.

Two young people named Ben and Jana met us at the check-in window and took care of our registration. The hulk was named Markem McClusky and was, he explained, a first year seminarian, while the fellow with the guitar, T. J. Whizzer," said he was "here to have a little Jesus laid on me."

"I've heard of you," I said. "You used to play backup for Iron Butterfly, didn't you?"

"Black Sunday, man!"

"Sorry. I'm more into Country and Western."

"Hey, I dig that, too! Applied with Buck Owens as Don Rich's replacement, but he said I didn't quite fit the image he was looking for."

Then Ben addressed T. J. "You have a guitar. I assume it's electric?"

"Yep."

"You plan on playing it much?"

"Only all the time. It's my baby."

"Well, we have a regulation here that states that all loud noises need to cease around midnight, so if you plan on playing after midnight, do it without the amplifier. Now, here are the keys to your rooms. Supper is served between five and six thirty."

"Are there any other seminarians living in the dorm?" I asked when it was my turn to register.

"Yep," was Ben's response. "We got this arrogant retired college professor. He's rooming with a second-year seminarian who's a converted Pentecostal. Then we got this real dumb shit living down the hall from you. His name's Rufus Pelmonte. And we've also got a beer-guzzling frat guy named Sam Church from some obscure college in Illinois. Oh, by the way, officially it's against campus rules to bring any alcohol on campus and in the dorm, so if you do, be discreet about it. It's not a rule that's rigidly enforced, but don't advertise it."

"I got no intentions of drinkin'!" said Markem. "I was told by someone close to me that the Lord don't like me boozing an' bein' a preacher at the same time!"

When five o'clock arrived, students from both dorms assembled in the dining commons for the evening meal. It became evident within the first fifteen minutes of our introductory conversations that both Laurie and Kathleen were sizing up the new male element of the seminary. Five minutes later, a student named Elmo Piggins walked into the commons, and everybody present broke out in a rousing ovation. One group of students even rallied together, singing a rendition of "The Streak." Turning bright scarlet, Elmo ducked his head and got in the food line.

"What was that all about?" Kathleen asked.

"Haven't you heard?" Ben replied. "That's Elmo Piggins. Some of the girls at the pool pantsed him. He didn't have a towel, so he had to run buck-naked back to the dorm. His roommate wasn't anywhere around, and he didn't have his key, so he had to climb in the window. You'll be seeing pictures of it, I'm sure."

"That's terrible!" Laurie cried turning to Ben. "And I think I know who did it too!"

"Well," Ben said, "whoever did it gave him a huge surge of popularity. I'm bettin' he's gonna have a huge bevy of babes out stalking him now. Especially after seeing that humongous goober of his! Hell, I didn't know anything that big grew on a white man!"

"Benjamin!" Jana cried.

"Well Jana," Ben said turning to his wife, "I'm only stating a fact."

"Elmo is studying to become a minister!" Kathleen protested. "We shouldn't be talking about him like this!"

"Hey!" T. J. chimed in, "Did you say Elmo Piggins, like in Elmo Piggins from Georgetown, South Carolina?"

"Well," Ben replied, "I'm not really sure where he's from. Why? What have you heard about him?"

"Well," said T. J., "if it's the Elmo Piggins I'm thinking of, he's related to that female Country-and-Western star Lawanda Paget. I crossed her path a few times playing gigs with my group."

"Lawanda Paget?" Kathleen exclaimed, "As in

Lawanda Paget and the Jambalaya Five?"

"That's the one," T. J. replied. "Changed her name when she made the big time. Somehow a name like Lawanda Piggins didn't quite cut it when it came to show biz. I got to know her when my group toured with her once. Her father was a minister and her younger brother was following in his footsteps. Just before Elmo went off to college, her father's church had a special laying-on-of-hands service for him. During the service, he started into preaching. Then he singled Lawanda out in front of the entire congregation and told her she needed Jesus. That was when she just upped and belted him in the face while everyone in the church was watching. Then she left and swore she'd never set foot in a church again."

"That's terrible!" cried Kathleen.

"Not really," T. J. continued. "Elmo just continued to preach, and he led his father's church to a revival. Of course this caused a bit of a rift in the family. I could tell it was all Lawanda could do to keep her cool when she talked about it."

"So," said Kathleen, "based on what you tell me, Elmo is a natural, and has all the makings of a real hellfire and brimstone preacher."

"Yeah," Laurie chimed in, "and based on what I've heard, since his arrival on campus, he's still a horny SOB."

"Well then," Ben replied, "he better either get himself hitched, do something about his hormones, or find some other calling."

"Ministers are human, too," Reginald said. "They've got hormones just like everybody else."

"Hey man," said T. J. "you gotta find a way to cool

them raging hormones! They'll mess you up every time!"

"And how would you do that, pray tell?" Ben asked.

"Easy! Give up eating meat!"

"Is that what you've done?" asked Markem, leaning over from his chair nearby.

"Hey, you see any meat on my tray? All veggies! An' a little Jello for dessert."

"Hell, I dunno how you keep alive eatin' so small a portion!" Markem responded. "I need to go back for seconds!"

"Seconds?" exclaimed Ben. "That's the sixth time you've gone back and refilled your tray! Give it a rest, man. This place is already goin' under as it is. Let's not create a food crisis too!"

"But I'm hungry!" Markem protested, picking up his tray and heading back for the food line, "I ain't had nothing to eat since lunch!"

Laurie looked at Kathleen. "Scratch one." Kathleen nodded. Laurie turned to me. "You've been very quiet," she said. "I don't remember catching your name."

Oh my God! I thought. Now she's sizing me up! "Ishmael," I replied. "Ishmael O'Donnell."

"Is that it?"

"What else do you want to know?" I felt put on the spot and a little out of my element.

"Well, everybody's got a story to tell. Where're you from? What did you do before coming here? What school did you attend? What was your major? What led you to attend seminary?"

"California. Secretary. University of California. Major in American Studies with minors in English and

American history. Hopefully, God led me here," I said with a rueful grin despite myself, "although some people seemed inclined to believe it was the other guy."

"They told you that?"

"Yep. I received absolutely no encouragement from my pastor. But, I'd like to believe my call was genuine, so here I am."

"Well, we're glad you are, aren't we, Kathleen?"

"Yeah, welcome!" was Kathleen's response.

"Thank you," I replied.

I appreciated their friendly interest. Never in my whole life had I invested so much in myself and the very thought of it paralyzed me with apprehension. I felt clearly out of my element in these surroundings, as if I were Alice on the other side of the looking glass.

Just about then Markem returned with his tray stocked to the brim. He sat down and immediately began wolfing down the food. "Gawd!" cried Rufus Pelmonte, a tall, slender albino. "I ain't never seen nobody put it away like you, Markem!"

"Whad'ya expect? I'm a growin' boy! An' wouldn't a fifth o' Jack Daniels go good right now to wash it all down!"

"I'll match you on that score," said Sam Church, a portly man with a pencil-thin mustache.

"Boy," Markem replied, "I'd drink your sorry ass clean under the table! That is, iffen the Lord hadn't o' already done tol' me to clean up my act."

"Now let me see if I got this right," said Ben. "According to what you told me earlier, God spoke to you through your pet alligator while you were getting drunk on Jack Daniels?"

The Call

"Yep," Markem replied as he lifted a big fork full of mashed potatoes to his mouth.

"Did it ever occur to you that you might have been drunk and delusional?" Laurie asked.

"Well, yeah. But what the fuck difference does that make? Oh shit, did I just say fuck? Oh fuck, did I just say shit?"

Everyone responded to Markem's words with varying degrees of shock or delighted laughter.

"Hey, anybody here know where I can find me a gig?" T.J. asked. "I need to land me some bread!!"

"You might try the Wagon Wheel," Ben suggested. "That's a club and restaurant that's located on the main drag. They have a band playing there every Tuesday, Thursday, and Saturday evening and they might be looking for another player.

Of the entire group around the table, a woman in her thirties named Ellen was the only abrasive one. After telling us that she'd been saved six months before, and that was why she intended to get herself "a good Christian education," she declared that the company she now found herself in was not what she had been expecting. After she had managed to make a critical comment about all of us, Charlie Donohue spoke up. "Hey, isn't there also something the Good Book has to say about sitting in judgment?"

"I'm basing my judgment on what the Good Book has to say," Ellen said stiffly, "and by the Good Book's standards you're all guilty as sin."

"Young lady," Reginald said, "I've been a professor of psychology for the past forty years and based on that I believe, the following proverbial adage is appropriate: 'Be careful of the words you use. Keep them soft and sweet. You never know for certain which ones you'll have to eat.'"

When we all laughed, Ellen departed our company, head held high.

The rest of the evening was spent quietly. Finding my quarters a bit confining, I decided to retire to the TV lounge, where a number of students were gathered watching the showing of the movie *Frogs*. "Are you a Religion major?" an acne-besieged student asked me when I sat down beside him.

"No. I'm a seminarian."

"Well, what's the difference?"

"Religion is a major you take while an undergraduate. Seminary is a graduate program for people preparing to enter the ministry."

"Were you a Religion major when you were an undergrad?"

"No, I was an American Studies major."

"Then how'd you get into seminary?"

"I applied."

"Why did they let you in? Don't you have to have some sort of background in Biblical studies?"

"I think you may be asking the wrong person on that one. All I know is that I applied and got in."

"I don't understand," the fellow on the other side of me said. "How can they let you into seminary if you haven't studied religion? Besides, you don't seem like the preacher type."

"I'm not," I told him, "At least not yet. I'm a

The Call 121

seminarian and I've got three to four years to hopefully mold myself to your expectations as to what a minister should be."

"But I thought ministers were born to be what they were supposed to be."

"Hope I haven't disillusioned you," I replied and went back to my room, tired of being the center of undergraduate attention. I had always valued my privacy, and it seemed clear that it was going to be a hard thing to come by here.

The day before the retreat, we were all called to assemble in the seminary building's coffee lounge. While en route, I ran into a man who introduced himself as Lawrence Viscount who told me that he had already been ordained by the Methodist Convention, and was almost a deacon.

If I felt out of place before, I did so with a vengeance now. Here I was with no credentials to my name and no support, even from my own church.

Dean Rupert Babcock was to preside over the meeting along with a few of his tenured professorial colleagues. Once the noise subsided, Professor Babcock briefly introduced himself and called for an introduction from each of us. Most of the neophyte seminarians proudly waved the banner of Parkins University, their undergraduate alma mater and now their base for graduate studies. There was a good deal of banter attached to the rivalry of the two most prevalent denominations which I found tiresome, but they clearly thought of as good fun. There was one member of the student population who shared my alma matter, a fellow named Jack Logan, who unabashedly came forth and stated that he had absolutely no experience in ministry. For a moment, I was tempted to make a similar disclosure. After all, apart from doing volunteer work at my church, I didn't have any true ministerial experience either. But not wanting to let on about it, I opted to keep silent.

When the introductions drew to a close, Professor Babcock addressed us. "On behalf of the faculty and the staff here at Parkins Theological Seminary, I would like to extend to you a cordial and warm welcome. We're all glad you chose us and we will make every effort to ensure that your decision is a wise one. Now let me tell you about myself. I'm the acting dean. I want to stress that by 'acting' dean, I mean I'm only the dean for the interim. Normally my status is just that of a plain old seminary professor. I teach New Testament and homiletics, which is preaching. I've occupied that role for the past thirty years, but I have never occupied the position of dean … even that of acting dean. One of you first-year seminarians was quick to point out that he had absolutely no experience when it came to matters of ministry. Well, I don't have any experience at being a dean. That's why I'm hoping this position gets filled before too much more time elapses, because I also have no experience at acting, either."

We all laughed.

"Now, I need to tell all of you assembled here that we've undergone some changes in the past few months, changes that have caused us a bit of administrative difficulty. Former Dean Archibald Shyster's call to serve a church left a considerable gap in the organizational side of running of this seminary. Such difficulties are always inevitable when there are changes in staff or faculty. But I can say, with a high degree of optimism, that these difficulties should not in any way impede the academic program and your educational matriculation while you are in attendance at this seminary. The faculty and the staff here at the seminary stand ready to provide you with a rich and rewarding experience that will more than equip you for ministry and we make that promise to all of you, even to those of you with no experience. You provide us with the raw material and we do the refining and cultivating, and, God willing, we will all reap the bountiful harvest promised us by the end of our journey here within these cloistered halls."

He went on to tell us that the next day we would be embarking on a three-day seminary retreat. This retreat would signify the beginning of our classes. It would be during the course of this retreat that we would be accorded the opportunity of acquainting ourselves with the faculty, be assigned advisors, signed up for the appropriate classes, and be afforded the opportunity to worship, fellowship, and have a whole lot of good fun ... sort of a last fling before the hard work starts. And particular emphasis was placed on the hard work. After all, as he pointed up, it was an integral part of the package.

Professor Babcock went on to mention that along with being the acting dean, he also taught a course in Advanced Homiletics and that during the course of the retreat, he would be treating us to a sermon or two, or as he put it, he would be showing us how it was done. He told us to look upon it as a sneak preview before enrolling in his class, which, he stated emphatically, was compulsory if we were entertaining any notion of completing the program.

"Okay," he said. "That's about it for the meeting. I'll see you all tomorrow, and we'll head out for Brisbane Camp, where the retreat will be held. We'll stick around here in the lounge for a while in case any of you want to talk to us. Coffee and doughnuts are in the back. Five cents for the coffee and ten cents for the doughnuts. Look upon it as a love offering."

As the crowd dispersed, a fellow came up and introduced himself as Jack Logan. "I understand we share a common alma mater," he said

"Yes," I replied. "U.C. but different schools."

"Yeah. I couldn't help but get the feeling that we're sort of looked down upon for our University of California affiliations. You know, take two steps back and three steps to the side."

"Well, we have something else in common. I don't have any real church experience either, except volunteer work."

"Well, that's probably more than I can claim. I'm presently working as the church janitor over at the Christian Church near the campus."

"I guess that's a start. Do you think the head of the field office has any openings for a church secretary? That's what I did before applying here."

"Don't know. I guess more will be revealed at the time of the retreat. So how do you feel about being here?"

"Scared as hell. This is a big step, and it's really overwhelming."

"Well, the Lord'll take care of you. That's what I keep telling my wife."

"And does she believe you?"

"I don't think so. She wasn't too hot on the idea of giving up the luxurious lifestyle I was able to provide as a businessman so I could answer the call. She's still not too hot on the idea."

It was clear to me that he was lonely, and a little confused, and oddly enough that helped, because I felt that way as well.

The next day we were all assembled in the seminary parking lot where three buses were standing by, ready to transport us to Brisbane Camp. The retreat not only included the seminary students and professors, but also their respective families. Certain undergraduate Religion majors could also attend if proper arrangements were made. Among the undergraduates was Elmo Piggins, who jumped at the opportunity of having exchanges with those who shared his aspirations to the ministry.

Most people crowded into buses, but some people like Reginald Dexter took their own cars. I overheard him mutter something about thanking God that this was the only weekend he'd have to spend in this madhouse, just before he started off. And I noticed that his roommate did not accompany him, which was understandable. Charlie was so friendly that living in cramped quarters with him must have been difficult.

The rest of us chose the buses. They were little more than renovated school buses, but they served their purpose.

During the course of the ride, I struck up a lively conversation with a lady in the seat just behind mine: Jessica Bently, already an ordained Methodist minister. Appearance-wise, she stuck me as every inch a plain Jane, a tad on the frumpy side. But she had a great personality and we were soon chatting away like good friends. She was, I discovered, planning to take a Masters of Divinity degree; that would mean better parish assignments. Not only that, but she was being sponsored by the regional Methodist headquarters, which enabled her to have her own apartment, "And what about yourself?" she said, turning the conversation over to me.

"Just my own savings ... and a scholarship the former dean promised me."

"Scholarship? I didn't know the seminary had the resources this year to provide any financial help."

"All I know is what Dr. Shyster wrote in his letter to me."

"Well, I hope for your sake they're able to make good on what he promised. I understand Dr. Shyster left this place in a big mess before he took off to Big Springs."

"He did?" I responded. It wasn't long after I heard that when Isaac, who had not been heard from for a while, began to laugh. It seemed all too clear to me that trouble was looming on the horizon.

"When Professor Babcock said yesterday that they were having a few administrative difficulties, I think he was kind of understating the problem," she went on. "I just hope we'll be able to carry out our course of study and finish our credentials here before the place goes under."

I shivered at her disclosure. I tried to shift the subject matter to lighter topics. "I see. So, what else are you into besides ministry?"

"Oh, movies, stage plays, dancing, romantic walks by the river, watching sunrises and sunsets, skating. I'd like to find a husband eventually. How about yourself?"

"Well, I've been working long hours over the past few years so I really haven't had a chance to develop many hobbies. I've always wanted to get into electric trains. I go to movies and stage productions. My favorite stage productions have been *Tartuffe*, *West Side Story*, *Hair*, and *Three Penny Opera*, …"

"You saw *Three Penny Opera*?"

"Yes."

"So did I! I loved it!"

We passed the time on the bus engrossed in conversation until we heard someone say, "All right, folks! Everybody out! We're here! We have just enough time to get ourselves situated before the noon meal is served! Men's dorm on the right! Women's on the left!"

"Well," I said, "I guess we can continue this conversation a bit later."

"You bet," Jessica replied.

Hmmm. I thought. Maybe there's hope for me yet. My heart skipped with a surge of optimism.

Professor Babcock, along with some other faculty members, had already arrived and was in the process of setting up advisory schedules and enrollment tables.

It was his secretary's day off, so both he and the other faculty members were left the arduous chore of organizing the materials.

Professor Randolph Hennessey, a tall, robust man with a full head of red hair, was first to confront Babcock with an issue regarding his list.

"Babcock!" he called out indignantly. "Just what the hell are you trying to do to me? Sign my death warrant? You realize how many of these students here on my roster you've marked as problems?"

"We *all* have problem students here," an older professor named Stephen Bildeberger told him. "You think it's wise to try to even consider eliminating them from the program given the mess we're in?"

"I can't compromise that much!" Hennessey exclaimed. "We have got to maintain academic standards! I mean, look at this one. The man's a plumber! No baccalaureate! Just vocational training! And don't tell me we have to make allowances for people over forty on the basis that they've had life experiences."

"Look," Babcock replied, "I know seminaries that require students to have a rudimentary knowledge of Greek and Hebrew before they'll even look at them as candidates. I admit that we're a bit more liberal in our policies of acceptance than that. But my main concern here is, how much more do we need to dumb down our academic program?"

"Enough to keep our ship afloat?" Bildeberger replied.

"The seminaries I'm referring to are doing fine, and they don't compromise!" said Babcock

"Look, I don't want to be the hatchet man who has to turn these students away," Hennessey countered. "But I actually have a former alligator wrestler on my roster of advisees! And look at all these you've marked as not being up to academic standards. You realize they're being backed by churches in our denomination. And you'd also better respect the students who've been endorsed by the Methodist headquarters too, or this ship will go down quicker than the *Titanic*!"

"Somehow I get the feeling that God is already sinking this ship," Babcock replied. "What about the ones who aren't affiliated with either of the two denominations?"

"Other than the Greek Orthodox student from Crete," said Bildeberger, "we have only one. The O'Donnell guy. He's a Baptist."

"A Baptist!" Babcock laughed. "Baptists don't go here!"

"He's an American Baptist."

"I don't believe we have any of them in this part of the country. Is he being subsidized by his denomination?"

"No subsidies. He's paying for it all himself and the scholarship Dr. Shyster dangled under his nose to get him here."

"I know. Dr. Shyster did that a lot."

"Oh yes, we also have a Unitarian."

"Yes, I know. I talked to him yesterday. Appears Dr. Shyster hinted at getting him one too, but he turned it down. Seems he's tucked away a sizable retirement nest egg. But Unitarian is not Christian! They do not ascribe to the notion of a God that is triune."

"Look," said Babcock, "if he wants to go through the program, let him go through the program. He's got a Ph.D. Maybe he can teach *us* something."

"Well," Hennessey replied, "all I can tell you is that it would be cruel to let some of these students into the program."

"It would also be cruel to cast us to the wolves," Bildeberger replied. "These students want to become ministers, and they may prove critical as to whether or not we stay afloat!"

"I know," Babcock sighed, "God help me, I know."

Later, back at the dorm, I witnessed Samuel Hill, a portly man in his late forties, lumber into the entryway with his baggage. "Is this the men's quarters?" he demanded.

"Yes, c'mon in, you gorgeous hunk!" Ben responded in a mock effeminate voice.

All of us, from year one to year three students, with a couple of doctoral students, were all gathered in one place. We had all chosen a cot and a locker to stash away our belongings for the next few days. It was now down to the business of acquainting ourselves with one another.

"Jack!" a woman from somewhere outside the dorm called. "Get your sanctimonious butt out here!" Bobby and Jack Jr. want to sleep in the guy's dorm. They don't want to be around a bunch of women. I told them they could."

"But honey," Jack replied, "we don't have enough room for any more."

"Find room! It's bad enough you dragging us away to this shoestring-type existence, and wanting me to have our next baby hippie style at home, but you are going to have to help out with these kids!"

"But honey, the men's dorm is no place for kids."

"Damn you, Jack! You are going to make it a place for kids or so help me, I'm gonna throttle you within an inch of your life right here in broad daylight!"

"Excuse me," one of the doctoral students said, "but this really isn't a place for children."

"If you think you're man enough," Jack replied, "then go tell my wife! If you can persuade her to take them off my hands, then more power to ya! Otherwise, they're staying with me!"

"Look," the doctoral student reiterated, "we've never allowed children here in the men's dorm. They've always stayed with the women."

"Times change. So do traditions. They're staying with me. And right now I'm more willing to go toe-to-toe with you on the matter than I am with my wife. So if that's what you or anyone else cares to do, then I'm more than willing to meet you outside! Otherwise, this conversation is closed. And I hope I don't have to have this conversation with any of the rest of you! Come on in, kids, and bring your stuff with you."

The two boys stood behind their father as he was making his assertion.

"Fine-looking brood you got there," Reginald said. "I couldn't help but notice they favor their mother."

"So I've been told," Jack replied.

"I also noticed you're wife's expecting another. Any idea what you're planning on calling it?"

"Quits, I hope. I had a vasectomy a few years ago, but somehow I think they botched it."

"And you're planning on going back to school with four kids in tow?"

"That's what the Lord's told me to do," Jack replied.

"Now that man is someone who has truly been called. Either that or he's crazy," Reginald said, turning to Charlie who replied that the Lord works in mysterious ways.

"I suppose," Reginald replied. "And who's the big bearded guy who thinks he's in charge of things?"

"That's Dean Marco. He's a doctoral candidate. He also teaches classes here at the seminary. Primarily, he deals with the practical aspects of ministry like family life and priority setting. He serves a weekend parish, and during the week he works as a counselor at the county mental health outpatient center. And along with all that, he's one of the head coordinators of the telephone crisis counseling service."

"Guy's got quite a full plate. Seems like a bit of an asshole, though, horning in on the domestic issues of others."

"Hey, don't kid yourself. He's a man who's highly respected and very knowledgeable about ministry. Used to be a Jesuit until he got saved. Soon after he was saved, God gave him a wife, and they've both worked together for a long time in team ministry. Yep, Dean Marco's a good man. I wish we had more like him."

I heard Reginald mutter something about not knowing what he was doing here, and from what I knew about him, I could understand his doubts. His stories about the summer he spent skydiving and his obsession with tai chi made me wonder if it wasn't his age he was struggling with in starting this new career. But I understood the uncertainty.

As the day went on, I had all the more reason to

wonder what this retreat was about. As I attempted to organize items around my cot, I was uncomfortably aware that the dormitory possessed all the charm of a men's locker room. Seminarians were congregating in clusters, talking about topics ranging from evangelism to sex. Samuel Church had gravitated over to Lewis Coppel, and both were absorbed in a conversation about sports. Norman Decantor was demonstrating his formidable vocal prowess to Lawrence Viscount who, in turn, was attempting to match him with his less-tempered Irish tenor, singing numbers ranging from *The Barber of Seville* to *Melancholy Baby* with a little *Ave Maria* thrown in for good measure. Meanwhile Elmo Piggins struck up what sounded like an awkward conversation with T. J. Whizzer.

During the interim, Leonard DeWilde was enjoying a late-morning highball. Both he and Lillian had packed some of their private stock away, figuring they would both need it to fortify themselves while undergoing the rigors of the retreat.

Over in a far corner, the lone figure of Jerry Cantrell sat glaring at all the proceedings, observing everyone's words and movements with intense concentration. I briefly returned his glance and could feel him look though me as if I were translucent when Dean Marco walked up to him and introduced himself. Jerry ignored his extended hand and when Dean mentioned the fact that he'd be glad to have him and his wife, both licensed psychiatric social workers, work with him at the county mental health outpatient clinic, Jerry said, "Possibly. What does it pay?"

"Well, it's sort of a voluntary thing."

"Then the answer is sort of no. If you want my professional expertise, you pay for it."

"Mr. Cantrell," Dean replied, "if I could just appeal to you in the name of Christian charity. This could fulfill your fieldwork requirements here at the seminary, and the clinic would benefit immeasurably by the services of both you and your wife."

"In case you haven't noticed, my wife and I are embarking upon a very expensive undertaking. That makes us akin to charity recipients. Taken in that context, your appeal out of charity is analogous to asking a drowning man to throw you a line. The answer is still no."

"Okay. But think it over."

"I'll think it over if you think over paying us. I can't claim to know as much about the Bible as you, but isn't there a passage in there somewhere that says something about a worker being worthy of his hire?"

Dean Marco made no reply. He bid Mr. Cantrell good day and proceeded on to other matters.

All in all, I was content to watch and listen. There were more unpleasant characters than I had ever seen gathered together in one place, which was a bit ironic in itself since all of us presumably shared a Christian philosophy. But I reminded myself not to make judgments. Heaven knows what others had to say about me.

The Cantrell's story was a simple one, I discovered. Jerry and Linda met, fell in love, and married while they were both working in the same psychiatric outpatient clinic in Denver, Colorado. Jerry was a moody and introspective man who was plagued with a case of prematurely advancing osteoarthritis. At the time he met Linda, he was in the process of authoring a book on the topic of Zen and how it might aid in the psychiatric process — sort of a Zen and mental health exposé, which had interested Linda a lot.

In the span of their shared career endeavors, they both reached the conclusion that religion might be one of the factors robbing a person of his or her sanity. They never professed any call to the ministry, but given what they encountered on a daily basis at the clinic, they both concluded that perhaps it might behoove them to supplement their clinical training with the spiritual. Perhaps with this background, they would be of service to the outpatients and draw a greater understanding of the functions of the human psyche.

Jerry and Linda were known for their intelligence and open-mindedness. However, none of the faculty or the students could ever get a true fix on where they stood theologically.

As I sat on my bed and watched my classmates laugh and debate with one another, my anxiety level continued to rise. I could feel my heart thumping rapidly, like a hammer. I saw myself in a room full of thespians and polished performers, and I had no place on that stage, and I cringed at the prospect of such exposure. How could I perform? I had nothing to perform with! Then I heard the echo of a sinister, maniacal laugh resonate in my brain until it sounded like thunder. It was Isaac's laughter taunting me, badgering me, mocking my existence because he couldn't bear to see me have what he could not. He repeated his mantra incessantly, "That's not yours! That's not yours!"

"Not now, Isaac!" I pleaded under my breath as I entered into the throes of desperation. "Don't expose me in public! Please! Go away!" And when the laughter persisted. "Why do you torture me, Isaac?" I cried. "It's not my fault you died!"

In the midst of this internal struggle, Elmo Piggins walked up to my bunk, put his hand on my shoulder, and shouted, "Praise the Lord, brother!"

And when I told him to go away, he not only told me that he'd come to me to spread some of God's love, he said directly, "Do you know Jesus loves you?"

"I believe we get the picture." Jerry said walking up to Elmo.

"But Jesus is the answer!" Elmo replied.

"I believe that depends upon what the question is," Jerry replied. "Now go. I can only address one clinical issue at a time."

"But …"

"Go!" Jerry shouted and, sitting down beside me, "Care to tell me what the problem is?"

"You'd never believe me," I replied. "And I've never really told anyone."

"I've worked in mental health for the past fifteen years. You'd be surprised at what I've encountered. And I can't believe you'd even be here if you had anything really wrong with you emotionally. If you're feeling anxious about being here, we all are to some degree. But when I start seeing someone convulse, turn pale, and break out in a sweat like you just did, I just naturally have to express my concern. Have you ever been in counseling or taken any psychotropic drugs?"

"I started going to counseling years ago. Then my old man came back from his overseas tour and abruptly put a stop to it. He said, 'You're my son. I didn't raise a nut. You don't need this.' And he wouldn't accept any evidence to the contrary."

"Well, no disrespect intended toward your old man, but I strongly suggest you get help. One thing I've learned from all my years working in the mental health field is we get the weakest at a far greater rate than we get the sickest. I don't know you that well, but just sitting here for the past hour observing everyone, I can name you a laundry list of prevailing neuroses ranging from delusions of grandeur, to insane fantasies like talking alligators, to just plain egomania. But they've all got strong personalities. And the strong prey upon the weak, I don't care how sanctimonious or well meaning they profess to be. Think about it."

I felt normalcy return. Jerry's words left me with much to consider. Here I was, miles away from home. The influence of family, friends, and familiarity were behind me, and now I discover that I might be in need of counseling. And what were psychotropic drugs? Did I really need them? And then I saw Charlie pointing me out to Reginald and I heard him say, "See Reggie! I told you that Ishmael was influenced by something, and I'm bettin' it's Satanic in nature, sure as I'm standin' here!"

"And I've got horns and a tail," was Reginald's response. "Charlie, why don't you come out of your fantasy world and back into reality? This is the twentieth century, you know."

"And the devil's as much alive now as he was back in Jesus' time."

"You didn't by any chance watch *The Exorcist* last year?"

"Well yeah, Reggie! How'd you know?"

"Lucky guess. Tell you what. If I see any of our fellow seminarians throw up pea soup, then I might have cause for concern. But until then, I'd really like to indulge in more rational conversations."

Heaving a heavy sigh of resignation coupled with a tinge of despondency, I resolved to keep a tighter reign on my emotional state throughout the rest of the retreat. After all, if one seminarian believed I was possessed, wouldn't there be others? And there was nothing like having people believing you were possessed by the devil as a way of getting kicked out of a seminary program. I didn't start out on this endeavor with the intent of failure, so unless I wanted to spend the rest of my life behind a typewriter I knew I had better find some way to pull my act together. Perhaps Jerry was right. After this retreat, I'd look into what resources were available. After all, it certainly wouldn't help if anyone here were to find out about my emotional instability, brought about, in good part, by Isaacs attempts to usurp my life.

As I was gathering my thoughts, Elmo Piggins persisted in bouncing about the men's quarters from person to person, trying to get a doctrinal fix upon all the prospective ministerial candidates. He wanted to know if everyone had been saved, if they had received the gift of tongues, if they had been slain in the Holy Spirit, how

The Call

they met their salvation, and numerous other queries that were often met with less-than-cordial responses.

"Do you know Jesus?" I heard him ask Dean Marco. And then Dean literally shrugged him off, muttering something about his being a nut case.

The women's dorm at the retreat was boisterous and chaotic. The majority of the occupants were wives of aspiring theologians who shared their varying views on the paths their husbands had chosen while tending to the arranging of furniture, clothing, and children in the marginal space accorded them. Sue Ellen Von Krumpke, the wife of the Reverend Randal Von Krumpke, was ironing her husband's slacks with her usual air of enthusiasm.

"This is so exciting!" Sue Ellen cried. "I can just feel the Lord's leading in this! Don't you just feel His presence, Elsie?!"

"Not really," Elsie replied as she placed the remainder of her clothing in her assigned locker.

"Aren't you excited about how the Lord has called your husband to his service?" Sue Ellen persisted.

Elsie turned and walked back to her cot where she sat down. "I don't think you want to know how I'm feeling right now. By the way," Elsie said as she pointed to Sue Ellen's ironing board, "is that men's briefs you're ironing?"

"Oh yes," Sue Ellen cried, "Randal just loves it when I iron his underwear! How about you? Don't you iron your husband's underwear?"

"He can iron his own damn underwear!" Elsie

snapped.

Renee Brennan shared a similar enthusiasm to Sue Ellen's, which she expressed to her bunkmate Jana Parson. "It's amazing!" she said. "Almost like a dream! Everything just came together so well! And now this! I am really excited! How about you Jana? How do you feel about you and your husband going into this?"

Jana looked up at Renee and shrugged her shoulders, "As long as it doesn't affect our sex life ..."

Carla Logan was perhaps the busiest and most occupied of all the women in the dorm. Not only did she have to tend to the arrangement of her clothing, but she also needed to address the needs of her disheveled toddler daughter, who remained less than content with her present surroundings.

"Mommy," her daughter whined as she tugged at Carla's side, "I don't like it here! I wanna go home!"

"There, there, Cassie," she said, kneeling down beside her daughter, "it'll only be for a couple of days."

"But why, Mommy?"

"Because of what your idiot father got us into."

"Is my father an idiot?"

"Not all the time, Cassie. Just lately."

"Where's Jack and Bobby?"

"They're with their father."

"But why, Mommy?"

"They wanted to be with men."

"But why, Mommy?"

"I don't know, Cassie. I guess because they didn't want a bunch of strange women seeing them naked."

Meantime, Linda Cantrell, in a fashion not unlike

The Call

her husband was keeping an eagle eye on the group, including one Lillian De Wilde who was downing a late-morning highball. "You're hitting the sauce a little early in the day, aren't you?" She inquired.

"Not nearly early enough," Lillian replied. "This place is really getting to me. I just can't believe my husband would do something like this!"

"Like what? Go into the ministry?"

"Whatever you call it!" Lillian's voice shook, as did her hand.

"Didn't the two of you talk it over?"

"If you can call it that! In all the years we've been married, I've never had to face anything like this! It's so surreal!"

"So what are you going to do about it?"

"Have another drink." Lillian told her. "That should at least numb the pain."

"Do you think that's the answer?"

"No. But it's the best I can do for the time being."

Three of the aspiring female ministerial candidates, Laurie, Sharon, and Kathleen were deep in conversation. "I'm serious, you two!" Kathleen said. "I've got no business going into this program! You guys have been great helping me through these past four years, and I'd have never completed my undergraduate studies without you! But the Greek, the Hebrew, the theological arguments, writing sermons …"

"Will you quit worrying about it, Kathleen?" Sharon countered.

"Yes," Laurie said. "We got you through your

undergrad studies, we'll get you through seminary. Trust us."

"Girls," Kathleen replied, "I trust you with my life! But you guys can't do the impossible! Did you know we all have to take Professor Babcock's New Testament course this semester? And do you know how much reading is required? Five thousand pages! Plus we have to do an exegetical paper, a biography of Paul, and three biblical critiques! And there is no way I can pull that off with my dyslexia holding me back! I've made some headway with it, but it's still not enough! What may seem like ordinary reading to you guys is like reading hieroglyphics for me!"

"Actually," Laurie said, "I've located a reading specialist for you in downtown Idle, and I'm sure she can help you with your problem. She's an advocate of the SRA program, meaning you'll be assessed and color-coded by your reading level. She practically guaranteed me that you'll advance to graduate level in no time. And she'll also double as your tutor. She's a deeply religious person, and she assured us that she'll take your case as seriously as she would a call from the Almighty Himself."

"But when am I going to find the time?" Kathleen asked. "Or maybe I should ask how can I afford to pay her? You know I've had to double up as both a dorm mom and a youth pastor just to pay my expenses. And I'm certainly not going to get any financial assistance from my parents! My father still completely refuses to acknowledge that I even have this problem … he says I wouldn't have made it this far if I had a reading problem. He doesn't realize what a miracle it is that I graduated from college, nor does he realize the miracle workers I've had carrying me all this time!"

"And we'll continue to carry you if that's what it takes," Sharon replied. "So try not to worry. And as for paying the reading specialist, I believe Laurie and I can help out there too, right Laurie?"

"Right," Laurie said. "Kathleen, you have too many gifts to be squandered just because of a reading problem. We've seen you minister to others. You're a natural with music, and you've performed wonders in your children's ministry. Sharon and I are not going to stand by and see you fail in your pursuit of the ministry. Whatever it takes, you're going to get this credential."

"So let's just take the work as it comes and try to enjoy this retreat," said Sharon. "By the way, girls, have you gotten a fix on the new single male seminarians? Who are they? What are they like?"

"I wouldn't get my hopes up too high," Laurie replied. "So far all I've come across is an arrogant forty-plus former insurance salesman, a super tall muscle head who used to wrestle alligators for a living, a burnt-out Jesus clone, a Satanic rocker, and you remember Lewis Coppel, don't you? Well, he decided to join us. And there's this former opera singer and a rather enigmatic guy from California."

Jessica Bently broke into the conversation. "Just a minute, girls. The enigmatic boy is mine."

"Oh really?" Kathleen spoke up. "What makes you subject to first dibs? Especially since you're a Methodist."

"He and I had a long conversation on the bus."

All the girls then gathered around Jessica. "Really?"

Kathleen cried.

"What did he say?" Laurie asked.

"Well," said Jessica, "he likes movies, the theater, electric trains, his father's a retired Army Lieutenant Colonel …"

"What church is he affiliated with?" Sharon asked.

"He didn't say. He just said he received no subsidies from his church and was promised a scholarship by Doctor Shyster."

"This should prove most interesting," Sharon said dryly.

"I don't know about you folks, but I pity Professor Babcock," said Laurie. "Dr. Shyster left him a whole lot of administrative entanglements."

"You know," said Sharon, "as sons and daughters of the cloth we've had a lifetime to comprehend the nature of the church and the political garbage that goes with it, but I bet that students who come in from outside the fold might have a tougher time understanding what they'll have to contend with. I'll wager we can anticipate some fireworks this semester, and I'll bet they'll begin tomorrow during class sign-ups."

"You might be right, Sharon," Laurie said.

At noontime the hand-rung bell summoning us to the dining hall where we lined up and were served cafeteria style. After we were all seated, one of the senior seminarians insisted that we say grace in unison to the Doxology, sung to the tune of *Hernando's Hideaway*. "Praise God from whom all blessings flow/ Praise Him all creatures here below/ Praise Him above ye Heavenly hosts, Praise Father, Son, and Holy Ghost. Amen." After we had a little chuckle, we began to eat servings consisting primarily of ham hocks, lima beans, black-eyed peas, and corn bread. For dessert there was peach cobbler. There wasn't too much food left over. Markem had gone back for six helpings and, as usual, was still hungry. As for me, I didn't have much of an appetite. I looked around for Jessica but couldn't find her in the crowd. Instead I wound up seated between Norman Decantor and Jason Tyler—not the company I would most readily choose, but it did make for somewhat of a colorful meal.

"Hey," Jason said, "what did ya think o' that Jack Logan bringin' his kids in to bunk with him?"

"Don't know," Norman replied. "Being single and childless and all …"

"Tell ya what I think … I wasn't gonna say anything, but those kids should be in with their mother."

"They're boys," I said. "They wanted to be with their father. Besides, Jack's got a daughter and one on the way. Seems only fair they go halves."

"I can tell you ain't never been married!" Jason spoke in an emphatic tone that grated on me like fingernails on a chalkboard. "It's the woman's place to look after the kids! As a husband, you have to make it known that childcare is her responsibility and that you're the one in charge! Otherwise she'll walk all over ya!"

"I don't think that's how things are in all families," said Norman.

"That's because there are too many men who allow these women to cut their balls off!" Jason responded. "The good Lord put us in charge, and the ministry ain't no place for henpecked husbands."

"You married?" I asked.

"No," Jason responded, "divorced."

"How'd it happen?"

"None o' your goddamn business!"

"You're right. But if memory serves, Christ died for the sanctification of his 'bride,' the church. Now, if a husband can go that far for the sake of his wife, I can find no fault with Jack for accommodating his wife in matters of childcare. And I haven't heard any theologians refer to Jesus as being a henpecked husband."

"Listen, boy!" Jason said brusquely. "Ministry is a fishbowl-type existence! That means you're on display twenty-four hours a day, seven days a week, 365 days a year. Those parishioners you minister to are just like vultures waiting to pounce on you if you make just one little slip or show any little signs of weakness or deviation from what they think a minister ought to be! And if they see their minister in any way give the impression of being dominated by his wife, then you might as well be prepared to kiss ministry good-bye or find another church! Paul notes that in his pastoral epistles!"

I rather doubt that, I thought, but I wasn't about to say it out loud. I found Jason to be a pretty scary individual, and I certainly didn't want to invite his wrath. If there was anything I didn't need it was an angry encounter with someone I scarcely knew.

"Certain ground rules have to be established with your spouse if she's to take to the role of a minister's wife!" he said, continuing his tirade. "And any departure from that needs to be dealt with quickly and dispensed with sharply! The man's got to be in charge of his house!

The Call 147

The ministry is no place for wimps! And meaning no disrespect, because I really don't know you all that well, but you come across as a wimp to me, boy!"

"I'm glad you prefaced that last statement with 'no disrespect,'" I told him, restraining my anger with difficulty.

"Hey," Norman shouted, "I see no reason to bring this discussion down below the belt. And besides, in case you haven't noticed, there are several female ministerial candidates amongst us. How do you perceive your hard-and-fast rule applying to these women and their husbands?"

"Frankly," Jason retorted, "I don't believe women have any business in the ministry! And furthermore, I seriously question the sanctity and viability of a church that elects a woman to be its pastor! I mean, it flies in the face of everything God's ordained as natural and sacred!"

Jason's arrogance was difficult to put up with, but I knew it would be folly for me to respond in kind.

As I struggled to keep my silence, I remembered an old Murphy saying: "Never argue with a fool. People might not know the difference." A certain definition of stress also sprang to mind that seemed quite apropos to the present situation: "Stress—the inevitable product that ensues when the mind overrides the body's natural impulse to choke the living shit out of some asshole who so desperately needs it." Finally I was reminded of an obscure passage of scripture, either Jesus said it in the context of the Synoptic Gospels or it was a passage in one of the Pauline Epistles. I remembered it saying something to the effect of "Insofar as is possible, be at peace with your fellow man." I concluded that the only way I could truly be at peace with Brother Jason and offer up to him the Christian love I was commissioned to give was to stay away from him.

"If you gentlemen will excuse me, this wimp will take his leave." I said, picking up my tray.

As I turned to walk away, I could hear Norman say to Jason, "You know Jason, I've met some assholes in my time, and you're sure one of them."

After the noon meal, we were all assembled in the meeting room to listen to lectures on the philosophy behind a seminary education. "Entering seminary is a lot like entering a dark cave with only a candle to light your way," one of the doctoral students said. "As you proceed on your journey through the cave, you ultimately venture into the darkest part. And as you reach that darkened area, somebody blows your candle out, and you are left to your own devices to get yourself out of that cave. Once you finally arrive at the exit, it really doesn't matter which exit you arrived at or how you arrived at it, what's important is that you remember how you made it there so you can pass that information along to those that follow."

"Very profound," whispered Charlie to Reginald, seated on my right.

"Lotta hot air," Reginald whispered back.

But what if you wind up in the wrong place? I thought.

Next to speak was a Professor Gene Molder, professor of ethics and public worship, who spoke at great length on the acquisition and maintenance of cosmic consciousness for the better part of an hour.

The Call

Professor Brian Wilson, director of field education, was the next speaker. He was a tall, slightly graying man in his late forties with bushy hair and a goatee. Probably well aware of the fact that Professor Molder's presentation had a soporific effect on many of us, he suggested that we stand up and stretch before he began. I managed to sit next to Jessica after the break, as a strategy for staying awake. After everyone was seated again, the professor introduced himself.

"My intention now," Professor Wilson began, "is to render a down-to-earth presentation regarding the meaning behind fieldwork. As Professor Babcock mentioned yesterday in the coffee lounge, the course of your seminary education will not only focus on the abstract theological but also on the practical. And these two combined elements are designed to last a total of three years, the same amount of time our Lord's earthly ministry lasted. During that time, even though our Lord ministered to the masses, he spent a lot of time with the twelve, teaching them how to minister, the equivalent of a three year seminary education."

Some of us laughed, and others groaned. But at least, unlike Professor Molder, he was getting some response.

"Don't laugh," he said. "There's something very significant about the number three here. I'll leave it to you to figure out. Suffice it to say that what Jesus needed to teach the disciples took the exact amount of time it takes, on the average, to matriculate through seminary. Now, as a few of us have already disclosed, the disciples started out with absolutely no experience. Jesus needed to start them out at ground zero. Then, when he felt they were ready, he would send them out to the neighboring towns and villages to perform acts of ministry. This is exactly what we're going to be doing with you and a few of the undergraduates who have applied through our field office. We have a number of positions available at churches in neighboring communities. Some are as far away as Oklahoma City."

"I have categorized these positions by way of levels based on a person's ability and preference. The first level is comprised exclusively of youth ministry and associate pastoring: this level is meant for those of you just breaking into the field of ministry. It provides an excellent training ground for beginners, and, while ministering principally to the youth, you will often get previews of what issues and dynamics comprise the task of adult ministry."

He went on to tell us about level two, a Sunday only pastorate, level three, a weekend pastorate, and level four, a full time field pastorate where the candidate would be residing in the town where the church s/he was ministering to was located. He stated that he would endorse only the most resilient and the most experienced seminarians for such positions. He further stated that if a candidate could survive this level, the candidate should have no trouble surviving ministry on the outside after completion of seminary.

He concluded with these words of assurance: "If you cannot, you may still be able to survive ministry on the outside, although I'd give serious consideration as to what degree you feel you can cope with the strain of it all. As I stated earlier, this is field education. It's also a weeding process, and some of you may fail. That's nothing to be ashamed of. Some of the greatest of saints failed in their first attempt at ministry. I might call your attention to John Mark as a principle example. At one point, the Apostle Paul wanted nothing to do with him. Then, later on in his epistles, he instructs his colleague to bring him along. 'He's useful to me' were his words."

"In conclusion, if any of you have any questions regarding field education, I will be available to answer them. I've already got your applications on hand, and some of the churches have already made requests to interview you. I have some of that information available as well. Thank you for your attentiveness. I hope this year proves to be a rich and rewarding one."

The crowd awarded him a standing ovation, not so much for the eloquence of his delivery, but for the brevity of his presentation. The students were once again free to mingle about.

"Your just being here helped keep me awake," I told Jessica. "Thank you."

"Happy to be of service," she replied, "but didn't you find Professor Wilson's talk interesting?"

"Oh, he was okay, but that Professor Molder …"

"Better get used to hearing him talk. I hear we'll be taking more classes from him than any other faculty member."

"Then I shouldn't have any trouble with insomnia these next three to four years."

"Now really, Ishmael, was he all that bad?"

"Worse. I feel like I need a nap right now, and I never sleep during the day."

"I was kind of hoping we could hang out during this free time."

"Well," I replied, "I guess if I really forced myself, I could stay awake."

Together we headed for a shaded area outside where the willows provided some shelter from the sun.

Meantime, Dean Marco and Reginald had started up a conversation.

"I understand you've been a professor of psychology at the University of Oklahoma for the past forty years." Dean said. "Matter of fact, I believe I've read some of your books and articles."

"That's nice to know," Reginald replied. "And here I was beginning to think that most of my works were just gathering dust on a library shelf."

"Oh gracious, no! You're quite renowned in your field! And that's what I've come to talk to you about. You see, I do counseling at the county mental health clinic …"

"So I've heard."

"Yes. Well, we could use someone of your expertise …"

"Listen," Reginald said, "If you're looking for someone to help with the counseling, it's only fair to warn you that I haven't done any counseling for more years than I care to remember. And there's one thing you ought to know about psychology."

"What's that?

"Most of it is pure crock!"

"Well, I've been counseling at the clinic for close to five years now, and I believe my associates and I have performed a great service to the community …"

"Belief is what keeps a person going. Knowing is an

entirely different matter."

"Well, you're going to need some units to complete your field education requirements."

"I've already worked that out. I'll be assisting my pastor during the time I'm back in Norman. Thanks for the offer, but no thanks. I've come here to branch out into a new field, not continue on in a field that retired me. Have a nice day." On his way back to indulge in a little tai chi, Reginald told himself he needed to exercise a little more patience. After all, he was dealing, for the most part, with people who were clearly several years his junior and hardly his intellectual equals.

"What can I do for you?" Brian Wilson said as, having left Jessica to enjoy the breeze, I approached him. "Are you as ready as that other guy? Elmo just told me that he's ready for his field assignment."

"No," I told him. "To be perfectly honest, I'm finding this whole scene rather scary. And no disrespect to you, but I found your talk to be rather scary, too." There was tension in every part of my body, and I could hear it manifest itself in my voice.

"Looks like what you've got is a bad case of stage fright," he told me. "Look, if you're worried, put your mind at ease. I'm not going to let you go into something you're not ready for. I mean, when you were first learning how to swim, were you just thrown into the deepest part of the pool and left to fend for yourself?"

"Yes, I was. Damn near drowned, too."

"Well, it doesn't work that way here. It's just like the acting profession. We don't put you out on center stage and expect you to assume the leading part right away. We either put you back stage to help with the lighting and props or we give you a supporting part. So relax. This is a learning experience … a growing experience. And lightning isn't going to strike you dead if you mess up every now and then."

His words were reassuring, the sort of thing I needed in order to remain as tranquil as possible, my best defense when it came to keeping Isaac at bay."

After the evening meal we were again summoned to the assembly room for a devotional and a sermonette to be delivered by Professor Babcock, who began by reading us a passage from Matthew, chapter 25, verses 14 to 30 regarding The Parable of the Talents:

"For it is as if a man, going on a journey, summoned his slaves and entrusted his property to them; to one he gave five talents, to another two, to another one, to each according to his ability. Then he went away. The one who had received the five talents went off at once and traded with them, and made five more talents. In the same way, the one who had the two talents made two more talents. But the one who had received the one talent went off and dug a hole in the ground and hid his master's money. After a long time the master of those slaves came and settled accounts with them. Then the one who had received the five talents came forward bringing five more talents, saying 'Master, you handed over to me five talents; so, I have made five more talents.' His master said to him, 'Well done, good and trustworthy slave; you have been trustworthy in a few things, I will put you in charge of many things; enter into the joy of your master.' And the one with two talents also came forward, saying,

'Master, you handed me two talents; see, I have made two more talents.' His master said to him, 'Well done, good and trustworthy slave; you have been trustworthy in a few things, I will put you in charge of many things; enter into the joy of your master.' Then the one who had received the one talent also came forward, saying, 'Master, I knew that you were a harsh man, reaping where you did not sow, and gathering where you did not scatter seed; so I was afraid, and I went and hid your talent in the ground. Here, you have what is yours.' But his master replied, 'You wicked and lazy slave! You knew, did you that I reap where I did not sow, and gather where I did not scatter? Then you ought to have invested my money with the bankers, and on my return I would have received what was my own with interest. So take the talent from him, and give it to the one with the ten talents. For to all those who have, more will be given, and they will have abundance; but from those who have nothing, even what they have will be taken away. As for this worthless slave, throw him into the outer darkness, where there will be weeping and gnashing of teeth."

"I've often pondered this biblical excerpt," Babcock told us, "and many times have been troubled by it. What troubled me most about the passage was the daring and almost cavalier attitudes displayed by the two servants with the five and the two talents, placing their master's money at risk in an effort to increase a fortune that was not theirs to toy with. I could almost liken it to gambling. The stakes were high and it was the luck of the draw, and boy would they have ever been in deep trouble had they lost. I always tended to relate more to the servant with the one talent. To my mind he was the wise and prudent one. He was entrusted with the responsibility of one of his master's talents, and he tucked it discreetly away to assure its safekeeping."

Babcock' audience sat before him, transfixed by his eloquence and inductive delivery. All of us held fast to his words, attempting to figure what lesson he was meaning to impart.

"And I have always been aghast at how the master treated this wise and prudent servant for his efforts," Babcock continued. "After all, based upon my conservative and provincial upbringing, all my life I had heard, as if they were mantras, such sayings as 'it's better to be safe than sorry,' 'a bird in the hand is worth two in the bush,' 'a penny saved is a penny earned,' 'waste not, want not.' So my lot in life was to always cleave to the safe and the sure and to never waiver from the straight and the narrow. After all, it was righteous, it was prudent, it was circumspect, and a tad on the boring side, but you learned to live with the drawbacks. But an inner voice kept churning in my brain, getting louder and louder with the passage of time, until finally I could suppress it no longer. One day a thunderous crescendo reigned forth saying, 'You foolish and slothful man! You wear my name yet deny the nature of my mission! Do you not know that mine is a ministry of risk? A ministry of sacrifice? A ministry of faith in something greater than yourself and your own self-serving precautions? Cast him into the outer darkness! For he is totally and completely worthless!"

When the sermonette ended, there was a long silence before people prepared to leave.

"Mr. Babcock!" Wanda cried with tears in her eyes, "I needed that sermon! I really needed that sermon!"

As for me, the notion of sacrifice did not sit well. After all, I didn't think there was much of me left to sacrifice. Then I remembered the passage of scripture that commanded the disciple to deny himself and take up his cross and follow Him. That's a pretty tall order, I thought. On the other hand, anything that was worthwhile was probably worth some sacrifice.

Back in the assembly room, Professor Babcock received another distress call from the cook regarding the food provisions running low.

"Impossible!" He cried. "Did you stock up?"

"I did," the cook replied. "Right to the brim. And we're still low!"

"This is going to run us over our budget! How late is the store open!"

"Until ten."

He handed her the credit card. "Here. We can't afford any slipups."

The cook took the card and headed for the car.

Babcock turned to Molder. "That's the second time she's had to go out and restock our food provisions! Now, I've known Lewis Coppel for the past four years. I know he's got an appetite, but it's never been anything that couldn't be satisfied."

"There is another student I've been observing," Molder replied, "and based on what I've observed, I believe he's insatiable."

"Right! It's that alligator wrestler! I can't believe

Shyster accepted him! Of course there're a lot of things Shyster did that I can't believe. And tomorrow we're registering these folks for classes, and if you'll pardon the expression, that's when the manure is really gonna hit the ventilator!"

"Rupert," Molder interrupted, "have you ever spoken to that Markem? Have you heard how intense and dynamic a speaker he is? On the basis of that feature alone, I think it would be well within the boundaries of this seminary's best interest to accept him and somehow get him through the program!"

"All right!" Babcock replied. "If you want to accept that line of reason, have you ever talked with Elmo Piggins? I'll wager he's just as intense and just as dynamic. I not only experienced his intense demeanor firsthand, but I've also received word from his home church regarding the revival he caused during the one Sunday he preached. And at least he's a high school graduate! And we're making him go through the undergraduate religion program. Seems a bit inequitable if you ask me."

"But Markem is over forty."

"Why is forty such a magic number? I've known people who were just as dumb at forty as they were at twenty. Only difference was they had twenty additional years to refine that dumbness."

"Trust me, Rupert. Follow Shyster's lead. I guarantee there was method behind Shyster's madness."

"'Madness' isn't quite the term I'd use to describe Shyster's method. I believe the man was grasping at straws, admitting anyone who had a pulse. He was so desperate for warm bodies he was willing to throw academic integrity and standards to the four winds just to keep the seminary afloat. Consequently, now the seminary can't even afford the luxury of an honorable death."

Back at the men's quarters, Jack was preparing his two sons for bed. Just then Dean Marco approached him with an outstretched hand. "I believe we got off to a bad start this morning. Name's Marco. Dean Marco."

"Jack Logan, and these are my two boys."

The boys gave Dean a shy glance.

"I may have been a bit out of line this morning," he said, "and I came by to apologize. Also, there's something that might interest you. We're putting together a class that we're encouraging all married seminary students and their wives to take. It's a class that also serves as sort of a support group. It deals with issues surrounding marriage, the family, and seminary life. I'd like to extend a personal invitation to both you and your wife to attend it."

After Jack said, rather grudgingly that he'd think about it, Dean approached Reginald, whose response was an emphatic "no."

"But…"

"No buts! The answer is no. My wife is busy with her legal practice. I'm retired and will only be here three days a week. And no wet-behind-the-ears divinity student is going to tell me how to run my marriage. End of conversation."

"Hey Reggie," Charlie called out as Dean left, shoulders slumped, "you think that was wise? Dean's got a great course. I ought to know. My wife and I took it and it did us a world of good. Besides, Dean's a doctoral student and he's got a degree in family counseling. He carries a lot of weight around here."

"Yeah," Reginald responded, "he *could* stand to lose a few pounds here and there."

"I swear, Reggie!" Charlie bellowed. "You have more impertinence than any man I think I've ever known!"

"Comes with gray hair. Now I've got to get some sleep. I don't think this old man can take too many more shocks to his system today without giving it a chance to rejuvenate."

We were all quick to follow Reggie's lead. I, for one, found great wisdom in his sentiments and was quick to find comfort under the covers.

Reginald arose from his bunk several hours before the rest of us. He was determined to maintain a remnant of his set routine despite the many disruptions imposed upon him during this period of seminary indoctrination. Now that his colleagues were tucked away in the land of Nod, he might just possibly be able to revert to his routine.

There was sufficient nocturnal lighting out on the retreat grounds to enable him to scout out an area fit for exercising. Having found a grassy clearing, he began to carry out his exercise ritual which began with a series of stretching exercises followed by a vigorous round of calisthenics—enough to get the heart pumping at a brisk rate. He then embarked upon his usual five-mile run. Upon arriving at the camp, he had scouted out a five-mile circuitous loop he thought would adequately suit his purpose.

After completing his run, Reginald took a quick, invigorating cold shower and began his tai chi exercises in the dormitory entryway. He preferred the solitude. At home, even his wife felt free to imply that his insistence on the routine was a sign of emotional instability. Now there was Charlie Donohue, who was convinced these exercises were of the devil. Reginald really didn't care to hear any more feedback of this nature from anyone. He knew people were inclined to condemn and ridicule things that were beyond their ability to fathom and during the brief interlude of the retreat, he felt suffocated by their ignorance. Ah, but it was this exercise regimen that brought him back into focus, giving him clarity of thought as it energized his body.

After about an hour, Reginald emerged like a recharged battery, refreshed, newly empowered, and ready again to embark upon the day of indoctrination that lay ahead of him. But more than that, he had been taken into a oneness with his future goal—that of reinventing himself, and no obstacle was going to deter him from attaining that end. As he continued his tai chi, he resumed his meditation, focusing on his Pastor's counsel, the words of the seven ascended masters, among whom was Jesus. By the time the first hints of morning were pulsating on the horizon, Reginald felt completely refreshed. One day at a time, he thought. Turning his eyes toward the east and the rising of the sun, he readied himself for the day.

Lawrence Viscount was next to awaken. His routine

was a much briefer one than Reginald's. He showered, shaved, dressed, combed back his dark hair, walked inside the main area of the dormitory as the rest of us were still sleeping, or at least we were until he began to sing "Rise Up O Men of God" in his shrill Irish tenor, wherein he was pummeled with a barrage of Bibles hurled at him by his less-than-receptive cohorts.

A half-hour later, we were all summoned to the dining commons for a hearty breakfast consisting of scrambled eggs, hominy grits, cornbread, and juice. After the morning meal, one hour of recreation was followed by a Sunday morning devotional led, of course, by Rupert Babcock. We were then given a short time of recreation. Class registration would follow about two that afternoon.

At registration, we were all introduced to our advisors who, in turn, lined us up around their tables. I was assigned Dr. Randolph Hennessey. Dr. Hennessey's first advisee was Lewis Coppell. "Lewis!" Dr. Hennessey exclaimed. "Good to have you with us!"

"Thank you," Lewis replied. "Nice to be had."

"Well, we consider it quite the honor. How's your father?"

"He's fine."

"And your mother and sister?"

"They're fine, too."

"Still shootin' them hoops?"

"You bet. Wouldn't want to give that up."

"You always were the sportsman. How's it going at your church?"

"Hey, the sports program is coming along magnificently. Why, just the other day …"

Just then, Reginald Dexter spoke up, "Excuse me,"

The Call

he said. "I don't mean to break up this round of socializing, but in case nobody's noticed, others of us in line need tending to."

"I see no cause for rudeness here, Dr. Dexter," Dr. Hennessey replied. "Everyone will be tended to accordingly. Well Lewis, I guess we'd better begin the process of scheduling your classes. Look, let's get together later. I really want to hear more about the sports team you've organized at your church."

The next person in line was Samuel Hill. "Where are your college transcripts?" Dr. Hennessey said, looking through his file.

"Don't got any," Sam replied.

"Excuse me?"

"I never went to college. I went to vocational school to be a plumber."

"Well look, in order to enter seminary, you have to be a college graduate."

"Dr. Shyster said I didn't need to be a college graduate 'cause I'm over forty."

"Well, Dr. Shyster is not the dean anymore."

"Are you telling me that what I was told was all a bunch o' crock?" Sam shouted.

"Listen," the professor defended himself, "this is the first time I've ever heard of concessions being made for those over forty."

"Well I got me the endorsement of the Methodist convention, so if you don't want to lock horns with them boys, I think you'd better knock off this bullshit and enroll me in them classes!"

"Now, calm down …"

"I'll calm down when you stop with all this b. s. about transcripts an' all and get me enrolled."

"Excuse me a minute," Hennessey said. "Professor Babcock. Could you come over here? This is Samuel Hill. If we let him in we're compromising our academic standards."

"Yeah, and if we don't, we'll have the Methodist convention on us like stink on manure," Babcock said.

"Since when have Methodists lowered their standards? I knew Baptists had, but …"

"The point is he's here with their endorsement. What can we do? Sign him up and see what happens. Like my secretary told me the other day, we've got to play politics … make concessions … although it goes against my grain."

Next it was Reginald's turn.

"You're a very cantankerous gentleman, you know," Dr. Hennessey told him.

"Comes with gray hair! Or perhaps it's because we Unitarians just aren't that high on the food chain, huh?"

"Well, Dr. Dexter, you see, you're the first Unitarian we've ever had attend this seminary."

"A dubious distinction, I'm sure."

"I assure you, it is Sir. Now, let me look at your file. Hmmm – a retired professor of psychology at the University of Oklahoma. Very impressive. I believe I've read a few of your works, and I've found them to be somewhat helpful in my discipline. I'm the professor of pastoral care here at the seminary, and I'm oftentimes called upon to cite works of various psychological orientations to convey effectiveness in my area of expertise."

"Yes, I can imagine that it would come in handy."

"Indeed it does. Now, because you are a Unitarian, I feel that it is only right to inform you that this is a Christian theological seminary, and we normally only accept students with Christian leanings."

"Dr. Shyster said he welcomed students with differing theological outlooks."

"Yes, but Unitarian is a bit on the extreme …"

"Well, let me put it to you this way: I've already paid my tuition, which means I've been promised by this school the right of entry. If you plan on reneging on that promise, I've got a wife who's a damn good attorney and …"

"Now, I didn't say we're reneging on anything, Dr. Dexter! It's just that a man such as yourself usually doesn't frequent places like this, not that we're not honored to have you."

"Thank you. Starr King Seminary's a long ways away."

"I'm familiar with that place," Dr. Hennessey said stiffly. "Now, let's get you signed up for classes. First off, we need to enroll you in the New Testament course entitled St. Paul and the Gentile Mission. Then there's Introduction to Theological Education. I believe that you said you are married? Because we have this one course that one of our doctoral students is teaching for the interim. It pertains to marital and family matters while in seminary and …"

"Don't even go there."

Things didn't get any better when the good

professor got to Markem McClusky. "It says here you got a tenth grade education," he said wearily. "Bit overeducated for this place, don't you think?"

"Yeah," said Markem with a grin, "an' I'm over forty, too."

Hennessey signed him up for the standard nine units of course work. Clearly he was too tired to argue with Markem about anything.

Next in line was T. J. "Ah," Dr. Hennessey said, looking over T. J.'s file, "twelfth grade. Standards are getting higher and higher. Let me guess. Dr. Shyster admitted you?"

"Yeah, man," T. J. replied. "Said I'd make a welcome addition."

"But you're not even forty."

"Yeah, but I'm a high school graduate!"

"Oh, well, silly me. Of course. That makes everything cool!" Dr. Hennessey signed him up for the standard nine units of graduate credits.

I was next. "You're a graduate of the University of California," Dr. Hennessey said. "And before that, you attended community college where you received your associate's degree. Tell me something. How come you managed to graduate with honors in your upper division course work, yet you fell short of maintaining a B average during your first two years of college?"

"Meaning no disrespect, Sir, but my letter of admission seemed to indicate that I was more than qualified for admission to this place, and now I feel I the need to justify myself as to my academic performance. I couldn't help but overhear you admit two people who've never even set foot in college. In fact, one of them didn't even finish high school."

"You're right. I never should have asked. Look, I'll sign you up for the standard nine units. By the way, I read over your senior research project regarding religion's role in twentieth-century American culture, and I think you did an outstanding job of research. Certainly you were very thorough in your coverage of the topic and very articulate in the presentation. Your theme and conclusion were something else, of course, but that's okay. I don't necessarily agree with everything I read. Are you being sponsored by your church or ecumenical body?"

"No, just me and the scholarship Dr. Shyster offered me."

Dr. Hennessey stared at me blankly. "Dr. Shyster offered you a scholarship?"

"Yes, he did." I handed him Dr. Shyster's letter.

Dr. Hennessey looked over the letter then looked up at me and said, "I'm afraid that we're not offering any scholarships this year."

"But Dr. Shyster said …"

"Dr. Shyster is no longer the dean of this seminary and, even if he were, he wouldn't be able to deliver on that promise."

"But …"

"I'm sorry Mr. O'Donnell. Unexpected budget constraints make Dr. Shyster's promise null and void."

"You mean to tell me that I gave up a nice, secure government job and traveled all the way out here to this god forsaken area of the country from California …"

"I'm afraid so, Mr. O'Donnell. Sorry."

"You know, on many occasions I've been called a

lousy Christian, but I do know a few basic tenets of the faith. Isn't there something in the Good Book about letting your yes be yes and your no be no … about not bearing false witness?"

"Yes, there is. I'm going to be straight with you. Archibald Shyster did not live by those principles, even though he may have been, and still is, a man who wears the mantle of Christianity. Dr. Shyster was first, and foremost, a politician. And often, like so many of them, he reverted to the old flimflam. Note the letter. It says you *may* qualify for a scholarship. That would be the way he would wiggle out of the commitment he made to you. It's sleazy, it's deceptive, but that's the reality of the situation. I'm sorry to be the one to have to tell you this. I wouldn't blame you if you told us all to go to hell. But from where I sit, I think you'd make a welcome addition to the student body, and I'd like to have you stay."

"Well, my funds'll only take me so far, and my church made it quite clear to me that I'd get no support from them. I was rather counting on the help I'd get from the scholarship."

"It says here in your file that you worked as a secretary before coming here. If it's money you need, we have plenty of typing jobs listed in our employment office. How fast do you type?"

"About seventy words per minute."

"Well then, you'd be a shoo-in for most of those jobs. Why don't you check them out after we finish this retreat?"

"Thanks. I might do that. Although I was hoping to get some ministerial experience under my belt."

"We can help you with that too. Just one thing."

"What's that?"

"Don't expect all the people, just because they wear the cloth, to be bastions of integrity. It's like any other occupation. We have our good, and we have our bad. You'll be finding out more along these lines as you advance in the program. Now, about your classes."

"Yes, could I have twelve units instead of nine?"

"That's going to be an awful big load for someone just starting out."

"I can handle it. Besides, how else am I going to finish in three years?"

"Many people don't. Many people take as long as four or five years. But I'll give you the twelve."

And so the enrollment process ended for me, leaving a bad taste in my mouth but some hope for the future.

After purchasing my textbooks and supplies, I acted upon Dr. Hennessey's counsel and paid a visit to the student employment center to see what options were open. By the end of the first week of classes, I managed to land a job as a typist working flexible hours for the city hall in an office located in the basement. I was given keys to the building so that I could work at night if I chose to do so. As for the number of hours I worked, they were not to exceed forty. The pay was not as much as I had made while working for the State of California, nor was I accorded any benefits, but all I needed to do was type the material placed in my in-basket, and there was always material in my in-basket.

Whether our work was secular or church related, we had to keep in sync with our classes. Those with church assignments worked only on weekends, while those of us who had secular assignments had to regulate ourselves accordingly.

Those of us who maintained secular employment found the juggling of work and academics to be a bit more burdensome. Leonard DeWilde, in particular, found it difficult to keep in step with everything that was placed on his agenda. He managed to attain a weekend church assignment, yet could not bring himself to let go of his engineering consulting position with the city that he worked in tandem along with his wife. Add to that, the rigors of academics, and he was inclined to believe the demands placed upon him as a CEO paled by comparison. He also had some marital problems that he hoped Dean Marco's class could help him and his wife to address, but it was like pulling teeth for him to persuade Lillian to attend, in good part because the course was in the evening and, after a day's work for the city, the last thing Lillian wanted to do was take part in academia.

On the other hand, Jerry and Linda were more than willing to enroll in Dean Marco's course. After all, the reason for their enrollment in seminary was to gather information for their research on religion and mental health, and why wouldn't marital dynamics figure into the overall scheme of the matter?

Jack Logan had the good sense to discuss the issue of enrollment with Carla before committing them to the class. She, in turn, expressed an almost eager willingness to partake in the class, much to Jack's delight. What Jack did not know was just how thoroughly their change of lifestyle had taken its toll on Carla and what a major axe she had to grind as a consequence of this adjustment.

The course workload proved to be cumbersome, particularly the reading part. The most irritating of the courses for most of the students was the seminary library class, which contained so much busywork and so much referencing detail that it drove a good portion of us to the brink of delirium. My weekends were relatively free and I was able to devote more time to the course work's completion, while the other students were at a disadvantage, because they had weekend parish commitments. Within the span of the first few weeks of class, I had the course nearly completed.

Next came the New Testament course pertaining to the travails of St. Paul as he tried to bring the Gentiles into the fold. The course was taught by Dean Babcock, and required five thousand pages of reading be completed by the end of the semester. It was during the course of this class that I noted something strange about the distribution of grades. One of his first assignments was for us to type out a three-to-five-page biography of St. Paul drawing material exclusively from his epistles. I spent several nights, operating on a minimum amount of sleep, thumbing through the epistles, jotting down significant items here and there, trying to piece things together to the point where I could submit a halfway coherent biography, for which effort I received a C+ along with a few notations stating that some of the incidents I had named were found only in the Book of Acts. Meantime, Kathleen McKensie, who had drawn a biography of Paul in crayon that was comparable to a first-grade picture assignment, with wording kept to a bare minimum, received an A. I would have liked to protest, but experience had told me that it was better to accept my lot, no matter how unfair.

Another class most of the incoming seminarians were required to take was Elementary Preaching and Pastoral Care. The director of field education, Brian Wilson, taught the course. In this course we would learn how to preach, do hospital calls, perform weddings and funerals, baptisms, comfort the bereaved, and other related liturgical practices.

It was obvious right from the start of the first class that Professor Brian Wilson was highly pragmatic in his attitude and methodology. "Good morning ladies and gentlemen," he began. "Elementary Preaching and Pastoral Care may be the title of this course, but in truth, it is a course in acting. After all, that is, for all intents and purposes, what a minister is … an actor. In fact, it's been suggested that if you ever fail at being a minister, then you might want to seriously explore a career in acting. Matter of fact, I've often wondered why they have academies of performing arts. If people really wanted to know how to truly render convincing performances, just send them to seminaries."

The class laughed. I felt uneasy. If there was one thing I was not, it was an actor. And the only time I felt comfortable addressing an audience was when I was reading from a fully prepared text.

"During the course of this ninety-unit curriculum," Professor Wilson continued, "you will be dedicating yourselves to honing this ability, to sensing the needs of those around you, and to adapting your behavioral attributes to the sole purpose of addressing those needs. In essence, you will become virtual chameleons. And this runs consistent with what St. Paul had to say about being all things to all people. A minister is someone who must maintain a readiness at all times. He must stand ready to preach or stand ready to pray at a moment's notice, or, if he's unable to perform these two functions, for one reason or another, he must be ready to run … fast! You're hearing it first in this class. And this will be reinforced over and over and over again within the context of this curriculum. As a man or a woman of the cloth, you are no longer your own! I'm going to give you a quick acting lesson right now. I'm going to assume the role of a grieving widow. One of you will be her minister. Let's have you up here, Leonard. I'll be a recently widowed woman." Suddenly he broke out in an hysterical bout of crying, "Why did he have to die?" he wailed, "Why couldn't I have loved him better when he was alive? Oh, God!"

Leonard was stunned by Wilson's tirade, and I was utterly relieved Professor Wilson hadn't chosen me for this designated role play.

"Okay, what are you going to do?" Brian said, suddenly stepping out of character.

The class broke out in gales of laughter. Most of us were relieved by the return to normalcy, and some of us were taken back by the stark contrast in Brian's modes of expression.

"Oh, you can laugh now," Brian said, "but this is a circumstance you're going to be confronted with again and again while in the ministry. Perhaps Leonard handled it the right way just by remaining quiet and allowing me to vent. Maybe it was and maybe it wasn't. These are issues we're going to be exploring throughout this course. And what about the prayers you render for the deceased? Or prayers for the suffering? It's just like what the rabbi said in the movie *Fiddler on the Roof*: 'There are prayers for every occasion.' It's your job to come up with these prayers, and to pray them spontaneously when the need arises. By the end of this semester, you will feel like you have run the gamut in the facets of pastoral care. But do *not* … and I can't stress this strongly enough… allow this feeling to be translated into fact! To paraphrase Karen Carpenter, at the end of this class, you've only just begun!"

Professor Wilson's class impacted us with a sizeable jolt of reality that was often quite stark in its presentation. But the impact was slight when compared to Introduction to Theological Education, team-taught by Dr. Stephen Bildeberger and Dr. Randolph Hennessey. While Wilson's course might have taught us that we were all actors, this one taught us the type of theater we were acting in—primarily the theater of the absurd, a theater that was in defiance of all principles one would normally ascribe to common sense and good judgment, where the ridiculous, the foolish, and the outrageous were considered the norm. To accentuate this truism, the first part of the class session might be dedicated to the expounding of excerpts from Becket's play *Waiting For Godot* or Twain's *Tom Sawyer*. Members of the class would read excerpts from Becket's play; these excerpts would portray characters waiting and anticipating the arrival of a hero who never shows. Near the end of the play, a messenger comes and tells them that the hero will arrive tomorrow. After the messenger leaves, one of the characters says, "Let's go."

The other character says, "Right."

And both are left standing there as the curtain draws.

Dr. Hennessey read the excerpt from *Tom Sawyer* in which Tom and his friends attend church, a section in which the preacher preaches and Tom and a good portion of the congregation endure. Only a few attending are truly cognizant of the minister's actual message. This example served to illustrate the desolate contrast in perspective when taken from the pulpit as opposed to how it is experienced from the pews.

The second part of the class session was devoted to the science of group dynamics and interpersonal interaction. The corresponding exercises dispelled any illusions that we were all Christian brothers and sisters drawn together in the spirit of love. The reality was, as we were all quick to discover, we did not even like each other. In fact, some of us hated certain individuals within the group.

One of the preludes to attending seminary was taking the Minnesota Multiphasic Personality Inventory. This test contained close to 500 multiple-choice questions, many of which were repetitious. It was designed to measure the multiple phases of one's personality, most likely administered to the incoming seminarians for purposes of enabling the faculty to know just what kind of characters they were getting in their program. I later discovered that the test was devised way back in the 1930s; and that it's standard for normalcy hadn't varied since its inception. Since back in the thirties, the standard for normalcy was an Idaho potato farmer with an eighth-grade education, we could all be viewed recognized as kooks and deviants.

Next, for Introduction to Theological Education we were given a stress test, which consisted of summing up the stress levels of certain life experiences. Death of a spouse rated top on the list, tallying a score of 150 points. It was followed by death of a parent, death of a sibling, moving to a different location, experiencing a change in income—even Christmas was accorded fifteen points. As Dr. Hennessey stated emphatically, "Stress takes its toll on a person. We want you to list the stresses you have tallied up within the span of a year. And we don't confine stress as being an exclusively negative occurrence. Even positive events ellicit stress in us, and the results are principally the same."

"I know of this one seminary student," he went on. "He had graduated from seminary and was accepted as an associate pastor of a church that was in the city of his first choosing. The congregation just loved him—so much so that when the head pastor resigned just a few months later, this man, who had not been out of seminary a year, was elevated to the position of head pastor. Just a couple months later, he met the woman of his dreams and they got married. The book he had written got published and became a number-one best seller. Letters and phone calls came from all over requesting his presence at speaking engagements and book signings. The momentum of this positive stress kept coming at him and coming at him, until the poor guy just up and committed suicide."

How about that, I thought. The man went and happied himself to death.

"The moral of this story is," he went on, "that when you're going through changes, it's important that you keep close tabs on your well-being—physical, psychological, spiritual—because stress kills. Now, if you've experienced twelve hundred points within a year's time, you can expect a minor health change. If you've experienced between eighteen hundred and two thousand points, expect a major health change. Over two thousand—well, all I can say is you'd better be on your guard. Seek out counseling, get into a support group, and start monitoring your activities very closely. I cannot emphasize this strongly enough. This program is no cakewalk, but we expect to turn out ministers, not corpses."

We took the test and when I tallied up my score I said to myself, "Son of a bitch. Over four thousand points, and I'm not dead yet. Guess miracles do happen."

Wanda Epperson, after seeing the results of her stress test, was quick to run crying to Dr. Hennessey and whine about scoring twenty-five hundred points.

"Poor Wanda," Ben Parsons mumbled. "Why don't you just go off somewhere and self-destruct."

Dr. Hennessey embraced the sobbing Wanda, in passing and told her not to worry, that her problem would be addressed in time, and then turned back to the class. "In fact, we want to address every one of your situations, both individually and in group sessions. Throughout this course, a part of the program will be your core and support group, and Dr. Bildeberger and myself will be your facilitators."

The next project was to write a detailed account of both our genealogy and an autobiography. This was an extended assignment that we had to pursue outside of class, and involved my having to contact my parents.

Finally, we were to be initiated into the "cutting edge" of the course, i.e., the core group. Half of us went with Dr. Hennessey, the other half with Dr. Bildeberger. Those of us who had Dr. Bildeberger as our chief facilitator went to a classroom in the basement of the seminary. There we sat in chairs that were positioned in a circular fashion about the room's perimeter.

"Alright," Dr. Bildeberger began, "we're here to explore the concept of group dynamics. It's been my experience that every group seems to take on a life of its own, as well as its own personality. So, it's going to be up to you folks to collectively decide what direction you think this group ought to take, what goals you think we ought to pursue and how we can achieve those ends. We're coming together now as strangers, for the most part. But regardless, it's my hope that whatever product we turn up during these next several weeks, our chief aim will be for us to draw closer together as a caring group, embracing a spirit of true fellowship. So, now that we're here, what do we do?"

Lawrence Viscount was the first to speak. "I've been the facilitator of groups before," he said, "and I have a method I think might be worth considering."

Lewis Coppel spoke up. "I believe we need more clarification as to why we're here."

"It seems pretty evident to me," Samuel Hill replied.

"We're here to form a group."

"Well, duh." Jerry Cantrell retorted. "I'll say one thing for you … you sure know how to state the obvious."

"I see no reason for derogatory comments," Wanda Epperson snapped.

"I need a reason?" Jerry asked.

"It seems as though Mr. Viscount had a workable method for getting this group going," I said. "I, for one, would like to hear what it is."

"I don't think I like you very much," Wanda said to Jerry.

"Go tell that to someone who gives a shit," Jerry replied.

"Now those are the types of attitudes and sentiments we need to explore," Dr. Bildeberger said.

"I thoroughly agree," Leonard DeWilde chimed in. "When I was a corporate head…"

"What concerns me," said Norman Decantor, "is why, all of a sudden, we have this negativity. I mean, we're just getting started and already…"

"Have we forgotten about Mr. Viscount's suggestion?" I asked.

"Reginald," Dr. Bildeberger said, "you have a background in psychology. What input do you have concerning why we're here?"

"No comment at this time," Reginald replied.

"I knew we'd be wasting our time conferring with that senile old codger," Jason Tyler remarked under his breath.

"I didn't quite catch that," Dr. Bildeberger said.

"Oh, it's nothing."

"'Nothing' indeed! If you're going to cast aspersions on any one in this room, you'd better speak up so we can all hear you."

"Forget about it," Reginald countered. "It's not even worth addressing."

"And I further see no need to discount anyone in the group either," Dr. Bildeberger said.

"Hey," I said, "anybody remember Mr. Viscount's suggestion?"

"You know," Leonard interrupted, "we seem to be drifting off into all sorts of tangents. We need to begin to focus."

"Could you clarify what you mean by that?" Lewis asked.

"I think my meaning is quite evident."

"I think what we need to do is define more closely what it is we want to achieve during these sessions," Norman interjected. "I see a need…"

"I don't know about you folks," Markem interrupted, "but I'm gettin' kinda hungry. You reckon we could serve refreshments during this class?"

"Why?" asked Ben Parson. "You'd just eat them all."

Laughter followed shortly after Ben's pronouncement. *It was amazing to me how easily everything could break down into irrelevancy, and I was tempted to say so. But experience had taught me to protect myself, and this time, at least, I said nothing.*

But what I perceived as counterproductive proceedings continued to display their prominence, I found myself growing impatient and uninhibitedly voiced my frustration. "I think this is all a bunch of shit!"

The Call 181

"I don't like your language," Wanda countered. "I'm sorry."

Dr. Bildeberger then pointed at me and spoke in a commanding demeanor, "You're too busy focusing on one thing and not taking into consideration the other factors taking place within the group!"

"Yes sir," I said.

After the first three days of classes, Reginald couldn't wait to leap into his car and floorboard it back to Norman. Was it because he missed his wife so much, or was it because he was so repulsed by life in the dormitory? At this point he was unable to tell. All he knew was how much he longed for comfortable surroundings and an absence of the madness brought about by the unique form of academia he perceived as exclusive to theological indoctrination. He also wanted to experience the comforts and conveniences the University of Oklahoma library provided as he pursued his research—and experience it he would, with a greatly enhanced appreciation.

As for the rest of us, with the exception of those who had already been given church assignments in the neighboring communities, we were stuck full-time in Idle in a claustrophobic setting, particularly those of us living in the dormitory.

Many of us found the antics of the undergrads to be a disconcerting cross between a Bible study group and a sex orgy. Much to our chagrin and amazement, the undergrads that preached to us most fervently and denounced our potential liberal leanings most zealously were among the ones we later discovered to be the most libidinal, promiscuous, and disruptive. Yet, each of us had our own distinctive manner of coping with our circumstances. Sam Church, a product of similar undergraduate surroundings, would often join in the gaiety, and did he ever like to drink. T. J. Whizzer, when he wasn't out playing gigs, would often don his headset and practice his guitar, much to the detriment of his studies. Markem McClusky was adept at browsing through his textbooks while simultaneously devouring junk food. Ben Parson remained as horny as any of the undergrads, but he had his wife Jana to satisfy his creature comforts when the need arose and if she was willing.

As for me, I had begun to feel the effects of sleep deprivation. Between my job, the pressures of academia, the worries I had regarding church placement, and the nocturnal noises of my neighbors on both sides that consisted chiefly of creaking bedsprings and orgasmic squeals, my sleep time was cut to a bare minimum. Earplugs helped, but I was still constantly reminded of how much fun I had missed out on as an undergraduate.

As raucous as the dormitory may have been during the week, its entire character shifted that first Sunday to a mood of somber piety. We were awakened at seven that morning to the sounds of hymns, played at a volume just loud enough to make further sleep impossible. After an early breakfast, we were all encouraged to prepare ourselves for morning worship. While wearing a suit and tie when attending church was considered optional in California, I was quick to learn that in Oklahoma it was something that was expected, which was a bit disconcerting since during my prolonged stay on the more liberal West Coast, I had never truly mastered the technique of tying a tie. It was a relief to find that T. J. was encumbered with the same disability, and could share with me verbal assaults such as, "You two ought to be ashamed of yourselves, going into the ministry and not knowing how to wear a tie!" or "A fine example of the clergy you're setting," or the ever popular "Damn hippie liberals! Can't even *dress* like God-fearin' men of the cloth!"

Markem McClusky *did* wear a shirt and tie. However, he wore them with his overalls. Apparently in Idle, Oklahoma, that mode of dress was acceptable.

After we had finished preparing ourselves to attend worship, we were all herded onto a bus to be transported to one of the churches that was a major sponsor of the university, a majestic structure comparable to that of Robert Schuller's Crystal Cathedral, although unlike Schuller's church, it was constructed of brick, mortar, stone, and glass, adorned with gold and jasper and pointed obelisks towering far above the walkways. The interior was garlanded with plush, blood red carpeting, and the spectacular stained glass windows featuring elaborate scenes from both the Old and New Testaments. Massive glass chandeliers hung from the ceiling.

The service that first morning was both lengthy and detailed. The choir was decked out to its fullest, the volume given more than subtle boosts by a highly sophisticated sound system, comparable to the one I experienced when I sat through the movie *Midway* and was made aware of the new "sense-around sound."

The sermon was entitled "New Beginnings" and focused on the welcoming, or the welcoming back, of the Parkins University students, the pastor deeming it worthwhile to mention that Parkins University was known for its high rate of marriages among the members of the student body. "So," he said, "take a good look around you, ladies and gentlemen, because your future spouse may very well be sitting nearby." His words, as it turned out, proved prophetic.

After what seemed like an inordinately lengthy service, it finally concluded, and we were all transported by bus back to the campus. A gap in time allowed for us to change from our Sunday clothing back to our usual collegiate grubbies before the noon meal. It was during that time when the mood of righteous piety once again dissipated and the atmosphere reverted back to the usual foray of irreverence and tomfoolery, with only a few exceptions. During the course of the noon meal, I found myself sitting among some of the undergrads. "Anyone know Sam Baker?" A student with a more than noticeable weight problem coupled with a semi-acute case of acne startled me by asking the group. I knew the name. He was the present husband of my childhood love, Becky Sutton.

Someone replied, "Yeah. Now there's one lucky son of a bitch! He's got himself a great-looking wife! How an ugly fuck like him ever rated a looker like that, I'll never know."

"Ugly guys always get the good-looking ones," another student chimed in. "Remember in Greek mythology? Who married Aphrodite? It was the ugly god of fire, Vulcan! And I don't mean Spock's home planet, either."

At that moment, I felt an uncomfortable, gnawing twinge in the pit of my stomach, a sinking feeling in my chest, and a supreme sense of violation. The distress of memories past coupled with unrequited speculation of what might have been, yet never truly was nor could never truly be, reared itself in all its hideous grandeur, as did the grating, maniacal laughter of my dual soul which reverberated in my head, followed by the searing taunt, "That's not yours! That's not yours! HAHAHAHAHAHAHAHAHAHAHAHAHAHAHAHA HAHAHAHAHAHAHAHAHAHAHAHAHAHAHAHA HAHAHAHAHAHAHAHAHAHAHAHAHAHAHAHA HAHAHAHOHOHOHO! NOTHING HERE IS YOURS! IT SHOULD BE MINE!" Isaac bellowed.

It was unbearable. Clasping my hands over my ears, I ran out of the dining commons shouting, "Go away Isaac! Go away!"

Laurie and Ben rose from their table and hurried down the hall after me, catching me just before I could enter my room.

"Hey, bud," Ben said, clearly concerned, "what was that all about back there?"

"It's nothing," I panted. "Really. Nothing at all."

"That was a mighty big nothing!" Laurie replied.

"Yeah," said Ben, "you keep up and you're going to be a bigger topic of controversy than Elmo Piggins's streak across the campus with his humongous goober."

"Look, Ishmael," Laurie said, "I know we don't know each other that well, but we're going to be in this program for at least three years. We need to learn to trust each other. Now I realize whatever is bothering you may be a hard thing for you to let go of, but we're here to help."

I was not particularly pleased, however, at the form their 'help' took. The following Tuesday, I was summoned to Dr. Hennessey's office.

"May I ask what this meeting is about?" I asked.

"I've been receiving some rather disturbing reports about the strange behaviors you've exhibited since your arrival here." Dr. Hennessey told me. "The topper came from Laurie and Ben concerning the histrionics you displayed Sunday afternoon in the dining commons. Who is Isaac?"

Although I certainly hadn't intended to say anything about Isaac, I heard myself mutter, "My twin."

"I didn't know that you had a twin." Dr. Hennessy said, frowning.

"Didn't think it was important," I told him, staring at the floor.

"Everything's important in this endeavor. That's why we have you take the tests we administered during the intro class. That's why we have you trace your genealogy. That's why we have you write an autobiography. It aids us in knowing what we have to work with. It also sometimes serves as a weeding process."

"You're not going to kick me out of the program?"

"No, but we do intend to address some issues, like these test scores, for instance. Ishmael, I've gotten the scores on all these tests, and of all the seminarians, your test scores prove to be the most unsettling. For one thing, you scored over four thousand points on the stress test."

"Well, I've gone through a lot of changes during the past year," I explained. "It's nothing to get disturbed about."

"You saw how disturbed Wanda Epperson got when she scored 2,500 points," he told me, "and a lot of her stress, we were later to discover, was prefabricated. And there's another thing. The Multiphasic test score depicts a tendency toward a severe bipolar disorder with schizoid tendencies. Have you ever been in counseling?"

"Once, back in high school. But my dad came home from overseas and abruptly put a stop to it. His words were, 'You're my son. I didn't raise a nut.'"

"And your mother?"

"She said it made her feel like she had failed as a parent."

"And what about your twin?"

"Dead. He died when we were just toddlers."

"I see. That explains a few things. Now listen Ishmael, I've set up an appointment for you with a psychiatrist who works as a consultant for the seminary. His name is Dr. Buddy Peters. The address is on the card, and I've arranged for you to see him this afternoon. I really feel it's important for you to be there. We'll be picking up a portion of the tab, but you'll have to take care of the rest."

"Wait a minute!" I said. "Am I the only one being singled out here?"

"Well, as of right now, you're the only one who's exhibited a need for this type of examination."

"That's crazy!" I protested. "You're singling me out? Man, you got a guy with a tenth-grade education who talks to alligators, a fraternity beer guzzler who's one step away from being an alcoholic, a burnt-out Jesus clone who's still stoned on perverted rock music and hardly takes off his headphones to study, as well as an egocentric insurance salesman, and you single me out as the one in need of psychotherapy?"

"Ishmael, the difference between them and you is that they are in charge of their abnormalities. You, on the other hand, have given cause for all of us to believe that yours have taken charge of *you*. I believe this warrants looking into."

"What's to look into? I had a nightmare during my waking hours. I'm sure I'm not the only one that's happened to."

"Ishmael, nightmares are a phenomenon that occurs when our conscious minds are at rest. What happened to you appeared to be more characteristic of a seizure, and if that is what it was, we need to see that it gets addressed properly. Now Buddy Peters is a nice man. He's very personable, and seeing him can do nothing but help."

I felt it useless to argue. If I were my father I would have told them to all go take a flying leap. However, I was only a product of his upbringing, and somehow, deep down, much as I hated to acknowledge the wisdom behind Dr. Hennessy's prognosis, I knew that resistance to his proposal would only make matters increasingly more problematic as the semester progressed.

As a consequence, one in the afternoon found me in the office of Dr. Buddy Peters, a bespectacled fellow with a slightly thinning crop of light brown hair topside who spoke in a languid western drawl.

"Congratulations," he said. "It appears that you are

The Call

the number one problem child of the seminary this year."

"Well if that's the opinion they have of me," I retorted angrily, "I'll just take my money back and go elsewhere!"

"It's only an expression. Do you always get that angry over the simple observations of others?"

"That was hardly a simple observation! It was more like a judgment! A judgment, I might add, no one has any right to make! Ever hear of toads calling frogs ugly?"

"It's nothing like that," Dr. Peters assured me. "We just want to run you through a battery of tests, ask you a few questions about your past history, and from there we can draw up an evaluation that I'm sure would be in your best interests. After all, that's what we're here for."

What could I say? If they were truly looking after my best interests, then resistance on my part would be folly. In the sessions that followed, Dr. Peters had me looking at inkblots, doing word associations, and drawing pictures of men, women, and my favorite pet. He asked about my mother and my father. He definitely wanted to know about my twin, a subject I never truly felt comfortable talking about. "You say your twin's name was Isaac and that he was identical? Tell you what, Mr. O'Donnell, our sessions are about up. But I'm going to write out a prescription for you. The drug is called Mellaril. I want you to take it three to five times a day. I have every reason to believe it will quiet these seizures you've been having."

"Seizures? Are you serious?"

"Oh, yes. Although you didn't express it in so many words, I have every reason to believe that seizures are what you're experiencing. Voices from within, profuse body sweats, flesh discolorations, and erratic behavior. I see definite signs of a bipolar disorder and maybe even borderline psychosis. I haven't ruled out Tourette's syndrome, although it doesn't seem typical in the way it manifests itself. I've ruled out schizophrenia. You appear to be quite capable of holding down a job. So I'd like for you to take this Mellaril and report back to me in a couple of weeks if you have the means to do so, and tell me how things are going. Perhaps we'll both know more by then. Of course, I have to say, you present a most interesting psychological profile."

When I left his office, I felt not only exhausted but downhearted. What would be the effect of all this on my standing as a student? What had I, in other words, let myself in for? What had happened to bring me to this state of being? And was I even capable of pursuing the endeavor I was purportedly called to?

After two days on Mellaril I felt wonderful. So wonderful, in fact, that I took advantage of the doctor's maximum recommended dosage, and as a consequence, experienced such a sense of euphoria that I walked around looking like "smiling Alfred." But the important thing was that I could really focus now. Furthermore, nothing seemed to bother me. Ben Parson, at one point, made a side comment to Jana when our paths crossed. "Have you looked at that Ishmael lately? It's like he turned on the light and left the house."

That Thursday, the core group once again convened and although everyone else displayed the usual animosity toward one another, I sat there smiling in a euphoric stupor.

"I think that as Christians we all behaved disgracefully during our first session!" Wanda said. "All we did was denigrate one another! We were discounting the other person, and we were all behaving in a very uncaring manner and I…"

"In other words, we were all being human," Lawrence said.

"No we weren't just being human!" Wanda cried. "We were being mean, malicious, cruel…"

"If you can't take a little heat, little girl, then…"

"Just like you're being right now!"

"And I'm beginning to note a little bit of projection on your part."

"Now just a minute, Mr. Viscount," Dr. Bildeberger countered, "exactly what is it you mean by 'projection?'"

Lawrence then pounded wildly on his desk and shouted at the top of his lungs, "I'm not excited!! You're the one who's excited!!" Then he spoke quietly, "Need I say anymore?"

"I think that was a very childish display," Samuel Hill observed.

"I'm more interested in getting Wanda's reaction," Dr. Bildeberger said. "Wanda, how did you just feel about what Mr. Viscount just did?"

"I resented it! I don't like Lawrence's implications! I don't like Lawrence's attitude! I don't like Mr. Cantrell's attitude either! And I certainly don't like that smirk on Ishmael's face!"

"You got something against a fella being happy?" I asked.

"Let's examine that statement," said Dr. Bildeberger. "What are you so happy about right now? I think you should share it with all of us?"

"I woke up this morning and guess what? I was breathing!"

The reactions of my colleagues were mixed. Some laughed. A few made sarcastic comments. Others told me to shut up.

"You know," Reginald said, "I can relate to that. In fact the only thing about that statement I find difficult to fathom is that it's coming from somebody who's a bit young to be making it."

"I'm inclined to agree," Dr. Bildeberger replied. "Although I must say I'm a bit surprised."

"We might use that statement as a springboard for what's to come," said Jerry.

"Now just a minute!" Wanda protested. "I feel discounted right now."

"Man," Lawrence bellowed, "what IS your problem? Just when things start to smooth themselves out, we have to listen to your incessant whining! I, for one, am getting real sick of it!"

"You, you! You make me so angry!" Wanda gasped, shaking her fist at him.

"I'm flattered. I must be a highly significant person to you."

Lawrence's response struck me as so funny I gave him a thumbs-up, thereby bringing down the wrath of Professor Bildeberger who snapped, "Now hold on!! None of this nonverbal signaling! If you got something to say, you say it so the rest of the group can hear it!"

I laughed and said, "Life is beautiful."

Dr. Bildeberger hollered back, "I resent ...!"

"Now hold on," Reginald said. "I happen to agree with the boy."

"Oh, come on now, Dexter!" Dr. Bildeberger exclaimed. "Are you shitting me? You got a Ph.D. in psychology. You probably know just as much, if not more than me, about appropriateness and inappropriateness in the area of group dynamics and…"

"And I'm sure we can both agree that we still have a lot more to learn."

"Touché, Dr. Dexter, touché."

"Well I'm still upset!" Wanda cried.

"Oh my God," said Ben, "back to square one!"

"Now wait a minute!" Dr. Bildeberger said. "We all have a right to be heard."

"Yeah, but she's monopolizing the time."

"The time is for everybody," Dr. Bildeberger said. "Right now, Wanda has issues…"

"Oh, she's got issues alright," Lawrence said, sliding down in his chair.

"And I believe she's entitled to address them to the group," Dr. Bildeberger said. "Wanda, could you please tell us what the real problem is?"

"Well, if you must know, I scored twenty-five hundred points on that stress test and neither you nor Dr. Hennessy think the matter is worth your time. Now I thought you were trying to create a caring community, and the way I've been treated so far, I feel unimportant and pushed to the side!" Breaking down in tears, she added, "I don't think you care that I might be on the verge of becoming an emotional basket case!"

When the session ended, those of us who lived in the dorm, walked back together. "Man!" Ben exclaimed. "What an experience! And to think we have to endure it once a week until the end of the semester! I tell you, it's enough to make me want to quit seminary and go sell widgets or something!"

"You're telling me!" Laurie replied. "And that Wanda! If I weren't such a libber I'd swear she was … "

"On the rag?" Kathleen inquired.

"That sounds a bit on the sexist side," said Reginald, "especially coming from two women aspiring to enter an occupation that's traditionally relegated to men."

"Yeah," Laurie replied, "but sometimes certain stereotypes come across so blatantly. And did you see the way she lit into Ishmael?"

"Yeah," said Ben, "All Ishmael was doing was sitting at his desk grinning and enjoying life when she…"

Reginald looked at me with narrowed eyes. "Have you been medicated?"

"I sure have," I told him, and wandered off toward the dorm, happy as a clam and, for the moment at least, free of Isaac at last.

Kathleen turned to Laurie and said, "You know, Laurie, we may be getting more than our fair share of nut cases this year."

"Maybe you're right." Laurie watched as I walked toward the dormitory. She looked worried.

Just across town, Leonard DeWilde was returning to his townhouse after a night of hitting the books at the seminary library. Upon his entry, he saw an assortment of suitcases near the door. "Hey, hey!" he called out.

The Call

"What's with all the suitcases?"

Lillian entered the living room with her raincoat folded neatly over her arm. "I'm leaving you, Leonard." Lillian replied calmly.

"What? What brought this on? What have I done?"

"It's not you, Leonard! It's this 'calling' you profess to have! I can't do it!"

"What do you mean you can't do it? Sure you can! You're my wife! My helpmate! My soul mate!"

"No, Leonard. That was when we were both engineers and on the same wavelength. I can't even relate to you now. Nor can I relate to this entire scene. Look, I've been in contact with the plant back in Detroit. They've agreed to take me back with no cut in pay. I'm hopping on board the first flight out of here. I'll send for the rest of my things. We can split our assets in half. I just want out!"

Just then a car honked outside.

"That's the taxi that's going to drive me to the Idle airport," she said, slightly breathless. "Look, no hard feelings. I wish you well in this. Really. It's just that you're going to have to do it without me."

And picking up her white-and-gold monogrammed suitcase, she made her departure, leaving Leonard to watch her getting into the cab without a backward look. The sound of the car door slamming cut the humid, Idle night in two.

Leonard stood frozen in the open doorway. He could see the silhouette of Lillian like an unreal cardboard cutout through the window of the taxi. The cab rolled efficiently down the street, the taillights getting smaller until they were only two red pinpricks. Leonard continued to watch until the car turned at a distant corner. "Oh my God!" Leonard cried. "I need a drink."

The campus of Parkins University was quickly evolving into a veritable beehive of activity. The sophomores were engrossed in the freshman hazing ritual, which included making the first-year students wear beanies. This enabled the upperclassmen to follow them around and torment them by making them recite the school motto or sing the school's alma mater, or carry their books. The two major selling points of this time-honored tradition rested with the fact that it was all in the spirit of fun and that it served as a great way for incoming freshmen to make many quick but lasting friendships. Of course, there were a few hard noses amid the current crop of new arrivals who said they did not want anything to do with the tradition, but they were, thankfully, as far as the sophomores were concerned, in the minority. Of course the juniors and the seniors likewise, felt they were above any observation of campus tradition and were just there to get an education.

In sync with these freshman follies, the bloodmobile made its yearly run to the campus giving the old hard sell, in an attempt to persuade the students to give up a pint of their precious bodily fluids shortly after the admissions office had drained them of their financial resources. In addition, the food costs at the dining commons must have been running exceedingly high because, shortly after the week of freshman hazing, the university called for a campus-wide volunteer fast so that "God would shower the abundance of his blessings upon the university as we went about the process of doing His will."

Knowing that the fast was strictly voluntary, I opted not to participate. Taking careful note of my nonparticipation, along with that of fellow seminarians Rufus, Markem, T. J., Charlie Donohue, Sam Church, Laura Parsons, and Reginald Dexter, was Ellen the overage freshman who demanded to know why we, as aspiring ministers, did not feel compelled to take part. Sitting down at the table where we were stuffing our faces as if food was going out of style, she began a speech about the redemptive qualities of fasting. "Why aren't the seminarians fasting like the rest of us?" she demanded.

I set my gaze back at her and said, "I don't know. Why don't you ask them?"

"I am asking you, right now."

"It's voluntary. I didn't volunteer."

At that point, I noted Rufus Pelmonte looking a bit uneasy.

"And why, if I may ask, would a seminarian, like yourself, and an aspiring man of the cloth who should be serving as an example for the rest of us, make such a selfish decision?"

"I guess because I'm a selfish S.O.B." I replied, taking in a big spoonful of red jello and mini marshmallow salad.

At that point Laurie Parson broke in. "Ellen," she said, "you're a new student here and from what you told me, a recent convert. It's good that you're enthusiastic and on fire. But don't expect everyone to be like you. The administration promotes this fast year after year, and we've just gotten tired of going through the same thing over and over again. So why not just live and let live?"

I then turned to Laurie and smiled. "Laurie, you're beautiful." I said as Ellen, red with rage, took her tray and departed. "Is it too soon in our relationship to talk about marriage?"

"Honestly, Ishmael," she sighed, looking into my eyes, "are you still on that Mellaril?"

That evening I ran into Reginald on the second floor of the seminary library. He glanced at me standing in the entryway and signaled me over to the table. The table he occupied was strewn with material pertinent to the courses he was taking. As I approached, he spoke with gusto in his voice coupled with a note of sarcasm. "Man!" he said, "Isn't this seminary education the cat's meow? Really spiritually enlightening." He picked up one of the journals lying on the table. "Look at this! It's for my Theology in America course! Cotton Mather! Now there was a real firehouse! And boy, did that man ever know his Latin! Look at this correspondence! Half of the letter he's chewing out this Anglican minister in Latin! And look at how he signs the letter! 'Yours from the bowels of Christ!'"

And then, switching the subject abruptly, "By the way," he said, "Laurie asked me to talk to you. It's about that drug they told you to take."

"You mean the Mellaril?" I sat down at the table.

"Yeah. I'd like to know what business it is of theirs, thinking they can give you that stuff?"

"Dr. Hennessy said it had something to do with the way I scored on my tests and the fact that I hear voices."

"How can you live in that godforsaken dorm and not hear voices? I feel by the end of my three-day stint here that I'm about to go off my rocker! I can imagine how you must feel being stuck there seven days a week!"

"Well, the Mellaril does help me cope," I told him.

"Listen: I don't trust those psychotropic drugs!" Reginald said earnestly. "You ever heard of an operation they call a lobotomy?"

"Yes. That's where they go in through the eyes and scramble the brain."

"Right! They outlawed that procedure some time back. Right now they're doing the same thing with the drugs. Kids are diagnosed with attention deficit disorder and put on Ritalin! It's like a *Clockwork Orange* society in the making! Look, do yourself a favor and try to get off that stuff. I know it feels good now, but you mark my word, there'll be consequences in the future."

Reginald's words broke through my euphoria, jolting me from my drug induced stupor, and awakening in me considerable cause for alarm. "I have an appointment to talk with Dr. Bildeberger on Wednesday morning," I told him. "I'll ask him about it then. Meantime, I'll switch back to the minimum recommended dosage."

I left him to put some finishing touches I needed to put on my autobiography before typing it up. It had to be done by Monday so Dr. Bildeberger could have time to read it by Wednesday. I also needed to write and type up a book report for Introduction to Theological Education, do an exegetical assignment for the New Testament course, and figure in the library course work as well. Between tending to all this course work and putting in my hours on the job, I knew sleep would be at a premium.

It was midnight Saturday when I pushed my typewriter aside and fell onto my cot, exhausted, having decided to forgo church services on Sunday and devote my time to wrapping up what I could of my assignments. It was a decision for which I was rebuked by some neighbors.

On Wednesday morning, I knocked on the door of Dr. Bildeberger's office and found him sitting at his desk with my test scores and autobiography spread out in front of him.

"Sit down," he said. "Make yourself comfortable. I'd like you to know that you are one of the few I've been most anxious to meet with."

I sat down facing him. "And what about the rest?" I asked.

"Routine, I assure you. Of course I'm trusting you not to go spreading that around."

"My lips are sealed." I told him. "But I'd like to know what it is about me that makes me such a special case?"

"Well, Ishmael, in all my years of teaching here at Parkins, I have never seen test scores like this. Given those and the autobiography, I'm quite interested in knowing exactly what it is that drew you to the ministry?"

"God, I would hope," I said. "Also a desire for purification, although the way things have gone for me since my arrival, I'm more inclined to believe I'm heading in the other direction."

"Based upon what I can perceive from the data you've turned in, it seems obvious you have a very high I.Q.," he said thoughtfully. "It also seems obvious that during your life you've endured more than your share of culture shock. Most of the students here have been nurtured. On the basis of this fact alone I can tell that your continued presence here at Parkins will serve as an interesting point in contrast. I note your father was a colonel in the Army. I also note your mention of having difficulty in school during your formative years. Could it be that you're dyslexic?"

"No. I've never had any problems along those lines."

"Are you sure? We have another seminarian here whose father was an Army chaplain. You probably know her ... Kathleen McKensie. Her folks moved around a lot and she had that problem, a problem, I might add, that her family never took the time, nor exercised the inclination to even acknowledge. I consider it a miracle she's gotten as far as she has. Many times parents get so wound up in the fulfillment of their own desires and wants that they overlook the needs of their children."

"I'm all too well aware of that." I assured him.

"I trust you're also aware of the notion that each of us have been programmed like computers to play certain tapes...to exude certain roles...to exemplify certain types. You, Mr. O'Donnell, and please don't take this the wrong way, seem to resemble the 'schlemiel' type."

"The only familiarity I have with the term 'schlemiel' is what I got from literature. Doesn't that mean 'wise fool, theoretically correct, yet practically absurd?' "

"Precisely! You probably know more than most of your fellow seminarians. But your methods of communicating are quite ineffectual. They're not taken seriously. That will serve to your detriment. I'd like to challenge you to adopt another method of operating."

"I'm not sure I can. I'll try anything you suggest, but I'm not really sure what my options are."

"Look around you," he said, raising his arms in a mock embrace. "See how the other seminarians act ... particularly the most effective and influential of the group. Try, at first, to imitate, then, perhaps, emulate. Imitate I know you can do. Let's see if you can do the latter."

I leaned forward. "What you're asking me to do is take on an entirely different persona."

"Exactly. Ever hear that passage of scripture where Paul says that he's all things to all people? As ministers, in many instances, that's what we're called upon to be. And I'm sure you've heard Professor Wilson say that a minister needs to be an actor, and how many roles does an actor play during the course of his career? To assume this calling you must do the same."

"Okay. Now I've got some questions for you. Number one: Why was I summoned to Dr. Hennessy's office? Number two: Am I the only one you guys saw fit to send to a shrink? And number three: Why was I given psychotropic drugs?"

"Good questions. Number one: Your test scores on the Minnesota Multiphasic Personality Inventory and the stress test indicated several red flags ... so many, we felt, that it warranted immediate addressing. The four-thousand-plus you scored on the stress test was more than enough to give us cause for alarm, but your personality test scores seem to indicate extreme schizoid tendencies, a severe bipolar disorder, and even a propensity toward lapses into psychosis. Of course, on a positive note, based upon your past history, you seem to have no problem in holding on to a job and you are quite functional in your academic pursuits. In fact, your undergraduate record notes that you graduated with honors. But, given the fact that these indicators revealed heavy negative markers, we figured that if we were to err in our judgment, it would be best if we erred on the side of caution."

Professor Bildeberger's words seemed to take on an air of analytical detachment that bordered on the ominous. I felt an air of disquietude come over me, as if I were akin to a lab specimen placed under a microscope for observation. It was at that moment that I would have given anything to trade places with Wanda Epperson, who only had to deal with prefabricated notions of stress.

"We did not feel qualified to deal with such matters alone," he continued. "We thought it best to enlist the expertise of one who specializes in them, in a word, Dr. Peters. We received the results of his findings yesterday, and they appear to correspond closely to the diagnosis rendered in our two tests. Also, in two instances, you were reported to exhibit what appeared to be seizures, once at the retreat, the other in the dining commons. There's also a notation about your being a twin."

"I haven't been a twin in over twenty years!" I told him, and unable to restrain my outrage at his inference, went on to tell him, in no uncertain terms, that Isaac was dead, all of which he listened to impassively.

"You've probably not had to face anything like this before, right?" he said when I had calmed down.

"Never allowed to believe it existed, actually."

"I'll be brief and direct with you, Ishmael. The ministry might not be where you belong. But, if you do decide it's truly your calling then it becomes a matter of 'physician heal thyself.' You're going to be called upon to minister to other lost souls and those suffering. To do so effectively, you have got to overcome your own demons. I assume that you'll be a stronger person for it. But, and I can't emphasize this strongly enough, the cure can oftentimes be worse than the sickness, and many times more painful."

Again, a chill embraced me coupled with a giant sized knot in my stomach. "In answer to your other two questions," he went on, "yes, you were the only one we sent to see a shrink. And based upon what I can deduce from the findings I have before me, I believe it to be essential for you to remain on that psychotropic drug. I can tell from your test scores that you've probably lived quite a stress-filled life, but unlike what's before you presently, you've always had a means of retreat no matter how tenuous that means may have been. While you're here, the retreat might not be as readily available to you. As my colleague Brian Wilson I'm sure has told you, you're on stage here. Every movement you make is being heavily scrutinized. The Mellaril should help you somewhat in coping with that pressure, but a lot will have to come from you."

"Didn't even Jesus need periods of solitude, rest, and quiet?"

"Indeed He did. And sometimes He could find it, sometimes He could not. One of the first steps you should take, in my opinion, is to move out of that hell hole of a dorm."

The Call

In my opinion, this man wasn't right about much, but this time he'd hit the nail on the head. Still, I left his office feeling not only angry but lost. Was I truly in need of that much healing? And would it ever happen as long as I was here?

As I stepped outside the building I saw Jessica Bently running towards me, waving. "Hey Ishmael, when are you going to ask me out? There's a theatrical production taking place in town tonight called *Charlie's Aunt,* and I'd really like to see it."

"You sure you want to go out with me?" I said, somewhat startled by her proposition. "I mean, what with you already being an ordained minister, I feel a bit out of my league."

"Hey, if I waited for every boy who truly felt he was in my league, I might wind up an old maid."

"Well, in that case, you've got yourself a date. Want to have dinner, too?"

"Sure. The play starts at eight. Could you pick me up around six?"

"You got it."

Before I knew what was happening, she kissed me. "Just sealing the deal," she said, and hurried off.

I stood there with my head spinning at several thousand rpms. Wow! I thought. Add at least another hundred points to my stress test score. I began my trek back to the dorm when I remembered that I had to call work to clarify a few typing assignments that needed to be completed by early tomorrow morning. I had classes all afternoon and a date that evening, so my only remaining option would be was to head toward city hall after my date. I walked to the pay phone inside the seminary building.

As I approached the phone booth I noted that Bob Osgood, one of the doctoral students, occupied it. He was a tall man who was balding on top and had a more than noticeable paunch. As I anxiously awaited my turn, I couldn't avoid hearing his conversation: "Man," he said in a loud voice, "these past two weeks have shot by like I was on the devil's own race course. I just put the finishing touches on my doctoral thesis, they're scheduling me for my oral this coming Tuesday, and at my church I'm scheduled to perform three weddings, four funerals, and a couple baptisms along with my standard duties, and my wife's probably got a honey-do list a mile long waiting for me this weekend. But tonight's my night to relax. I'm just gonna kick back, open up a cold bottle of Bud, read my *Playboy,* and shut out reality for awhile." He looked at me and grinned knowing I'd heard.

As he hung up the phone and vacated the phone booth I asked him, "You read *Playboy?*"

"Oh, hell yeah. I never miss an issue. I just love looking at those babes on the folding pages." He winked, and then departed.

Hmmm, I thought. Somehow, I don't think I picked the right place to come for purification.

That evening, Jessica and I enjoyed an excellent meal at Harvey House, one of the finest dining places in town, and took in a play that was so funny that we both laughed so hard our sides hurt. When I took Jessica home to her apartment, she asked me in for a drink. Needless to say, I was more than willing.

The Call 207

Jessica was, I discovered, living pretty well for a seminary student. While she poured the drinks, I admired the furnishings, which ran to Danish modern. But there was a touch of the religious everywhere, as well, in paintings that featured biblical scenes.

"Tell me, Ishmael, what do you think of women in the ministry?" Jessica asked, sitting on the sofa, close to me.

"Well," I replied, "it's really not something I've seen a lot of. I guess it's sort of intimidating. Like right now, I'm really not sure how to act."

She seemed slightly exasperated, "You can start by acting the way you do with any other woman!"

"And how might that be?" I said. I felt I was being put on the spot.

"Well," she said, taking my arm and placing it around her shoulder, "you can put your arm around me so I can snuggle up next to you. You know, Ishmael, all my cohorts seemed to have turned the issue of women in the ministry into some women's lib issue. I don't quite see it that way. I'm in it because I sensed I'd been called to be in it. And you don't argue with a call. Unlike my more liberated counterparts, if I had my say I'd rather be just a housewife and mother. Of course, in order to do that I'd need a husband who was willing to be the sole bread winner."

"When did you sense this calling?"

"Oh, I sensed it as far back as childhood. Somehow I knew I had been singled out to serve God. When I was nine I was baptized. I remember emerging from the waters and expecting a dove to descend upon me and hear a voice say, 'Behold, this is my daughter...'"

"Jessica Bently, Daughter of God."

"Yes, kind of has a ring to it, doesn't it?"

"Yes. It reminds me of a cartoon I once saw."

"What cartoon was that?"

"A cartoon where Mary was looking up and asking God, 'But what if it's a girl?'"

We both laughed. It was wonderful, I discovered, not only to be out of the dorm, but in the company of a woman I could like and admire, and I determined that this was one relationship that would last. But it didn't.

By the midpoint of the semester, fraternity and sorority initiations were underway. Like the freshman hazing, this was an occasion left principally to the sophomore members and the freshman pledges. Pledges received their invitations on the basis of politics and breeding. In other words, if a member of one's family had been a member of a certain fraternity or sorority, chances are membership would be open to that individual as well. There were three fraternities on campus, each of which had their sister sororities. As a rule, once you were a member of one of these organizations, your cross-gender fraternization usually confined itself to the sister sorority or brother fraternity. This is where the breeding part came into play. Such cross-sexual interactions by and large extended themselves into the aspects of dating, courtships, and even the marriages that occurred with such great frequency on this campus.

Everywhere you looked, pledges were undergoing their ritual hazing, carrying fishbowls of live goldfish, or being hustled off campus by car to places unknown, or being doused with food coloring. Sometimes I felt like I had traveled back through time. Certainly, nothing like this had gone on in California when I was a student at Davis. Here, once a student pledged, he or she had sealed their fate when it came to personal relationships, drawing confines around marriages as had been the case for Becky Sutton. A little world had been created, one closed to me that was, during the pledging season, at least, a bitter pill for me to swallow.

And what about us seminarians? Well, our sojourn to these cloistered halls had us scurrying about in a multitude of directions. T. J. was inadvertently taking a self- destructive course, devoting more of his time to gigs and practice, seemingly all but oblivious to his classroom assignments. He said he needed to keep jamming to score the bread he needed, but music to him was like dope; it was in his veins and he needed that fix.

Markem was busy eating the school out of house and home. He was also active in youth ministry at the church where he was assigned and was so popular that the kids at his church followed him about like he was the Pied Piper of Hamlin. He delighted in dazzling them with such feats of strength as tearing phone books in half and lifting tremendous weights.

He also demonstrated a remarkable degree of charisma in the pulpit when allowed to preach. This allure served him well when conducting the youth activities, but his lack of education severely handicapped him when it came to the academic end of ministerial preparation. However, the seminary was not above granting concessions where it saw the need and where it could perceive an opportunity—a supercilious legacy handed down by its erstwhile dean, Archibald Shyster.

As for Sam Church, he was still guzzling beer and trying to keep abreast of his studies. He had been hired on as a youth minister at one of the local churches, but had been asked to resign after only a few weeks, the pastor having told him he felt the Lord was calling him to serve elsewhere which, in ecumenical circles often translates to, "Get out of here! You stink!" It's been said a minister needs the hide of a rhino, yet, even a rhino can expire once a bullet pierces its heart. For Sam Church that bullet went deep, but he didn't want to let it show. During one of the sessions in the Elementary Preaching and Pastoral Care course, Professor Brian Wilson, always the one to give way to theatrical analogies, likened Mr. Church's plight to that of a neophyte vaudevillian whose performance brought about a barrage of rotten tomatoes from a disgruntled audience. Everyone laughed and Sam forced himself to grin. He knew that thespians needed to wear makeup, and that a smile was the one cosmetic that could often conceal a wealth of anguish.

Leonard DeWilde was having a terrible time after being deserted by his now-estranged spouse. He withdrew from the Marriage and Family class, was falling behind in his studies, and the church he was serving was sending less than favorable reports to Professor Brian Wilson at the seminary field office. The hours he was accorded employed by the City of Idle for his engineering consultation work were winding down, and his financial holdings were becoming increasingly nebulous as the semester wore on. On top of this, he knew his wife would be contesting for her fair share of their marital assets, and it was just a question of how much she deemed that fair share should be. Leonard knew that Lillian held all the cards in this matter. She was in a position where she could enlist the aid of an attorney, while Leonard, saddled with the expenses brought about by academia, had to rely solely on the generosity of his soon-to-be ex-wife. The only proactive measure Leonard saw open to him was a job opportunity the City of Idle offered for of an entry-level engineering position. It was beneath his qualifications, but after accepting that his situation was desperate, he now decided it offered a modicum of financial solvency.

Some of the more astute among us could see that something was wrong, but Leonard, being a private person, refused to discuss any issues pertaining to his personal life. In his former life as a CEO, such disclosures would open him up to being vulnerable, and being vulnerable carried with it a high degree of danger and liability given the fact that cutthroats abounded in the corporate setting. It was, as a result, essential for Leonard to stay one step ahead of those who might covet his position by distancing himself from the jackals that were all about him.

It was after one of the core group sessions that Dr. Bildeberger called Leonard to his office and rebuked him for not having kept the last three appointments, making it clear that he resented having to more or less "capture" him after class in order to talk to him.

"Well," Leonard replied, "I really don't know what there is I can tell you."

"First, I'll address the concerns of Professor Wilson," Dr. Bildeberger began. "He's been receiving complaints from the elders at your church about your preaching. Your sermons have been extremely short, and along with their brevity, there's an obvious lack of thought and preparation going into them. Furthermore, your delivery is sloppy, rambling, and oftentimes without any meaning."

"Also, there's the matter of the conspicuous absence of your wife during the past five Sunday services. I know you made it clear that she was not to be looked upon as a 'minister's wife,' but 'the wife of a man who's a minister.' However, what you're dealing with in these congregations is a rural mind-set that places an abiding emphasis on the role of …"

"My wife and I are separated," Leonard countered. "She returned to Detroit and her old job. I'm just waiting to be served with divorce papers."

"I'm so sorry!" the professor said "Any chance for a reconciliation?"

"I suppose there might be, if I give up my pursuit of this endeavor and return to my former occupation. That, and do a lot of crawling and begging."

"And what do you feel about doing that?"

"No way," Leonard said, looking Dr. Bildeberger straight in the eye. "When I received this call I took it very seriously. I'd like to think my call to His service was genuine."

"Okay. That's a start. But what about your wife?"

"She said she couldn't cope with all the changes."

"So where does that leave you?"

"I came here to answer a call, and I'm going to

The Call

answer a call."

"Okay. Good. Now we're halfway there. I've said this before and I'll say it again: It all boils down to the old saying: 'Physician, heal thyself.'"

"Right," Leonard responded. "Of course there might be some monetary issues I may need to contend with. But I'll address them the best way I can."

"Good. Just so long as you're aware that oftentimes answering a call of this nature is synonymous to answering a call to sacrifice. Do you feel prepared to make such sacrifices?"

"I'd like to think I am. I can't say I'm one-hundred percent certain."

"Well, you might want to ponder that question while you're in the throes of this marital crisis. Now, on to matters of *my* concern. I've been looking over your test scores. You received the second highest score on the stress test, and in light of what's just happened, it's probably quite a bit higher now than it was at the time of its issuance your test Your newly expressed resolve to address your calling is not going to be sufficient enough to carry you through the remaining pressures of this program. I seriously suggest you seek out some form of counseling. By the way, your personality profile seems pretty well balanced. That could be one of your saving graces."

"Fine. I'll probably need all the help I can get."

"If your call is as genuine as you assert that it is, I have no doubt you will receive the help you need. Remember, prayer works, as a first, last, and even middle resort. Of course, I still suggest you get that counseling."

"Right."

The conversation concluded shortly after. Leonard stepped outside desperately in need of fresh air. Shit. He thought. It was just one damn thing after another.

Linda and Jerry Cantrell were veritable godsends to the mental health clinic, winning raves from everyone who had anything to do with them. In turn, Linda and Jerry were provided with a stipend that served as a welcome means of meeting and defraying the many costs they incurred while embarking upon their academic and research venture. The clinic and the Marriage and Family class continued to provide them with the crucial data that would serve them well in the compilation of their research project. But just when matters appeared to be going along smoothly, Professor Wilson threw them a curve.

Given the many favorable reports they received by way of Dean Marco, Professor Wilson dropped by the clinic one afternoon and asked if he could speak to both of them in private. After making his request, Dean Marco escorted the three of them to a private office. After commending them for their good work, he told them that, on that account, he had a proposition to make. "I have a church in a nearby community that would like to hire a team ministry of sorts—to be more specific, a husband/wife team," he said. "I believe you two would be ideal for the position."

"Whaaaat?" Jerry exclaimed.

Linda then gave Jerry a quick kick to his in-step.

"Owww!" Jerry shrieked.

"I think we'd be delighted to take it, Professor

The Call 215

Wilson," Linda said.

"Next Sunday would be the time you start," Professor Wilson said. "But I want you both to be sure of this," Brian said. "This is for a *team* ministry. They expect both of you, so you need to be prepared to work in tandem."

"No problem," Linda replied.

"Good. I'll see that you get proper directions."

After Wilson had departed, Jerry shouted, "Are you crazy!?"

"Keep your voice down," Linda hushed.

"I thought we had agreed to steer clear of this aspect of seminary training! You realize you just volunteered us to co-pastor a church?"

"Sure. Don't you get it? An opportunity like this will provide us with an even greater opportunity to gather the data we need for our research project!"

Jerry pounded his fist on the table and shouted, "Yeah, if lightning doesn't strike us first in the process!"

"Now, Jerry, quit being silly."

"I don't think I'm being silly when I say that there are certain boundaries you do not cross! And you know as well as I do, we have no business pastoring a church!"

"You know that and I know that, but *they* don't have to know that."

"It's not even a question of what they know! Look, I've never been too religious a person, but I've always reserved a healthy respect for powers unseen! And I believe it unwise to tempt their wrath!"

"Oh, come on, Jerry. All we're going to do is pastor a church. Don't tell me you're afraid of hellfire?"

"Linda! You know good and well, I have no business pastoring a church!"

"And what is so wrong with you pastoring a church?"

"Well, for one thing, it's a Christian church!"

"So?"

"I believe I've already told you, I'm Jewish!"

"So was Jesus."

"Linda, I cannot believe you are taking this so nonchalantly! Our very presence there in that capacity reeks of blasphemy!"

"Oh Jerry, you're overreacting. Trust me."

"I ought to have my head examined, letting you talk me into this! I truly should put my foot down!"

"Then you'll go along with it?" Linda asked. Her eyes lit up with excitement.

"I suppose," Jerry replied.

"Great! Now after we finish our shift here, let's grab a quick dinner at the deli. Then we need to go home and start making preparations for Sunday."

"Oyyyy! I never thought I'd be in a situation like this! Oy vey! And which one of us is to deliver the sermon? I hope you're in good speaking voice; it was your mouth that got us into this mess!"

"Oh, honestly Jerry …"

Elmo Piggins was moving rapidly in his studies with a single-minded determination comparable only to that of a horse with blinders on. On Sundays, he attended the church where Jack served as janitor. Jack taught the college students, and Elmo readily assumed a spot in his class.

While attending the class, Elmo met Christy Boyd, a pert, voluptuous yet wholesome senior who was earning her teaching credential. Both shared comparable conservative theological outlooks, and felt that God had brought them together. They were both intense believers, and neither had any compunction about calling others to account for any hint of liberalism that they called, "the devil's work." After an intense six-week courtship, they decided to perform a fleece to see if it was truly God's will that they take the plunge into marriage. But unlike Gideon, who actually used the fleece of a sheep as a means of making a decision, their fleece was comprised simply of the rolling of dice. Christy and Elmo prayed over the dice before rolling. With a bit of proper nudging, the "fleece" rendered an affirmative nod. Their marriage was planned for the end of the spring semester.

Meanwhile, good fortune continued to smile upon young Elmo. Brian Wilson, through his field office connections, was able to set Elmo up on a series of church interviews and it wasn't long before he was called to a youth pastorate at one of the churches in a neighboring community. Once again, Elmo was given ample cause to swell with satisfaction knowing that he was being made an instrument in God's plans, particularly on assigning him with Christy Boyd. Not only were they matched theologically and in temperament, but also hormonally. St. Paul once said he would rather people marry than burn. In the case of Elmo and Christy, marriage appeared to be their only option since the fires raged like an inferno in both of them.

Brian Wilson was also able to arrange a number of interviews for me—positions at various churches in the neighboring communities. However, none of them led to employment. As a result, once again my typing job was the only thing that stood between me and destitution. When one of the interviewers asked me what my views were, regarding the practice of talking in tongues, I wasn't sure what she meant. But not wishing to appear ignorant, I suggested that anybody who wanted to regard himself as truly educated should avail himself of the knowledge of at least one foreign language, and that I had a working knowledge of both German and French.

Somehow, I got the feeling that this was not the answer she wanted to hear. The interview concluded on a rather abrupt note.

An interviewer at a different church asked me what my views were on the issue of virgin birth. I told her that it was an integral part of Christianity and something that was ascribed to the birth of Jesus. She then asked me if I had anything more to add on the topic. I told her I did not know what more I could add. Apparently, as I was later to deduce, my answer was too straightforward for her tastes. She asked me how I felt about the issue. I had no answer to give. It was instances such as these that contributed to my remaining among the few seminarians who did not have a church assignment.

However, there was a plus side. Since I was among the few seminarians that did not have weekend church responsibilities, I could devote a large measure of my weekend pursuits toward the dredging up of information the seminary library course demanded. With this advantage at my beck and call, I was able to come close to completing the course near the end of October while the rest of my fellow first-year seminarians were still struggling at getting through its the first half. The course also held a greater significance for me in that it marked my last noteworthy encounter with Jessica Bently. It was midweek when I met her in the seminary library, where she told me she was falling hopelessly behind and was overcome with gratitude when I offered her copies of my completed assignments. Before she left, she told me, "Ishmael, you just saved my life! I sure am glad you're a pal!"

Taken in retrospect, I could visualize many other men seeing her articulation of gratefulness as a window of opportunity in the matter of rekindling a romance. But I opted not to go that route. Instead, I chose to content myself with just being a "pal." I perceived such a decision as being less stressful somehow, and seeing that I had already scored in excess of four-thousand points on a certain stress test, any situation that might harbor the potential of thrusting more anxiety my way, I felt, might be wise to avoid.

Shortly afterward, Ben Parson also came to me with a similar problem with the library course. "I hate this damn course!" he whined. "It's not enough that I have to be at my weekend church assignment and read over all the material for my other classes, but then I have to do this damn busy work."

I handed him a copy of my completed work. "You think this'll help?" I asked.

"Yeah," he replied. "But what about all the crap I have to fish out of the card catalog?"

I helped him, just as I had helped Jessica, but with very little thanks. Still, it didn't matter, because it gave me a feeling of being somewhat useful, like being one who ministers to the ministers, who, like me, needed all the help they could get.

Choir practice turned out to be another rigor that taxed our stamina, especially mid-semester when midterms were scheduled. The choir director was a taskmaster. His name was Curtis Jones, a dark haired, rustic, countrified person who taught principally in the undergraduate music department. He made it clear during the first session that no allowances would be made, in case of tests or crucial assignment deadlines. In his own words, "You need the therapy."

The choir's part in weekly chapel services, like everything else, was carefully choreographed, right down to the so-called "spontaneous testimonials," of the sort I had taken as the real thing at the Campus Crusade for Christ meetings back at U.C. Davis. As I witnessed the planning of these chapel services, I noted how each move was carefully coordinated and tightly rehearsed. During one service, I remembered seeing a group of seminarians clustered together in an attempt to give what appeared to be a series of "spontaneous" testimonials.

It was fascinating to watch this rehearsal. "Okay, have we all got our testimonials down and memorized?" someone asked. "Good. Now, Bob, you situate yourself in the third pew near the center aisle. Dave, you take the third pew from the back, opposite end, also facing the center aisle. Joe, we have to make this look authentic, so you choose a spot somewhere in the center, situated amongst the attendees. Art, you do the same, only make sure the two of you are on opposite ends of the center aisle. Finally, Perry, you'll be our fifth and last speaker. Situate yourself third pew to the front, on the right end. Okay, we've got five minutes. Take your seats and break a leg."

That day the chapel was filled to near-brim capacity. It was near the end of the sermon when the presiding seminarian called for testimonials, at which time, like proverbial clockwork, a man to the left of me jumped up and said. "I have a full-time parish ministry, a wife and kids, and am still in the process of preparing for my doctorate. It's a cumbersome load that I sometimes feel ill-equipped to assume. But the Lord is there to strengthen me, and with Him I'm assured that nothing is impossible. I know the Lord is capable of taking on the mightiest of burdens, and during the times that I do buckle under the strain, he carries me. All I need do is to keep rightly focused on my God and I know I can persevere."

The next testimonial was equally revealing. "I have a church in the field, a wife and three kids, and am taking a full load in seminary." We were told, "I too, am burdened almost to the maximum of my capacity. Many times I've faced going into a church service feeling totally unprepared or ill-equipped for the task, and I remember lifting my head to heaven and saying 'Lord, I can't do it. You do it for me.' And He's never failed me yet. I know if He can do it for me, He can do the same for you."

"Money has been the big issue with me," the next seminarian declared. "Seminary is expensive. During the summers I've had to work at both my church job and take on a secular job to make ends meet and to pay for my tuition and books. With family obligations to meet, there have been times when things have looked mighty bleak. But when they do, I always turn to the Lord. There are no limits to His resources, and I've found Him always willing to share, and He never charges more than ten percent interest. So, when you're feeling you've reached your limits," he added when the laughter died down, "whether those limits be financial, physical, or even spiritual, you can always call upon the Lord to shower you with His excesses. I know it works for me, so I'm certain it can work for you."

At this point, I was literally floored by the audacity that was on display at this service. I might as well be watching a theatrical production, I thought. Then I remembered Brian Wilson's assertion that being a minister is just like being an actor. Recalling his pronouncement gave me cause to laugh a little as I sat back and, in a spirit of irreverence, took in the show.

"This is my last semester here at Parkins," the next speaker began, "and it was my hope that after three years in Idle, I could get a church somewhere out on the West Coast in a town like Beverly Hills. But I was soon to learn that the Lord had other plans for me. It was His will that I remain in Oklahoma and be placed in a town even smaller than Idle. Well, I was angry at first. But then I remembered the prayer of Jesus in the Garden of Gethsemane when he said, 'yet not my will but Thine be done.' I also remembered the scripture passage that calls upon each of us to deny ourselves and take up our crosses and follow Him. So, that's what I'm doing, because even though it's not what I want, the Lord knows best what I need and where He can best use me. And that's what I, as His servant, need to keep focused upon, and it's a lesson I need to keep learning and relearning every day, every hour, every minute that He has given me."

Finally, Perry Martin, another doctoral candidate, slightly older than the rest and somewhat gray, rose to give his testimony. "I'm finally on the verge of getting my doctorate," he began, "and let me tell you, it's been quite a struggle. I've always been one who values education. In fact, I must confess to my shame, sometimes I've been guilty of giving it top priority in my life. But I always have to stop and remind myself, without God's blessing, all our endeavors are vain. So, with that in mind, I can't really call it my doctorate. It belongs to God, and I must appropriate all that goes along with it to God's glory."

After the service, as I was hanging up my choir robe, I witnessed the presiding seminarian thanking the five for giving their "spontaneously rehearsed testimonials."

Reflecting back over the service I recalled the closing hymn being entitled *Have Thine Own Way, Lord.* I concluded the purpose of such a song was for purposes of ending the service on a note of reverence. However, after seeing what I just saw, the only number I could think of and sing under my breath was *There's No Business Like Show Business.*

Our education was not always confined to the classroom. During the course of one of the "Introduction to Theological Education" sessions, Sam Church gave an account of having attended services one Sunday at the First Church of Fundamentalist Brethren, the biggest church in town. During the course of his visit, he was forced to listen to the minister rave for a total of fifty-five minutes, his subject being the heretical follies of Parkins University's school of religion and seminary, a rant interrupted from time to time by "Amen" and "Preach on, brother!" Apparently, the students of Parkins Theological Seminary were viewed by many of the church bodies within the town of Idle as minions of Satan.

Sam Church wasn't the only one to experience chastisement from the pulpit. On Wednesday evening I ran into a similar occurrence at one of the Assembly of God churches. I had agreed to drive a couple of undergraduates there, but with the icy roads, the car had skidded into a snow bank. By the time we had managed to dislodge it, my shoes were soaked and, having reached the church, I removed them and left them to dry in the vestibule.

After singing a series of hymns, I was soon to learn that the church would be showing a film pertaining to a projected period in our Christian history scholars had labeled "the Eschaton" but was popularly referred to as "the Rapture."

"Brothers and sisters," the minister declared when that part of the service was over, "we've all seen by this film that not everyone who calls himself a Christian will be caught up in the Rapture! It says so right there in the scriptures, 'not everyone who cries Lord, Lord!' No, good brothers and sisters, I say that some of you here tonight, if the Lord were to call, might find yourselves left behind to suffer the scourge of the tribulation, yea, even those of you seated tonight in these very pews! Yes friends, the Lord seeks only those who devote total commitment to the doing of His will!"

Now, there is a real ham actor, I thought. Comes complete with both voice and body language.

"Only they will be the ones the Lord will be calling when the end comes!" he continued. "Total commitment means if the Lord calls you to cut that shaggy, faggy hair, you'll cut that shaggy, faggy hair!" He resumed, "If the Lord calls for you to put on a suit and tie, you'll put on a suit and tie!"

At that point, I began to wonder if, given the fact that I was wearing rumpled jeans and sweatshirt, he was talking to me. The minister continued his oration, "If the Lord calls for you to quit drinkin' and smokin' those funny cigarettes, you'll quit drinkin' and smokin' those funny cigarettes!" he went on. "Yes, brothers and sisters, that is what we are going to be calling on you to do tonight! After this meeting we'll all be gathered in the back for a prayer of total commitment! We pray the room'll be full, and spirits will be willing, and the Lord will have touched all your hearts! Yes friends, I sense a great revival will be taking place here tonight! Amen! Hallelujah! Let us now bow our heads in this prayer of total commitment!"

The rest of the semester passed uneventfully. I completed all my reading and written assignments on schedule, with the exception of the thirty-five page exegetical paper that needed to be ready for Dr.

Babcock's New Testament course shortly after the Christmas break.

Thanksgiving had arrived, and most of the students vacated the dormitory for the holidays. As for me, I spent the major portion of that Thursday writing out the rough draft, after which I got a turkey sandwich and a can of Mountain Dew, along with some Ho Hos for dessert from a little convenience market not far from the campus.

My draft was completed that weekend. It now became just a matter of getting the paper, which was due that Tuesday, typed up and submitted to Babcock. A number of seminarians had to cash in on the option of getting a three-day extension on the assignment. As for me, the day before the assignment was due, I spent the entire night typing the paper. My next-door neighbors, two of the biggest noisemakers and hell-raisers ever to grace the campus, felt obligated to come into my room and complain about the racket my typewriter was making. But what was important was that I was able to submit an exegetical paper totaling fifty-two pages, plus a three page bibliography to Professor Babcock at eight the following morning.

Following the paper's submission I had an appointment with the shrink. Then it was one class after another after another. Because I'd spent all night typing, I came close to nodding off during Rufus Pelmonte's sermon on the workings of the Holy Spirit. However, I managed to remain awake during Reginald Dexter's sermon on the Unitarian view of the Bible, perhaps because, after forty-some years of teaching, the man seemed to have a knack for keeping a person involved in spite of the subject matter.

The Call

Finally, there came a break in classes with the advent of chapel services. Fortunately, the seminary choir was not required to perform that week, so I took advantage of this reprieve and retired to my room for a much-needed hour-long nap. Once again, at the noon meal, Ellen was present to ask why none of the seminarians attended the chapel service. Naturally, her eyes were fixed squarely upon me.

"Our presence wasn't required," I replied, "so I took a nap."

"Your attendance would have edified you more than the nap!"

"I was up all night, typing an exegetical paper. To my mind, that makes sleep the most edifying substance in all of God's creation."

"You seminarians are supposed to be setting an example for the rest of us!"

"And just what type of example are we supposed to set?" I snapped back. "We sleep when we get tired! We bleed when we cut ourselves! We…"

Ellen picked up her tray and moved elsewhere.

"You know, I wish somebody would shut her mouth!" Ben seethed. "Just who does she think she is?"

"Oh, calm down," Reginald replied. "Everybody's got an ax to grind."

"Yeah." Ben muttered, "An' I'd like to grind mine right up her…"

"Don't say it!" cried Markem. "I'm tryin' to break my own nasty habit of havin' a foul mouth! An' I'm askin' you to help me with it by keeping yours clean!"

A few days before Christmas break, I received a call from my dad. "Hello, Ishmael? I was wondering if you could tell me when the Christmas break begins so I could make your plane reservations."

"I can't come home, Dad," I replied. "My job won't let me."

"But your mother and I would really like to see you. It's been several months now."

"Well, I'd like to come home too, but like you always told me when I was growing up, you can't always have what you want."

"So you're going to spend Christmas by yourself all alone in that dorm?"

"Looks that way," I said. "But it can't be helped.

The prospect of solitude did indeed fill me with a sense of dread. I had never been alone on Christmas before. And spending time in an empty dorm was unsettling. But my time was not spent in total solitude since the winter break enabled me to put in a solid forty-hour workweek at my place of employment. There I was able to socialize with the office staff and take part in all the yuletide activities the city hall sponsored, activities that included a potluck, a gift exchange, and a Christmas Eve luncheon. Despite the near-zero weather with the 72-degree-below-zero wind-chill factor, the City of Idle saw fit to stage their Christmas parade. I stood on the crowded sidewalk, watching the parade while holding a cup of hot cocoa, and growing more numb by the minute. On Christmas Eve, I attended a late-evening service at a church near the university. But on Christmas day, I not only found myself alone in the dorm, but, since Idle had just experienced one of the most severe storms in the past

The Call

ten years, I was snowed in. It was the loneliest day I could remember. Given my state of solitude on the Lord's birthday, I felt black and white, with the rest of the world in color.

I was not the only seminarian besieged by solitude on our Lord's birthday. Leonard DeWilde spent the day slouched on his divan in a state of near-drunken despondency. In his hand, he held a notice from his wife's attorney that he had received a few days prior stating that all marital assets were to be sold and the proceeds split up accordingly — sixty percent for her and forty percent for him, which, Leonard knew, would mean that she would get the townhouse and all its furnishings. Adding to Leonard's woes, the City of Idle had informed him that, as of January 1, there would be no further need for his consulting services. As for the Engineering 1 position, although Leonard had received a top score on the written test, he had failed to remember one factor, in the aspect of nepotism—always rampant in small-town life. The position, Leonard discovered, would be awarded to the son of the department head.

To make matters worse, the church he had pastored over the past semester had asked for his resignation to go into effect after the first of the year. Somehow, the pulpit steering committee could not countenance having a divorced man as a minister. Professor Wilson consoled Leonard by informing him that there would be other churches in need of pastors due to vacancies left by graduating seminarians, and Leonard could also take a modicum of comfort in knowing that with his share of the marital assets, he would probably have enough funds to carry him through the remainder of the seminary program. However, the part of the scenario he dreaded the most was the fact that, in order to continue the financing of this endeavor, he would have to drastically change his lifestyle. This meant he would need to secure cheaper living quarters, perhaps even move into the dorm.

And so it was. Among the seminarians gravitating to this nebulous shelter at the beginning of the next semester was a disheveled Leonard DeWilde, now forty-two with a finalized divorce attached to his credentials and unemployment and destitution dogging his footsteps.

The snow melted the day after Christmas, and the sunshine returned, bringing the temperature up close to seventy degrees. It appeared that Will Rogers had been right when he had once said of the weather in Oklahoma, "If you don't like it, wait a day."

Since the admissions and records office had been open during break, I checked in sporadically during the winter break, hoping for an apartment to become available. It was on a Wednesday of the second week that the office informed me that there would be a vacancy on the twenty-eighth and that my name was at the top of the list. I knew it would entail more expense, but it would definitely be worth it to getting out of that dorm.

Meanwhile, the campus bookstore was looking for part-time help restocking merchandise for the spring semester. I managed to work in the bookstore in the evenings when I wasn't performing my day job at city hall — anything to defray expenses while I still had time to do so.

Leonard felt a monumental measure of numbness

The Call

clutching at his insides coupled with a considerable degree of alienation as he was thrust into an environment comprised mostly of students who were less than half his age. He didn't know whether to bless or curse the impulse that kept him proceeding along in this sanctified endeavor.

Before making his move into the men's dormitory, Leonard had a conference with Professor Brian Wilson about securing another church assignment. The good professor, sensing his plight and taking compassion upon Leonard and his predicament, quoted him the Epistle of James, chapter one, verses nine and ten: "Let a brother in humble life rejoice when raised to a higher position; but a rich man should rejoice in being brought low, for like flowers among the herbage, rich men will pass away." No doubt, Leonard knew he was being brought low. How to rejoice in being brought to that state he had yet to discover, if such a discovery was his to make.

It was with reluctance, coupled with a sense of nausea that he headed toward the reception window presided over by Ben and Jana.

"You got a room?"

"We most certainly do," Jana said.

"And I understand that for a few dollars extra I can have a private room?"

"Nope!" Ben replied. "Not this semester. It appears we have a lot of midyear first semester students, so everyone has to double up. Ol' Reggie and Charlie are occupying the guest quarters. Rufus is rooming with Sam Church. Of course, Rufus might be getting married before the end of the semester. Markem is rooming with an undergraduate, Elmo Piggins. As for you, we have you down to room with an incoming freshman by the name of Timothy Hobbin.

"Hmmm!" Leonard said.

"Well, it's either him or the outside."

Leonard sighed. "Give me the key to the room then."

Overcome by foreboding as to what would come next, Leonard made his way down the corridor toward an uncertain future.

A few days had passed when I heard a loud knock on the door of my apartment. I opened the door. It was Laurie. "Where have you been?" she cried. "You're the only one on the roster that hasn't signed up for the two day retreat at the Brisbane Camp! For class signup!"

"In this weather?"

"Yes! In this weather!"

"Why can't we just have it in the seminary building?"

"Because there's a large number of new seminarians who have enrolled this semester and Babcock feels that meeting at the Brisbane Camp would be a good means of indoctrinating them into seminary life!"

"But the roads … the driving conditions…"

"Can't you get snow tires?"

"Oh, shit, Laurie! Do you think I've got an inexhaustible bank account?"

"Then take the bus! It'll be fun!

With only a few more words exchanged, I soon found myself being towed by Laurie to the seminary building where registration was taking place. It was only

The Call

two hundred yards from my apartment to the seminary building, but the zero-degree temperature coupled with the 72-degree-below-zero wind-chill factor, the trek seemed a bit longer than the actual measurement.

Upon our arrival, Laurie ushered me to the seminary's main office. There, at her desk, sat the secretary, Ms. Shirley Adams.

"We were wondering what happened to you," she said to me. "We need for you to sign this reservation slip right away!"

"Uh, excuse me," I replied, "but given the weather and the hazardous road conditions, wouldn't it be better for registration to take place here on campus?"

"Oh, nonsense. It's the beginning of a new semester. You folks need this! A lot of new students are entering the seminary this term, and we feel this is the best way to usher them into the spirit of fellowship that's part of the seminary experience!

"Well, in that case, could I arrange to register for classes here and be excused from the retreat?"

"I am shocked that you'd make such a request," she exclaimed. "What could you possibly have going on that's more important than the retreat and a reunion with your fellow students?"

"Well, for one thing, I figured on putting in a little more time at my job before classes started—you know, get a little more money stashed away before the big drain of academic expenses sets in."

"There are certain things in this life that far outweigh the pursuit of money!"

"Only if you have enough of it."

"Well, what you're asking is out of the question. You need to take part in the retreat. It marks the beginning of your classes. Besides, it'll be fun!"

Yeah. Fun. I thought. Right.

Two days later, bad weather and hazardous road conditions not withstanding, we boarded the buses for the Brisbane camp. With the exception of a handful of us, spirits were at an all-time high, and the buses were filled with laughter and boisterous banter. Midway to the camp Wanda Epperson, guitar in hand, stood in the center of the bus and led us in a rousing chorus of *Pass It On*. Other songs were quick to follow.

I was seated next to Sam Church, who was giddy about the proceedings to come.

"Isn't this fun?" he demanded. "And look at all the snow! I love snow!" Then he noticed me reaching into my coat pocket and pulling out some capsules. "What are those things? Are you becoming an even bigger pill head?"

"Vitamin C," I replied. "Unlike you, I catch cold or get the flu when I'm exposed to snow."

"So do I! But that doesn't keep me from loving the snow and having fun out in it!"

"Well, bless your heart." I replied.

Just in back of us, Leonard was seated next to Ben. In spite of the atmosphere of merriment, Ben could not help but notice Leonard's dour and unresponsive expression. "What's shakin', Leonard?" Ben asked, giving Leonard a gentle nudge on the shoulder with his fist. "You found work yet?"

"Yep. Flipping burgers at McDonald's."

"Well, that's better than a poke in the eye with a

sharp stick! Praise the Lord! And how's the roommate situation going?"

"I try to avoid him."

"Man, you need to get out o' yourself!"

"I wouldn't be so quick to judge if I were you," Leonard snapped. "You still have Jana."

Meanwhile, Jerry and Linda were seated together at the opposite end of the bus, and appeared to be having something resembling a marital squabble. "Will you stop your fussing, Jerry!" Linda pleaded, "You're going to blow our cover!"

"How can I help it?" Jerry said. "You know what we have to do when we get back? Or better, I should ask, do you know what *I* have to do?"

"Of course I know. But that's what ministers do!"

"But not me!"

"And why should you be an exception?"

"You know why! I'm Jewish!"

"Shhhh!"

"All right! I hear ya! But it's still not right that I do this!"

"Jerry, all you have to do is perform a baptism. You know how to do it. We were taught how in Professor Wilson's class last semester."

"But Reformed Jews do not baptize!"

"Well, neither do Presbyterians."

"Yes, you do."

"Well, we do, but not in the way they're having us do it."

"Sprinkle, immerse…it's all the same! It's baptism, something Jews don't do! *Better you should do it!*"

"But they want you to do it!"

"Why me?"

"I guess because you're the man and they figure it's more the man's place to perform such rituals than it is the woman's. You've got to understand, Jerry, this is rural Oklahoma we're talking about, and you know what Professor Wilson told us! It's all they've been able to do to get these congregations to warm up to the idea of female pastors! So it stands to reason that they would still assume the man as the head pastor."

"But we know differently, or at least I do! *Otherwise*, I'd have never let you talk me into this!"

Overhearing them, Reginald found himself remembering happier excursions he had taken with Eleanor at his side and opened his heart to despair.

We arrived at the camp and headed toward our respective dorms, after being informed that the noon meal would be served in half an hour. Plopping my baggage down on a bunk that was situated in the center of the dorm, I sat down on the cot in hopes of regaining my bearings. I felt dizzy and could sense the first phase of a cold setting in. There was a slight tenderness in my throat, coupled with an accelerated amount of sinus drainage that I knew could not be accommodated by the two handkerchiefs I had in my possession.

It was clear that there were many more students at this retreat than at the last, probably because some of the new seminarians had brought their wives and children along. Whatever the reason, it was soon obvious that there were not enough cots to go around.

Just as I was getting set to blow my nose, a young

man, barely in his twenties, introduced himself as Orville Stapleton, a former fullback from Baylor University, and after assuring me that he was here to serve the Lord, demanded my bunk.

"Well," I replied, "this bunk is already taken."

"I know, but I'm sort of asking you to relinquish your claim to it."

"And I'm sort of telling you that you need to find an unoccupied bunk just like the rest of us."

"Wait a minute. I don't think you quite understand. I played football for Baylor University. We football players always receive preference."

"This is not Baylor." I reminded him.

"I've tried to handle this in a Christian way, but you're not making it easy!" he said abrasively. "So I'm telling you again, I want this bunk!"

"And I'm telling you again that this bunk is already occupied." I replied as Markem joined us.

"Is there a problem here?" he asked.

"No problem here," Orville told him, clearly noting the fact that Markem outmuscled him. "No problem at all." He then departed.

"Thanks, Markem." I said as Orville beat a retreat.

"No need to thank me," Markem replied. "Just get your junk off my bunk! Here, I'll help you get started."

"What the f... !" I exclaimed.

"And no cussin'! The Lord don't like it when you cuss!"

"Damn right!" I heard another seminarian say.

Markem turned and glared at that seminarian and said, "I'm serious!"

"And what about thou shalt not steal?" I retorted.

"I ain't stealing! This bunk don't belong to you! It belongs to the camp! And I sort of had my eye on it, ya know!"

Rather than provoke a full-scale confrontation, I gathered up my things and started looking for another bunk. Not finding one, I found my only option was to bring the matter to the attention of Rupert Babcock, the chief coordinator of the retreat and still the acting dean, only to find that he was enduring a siege by a good many others with the same complaint as mine. During a meal of ham hocks, black-eye peas, cornbread, and punch, he made it clear that he expected one of his colleagues to come up with a magical solution to the problem.

"Well, I hate to say I told you so," Professor Wilson said, "but you should have conducted sign-ups at the seminary. Having a retreat in this weather was just sheer stupidity on your part."

"I want suggestions, not I-told-you-so's!" Babcock retorted.

"Alright! Here's my suggestion! Let's call off this retreat and go back and conduct sign-ups at the seminary."

"I disagree," Stephen Bildeberger countered. "I think the retreat at this setting is essential to the program! I mean, why should the incoming students be deprived of the seminary initiation proceedings just because they're entering midyear? After all, we're a community, and these newly arrived students are entitled to the same sense of belonging as the fall students, and I can think of no better time or place for this initiation process to begin than right here at this camp, right now!"

"I can," Professor Wilson replied. "How about the Holiday Inn in town?"

"Certainly not!" Professor Bildeberger snapped. "For one thing, that's too expensive. And furthermore, it would spoil the rustic, tent-of-meeting effect that scripture espouses!"

"In case you haven't been keeping up on your geography, that tent of meeting was designated for the spring. Furthermore, it's a lot warmer in Israel this time of year than it is in Oklahoma."

"All right, you two!" Babcock shouted. "This bantering isn't solving anything! I agree with Stephen. We do need this retreat! But there's still the issue of not enough cots!"

"That's a minor detail!" Professor Bildeberger replied. "Most of these students are so hyped up, they won't even be bothered by that little inconvenience! Besides, what's a little roughing it?"

"Excuse me for throwing cold water on your fervent assertions," Babcock replied, "but I just got through hearing a number of complaints that go counter to your assumptions!"

"So, we've got a few malcontents! We can't let the whining of the minority ruin it for the rest of us."

It was then that Dr. Hennessy came up with a suggestion. "Folks," he said, "if memory serves, there's a shed behind the dining commons that has a bunch of mats stored in it. Maybe after the noon meal and the afternoon's meeting and fellowship, we can have the students go out to the shed and fetch the mats."

"Wouldn't they be a little dusty?" Babcock asked.

"I believe the custodial staff hosed them down this past November." Dr. Hennessy replied.

"Great," Professor Wilson responded. "So now the students will have to contend with moldy mattresses."

"I hardly believe we'll have that problem," Dr. Hennessy responded.

"It's obvious you don't know our custodial staff."

"Alright!" Exclaimed Bildeberger. "So there might be a little bit of mold and dust on the mats! I doubt that most of them will notice! Besides, why should a little mold interfere with the fun and festivities of the retreat?"

As the afternoon proceedings ended, the announcement was made concerning the cot shortage. Professor Babcock issued the directive that we were all head to the shed out back where the mats and blankets were stored, after which we could have some free time to frolic in the snow. Some of us, the few malcontents to whom the good Professor Bildeberger had alluded, decided to give the frolicking a pass.

While I reclined on my mat, my head propped up on a moldy blanket, Jerry and Leonard engaged in a spirited dispute over whether or not, what with my coughing, I might infect them. Jerry still had his cot, thanks, he said, to showing the football player from Baylor a few hand-to-hand moves he'd picked up in the marines.

Jack Logan was also present among us malcontents. He could be seen slumped over on his mat with a look of despondency about him. He did not want to be at this retreat and could find no room for the spirit of merriment shared by the major part of the attendees. He wanted to be home with his family. His mother's health was taking an increasing turn for the worse and he knew she was not going to be around very much longer. In fact, there was the lingering fear in the back of his mind that she might not make it through this three-day retreat he was compelled to attend. He longed to hear her voice just one more time. He also desired the presence of Carla and their newborn daughter. For Jack, answering the call at this moment was akin to the bearing of a cross, and he could feel his spirits buckle under the load. Yet, he endured in silence.

Later that evening, after dinner, we were all gathered in the meeting room, and situated on the floor in a semicircle to listen to a presentation by Dr. Stephen Bildeberger.

The murmurings of the crowd gave way to silence as Dr. Bildeberger walked to the center and stood before us. He wore full black. His posture was erect. His facial features held a grim and forceful look about them. He carried a Bible in his right hand. He looked about his audience and said, "Good evening, folks. I'm Dr. Stephen Bildeberger, and on behalf of the faculty and staff here at Parkins Theological Seminary, I welcome you to our spring semester retreat. I want to bestow a special greeting to our newly arrived students. You made a good choice in your selection of seminaries, and we intend to make your next three to four years at this seminary a reinforcement of that statement. As for the rest of you, why do we hold this retreat?" Dr. Bildeberger's eyes scanned the faces in the audience. "I've been watching all of you since our arrival here at Camp Brisbane. Most of you, I've noticed, have been using this as a time to have fun and go out and play in the snow. Then I've noted a handful of malcontents who really don't want to be here. These moaners and complainers have seen fit to isolate themselves from the rest of you folks, generally questioning the feasibility of having this retreat. After all, the weather's bad, their routine is disrupted, and there's just generally better ways to spend one's time."

Dizziness began to overtake me, so I got up from the semicircle and moved over to one of the couches.

Dr. Bildeberger continued, "What comes to mind now is the scriptural passage of Matthew 16: verse 24 which says, 'If any man come after me, let him deny himself and take up his cross and follow me.' This means that as His suffering servants we are called upon to put aside our individual concerns and selfish motivations, and even stop frolicking in the snow if circumstance necessitate it, and focus on the broader picture … focus on the mission … the calling."

Mission. I thought. Where had I heard *that* word before?

"What is the reason for this retreat?" Dr. Bildeberger resumed. "I'm not going to give you a reason for this retreat. Instead, I'm going to read to you the Book of Jonah." And read it he did, from start to finish. After he finished reading, he closed his Bible, looked at us, and said, "What we have here is the portrayal of a prophet of God who doesn't really want to perform his prophetic duty. This duty is to preach to the people of Nineveh. And on that note a bit of historical data might be in order. Jonah was a native of a place called Gath-hepher in Israel. He served during the reign of Jeroboam II from 782 to

653 B.C. Now it would behoove each one of you to take note of this bit of history because it will be covered again during one or both of your Old Testament courses."

The audience began to fidget.

"Jonah was a contemporary of the prophets Hosea and Amos and was instrumental in regaining some of Israel's lost territory by predicting the conquests of Jeroboam II. You can find references to this prediction in Second Kings versus 14 through 25. Now, according to biblical historians, the city of Ninevah was then the capital of Assyria. At that period in history, just as it is true today, Assyria was causing problems for Israel. It still causes problems for Israel, but it goes by a different name. Thus, to preserve the city of Nineveh was to preserve a potential enemy, and Jonah, being the typical Israelite of his day, did not want to see this enemy preserved. And just as with the cities of Sodom and Gomorrah, God's judgment was coming against Nineveh because of the inhabitants' exaggerated perversion. By divine commission, it was Jonah's task to preach a message of repentance to the people of Nineveh so that they would turn from their wicked ways and turn back the fearful wrath of an angry God. But Jonah didn't want to preach to the people of Nineveh for two reasons: One, Assyrians didn't like Israelites, and Jonah was probably in fear of his own safety. And two, Israelites didn't like Assyrians, and Jonah, being the typical Israelite, would probably have preferred to see the entire nation go up in flames without the benefit of any warning. And there was a third reason, if Jonah was capable of seeing into the future. A ways down the road God would use Assyria to destroy Israel—a feat accomplished in part by the deliverance of Jonah's message. You see, God's mind doesn't work the same way our minds do. Our minds may be centered more on the immediate. God, on the other hand, has a mind continually centered upon eternity. And oftentimes these two differing mind-sets come into conflict with one another. This is where we, as the cultural shaman, the called ones of God, need to pay heed to the words of Jesus found in the scriptural passages of Matthew 16 verse 24: 'If any man come after me, let him deny himself and take up his cross and follow me.' We are called to let go of our human pettiness, our small-mindedness and self-centeredness and attempt to attune ourselves to the mind of God and the bigger picture. Is this an easy task?" Dr. Bildeberger's voice then resonated in a shout, "No! It is hard as nails! Could Jonah at that time do it? No, he could not. But did God let go? No, He did not! He never let go of Jonah! Even at our worst, God does not let go! And even in our disobedience, God still uses us as He used Jonah. Jonah, wishing to see destruction befall Nineveh, departs in the direction opposite the city. As a result of Jonah's attempt to escape God's command, God summons a storm to overtake the ship Jonah has boarded. During the course of the ship's plight it is revealed that Jonah is the cause of the tempest that besieges the ship. It is then that the crewmen take the hapless prophet and toss him overboard, where he is intercepted and swallowed by a whale." Dr. Bildeberger then briefly paused. "One interesting aside to this story." He noted. "Did you know it is possible for a man to survive for a certain length of time inside the belly of a whale? It's true. Some seventy years ago a sperm whale

The Call

off the Falkland Islands swallowed a sailor by the name of James Bartley, who sailed on a ship named Star of the East. About thirty-six hours later, his fellow sailors caught the whale, killed it, and opened it up. There they found Bartley, unconscious but alive, inside the belly of the animal. As the story goes, he was eventually restored to complete health, but as a result of being bathed by the whale's digestive juices for the thirty-six hours he was in the whale, all pigmentation was washed away and he spent the rest of his life as an albino. So yes, you can survive inside the belly of a whale. You might not like it. I hear the temperature inside the whale is around 104 degrees with a matching humidity."

The audience resounded with oohs and aahs.

"James Bartley only had to endure thirty-six hours inside the belly of the whale. Jonah, on the other hand, was inside that belly three entire days—the same amount of time Jesus was in the tomb. Once again God is using Jonah to foretell the coming of his own son — selfish, narrow-minded, bigoted Jonah is being used to forecast Jesus Christ,—King of Kings and Lord of Lords. And just as Jesus rose from the tomb as Christ, the Risen Lord, so Jonah was called out of the belly of the whale and again commanded to preach to the people of Nineveh. But this time Jonah exhibited no signs of resistance. Instead, Jonah lent himself willingly to the task with a supreme sense of brokenness about him. And that's when God can truly use us—when we are broken. And I'm only conjecturing right now, but I believe there was something else about Jonah, something in his appearance, that made the people of Nineveh all the more attentive to the message he was bringing them. If James Bartley looked like a washed-out phantom after only thirty-six hours inside the belly of a whale, I can only imagine what Jonah looked like."

The audience laughed.

"The people of Nineveh repented almost instantly, and were spared God's wrath. But Jonah was angry because God did not reign down destruction on the city of Nineveh, and he was confused and disillusioned as to why he was made to undergo all the trials that had brought him to this moment. And standing here before you, I can say with all confidence that I doubt if the answer God gave him was sufficient to his mind. And so it is with you folks here this evening. Some of you may think this retreat is just a bunch of crap. The rest of you would think of the occasion as an opportunity to play in the snow. But the retreat is not over, and our agenda is not yet fulfilled. Even after it is, you may not see the purpose of it. That's where our mind-sets differ from yours. You may only be thinking in the immediate. But by necessity, our thought process has to be more long term. We're here to facilitate the turning out of stalwart men of God. So, some of the things we give you to do, you may find to be a waste of time, and an inconvenience. But you're going to do them, just as Jonah had was to do what God had commissioned him to do."

The crowd dispersed shortly after the conclusion of Dr. Bildeberger's talk. Wanda Epperson approached Dr. Bildeberger with tears in her eyes, embraced him and said, "Dr. Bildeberger, I needed that sermon!"

Leonard DeWilde rose to his feet with a sense of resolve about him and said to Jack Logan, "Well, I guess it's time I collected myself and get on with doing what I set out to do."

"Me, too," Jack replied.

Jerry Cantrell turned to Linda and said, "I've got to say, that was an interesting take on Jonah."

Linda beamed effusively as she asked, "Wasn't it inspirational?"

"No, but it was interesting."

Charlie Donohue, also caught up in the fires of inspiration, turned to Reginald and asked, "Didn't you just feel saturated with God's blessing after hearing that sermon?"

"Kind of boring," Reginald replied.

It wasn't long before a large group of seminarians and a few faculty were gathered together in a Christian songfest. During this time, I saw Professor Babcock call Markem McClusky to one side. "You've shown a type of charisma we rarely see," he said loudly enough for me to overhear. "We think you have what it takes to be an outstanding evangelist. But your grades are terrible. So, what I'm going to do is assign you to a peer mentoring program. One of your mentors will be Ishmael O'Donnell. He's excellent academically and it would be to your advantage to stay on good terms with these mentors, because your size will only get you so far in this life. I think you know what I'm talking about."

Later on that evening Markem approached me with an outstretched hand. "Ishmael," he said, "I was wrong to take your bed from you. Can you ever forgive me?"

I looked directly into Markem's eyes. They were truly a picture of remorse. "No problem," I replied. "Does this mean I get my cot back?"

Markem grinned and said, "Hell no." He then turned and headed toward his cot.

Dr. Bildeberger's speech was quite prophetic. The next day was filled to excess with lectures, drills, statements of policy change, and announcements of added classes. Class registration took place. Afterwards we had a short devotional and boarded the buses back to town. Upon our arrival, most of us made a mad dash to the bookstore. As for me, I needed to visit the school's clinic. The doctor on duty was quick to diagnose my symptoms as that of the flu, issued me the appropriate medication, and sent me home to bed.

Wednesday evening found Jerry and Linda at home engaged in diligent preparation for the coming Sunday.

"The congregation keeps asking about you delivering the message, Jerry."

"Oh, right!' he said with a slight grimace. "And just suppose I inadvertently deliver a Jewish message?"

She ignored him. "Look! Just keep within the boundaries of the New Testament as your principle point of reference, and you'll do just fine."

"But I've only had one course in the New Testament! And up until the time we enrolled in the course, I just regarded it as a work of fiction not even worth reading!"

"You can use several reference guides for drawing up a sermon," she told him. "And I'll help you out. Besides, we've got Babcock's Advanced Homiletics course this semester. That'll give you even more clues about what's needed."

"I sure hope that's enough!"

"Jerry, first things first. You have a baptism to perform, and you said yourself you need the practice. I'm here. You can practice on me. Here, Jerry. Give me your right hand."

"Now, Jerry, if you can't remember Professor Wilson's class session we had on baptism, then surely you remember a few years back when we took the Arthur Murray dance course and how you learned how to dip me?"

"I didn't know romance figured into this."

"Look, enough kidding around! You'll be doing something similar with Elmer Ponks, only you won't be supporting him with your left hand."

"So how do I bring him up again?"

"I'm getting to that. As you can see, both my hands are gripping your right hand. Now, raise your left hand above your head. Kind of like the Statue of Liberty. Now say, 'Elmer Ponks, I now baptize you in the name of the Father, the Son, and the Holy Spirit.' And then you lower me down into the waters until I am completely immersed. That's right. Now, A little lower…"

"Ow! This is hurting my arm!"

"Oh, quit being such a baby! A little lower… Okay! Now bring me up! Why are you looking like that?"

"I think I sprained my arm a little bit during my encounter with that Orville Stapleton guy," Jerry said grimacing. "It's been awhile since my Marine Corps days. And what bothers me is Elmer Ponks is bigger than you and weighs quite a bit more."

"The answer to that problem rests with physics. The

water should offset the weight. And before immersing him in water you might want to ask him to affirm publicly his faith in Jesus Christ as his Lord and Savior."

"Do we have any liniment in the house? Incidentally, where am I supposed to get the hip waders."

"Don't be silly," Linda told him. "You'll have to wear Bermuda shorts."

"Bermuda shorts? Couldn't Elmer put off this baptism until the weather gets better?"

"No. He wants to get baptized as soon as possible. Remember, in the Campbellite religious tradition, baptism is essential for the soul's salvation."

On Thursday Leonard DeWilde was called into Professor Wilson's office. "How are you feeling today?" he asked as Leonard slid back on the vinyl sofa.

"I'm still here," he said.

"I take it you're now living in the dorm?"

"If you can call it living."

"Are you taking advantage of our counseling program?"

"Yes. I can't afford not to."

"And how are finances?"

"Money's coming in, although I'm not all that crazy about what I have to do to get it."

"Still not to the point where you can rejoice?"

"No, that's going to take awhile."

"I can understand that. The reason I called you in this morning is that I have an opening for a Sunday only pastoral position at a church about forty miles from here."

"I'll take it!"

"No, it doesn't quite work that way. They have to

The Call 251

decide if they want *you*. You'll enhance your chances of getting the position if you can put your divorce behind you, at least for the duration of the interview and for the Sundays you serve as their pastor. After all, they don't need to know about your personal life. You did the right thing by filling out another application form. As far as they're concerned, you're just single. You don't have to expound any further on the matter. The interview is this coming Tuesday. See you then."

As Leonard started back to the dorm, he encountered a vivacious young coed with blond hair framing a heart shaped face. "You don't remember me, I suppose," she said breathlessly.

"No," Leonard replied. "I'm afraid I don't."

"I'm Lonnie Peterson! Remember? I was sitting with friends at the same table that you were sitting at yesterday at dinnertime! Jana and Laurie told me all about you!"

"And knowing all that you still want to associate with me?"

"Sure!" Lonnie replied. "Laurie told me you were once a millionaire corporate exec, but you left it all behind to answer God's calling! I think that's wonderful!"

"Really?" Leonard replied. "I know a good many who would be inclined to disagree with you."

"Well, that's because they don't see the overall picture! My daddy's a minister and he did something similar with his life before I was born! In fact, he went to seminary right here at Parkins. I guess you could say he started a tradition in the family. I just started here this semester and my brother's coming here next year. Daddy always says the main thing you should do in this life is to keep your priorities right and in focus. And what higher priority is there than God?"

And even though Leonard did not commit himself to an answer, just then, she took his arm and announced that they might as well have lunch together. It was clear to Leonard, right from the start, that he had encountered a force that was considerably stronger than he was.

After a good deal of rehearsal, the much-anticipated Sunday, during which Jerry would endeavor to baptize Mr. Elmer Ponks — all six feet, five inches and 340 pounds of him, arrived. Along with a change of clothes for her husband, Linda packed a tube of Ben Gay.

"Will you please calm down?" Linda said when they arrived at the church approximately two hours before the service was to begin. "There's the proper amount of water in the baptistery; it's just the right temperature so you won't catch your death of cold or contract hypothermia. We've rehearsed the procedure to the point where you ought to be able to do it in your sleep, and I'm quite certain lightning isn't going to strike."

"Linda," Jerry replied, "one of the reasons we Jews don't believe in Hell is because we have a wrathful God who will zap the life out of you if you step out of line! By performing this baptism, I will *definitely* be stepping out of line!"

"Look, try to calm down." She told him impatiently. "Why don't you take your clothes into the baptistery dressing room and change. You know the baptism takes place before the service. I'll hand out bulletins."

"What about Elmer? Somebody has to instruct him

The Call 253

where to go, and I don't want to parade around the church in my Bermuda shorts and bare feet."

"I'll take care of it. Take a few deep breaths, do some stretching exercises…"

"I think I'd better relieve my kidneys too!"

"Yes, by all means, do that."

As the congregation began to trickle in, Linda stood at the church door to greet them, including Elmer Ponks who grinned from ear to ear as he shook her hand. "This is the Sunday I get myself saved! Right here's my change of clothes."

Linda placed her hand on Elmer's shoulder and said, "Yes, we'll be ready to begin in about fifteen minutes. My husband's in the baptistery dressing room."

"Now don't be nervous." Jerry told him, pale with fright himself when Elmer joined him in the baptistery dressing room.

"I ain't nervous. I'm excited!"

"I wish I could say the same," Jerry mumbled under his breath. "I can hear Linda reading the invocation. Okay Mr. Ponks, it's time." The baptistery proper was like an elongated bathtub filled with water almost hip deep. Elmer was the first to step into the waters. Jerry followed, first descending the steps then onto the floor. Once his foot gained contact with the fiberglass surface, however, Jerry lost his footing, knocking up against Elmer, submerging them both beneath the waters.

Rumblings were heard in the congregation. From the pulpit, Linda could see faces with mixed expressions. Some laughed, others looked disturbed, others indignant.

Elmer was the first to surface shouting jubilantly,

"Hallelujah! I'm saved! I'm saved!"

"Wait a minute, Elmer," Jerry said, "That one didn't count. I slipped. We have to do it the right way."

Elmer turned to Jerry and said, "What? You mean I ain't saved?"

"Not yet, Elmer. I slipped."

"You mean I gotta go under again?"

The congregation again began to rumble. There were sounds of laughter. There were gasps of amazement and indignation.

"If we're going to get it right, you do." Jerry said, and extending his right hand, said,. "Here. Grab hold of my wrist with both your hands. Have you accepted Jesus Christ as your own personal Lord and Savior?"

"Yes, I have." Elmer replied, almost defiantly.

"Elmer Ponks, I now baptize you in the name of the Father, the Son, and the Holy Spirit." Jerry declared, beginning the submersion process. It was then, just as Jerry had feared, Elmer's weight was too much for him, and he joined the communicant in the water.

After the service while driving back to Idle, Jerry was applying the Ben Gay like it was going out of style. Linda said, "Well, you haven't been zapped by lightning, even after botching up a sacred ritual. I guess that goes to show, even your wrathful God has a sense of humor."

It was Monday morning, the second week of the spring semester when Professor Wilson gathered all of us together for the class in field education. With a look of profound weariness, he took his place at the front of the classroom, "Ladies and gentlemen," he said, "welcome to Field Education. I've had a rough time putting things

The Call 255

together for this course—a lot of administrative tasks and such—and there's still a lot more work that needs to be done. Right now, I feel the need to ask for a little help. Please join me in a word of prayer. Heavenly Father, it is as thy servants we come to thee seeking thine empowerment to do thy will. We are weak and seek the strength only Thou canst provide. It is in thy son's name we beseech thee O Lord in this time of need — Amen."

He went on to impress on us that this was a required course, one of the nine one-unit courses we would have to complete, and explained that its purpose was to monitor our time out in the field and provide us with feedback about both our personal and professional achievements, a sort of practical side to theology, pertaining to both the Gospel and human relations.

"As some of you may be aware," he said, "ministry is fraught with all sorts of pitfalls that must be addressed both in the light of the Gospel and human relationships. I always contend," Professor Wilson continued, "the church is like a theater and its minister is the lead thespian." Then he fixed his sights on Jerry Cantrell. "The employment of slapstick in the context of a theatrical production still falls within the parameters of acceptability. And if I may cite Shakespeare, your performance this past Sunday, I'd say, was a true 'comedy of errors.'"

Jerry blushed as laughter broke out.

"Excuse me, sir," I said when the laughter died down, "but it seems obvious to me that this course is for people serving churches out in the field. No church has seen fit to hire me, nor am I serving in any ministerial capacity at present. Matter of fact, I haven't had a ministry since my arrival here at seminary. I've been supporting myself via secular employment, and all I've done of any significance since I've been here is enhance my typing ability. Given this set of circumstances, maybe I should just pull out and enroll in secretarial school."

"Yes," Professor Wilson replied, "I've been thinking about you. Some of us do not serve churches. For you folks we have alternate ministries. One such alternate ministry that I have in mind for you is the County's alcoholism rehab outpatient program. Many of these patients have done stints in the mental health facility and have since been released on their own recognizance. However, due to their probationary standing, the county has deemed it necessary to monitor their progress, or lack of it, using caseworkers. To help fulfill this end, the county has allowed the seminary to send them volunteers."

"Sounds more like social work than ministry," I said.

"On the contrary," Professor Wilson explained. "What you'll be doing is ministry in the truest sense of the word. Look upon it as paying a pastoral visitation. You'll be aiding these people in dealing with their own personal demons and in every way assisting them in a life-and-death struggle. Not only that, you'll be needing to come to grips with your own demons as you do, and that's what this field education course will be about as well." Professor Wilson went on to explain about the class format, its requirements, and how its meetings would be scheduled. He then briefly entertained questions.

"Now, if there are no further questions," he concluded, cutting matters off abruptly, "I'd like to dismiss early. Like I said, I still have quite a few administrative matters that demand my attention. For those of you participating in the alcohol rehab program, please see me after class. I need to give you the name of the contact person you'll be reporting to."

There were only two of us taking part in the alcohol rehab program: Sam Church and myself. The contact person for the program was a licensed psychiatric social worker, a slender, officious woman in her early forties, named Mindy Grover who insisted that we, as volunteers in the program, conform strictly to policy and procedure. As she put it, "Brian Wilson may have sent you guys to me with the intent of allowing you to play preacher, but as long I'm your supervisor, you are case workers! That means you follow my agenda. This program is funded by state tax dollars and we are subject to tight regulations and to stringent reviews by state officials. That means your principle responsibility is to gather the appropriate data on these individuals."

Handing us a four-page listing of the data she needed, she told us that this information must be gathered during the course of each visit and that there should be no deviation, since this fact finding was essential to providing outpatient service.

"Once you have completed the gathering of this data," she continued, "it is then, and only then, that you'll be allowed to play preacher. Clear?"

Before leaving Mindy's office, we agreed to turn over transcripts of our visits along with the data sheets.

My first day of fieldwork found me wandering about the older section of Idle. As I drove to my destination, I could see the neatly kept dwellings occupied by the town's professionals giving way to the poorer part of town where my client, one Rudy Sellers, reputedly lived in either the house on the right or left hand side of the street, depending upon his state of sobriety.

I found Rudy in the rundown dwelling on the left hand side of the street, strewn with an interesting assortment of garbage. Though he was only forty according to my records, he looked much older.

"Hmmmm," I said, situating myself on a chair across from him, "according to our records it appears you've been on and off the wagon more times than a rusty lug nut. So why do you keep returning to the bottle?"

"I need to drink," was Rudy's succinct reply.

"It also appears you've had some rather serious liver problems," I continued in a business like manner. "Seems like what you say you need is also proving to be your undoing."

"He gets a terrible case of the DTs when he stops," Sally Ann said.

"Orange juice and honey can address that problem," I replied.

"I like my White Port." Rudy said with an astonishing display of outraged dignity. "I think you'd better leave now."

"Okay, I'll go," I said. "But if you ever decide you want help, you know where to call. After all, a man has to want to be helped." I then left the house.

Midway through the semester, Mindy Grover told

Brian Wilson and a few of my seminary colleagues that she felt that I was the best caseworker who had ever been brought into the program, which was, she was told in return, extraordinary since I had displayed so few ministerial attributes.

Meanwhile, Samuel Church, whom Mindy Grover had assessed as the biggest screw up she ever had to deal with, received a far higher rating from Professor Wilson who based his assessment on his opinion that Sam displayed more "pastoral savvy," whatever that was suppose to mean. Somehow I never was quite able to fathom the basis Professor Wilson used as a means of drawing up such assessments.

Despite my rave reviews, however, the longer I stayed in the program, the more clearly the alcohol rehab program appeared to be an exercise in futility and an expression of absurdity. Those whose lives had been claimed by this substance were, for the most part, doomed to a pattern of extended repetition, playing their con games on those whose lives they touched and, ultimately, upon themselves. Nothing I could do would make much difference. Jesus put it well when he said, "Aside from me, you can do nothing." I was humbled by this recognition, and for once the attitude of people like Sam Church, who called me defeatist, made little difference.

It was on a Saturday morning a little past the semester's midway point when the Logan family received a call from the hospital, telling them that. Mrs. Martha Logan, the family matriarch, was in the throes of a losing battle with cancer, and that she was requesting their presence. In fact, she died soon after they arrived at her bedside.

Hearing about Jack's loss, I called him the next day to offer my condolences. I asked him if there was anything he needed. "At times like these," I said, "I really don't know what to say. To say I know what you're going through would be a lie, because to tell you the truth, I don't. All I can say is: call if you need me."

When several days went by, and I hadn't heard a thing from Jack, I decided to call upon him at the church where he still labored as janitor.

"I hadn't heard anything from you, so I thought I'd drop by," I said when I found him mopping the floor in the social hall, "and see how you were doing."

"I feel real bad, Ishmael," Jack replied. "At first it wasn't so bad, but now ... I'm really worried about my dad. He's so sad. I can't concentrate on my studies and ... things are just all around bad."

"I'm sorry to hear that, Jack."

"That Ministry and the Family class ... that's become a real joke. The folks in that class act like they're afraid to even talk to Carla and me. Matter of fact, it seems to be the way it is with most of my classmates. Everyone is so uneasy when they're around me."

"Death hits different people different ways, I'm told."

"But we're supposed to be studying for the ministry!" he protested. "We're supposed to be helping people with grief issues! What good are we if we can't even talk to our peers about it? Shoot, you're the only one who's been able to talk to me."

"You're my friend, Jack. I want to help."

"I appreciate that. By the way, you know that Dean Marco?"

"Yes."

"He's the biggest putz I've ever met. He tried to start a discussion about my mother's death in the class after I shared my belief that my mother had finally lost a prolonged battle with cancer, and that in my mind her death was a victory—that the Lord in all His mercy had seen fit to alleviate her pain and draw her to His side. Do you know what that idiot said? He disagreed with me. He said that after his experience in Vietnam, he could state unequivocally that death was not a victory. Now I ask you, what kind of minister is that?"

"A very opinionated one, I would say."

"I tell you, Ishmael, I'm getting real disillusioned with this place. I'm beginning to feel like I don't belong here."

"I'm sure you're not alone, Jack, and remember that you don't have to listen to Dean Marco. All he was doing was giving an opinion, and you know what they say about opinions. They're like you-know-whats—everybody's got one. If you believe your mother's death is a victory, then who are we to question it? She's not suffering anymore. That in itself is a victory. I just wish there was something I could say or do for you to help."

"You have, just by being here." We stood up and grasped hands. It was another healing experience. I reached out to someone, and I could see from the look in Jack's eyes that he was grateful. Once again I gained a tenacious awareness of a strength I had not recognized before.

Well, I thought, at least I was able to minister to Jack. Maybe there is a point to my being here.

Elsewhere amongst the student body, Dr. Reginald Dexter was evoking his full prowess as a scholar and dazzling everyone with a brilliance that rivaled that of a cosmic body, not only during the course of his in-class presentations in Church History and Theological History, but also in the Old Testament Prophecy course taught by Professor Joseph Flowers.

Flowers, who sported a gray, craggy beard, was quite the Old Testament scholar and a student of Middle Eastern archeology. During the course of his twenty-year tenure at the seminary, his somewhat unorthodox theological teachings sometimes came across as threatening to the more conservative students. For instance, Dr. Flowers had no compunction about shattering certain preconceived beliefs his students had about the Bible, particularly with regards to geographic and archeological findings. One discovery he shared with his class had taken place during the time he had spent working at the Tel Hesse dig. His team had unearthed the remains of what were reported to be Philistine penises—and these penises were revealed as having been circumcised. The report of such findings profoundly disturbed some of the more conservative students, who were taught to hold tightly to the belief that only the Philistines were uncircumcised.

Another controversy concerned the passage of scripture where the story relates that Ruth lay at the feet of Boaz, her kinsman redeemer. As Dr. Flowers was quick to explain, the term feet, in Hebrew, was a euphemism for genitals, a disclosure that profoundly shocked many members of his class. How could this be? Could this be referencing the same Ruth they had heard so much about during their women's day programs? Could this woman's virtue have been compromised? Could a godly man like Boaz really have a penis? And if he did, could he really have used it?

Dr. Dexter had none of these preconceived notions and would, in turn, deliver Professor Flowers a blow of a comparable nature as he embarked on his exegetical assignment. This blow backfired, much to Dr. Dexter's chagrin, and he found himself on the receiving end of something he was definitely not accustomed to getting.

One evening, on the second floor in the seminary library, I ran into Dr. Dexter who was grumbling as he pulled a book from the shelf in the pastoral psychology section. "Damn narrow-minded old farts," he said. "Think they're so damn liberal and progressive, but as soon as they come across something they don't understand they invalidate it as heretical, sacrilegious, and unsuitable. Kind of puts me in mind of the Dark Ages when the Catholic Church had everybody subjugated."

"What brought that on?" I asked Reginald.

"You ever notice how people fear things they don't understand?"

"Yeah. I've often had that tendency."

"Well, at least you admit it."

"So who didn't understand what?"

"Oh, that old fart-faced Flowers."

"You mean ultra-liberal, progressive Professor

Joseph Flowers, the scourge of fundamentalism?"

"He's not liberal. He gave me a 'B' on my paper."

"Well, he is a tough grader."

"He didn't like my paper at all."

"Well, if you got a 'B' from Professor Flowers, I don't think you have much cause to berate yourself. What was your paper about?"

"It was about Ezekiel. My paper said he was crazy."

"Whaaat?" I raised my eyebrows in surprise.

"I based my conclusion upon several expert sources that lend credence to the fact that his visions, the wheel within the wheel, were actually schizophrenic models portraying the classic psychotic mindset. Of course, Flowers didn't understand about seventy percent of the terminology I used to lend credibility to my prognosis, so he continually had to run my paper over to Dr. Hennessey so he could get interpretations of my findings. It was a fifty-page paper, complete with extensive footnotes and annotations, the stuff doctoral dissertations are made of, and he gave it a 'B'."

"Have you presented a grievance to our acting dean?"

"He said he didn't understand it, which isn't a great argument, since he could have read it with the intent of learning something. Flowers is into archeology. What's going to happen if one day he should suddenly unearth the skeleton of Jesus? What's going to happen to him then? Where's his well-placed mindset going to be after that discovery is made?"

"You make some very challenging statements."

"What about you? Do you think you could adjust to this find?"

"I think I could. Of course, it would take quite a bit of creativity and growth on my part to do so. One of the major cruxes of Christianity is based on the notion that Christ rose bodily. Take that away and we'd be facing some agonizing reappraisals."

"I'll bet you're probably one of a very few who could. I'm betting most of the people around here, including Flowers, would be lost in a quagmire."

To my certain knowledge, Reginald never could overcome this setback. Certainly he carried the insult with him up to and beyond the period of graduation.

Leonard DeWilde was a classic example of the walking wounded. Yet, through his own stubborn tenacity he toughed it out, and circumstances in due course turned in his favor. He was able to obtain a level two Sunday-only church assignment. To add to that, when February arrived the City of Idle once again requested his engineer consulting services, and guaranteed him a long-term stretch of employment, involving the construction of a new power plant a few miles outside the city limits. It was a challenging prospect, and Leonard wasted no time in dropping his burger-flipping job.

The money he garnered from his consulting job also provided him with the option of seeking out more suitable living quarters. He couldn't stand dormitory life, and the roommate they had saddled him with was testing the last delicate strands of his sanity. Ben and Jana often rebuked him for his "less than Christian" attitude toward the young lad, a fact that only enhanced his irritability.

After having endured the monumental financial

setbacks accompanying his divorce and suffering a prolonged exposure to near-destitution, Leonard selected a modest campus apartment as his place of residence. At last he had his own space. Anticipation of this luxury fueled him with adrenalin. He couldn't move from the dorm fast enough. Once settled, there was only one other item to make this fortuitous change in quarters complete-- a cocktail. It seemed like ages since he'd had a good drink, but it was nothing a trip to a liquor store couldn't remedy.

Leonard was quick to acquire his libations and head back to the apartment. He got out the appropriate glass—a long-stemmed blue glass from Tiffany's that Lillian had overlooked—mixed the ingredients in proper proportions, and poured himself his much-anticipated cocktail, a chilled martini. But before he could take the first sip, he heard a knock at his door, and Lonnie Peterson made her appearance.

"Well," she said, "are you going to invite me in?"

During Leonard's dormitory stint, Lonnie had kept turning up. She was the daughter of a minister who, like Leonard, had turned his back on a position of considerable wealth and affluence to answer the call of God. Lonnie idolized her father, and it was because of him that after early graduation from high school, she served in a group called Youth With a Mission, which meant going into various communities to spread the Gospel. Because of that and her father's influence, it was easy for her to gain entrance into Parkins where she had followed in her father's footsteps by majoring in Religion.

The Call

When she saw Leonard in the dining hall, she told herself that he was the man she was going to marry. Her principle means of getting his attention was to ask Leonard for help with her homework. Knowing that he had an engineering background, and having to fulfill certain course requirements in the natural sciences, she felt compelled to tap into his knowledge of math and physical sciences.

Appealing to Leonard on an intellectual level had to suffice while the weather remained inclement. But as winter gradually subsided, Lonnie embarked on a more direct approach, one that included dressing in tights that showed off her perfectly round buttocks, slipover blouses with spaghetti straps, sleeveless halter tops, and short, blue-jean cutoffs. Counter to the instructions she received from the Christian family during the time she spent with Youth with a Mission, Lonnie wore her hair down and wild, although she wore glasses with clear lenses for the sole purpose of making herself look more intellectual. As they read assignments together, she always sat as close to him as she could.

Tonight, standing at Leonard's doorstep, Lonnie was wearing a halter-top that showed off her shoulders and the sides of her breasts, short jeans cutoffs, and sandals. She asked to see the apartment.

"Could I have some of what you're drinking?" Lonnie asked as she reclined on the sofa.

"This is a cocktail," Leonard explained. "You sure you want this? I mean, have you ever tasted one of these before?"

"Sure."

"And didn't you say you were nineteen?"

Lonnie gave Leonard a coy look and replied, "Well, yeah."

"Okay, I'll fix you one." Leonard said. "But just one."

"Come sit with me, Lonnie said as he handed her a drink. Why didn't you tell me you were moving? I had to do quite a bit of asking around to find you."

"Well, I've been pretty busy, between the day job, class assignments, moving …"

Lonnie took long drink.

"Sip," Leonard warned her, "don't gulp."

"It tastes wonderful," she smiled.

"Maybe, but you've got to ingest it slowly. You know what they say about too much of a good thing."

Lonnie leaned over and kissed Leonard on the cheek. "Like you?" she replied with a look of adoration on her face.

"I have an ex who might tend to disagree with you. And besides, I'm forty-two. Doesn't that make me a little old?"

"Your ex is an idiot. I think you're wonderful. Besides, you're more mature than the boys in the dorm."

"Maturity comes from living long and falling hard, I'm afraid. It's not an attribute I'd be too hasty to acquire."

"You're also very wise."

"Wisdom too, is painful in its acquisition. But I don't want to appear too negative. Things are beginning to look up again."

"Am I a part of that?"

"You're very much a part of it. Have you eaten

yet?"

"No. I was kind of hoping you'd take me out."

"Dorm food getting to you, huh?"

Lonnie stuck out her tongue like she was gagging. "You know it."

"Unless you'd like to go back to the dorm and change, I suggest we eat at Henry's."

"I'd love to eat at Henry's."

"Thanks," he said grinning, "for being so easy to please."

After dinner, they went to the movies, where Lonnie, complaining she was cold, coaxed him to put his arm around her. It was well after dark when Leonard steered the car toward campus. "Don't take me back to the dorm," Lonnie said in a low voice. "I don't want to go back. I want to spend the night with you."

Leonard felt as though he was about to leap from a very tall cliff. Lifetimes flashed before him. He took her in his arms and kissed her long and tenderly. Drunk on kisses, they finally made it into his apartment. Once there, they both fell into bed and made passionate love through the night. Morning found them crumpled together, still lying in each other's arms. After a prolonged shower, they made love again.

In the weeks that followed, Lonnie continued plying the domestic skills her parents had instilled in her, energetically helping with the cleaning and upkeep of Leonard's apartment and preparing him sumptuous meals—Yankee pot roast, veal parmesan, and roast leg of lamb—all the recipes handed down to her from her mother and grandmother. All in all, their relationship was a sensual awakening on many levels. She enjoyed an openness of expression with him transcending that of any other human rapport. There was nothing she found she could not talk to him about, no question she felt she could not ask, no feeling she could not share. Leonard experienced the same high degree of fulfillment in the relationship, and for him Lonnie's presence more than filled the void left by Lillian. Leonard reveled in the newness and zeal of Lonnie's adoration, coupled with her youthful enthusiasm. He began feeling younger, and energized with a renewed desire to achieve. And he learned to laugh again.

Leonard's contribution to the relationship was recreational in nature. They would go jogging in the park in the early morning or the evening hours, play tennis on the campus courts, and go out dining and dancing at swank places in Oklahoma City and Tulsa. He would also take her on extravagant shopping sprees at malls, where she would buy dresses and new outfits. They were both enthusiastic about hang gliding, and one time they experienced their romantic zenith by going up in a hot-air balloon. Soon Leonard became oblivious to the difference in their ages.

But even the most torrid of romances needs to take a back seat at times to the demands of academia. One evening, when Leonard had to attend a class and Lonnie was back in the dorm putting the finishing touches on a paper that was due the next morning, her dorm parents, Laurie and Kathleen arrived.

"It's been brought to our attention that over the past several weeks you have been absent from the dorm, particularly at night," Laurie said. "Now we have rules in place, and one of those rules is a curfew that mandates your presence in the dorm no later than ten p.m. on weeknights and midnight on Fridays and Saturdays. Although we don't enforce these rules rigidly, when it's reported that someone is habitually absent from the dorm during the night, we feel it's necessary to look into the matter. So Lonnie, what's been going on? Where have you been staying? What have you been doing that necessitates you staying out all night? As your dorm parents we have the right to know. Not only that, we also have an obligation."

At that, Lonnie confessed that she had been living with someone off campus. When she had finished, without revealing Leonard's name, Kathleen asked her if she thought her father would approve of what she was doing.

"I really haven't thought about it. My boyfriend and I are in love and he's going to marry me."

"Has he asked you to marry him?"

"No, but I know he's going to."

"And how do you know that?"

"I just do. A girl can tell."

"Really? Well, just for argument's sake, do you actually believe sleeping with him will help the process along?"

Lonnie blushed. "Well," she said, "maybe we should have held off, but we couldn't. The tie between us is so strong. We're in love. And that makes everything okay."

"We'll leave it at that for the time being," Laurie answered as she and Kathleen turned to exit. "But remember, we have rules that are firmly in place, and we most likely will be talking to you again."

"Can you imagine that?" Kathleen exclaimed, once they were out the door.

"Oh, don't sound so shocked," Laurie replied. "We've been at Parkins for going on five years now, and we've both seen what goes on. What's it they say? 'The only recreation is procreation?' Hers' might be one of the many wedding invitations we see plastered each year in the dormitory reception window."

"Yes, but she's so naïve. I wonder who this guy she considers Mr. Right to be is."

"Well, if it were an undergrad, I believe she would have said so. That leads me to believe it's a grad student. And seeing that we have only two graduate programs here at Parkins, I believe we can clearly deduce that he's either a seminarian or a speech and hearing student. And given the fact that Lonnie has such strong ties to her father, I think we can clearly assume that her lover is a seminarian, and most likely is one of the single ones."

"That narrows it down considerably. But which one?"

"Well, let's go down the list. Rufus Pelmonte is already engaged. T. J. Whizzer's not a student here anymore, but a teacher in the music department. I can't believe she'd be attracted to Markem McClusky."

"Well, you never can tell. Stranger things have happened."

"Kathleen, this is Parkins, not the Twilight Zone!"

"You're right. Scratch Markem. Ishmael O'Donnell?"

"Possibly. But somehow, I have my doubts. He's got too many other issues to contend with right now."

The Call

"Leonard DeWilde?"

"Nah, too old."

"Norman Decantor?"

"Also too old. And too narcissistic."

"You noticed that too. How about Sam Church? Of course, there'd be no accounting for taste."

"Well, I'm certainly at a loss. But one thing's certain. If he is a seminarian, then he needs to be made aware of the regulations put in place with regards to sexual misconduct."

"Oh get a life, Kathleen! Dormitory curfew rules haven't been stringently enforced around here since the early sixties, and as for the conduct of the seminarians, as long as they're discreet, who are we to be snooping around in their private lives?"

No doubt, she had a point, Kathleen thought. Certainly hearing about Lonnie's love life had made her more aware than usual that something was lacking in hers.

As my first year of seminary was ending, I was faced with the nebulous and cumbersome prospect of writing a resume. The alcohol rehab fieldwork provided me with some leverage, but my prospects for actual paid pastoral assignments were nil.

During this same time, Rufus Pelmonte's church assignment had ended due to lack of funds. Now unemployed, Rufus and Judi resolved to postpone their wedding plans until the following fall. That would provide Rufus with the time he needed to scout out other existing prospects.

Rufus and I attended a presentation in the seminary break room by a group known as Park Ministries, Inc. The presentation included a film showing our national parks in all their beauty and sending the message that tourists needed to keep in mind the source of these marvels of nature. Those of us working in the Park Ministries program would be expected to fill such secular roles as restaurant workers, trail guides, and waste disposal workers. The presentation ended with an appeal for all of us to sign up.

A meeting was held in Oklahoma City later on that provided us with the grander scheme. The park workers were to be paid $1.09 an hour for a twenty-four hour workday, which meant that we were to be at the park's beck and call twenty-four hours a day. Any tasks we were called upon to perform, from the cleaning of the port-o-potties to disposal of sewage, were to be performed cheerfully. We would be given two days a week off, but that didn't mean we wouldn't be expected to work on those days. We would be held to strict standards as to how we would dress, how long we could wear our hair, and with whom we could fraternize, and we would be provided with room and board—the rooms being dilapidated structures and the board being whatever food the tourists did not finish eating.

Basically, the signing of the contract gave the program the license to work our asses off performing secular functions. As one potential recruit put it, "Who's going to have the energy to perform the Lord's work after being worked to death by the secular task-master?"

I glanced over the contract and said to Rufus, "Scratch that. I'd be better off working for the City of Idle this summer. The pay is better, the hours are more reasonable, and at least they don't make me clean up shit."

Rufus agreed.

Hearing of our dissatisfaction with the Park Ministries program, Professor Wilson called Rufus and me into his office. "I understand the both of you turned down the Park Ministry job," he said. "How come?"

"Well," Rufus said, "most everybody there at the meeting was pretty unhappy about the terms of employment."

"And what was so wrong about the terms of your employment?"

I handed Professor Wilson the contract stipulations. He gave them a thorough looking over then looked up at us and said, "This is really not too bad a job. I mean $1.09 an hour doesn't sound like much, but it pays you twenty-four hours a day, and you're getting room and board."

"Yeah," I replied, "they're quite specific in the outline of this contract and only an idiot would buy the way they sugarcoat the wording. Besides, we got to talk to some of the people who've worked there before. We'd be staying in condemned buildings. Then we get to ingest all the leftovers! And I'll just bet they'll be calling upon us to earn that $1.09 an hour around the clock!"

"Well," Professor Wilson replied, "you wanted ministerial experience and this is one way to get it. You know you have to learn to crawl before you can walk. And remember, it was our Lord Himself who called us all to be suffering servants."

"Being a suffering servant is one thing," I snapped,

"being a sucker is quite another! I don't recall our Lord saying 'thou shalt be a patsy, a fool, and a rug for people to walk on!'"

"I think you're being a bit too harsh, Ishmael."

"A lot of the people there had the same opinion," Rufus said.

"And I could make just as much money working at my clerical job forty hours a week this summer," I added.

"You could," Professor Wilson replied, "but then you wouldn't be getting any ministerial experience."

"I doubt I would be getting much with that Park Ministry program either."

"Whatever. Summer's almost here and we have a number of churches in the surrounding areas, some even as far as Arizona, that want to hire youth workers for summer positions. You did a great job with the alcohol rehab program," he said. "That's something you can add to your resumé. Now, do you want to apply for the summer youth worker positions, or do you just want to hide behind the typewriter for the duration of the summer?"

I didn't know what to say at first. A part of me wanted to play it safe and stay hidden behind that typewriter, but I hadn't traveled all this distance to be a typist. So, I chose the more difficult path, because being a youth worker at one of these churches would make a welcome entry to my resumé. So, Rufus and my names were added to the candidate list.

A Christian church located in Wichita, Kansas, at which the minister traditionally headed a pulpit committee, was the first to interview me. I was asked a series of questions concerning my theological leanings, my denominational background, and what I felt might be suitable activities for a summer youth program, all of which I answered satisfactorily. But then came the clincher: the question regarding my preference in living quarters.

"Mr. O'Donnell," the minister began, "suppose we were to give you a choice as to what type of living quarters you'd prefer, your own apartment or living with one of our church families. Which one would you choose?"

"The apartment."

"And why would you choose the apartment?"

"Well, I prefer to do my own cooking. I've grown sort of accustomed to it."

"Okay. Suppose this family extended kitchen privileges to you. What would you choose? The family or the apartment?"

"The apartment," I replied, "because after tending to the needs of others, I need some time to myself. Besides, it's not my family. I'd be coming in as an outsider, and I really don't feel too comfortable about that arrangement."

Somehow, I didn't think my chances of getting that position were too great, and I was right. They wound up choosing an undergraduate Religion major by the name of Alice Masters, who gave them the answer they wanted to hear. That answer being, "I'd choose the family. By living with the family, I'd be able to continue enjoying fellowship and I'd be able to minister to them as well as minister to the youth." Of course I was later to hear that her period of ministry did not go as well as she would have liked and a few of her high ideals regarding the noble calling had been shattered as a result of the experience. Before accepting the position, she had not realized how severely scrutinized by the congregation she would be, as well as how little privacy living with one of their families would give her. She also grew to not like the family very much.

I received several brush-offs and was soon resolved to spending my summer typing for the City of Idle. Just before my last final exam of the semester, I received a long-distance call from my father who wanted me to spend the summer at home, helping him take care of my mother whose rheumatoid arthritis had taken a considerable turn for the worse.

Dad was never one to take no for an answer, especially from me. But this time I didn't feel like offering him any other option. Of course, I knew there would probably be a penalty to pay at a later time, but I couldn't waste time agonizing over that issue. I needed to focus.

I finally received an offer as a summer youth director at a Christian church in Roswell, New Mexico. It was an offer Rufus had already turned down because he didn't relish the thought of being that far from home and his fiancé. The position lasted for three months. It was the most exhausting, emotionally draining experience I ever had.

I remember Jason Tyler telling me that ministry was a fishbowl type of life, and during that summer in Roswell, his meaning became abundantly clear. People took note of my every quirk, my flaws, and behavioral idiosyncrasies. The congregation's expectations were high, and their judgments were harsh. Near the end of my

The Call

summer hiatus at that church I started feeling paranoid, and grossly inadequate, constantly afraid that I would say or do the wrong thing.

At the outset of my ministry, I was told that, because of the promiscuous tendencies of the church youths, it was the congregation's expectation that I would turn their children around. As one of the elders put it, "You reckon you could get Johnny to read his Bible more?"

When the time came for church camp, I served as one of the counselors. I later found that our church camp was the only camp that allowed coed swimming. We didn't monitor the youth as closely as did the other camps in the area and received criticism from the other denominations, stating that our young people "just weren't spiritual enough to call themselves true Christians."

One night some of our high school teens went to one of the Baptist camp revivals. The gathering took place at an open-air chapel structure. The weather was still hot and sweltering. The speaker stood on an elevated platform, while the students all gathered about a cemented patio around the podium. "You can always tell the Christian by their behavior," the speaker declared, "as well as their attitudes and dress."

It was interesting to note that all the Baptist campers were dressed fastidiously while our gang stood around in blue-jean cutoffs, tank tops, halter tops, bikini tops, ragged t-shirts, and disheveled hair. Some of the girls even had their hair up in rollers. Knowing full well who in the congregation needed saving, an altar call was made near the end of the service. At this time the minister said,

"Now I know there are a group of people standing in this congregation who need to come forward, who need to repent of their sins, and experience cleansing by the blood of Jesus!"

No response. A second altar call was made, followed by a third and a fourth. Not one of our teenagers answered these calls. Finally one girl in our camp turned to a friend and said, "Gee, I wish whoever it is that needs saving so bad would hurry up and go forward so we can all go back to our camp and go to bed."

Those within hearing range started to snicker.

I didn't think it had been that long since I had been in my teens, yet for all I could recollect about that time of my life, my experiences and observations that summer in Roswell opened my eyes to the sobering realization that it might as well have been light years away. And yet, the congregation expected me to set their kids straight regarding their sexuality, a subject about which the kids probably knew more about than I did. They would marry as early as seventeen. I was told that it was not unusual to see a husband and wife sitting in a twelfth-grade sixth-period math class with the wife being eight months along in her pregnancy.

Many of the boys, upon graduation (and some even before, if physically capable), went to work on the oil rigs in neighboring towns. It was there they drew a wage of nine-hundred dollars a month, more money than I had even seen or perhaps could even hope to see even with an advanced degree. They liked to drink and carouse, and they loved sex. The divorce and infidelity rates were high. I saw a most disturbing cycle disseminate itself from one generation to the next and couldn't help but wonder how the parents could logically expect me, an outsider, to turn things around for them when the problem was a self-perpetuating one.

After several weeks enmeshed in this social quagmire, I heard Professor Wilson's words thunder in my brain. "You're an actor, son! You're on stage now! Give them their money's worth!"

I also heard sporadically from Isaac, particularly when my pills were running low. He never seemed to tire of reminding me that what I was doing was not mine, and he would laugh robustly and derisively whenever I would fumble and miss the mark.

I kept hearing of a youth minister who presided there back in 1968. He was the stereotypical hippie, Jesus freak, establishment baiting rebel with a cause. But his cause was Christ, and did he ever put on a show for these folks, displaying charisma and magnificent leadership qualities. Even his exit was fraught with drama since he died in an auto accident right at the end of his sojourn with the church, leaving the congregation stunned. As one member put it, "Truly he was one who was called by God!"

It didn't take me long to become aware of the fact that I was not a leader, had no flair, no charisma, and was, in fact, quite dull. To top it off, once back in Idle, I received a letter from my Roswell pastor about whom, during the course of my internship, I had learned nothing but how futile the entire process was. The letter read as follows:

Dear Mr. O'Donnell:
I found you hard to believe. During your time here, I

was stunned and nearly appalled by the fact that someone your age could be so ignorant to the ways of proper protocol and interpersonal relations. I found you to be highly self-centered as well. Don't you realize that as ministers we are called upon to deny ourselves and be the suffering servants of others? I see none of that in you and it's a shortcoming I'd take great pains to rectify if you expect to continue in this endeavor.

Your interactions with the parishioners left much to be desired as well. I received many complaints from members about how they felt rejected by you, or overlooked, particularly when you would not look them straight in the eye. I would think your parents would have taught you better. Are your own self-centered needs so great that you cannot cast them aside to provide these folks with the most basic of affirmations?

Furthermore, your social ineptitude included a slovenly manner of dress. You may be able to get by with what you exhibited in California, but this is not California and in the words of the Apostle Paul, we are called to be all things to all people. You were expected to minister to children, and yet you seemed totally clueless as to how to relate to their problems. I find this incredible knowing that it wasn't that long ago you were their age. Knowing all this, can you truly regard yourself as one who is justly capable of carrying out this divine commission?

I know this is a harsh letter, but I'm telling you this because I know it is what you truly need to hear and I pray you give much consideration to my words if you wish to succeed in ministry.

God be with you,

Rev. G. Millard Duncan

His words pierced my heart like a dagger. It did not help to know that he had sent a copy of the letter to Professor Wilson. Therefore, it was no surprise that, the next day, I was summoned to his office.

Professor Wilson summed it all up for me. "It all comes down to one thing O'Donnell," he said. "You're a lousy actor. Now you can let this letter destroy you or you can learn what you can from it and move on." I wanted to move on, but the impact of the reverend's words left me with a paralysis that would take quite a bit of time to heal.

"I don't know if I'm quite so resilient," I replied. I felt as if someone had struck me hard below the belt. And in my brain I could hear Isaac laugh and laugh and laugh.

III

The Instruction Continues

The fall semester of our second year marked its start with another retreat.

I was intent on not attending, but Kathleen McKensie, who had been elected student body vice president and chief coordinator of said retreat, confronted me face to face.

"Ishmael O'Donnell, what's this I hear about you not going to the retreat?" she demanded. "I'll kick your ass if you even hint at some truth to that vicious rumor."

"How can I resist so gracious an invitation," I replied. This time, instead of riding the bus, I took my own car.

Jason Tyler had taken a semester off from seminary to follow another academic pursuit at Oklahoma State University in Stillwater, something to do with counseling. It soon became apparent that the academic pursuit was not all he had been tending to. The first evening of the retreat, I met him walking with a plump, curly-haired woman who was carrying an armload of baby paraphernalia, while he pushed a stroller. When I said that I'd heard he had gotten married, his only response was to call me a smart ass.

Interestingly enough, he was even more cocky and arrogant upon his return to seminary. One night we gathered in the woodsy lodge decorated in circa-1950 L. L. Bean complete with old stuffed couches, beat-up tables, and lamps shaped with silhouettes of jumping fish. A group of us had gathered around the fireplace and Jason began voicing his opinions, with blasts of incontestable authority in a tone that would make a gentle person

The Call

cringe. "Let me tell you something," he said, "something I learned during my hiatus that I found out to be an undisputable truth! When you preach, you have to preach the Lord, and you have to preach Him boldly and with absolute deliberation! I know this for a fact! I did it and I reaped the fruits of it! Not only did I grow in the Word, the Lord blessed my ministry. He allowed me to get married again, He gave me a son, and I sit before you a better person because of it!"

Charlie Donohue said, "Well, I'm from Missouri and…"

"I fail to see where your regional bearing has anything to do with what I just said!" Jason retorted. "I'm telling you the truth, and you'd all be wise to test it out!"

Once we were back in the dorm, I disclosed to Jack Logan the various problems I had encountered at my assigned church. Jason, being within earshot, continued his erstwhile tirade, focusing it in my direction.

"I see an appalling amount of self-centeredness coming from you!" He told me. "Along with that I see a lot of craven cowardice, a lack of conviction, and no sense of initiative. The souls of those children were placed in your charge, and you failed to boldly lead them into the path of righteousness and away from all those sinful pastimes! The Lord issues a harsher judgment to those of us called to lead in such matters, and the Lord is judging you now for this failure on your part!" He walked back to his bunk.

"What an asshole," Jack commented, as soon as Jason was gone. "Don't look so crushed. Consider the source. He doesn't know any better."

Jack had made considerable headway during his first year, so much so that Professor Brian Wilson had approved him for a level four position at a church in a neighboring farming community. He appeared as one born to the role of minister and reveled at the rapport he had established with his congregation. He even began to speak with the accent of an Oklahoma native. Carla, too, had made her adjustment to small-town life and her role as a minister's wife.

In many ways, the retreat came across as a repeat of last year's. There were talks, mini-sermons given by Professor Babcock, games, and finally class registration. Even the food was the same old ham hocks, black-eyed peas, and corn bread in the same limited supply.

During the retreat, Professor Wilson informed me that he was going to place me, bad evaluation and all, among the candidates for church positions. This time, however, he also advanced my eligibility to a level two Sunday-only pulpit ministry.

"Level two?" I exclaimed. "After the mess I made in Roswell?"

"Believe it or not, Ishmael," Wilson replied, "I've seen worse. Besides, what happened back there wasn't all your fault. I've known Reverend Duncan a long time and he's had to deal with his own share of setbacks. You probably know, he's not very well liked in his church. So, somebody had to be his scapegoat, and you were the lucky one to fill the role this past summer."

"That's dirty pool!" I retorted.

"Hey," Professor Wilson replied, "don't think for one minute that just because someone wears the title of 'reverend' next to his name that he holds a monopoly on all that's good and decent. When God recruits, He recruits from the human race. And let me tell you something, He recruits some real sons of bitches. You'll be finding that out this semester when you take Professor Flowers' Old Testament course. I remember sitting in on a few of Flowers' lectures and as I recall, David was perhaps the biggest son of a bitch ever recruited by God. And Jesus was his direct descendant."

A few days after the retreat, Professor Wilson set me up with an interview for a level two position at a church in a neighboring community. As before, I was unsuccessful at obtaining the church position. They wanted a hellfire and brimstone type of preacher. They also wanted their pastor to be married with a couple of children. When they saw that I was single, they asked me if there was any chance that I would change my status. I told them that there was always a chance, but it would have to wait until after I finished seminary. That was not the answer they wanted to hear.

Once again, my field education requirement was fulfilled by way of the alcohol rehab program, although sporadically Brian Wilson would send me out as a one-shot pulpit fill-in to churches that had no regular pastor or whose pastor was absent for one or two weeks. Oddly enough, I was pleased to return to my regular job in the same position I held before my ill-fated excursion to Roswell. It was, I found, a relief to be doing something that I did well, among people I liked. It was, perhaps, a pity I did not put two and two together and get four.

Due to Elmo's busy schedule and youth ministry,

and Christy's having to teach the summer session at the Glenwood elementary school to earn the needed extra funds, the couple had to postpone their nuptials, but occur they did in keeping with, as Elmo put it, "God's own timetable." Elwood tried to convince them to wait until graduation, but thanks to hormonal prodding, they insisted on tying the knot as soon as possible. So, once again, Elwood was faced with his son's one-upmanship, and reluctantly officiated over the marriage ceremony.

It was an elaborately staged ceremony. The church sanctuary was arrayed with peach and white décor. A red carpet was rolled down the center aisle and white, yellow, pink, and red roses decorated the pulpit area. Christy's bridesmaids were flown in from her hometown to take part in the event, and friends and relations inundated the building. Elmo wore a white tuxedo with a peach cummerbund, and, Christy wore a full-length white wedding gown and carried peach-colored roses and white baby's breath.

Prior to the wedding Elmo insisted that Christy's vows be to love, honor, obey, and be subservient to. Christy agreed. Elwood and Ellen thought such vows were sexist and quite outdated given the present-day climate. But Elmo insisted that it was a Christian's duty and responsibility to keep in adherence to God's plan for marriage.

The wedding came complete with a catered meal of prime rib, baby new potatoes, delicious creamed spinach, a salad bar, and glazed carrots for all the guests. Elmo and Christy's church picked up the tab. Elmo and his bride endured an endless stream of congratulatory plaudits. Shortly after the reception's close, Elmo and Christy

The Call 291

changed clothes and boarded a train that would carry them to their honeymoon destination at Cape Cod. It was a torrid and passion-filled two weeks spent frolicking about the countryside, making love, sampling the many seafood restaurants along Cape Cod's shoreline, making love, walking along the beach, making love, seeing the sights, and making love. Christy wound up getting pregnant on their honeymoon, and Elmo and Christy were ecstatic at the news. All Elwood could do upon hearing their announcement was shake his head. He then turned to Ellen and said, "You know, ever since our son returned from the Navy, there's been something about him that seems almost surreal. And I find it scary."

Elmo and Christy set up housekeeping in an apartment near the campus just before the start of the fall semester. Christy took another teaching position at one of the schools in a neighboring community, while Elmo once again signed up for eighteen units and continued with his youth ministry position. Christy's mother lived nearby and always stood ready to lend a hand after the birth of their first-born. This worked out nicely when Christy was away at work and Elmo was in class. As for weekends, Christy would join Elmo and assist where she could in his youth ministry.

The pace they maintained seemed maddening to any onlooker, yet their moods appeared outwardly joyful and their morale consistently inclined itself at the highest pinnacle.

When asked what their secret was, Elmo was always quick to say, "It's no secret! God sustains us and provides our every need!" Time itself bore witness to this supposed truism and rendered testimony to the extent of their endurance, for by the end of the spring semester of Elmo's third year of college, he had aced all eighteen units of his course work, and Christy was pregnant again.

My second year at Parkins took on all appearances of a repeat of my first year. When I queried why it that was so, the only answer I received was, "It's tradition!" Thus I knew that for as long as I would remain at Parkins, I would see the same things repeat themselves over and over.

Tradition extended itself into the seminary community. A good number of the seminary students were university alumni. Wanda Epperson was one such example. During the beginning of her second year of seminary, she and her sweetheart, a fellow from the fraternity affiliated with her sorority, had announced their intentions to marry. He had entered seminary after graduating with a bachelor's degree in Religion. Together they planned to form a husband/wife team ministry.

Wanda first announced their intent to wed at her parent's place that Thanksgiving. The announcement came about while she was saying grace. "Oh Lord," she is said to have prayed, "please extend your blessings upon this house and help my parents extend themselves warmly to Dave, that his entry into this family be a welcome addition when we get married." Her grace startled the members of her family, and that was Wanda's intent. After all, as Wanda disclosed to Sharon McMillan, "We're only going to get married once. We might as well do it right."

Married life seemed to agree with Wanda. She could

be seen traipsing merrily through the cloistered halls daily wearing a big broad grin on her face. Lawrence Viscount, who never was able to stand her, remarked one time, "Wow! So it took getting married and having sex on a regular basis to keep her from being so bitchy all the time! I gotta say I don't envy Dave one bit!"

Lewis Coppel was also soon destined to walk down the aisle with his sorority sweetheart. All his "brothers" flocked together to give him a bachelor's party complete with several kegs of brew and painted his testicles green, transforming them into fertility symbols, another time-honored tradition. As for me, I had been warned that it was not wise to mix Mellaril with alcohol. So, guess who was sent out for more booze?

Rufus Pelmonte also took the matrimonial plunge that semester, although unlike his fraternal brother, Lewis, he did so without any of the standard fanfare, due to the insistence of his prospective wife-to-be..

Norman Decantor also found the girl of his dreams, the choir director of the church he was pastoring. She was nineteen years his junior, but, as he put it, "What the hell, women age faster than men."

In the midst of this matrimonial climate, Leonard DeWilde popped the question to Lonnie over a candlelit dinner at an exclusive club in Oklahoma City, a proposal that was met with squeals of joy as she cried, "Yes! Yes! Yes! Yes!"

"Now calm down, Lonnie," Leonard replied. "This is a public place, you know."

"Oh Leonard! I'm so happy!" she cried, tears rolling down her cheeks as he slipped the ring on her finger. "I can't wait to tell my folks."

After they finished eating, they headed back to their hotel room with arms wrapped around each other. Once they had reached their room, Lonnie made a mad dash to the phone to call her folks.

"What?" Her mother shrieked. "But how? You haven't even been away from home a year and…"

"Oh mother, he's the most wonderful man in the world and you and Dad just have to meet him! I'm so excited!"

"Just when do we get to meet this young man?" her father said, taking the phone.

"How about this weekend? Saturday?" Lonnie said.

And so it was that the following Saturday Leonard was being introduced to Lonnie's parents who had some difficulty hiding their surprise at Leonard's age. Her mother said, when they were alone in the kitchen, "Lonnie, when I told you to find a man like your father, I didn't mean find a man as old as your father!"

However, Reverend Peterson was impressed, not only with Leonard's engineering background and his enterprising approach to his seminary experience, but also by the fact that he owned a yacht docked in the harbor just off Lake Michigan.

Leonard and Lonnie were married several weeks later in her father's church where her father filled the dual function of giving away the bride and performing the wedding ceremony. After a gala reception, they were off on a three-week honeymoon in Hawaii. For Lonnie, the trip was the adventure of a lifetime, while Leonard reveled in a sense of renewed vigor.

After the honeymoon, Lonnie and Leonard returned

The Call 295

to their campus apartment at Parkins, where Lonnie applied herself to the task of setting up housekeeping. Before marriage they both sought to keep a low profile regarding their relationship. But since their marriage, they reveled at being able to come out into the open. They could frequently be seen walking arm-in-arm across the campus, lost in the rapture brought about by each other's company. Two of the many onlookers were Laurie Parson and Kathleen McKensie. One day, as they glanced at Leonard and Lonnie walking arm-in arm, Laurie said, "You know, there's something about seeing those two that borders on the obscene."

"Are you jealous?" Kathleen asked.

"You bet your life I am. But there's something more to it than that. She breaks dormitory regulations, she acts in ways that fly in the face of her Christian upbringing, and she winds up living happily ever after! Meanwhile, you and I play it straight, try to suppress our hormonal urges, behave righteously, and what does it get us? I'll tell you what it gets us! Nights alone with our textbooks!"

Of course, not all went well with the happy couple. That Sunday, Leonard brought his new bride to the church he was pastoring. Lonnie greeted the parishioners alongside her husband. While in the process of shaking hands, one of the parishioners, an aging farmer with a graying countenance, asked Leonard, "Who's that? Your daughter?"

"No," Leonard replied. "She's my wife. We just got married a few weeks ago."

That Tuesday, Leonard was summoned into Professor Wilson's office. "This is a bit awkward for me because I've never had to deal with a situation like this before." Professor Wilson said. It seems you've been discharged from your church. Certain members of the congregation really don't feel comfortable about their minister having a child bride. At least that's what they call her.

"What the hell business is it of theirs who I marry?" Leonard demanded.

"These are things a minister needs to contend with all the time."

"No way! It's discriminatory, it's biased, it's narrow-minded, it's old fashioned, it's … !"

"Look Leonard, I've heard rumblings around the campus that one of our seminarians was conducting a clandestine sexual liaison. Now even though certain rules around here are not stringently enforced, they are still in place. I'm not directly accusing you of being this seminarian, but I am informing you that there has been traditionally certain rules of conduct to which we have been called upon to adhere, and one of them pertains to sexual conduct. And we're a lot more lenient here in the enforcement of that rule than the denominational headquarters would be."

"What sexual misconduct? We're married, for God's sake!"

"Alright, you're married now. That's good. But outward appearances do not point in your favor. Remember what the Good Book says about avoiding all appearances of evil?"

"And what's so evil about two people being in love?"

"I understand. But we're dealing with a more

parochial mind set when we minister to folks in these rural farming communities."

"So what am I supposed to do? Get a divorce so I'll once again uphold the façade of righteousness and purity?"

"No. We'll just have to find you another church. You could get your child bride to present herself in a more mature fashion. You know, dress a little frumpier, wear her hair up in a bun, stuff like that."

"Shit."

"I know. It's rough. But that's the way things are."

It was Leonard's and Lonnie's first marital crisis, and as Leonard told us later, it was a great relief that he discovered that Lonnie, having been raised as a minister's daughter, understood. It was, as I told him, the luck of the draw. And I found it amazing how so many of my fellow seminarians were drawing aces, while I continued being dealt a losing hand.

In the fall semester of my third year, the seminary acquired a new dean—a tall, rugged, handsome individual in his late thirties with jet-black hair, steely blue eyes, and a strong jaw. Dr. Glen Joseph Glenn delivered sermons and gave a lectures with such an air of authority that even his rendition of a genuflect at the end of a presentation was dramatic.

Professor Rupert Babcock greeted Dr. Glenn's appointment with relief. Now he could step down from his post as acting dean and concentrate his efforts exclusively on what he regarded as his principle calling, teaching. The timing of this transition had an element of divine influence, as well, since this was the semester he was due to teach his Advanced Homiletics course. For many of us who had taken Brian Wilson's Elementary Preaching and Pastoral Care course, Professor Babcock's course turned out to be a bit of a contrast. He tended to downplay the acting angle and concentrate more on the development of such skills as storytelling, inductive reasoning, and the sifting out of the theological from the secular.

At the outset of the class, he told us that it was of tantamount importance that we read a verse of scripture a day, one poem a week, one short story a week, and a novel a month. (It could be any kind of novel—a trashy novel, a science fiction novel, a Hardy Boys/Nancy Drew novel, a pornographic novel … whatever.) We were also advised to keep a journal of impressions that could be analyzed theologically. Some people, he maintained, were even able to obtain theological impressions by flushing the toilet. The only boundaries were our fertile imaginations.

We would also be expected to write five sermons. Three would be simply written sermons, one would be audio taped, and one would be videotaped. In addition, Professor Babcock informed us that he would be keeping a signup form on his office door, and he planned to have a single one-on-one counseling session with each of us regarding our style, technique, and other features of our preaching sometime during the semester.

I had no problem finishing and submitting my three written sermons. However, since I was not pastoring a church, I needed to get Brian Wilson to send me off on a pulpit fill-in mission for the audio and video-taped sermons. And what topic would I preach about?

One evening, early in March, I was returning home from a visit to the girls' dormitory. Unaware that love was about to draw me in, I passed by a university-owned house, where one of the senior seminarians and his wife lived. On the porch, I saw a bed made up for a family pet. Pets were not allowed in student housing but many of the grad students tried to get around this rule. Some could successfully elude it, and some got caught.

Just beyond the porch stood a brown female bulldog with a stub for a tail, prancing about, begging for attention. Sitting down on the grass, I let her lick my hand and held her. It was clear she was starved for affection, and so, I suppose, was I. Oblivious to the cold, I spent the night holding her on my lap, petting her, stroking her head and neck. Observing her up close, I could see the dog was pregnant.

As we parted company at dawn and I headed home, memories of the animal flooded my brain accompanied by recollections of an episode of Kraft Mystery Theater entitled "Feral Dog." The feral dog was a manifestation of Christ, I thought. Then I remembered reading a book entitled *Parables of Peanuts*. In it, I recalled references being made to Snoopy as the Christ figure within the comic strip, and I remembered the author observing that "dog" was "God" spelled backwards and citing several theologians who thought this was significant. And now, after the unexpected experience, I made what appeared to be an obvious conclusion that the closest tangible, earthly manifestation of God's love is that of a dog. A dog accepts you unconditionally, never lets go of you, and is loyal to you until the end. Suddenly I knew that I had the makings of a sermon for Babcock's class, a sermon that might make people take me more seriously as a candidate for the ministry.

When the time came for me to deliver my sermon in Clinton, I brought my tape recorder, recorded it, and was delighted to find that it was well-received by most of the members of the congregation. One woman was so touched when I told of having to put my dog to sleep, that she had to leave. As I was later to discover, she had to put her dog to sleep the week prior.

The following week, I played the sermon for the class. Most of my colleagues were quite receptive. Wanda didn't like it, but Lewis said it was the best sermon he'd ever heard, and Reginald expressed a bit of awe at the intellectual prowess of my sermon's composition and my articulate delivery. He said he had never dreamed I had it in me. Leonard DeWilde said the sermon left him confused. Jerry Cantrell said it really "spoke" to him. As for Babcock, he said I might have given my congregation a little too much to absorb.

"I have been very impressed with all your work," he told me when he met with me later. "You're a voracious reader with an intellectual prowess that is second to none. Your sermons are terrific. They actually have the Gospel in them. Most of the people in my class seem to be afraid of the Gospel, but you go in and tackle it head on. I remember saying to my wife once that you have more raw material to offer the ministry than practically anyone here. But you also have your fair share of rough edges that need to be smoothed out. Have you ever thought of taking a unit in Basic Clinical Pastoral Education?"

"I'm not sure I know what that is, sir," I replied.

"That's where you perform chaplaincy work within the confines of an institutional setting. That setting could be a mental health setting, a regular hospital, a hospice…"

"Sounds intriguing. How do I apply?"

"I'll get the literature from Dr. Hennessey and have it for you by next class session."

At last, I was beginning to see a beacon of hope. To my surprise, I received a totally opposite signal from Dr. Bildeberger the next day when I attended my weekly field education class. For the past year, Mindy Grover had held me in high regards as the best case worker ever to grace the alcoholism outpatient rehab program. Yet, despite Grover's glowing recommendation, Dr. Bildeberger saw fit to call me to one side after class and tell me point blank, that, although he thought I was brilliant, he did not think I was suited to serve a middle-class church congregation.

It was a hard time for me, but I had the companionship of my fellow seminarian's dog. When she gave birth to a littler, her master named one of her pups Pooh. Dog and pup were a buffer for me against the world. And at the time, I needed that.

I received an invitation from one of the Christian Churches back in my hometown in California to give a sermon during the Christmas break. The minister was an alumnus of both Parkins University and Parkins Theological Seminary and, at varying points, had taken an active interest in my pursuit of the ministry and in his alma mater. Needing to go out of town the Sunday after

Christmas, he figured that I was the perfect stand-in. The associate pastor would still be present and could take charge of the rest of the liturgical details surrounding the service. All I would need to do was give the opening scriptural reading, deliver the sermon, and conclude the service with a closing prayer.

So what was I to preach about? It was still the Christmas season. Should I preach a Christmas sermon? No. According to both the pastor and the associate pastor, the people had already had their fair share of Christmas sermons. What about the New Year? Possibly. Then I recalled my dog sermon. It was the sermon for which I had received the most plaudits. Lewis Coppell had even mentioned it in one of Professor Gene Molder's classes. So, I opted to go with my power.

Work had stopped temporarily at the Idle City Hall during the holidays, leaving me with little reason to stay, and my folks were more than happy to have me pay them a visit in light of the fact that I had not made it home the previous year.

But to my surprise, I found the prospect of preaching at this church terrifying. Although I took great comfort in the church while I was only a part of the surroundings, I found the prospect of being its centerpiece, even for that one brief occasion, scary beyond reckoning.. My parents would not be able to attend because of their declining health. I was grateful for their projected absence. I was certain their presence would only have accentuated the already acute stage fright I was experiencing.

As the congregation gradually grouped in the foyer, I paced about fretfully in the vestibule, unable to suppress my mounting anxieties, drawing several cups of water from the cooler in an attempt to quench a nervous thirst, and the process of downing the maximum dosage of my prescribed psychotropic drug. All I needed now to compound this anxiety was to hear from Isaac.

As I emerged from the men's room, the associate pastor, Lynn Conklin, appeared before me as a veritable icon of the church. "It's that time. You want a robe?" She asked.

"No thank you," I responded. It was not something I was accustomed to wearing, and at that moment I was so overwhelmed by my surroundings and the circumstances before me, that I could not bring myself to take on anything else outside the realm of familiarity.

We proceeded down the aisle as the opening hymn was sung, past wall-to-wall rows of people on both sides of us, Lynn leading with a stunningly vibrant soprano that made me feel dwarfed. As I assumed my seat on stage, I realized that I had never beheld such a huge congregation, and all eyes were upon me. "Please take hold, pills!" I pleaded silently.

Lynn introduced me to the congregation. When I stood in acknowledgement, I became aware that, in spite of all the water I had consumed beforehand, my throat felt constricted. Even worse, my kidneys were starting to scream. Finally the moment of the inevitable arrived. It was time for me to mount the lectern and begin my reading of the scriptural passage. I opened the Bible to the place I had marked and began to read the passage from the Gospel According to John, chapter 13, verses 1 through 9. It was fortunate I had memorized this passage, because I was finding it more and more difficult to focus. I managed to get through the story of Jesus washing the feet of his disciples. When Peter refused to let him do it, Jesus told him that, unless He was allowed to wash his feet, He would have no part of him, to which Peter said, "Not just my feet, Lord, but my hands and head as well." As I read, my voice was raspy and my vision began to blur.

After another hymn, Lynn Conklin's lead us in the pastoral prayer. Finally, it was my turn to deliver the sermon. Anticipating that I would be nervous, I made sure the sermon was meticulously prepared in manuscript format and that the pages were all in order. The text of the sermon was set up in large type, so I knew it would be easier to read than the scriptural passage. Again I glanced furtively at the congregation and swallowed hard. Clearing my throat, I began, "Who was the man called Jesus? Throughout the context of the Synoptic Gospels, and even in the context of the Gospel According to John, we see an exalted figure—a bearer of wisdom, a teacher, a man of authority. Yet, when we come to the thirteenth chapter of John, we see Jesus washing the feet of the disciples—a very humbling task—a task that was only performed by the lowliest of servants."

Gripping the lectern tight with both hands, I continued my sermon, developing the man/dog analogy. Almost at once, I could sense the congregation was uneasy. Add to that, my throat felt as though it was filled with sand, and my bladder felt like it was about to explode. As I continued my sermon on the man/dog analogy, I could sense the congregation's disquietude. Unlike the positive accolades I received when I first gave the sermon to the rural Oklahoma congregation and the warm plaudits that were heaped upon me by Rupert Babcock and my fellow seminarians, this urban, West Coast congregation scrutinized my performance very critically and took great displeasure at my quirky delivery and eccentric demeanor. Endless minutes passed as I struggled toward closure.

When it was finally over, Lynn and I stood at the door, shaking hands, and it was soon apparent that my sermon had not exactly been a hit. I knew one of the members of the church's pastoral staff would want to confer with me during the week about my performance at their pulpit, and I dreaded the thought of facing them. I took marginal comfort in knowing I would be accorded a few days' reprieve since it was Sunday, and they were off on Monday. Perhaps by midweek my nerves would settle.

On Tuesday, Reverend Jones called to set up an appointment to confer with me the next day. I wasn't sure what to expect. My gut feeling was one of trepidation, a sensation I had become quite accustomed to over that past few years. Reverend Jones was a likeable man, personable and affable, but I was about to see quite a different side of him. As soon as I arrived in his office, he handed me a note from Lynn. "Here," he said, "I want you to read this."

The note read as follows:

Dear Mr. O'Donnell:

I'm afraid in your case I must speak bluntly. After viewing your performance in our church this past Sunday,

I must say that I am deeply shocked and dismayed by the fact that you have pursued this endeavor for as long as you have without giving some serious thought to the repercussions that might ensue in matters regarding both yourself and your future parishioners. I see a lot of hurt in you—hurt you dare not bring into this most sacred of callings. This hurt was made manifest to me by your uncontrolled nervousness and your inability to take even the most elementary of cues. As you addressed the congregation I saw in you a deplorable inability to read the audience you were called upon to minister to. And likening God's love to that of a dog was the pinnacle of embarrassment. It was like you were giving a lecture rather than delivering a sermon. It was our Lord Himself who admonished us to remove the plank from our own eyes before removing the speck from our brothers. "Physician heal thyself" is another axiom I would apply to you, particularly before you should entrust yourself to the caring of others.

I speak this truth out of love, Ishmael.

God be with you,

Lynn

I faced Bill with foreboding.

"I happen to agree with her," he said. "You are not ready to assume the role of pastor. You are not ready to serve a church. The ministry is not like going into medicine, where people want you to cure them of a physical affliction. It's also not like being a lawyer, where you're charged with helping people get what they want or avoid what they don't want. It's a calling in which you are commissioned to prophesize certain eternal truths and stand with people on the precipice facing that eternity. To do that we need to have our own misgivings worked through. I strongly recommend you receive extensive counseling."

"I already have."

"And what were the findings."

"Well, I'm bipolar…"

"Now that's quite a burdensome thing to take into the ministry."

"So how do I get rid of it?"

"I don't know, but I'd give the matter some serious thought before continuing. Is this really the right place for you to be?"

I walked away, seriously shaken by Bill's words. Where was I to go from here?

Reverend Jones had given me a huge downer to carry into the spring semester. Just when I thought I had managed to rise above what the Reverend G. Millard Duncan had considered an inept performance the previous summer, these people had actually questioned my calling. Their assertions thrust me into the throes of depression and uncertainty—misgivings I carried with me as the semester progressed.

My course work continued to be a persistent source of discomfort to me, particularly the course in systematic theology, which my colleagues seemed to eat up. But between the classroom lectures, discussions, and the reading assignments, the wedge of ambiguity and doubt planted by the Reverends Jones and Conklin only drove itself ever deeper into the core of my awareness.

I was again assigned to a unit of field education, and that field education was again comprised of casework for the county alcohol rehab outpatient program, although I enjoyed making the visits and writing the reports far more than I did the class sessions presided over by Stephen Bildeberger. The good professor had this tendency to pontificate, and when it came down to discussions pertaining to my reports, he concentrated squarely upon my lack of theological insights and all-to-apparent absence of pastoral savvy. It was confusing to attempt to balance the positive plaudits I consistently received from Mindy Grover, with Stephen Bildeberger's conviction that I was not fit to minister to a middle class congregation.

As for counseling, I could only go so far within the context of the limited sessions. So many issues and hidden dynamics were present that I could not bring myself to face, especially when it pertained to my dual soul. I was afraid if I shared that aspect of my makeup with anybody I would wind up in a padded room with a jacket that fastened in the back. But I did share with Brian Wilson the possibility that perhaps, thanks to my botched performance at the church in California, I might as well drop out of seminary for a year or so and enroll in a few courses in acting at a conservatory or a community college.

I felt most comfortable while doing clerical work at City Hall where I enjoyed an easy rapport with the office staff and my immediate supervisor was more than happy with my job performance. I knew that I could become a full time employee at that job, complete with benefits and a retirement package. Yet something kept pressing me to attempt to succeed in ministry. After all, if I had wanted to continue in clerical work, I could have continued my employment with the State of California. Something inside me kept pressing me to succeed in ministry and refused to allow me to settle for what was comfortable. No, it was ministerial training that I came here for, and ministerial training I would continue to pursue. So, summoning up all the strength and perseverance the Good Lord chose to give me, I pressed on independently. Normally Professor Wilson would take care of church placement for students. But since, in the past, I had little success going through his office, I resolved to go outside his parameters and apply at every regional office endeavoring to recruit ministerial candidates for summer intern programs. I coupled this effort with applications to places that offered clinical pastoral training. A barrage of rejection letters hit me. Charlie Donohue heard me speak of my long run of rejections and commented as follows: "That's good! A rejection means the Lord's got something even better for you!" which was, unfortunately, of little consolation.

Also, even though I put in as many hours with City Hall as possible, I still found myself running low on funds. In the course of correspondence with my home church, I discovered that my two fellow ministerial candidates, Sol Pickering and Mary McMillan were breezing through their studies with the generous scholastic aid being granted them by both the church and the regional conference. It seemed reasonable to me that my church might deem it feasible to accord me with a like financial arrangement. I submitted my request, only to secure a one-sentence refusal from the chairman of the finance committee. Given their attitudes in the past, I was not surprised.

Near the end of the spring semester, after receiving a bombardment of rejection letters for church and clinical pastoral positions, I received a letter of confirmation granting me acceptance into a summer quarter of Basic Clinical Pastoral Education at a mental health facility in a small town in Texas. I also received an insistent call from my father urging me to come home because of a decline in my mother's health. Since the clinical pastoral education unit was scheduled to start in the middle part of June, I had about a month to tend to family matters, thus having to terminate my secular job earlier than I had anticipated.

It took three days of hard driving to reach home in California. I parked in the street in front of the house, under the shade of the old walnut tree, walked up, and knocked on the door. My dad, his face grayer with dry-looking small lines etched across his forehead, answered. My mother, wearing an old housecoat, her face wan and spectral, was in the kitchen rinsing off the dishes and loading them into the dishwasher. After greeting me, she hobbled to the living room, relying heavily on the walls to keep her balance as she made her way to the brown contour chair just adjacent to the stereo. Her eyes bore the look of death, and her voice trembled as she spoke. She asked me about my trip. Only then, could I see some vestige of the mother I used to know. Even at the peak of

The Call

her despondency, she had always held that maternal glow she had always reserved for me. When I asked her what was wrong, I was horrified to discover that she actually believed that in order to have the joint replacement operation she needed, they would have to chop off her leg.

"I see the Army physicians have explained the procedure to you with their usual high degree of finesse." I said dryly.

Father appeared to be quite traumatized as well, but did his best to keep up the authoritative front he had consistently strived to maintain since my first conscious memory of him. "Ishmael," he said, "this is no time for your sarcastic quips. We have something very important we need to discuss with you and I'm going to say it right now! I want you to seriously consider a career as an Army chaplain." There was firmness in his voice.

I felt like a bombshell had been dropped in my lap. Did he still, after all these years, think he could plan my life for me? I was floored by his audacity, even though I had seen it displayed countless times before. "All right. Consider it considered, and the answer is no."

"Now just hold on a minute!" he said, wheezing, as he lit another cigarette. "There are other things I need to point out to you! Don't ask me how I know, but there is going to be a war starting up in the near future, and I'd rather have you in the military as a chaplain than as a grunt soldier."

"I'm finding this conversation to be absurd. I'm going to bed."

"I know this chaplain down at the Presidio!" he

persisted. "I talked to him about you. Your mother and I have appointments at the Presidio tomorrow and I'd like for you to come along so we can talk to him while we're there. He's a good man and I'm sure he'll convince you that the chaplaincy is the way to go."

"Oh I'll talk to him, as long as you realize that nothing he says is going to change my mind about this." I said, hoping against hope that for once he would understand that my life was my own.

Father abruptly leaned forward in his chair and pointed his finger at me. "That is the most narrow-minded... look, the military chaplaincy is an honorable way to serve both God and your country! And look at your other options! You actually want to spend your time being a minister at a church in some hick town? Or let's say you don't succeed at all! What're you gonna do then? Go back to typing and taking dictation for the rest of your life? That's all you've been doing since you've started seminary. You *need* the Army! The chaplaincy will be good for you! The Army will be good for you! It was good for me! You're my son. It's your legacy, and you'd be damn stupid to deny a legacy."

"Dad," I said, "there's something you should know before insisting upon such a thing. At the very beginning of the program, we were all given a psychological screening. Since that screening I've been diagnosed as being bipolar, having a schizoid personality and a few other psychological afflictions I'd rather not go into. But because I believe in the call I received, I've been just hanging on for dear life trying to get through the program, and I doubt the military wants people who have what I have, based upon what I know of their admission standards"

"Psychological afflictions, my ass!" my father shouted. "Ishmael, there is nothing wrong with you! And the more you think there is, the worse it's gonna be for you! You need to quit listening to these sanctified know-it-alls and get with the program! You need to stop looking at imaginary things and face reality! You need the Army! And the sooner you face that reality, the better off you're gonna be!"

I forced myself to accept the fact that nothing would ever change. This man didn't know the meaning of boundaries. It was, I thought, a wonder that I hadn't suffered more emotional damage than I had.

The next day found the three of us driving toward the Presidio in San Francisco. Mother needed to get more preoperative treatment, while father was undergoing his usual checkup and treatment for his emphysema. I sat in the office while the doctor lectured my father in vain about the folly of continuing to smoke, and listened to my father take change of the session, demanding the medication he thought he needed for his emphysema.

After finishing with the doctor, Father drove me over to the chaplain's office. "What direction do you see yourself heading presently?" the chaplain, one Major Farrell, asked after my father had sketched in my background.

"Well," I said, "in another few weeks I'm scheduled to begin a unit in Basic Clinical Pastoral Education in a psychiatric lockup facility out in the eastern part of Texas. It's located in a small town near Tyler."

"Then what?"

"Then I return to seminary and resume my studies. Hopefully I'll be able to land a student pastorate in one of the neighboring communities. If not, I'll continue my field education requirements through the county alcohol rehabilitation program and support myself with a secular job. Actually, you should know that I just came here to appease my father. The military is really the last place I want to be."

"Well," Major Farrell responded, "if that's the case, then I would strongly advise you not to enter it."

"Whaaat?" My father exclaimed.

"The military's not for everyone, Colonel." Major Farrell replied. "The man of God needs to go where the Lord leads him, and I don't get any inkling of a notion that He is leading your son in the direction of the military."

"I just went through a whole slew of rejection notices trying to attain a summer position, and I really don't appreciate your interference in this matter!" I told my father.

"The Lord has already led him to this place in Texas, and he is not yours anymore," the chaplain supported me by saying. "He belongs to God. That is a reality that needs to be faced and respected."

Father and I left Major Farrell's office shortly afterwards. As we walked back to the car, I could hear Father curse under his breath, "Damn chicken shit chaplain! They're supposed to be recruiters first and foremost!" Then he turned to me and said, "Look, there's this colonel chaplain I'd like for you to talk to!"

"I think we'd better see how Mom's doing," I replied.

The Call

The next few weeks were a bit tense around the house. Father was not able to make connections with the colonel chaplain. The places that offered clinical training in California were filled up and did not pay anything. Father was a man who was used to having his own way, and it rankled him fiercely when he did not. Both Mother and I shared in the tension that mounted by way of his discontent. He was more than adamant about the military being the proper place for me regardless of what the chaplain had had to say.

My time at home was turbulent, since my father's response to being thwarted was to be enraged with anyone or anything that stood in his way. But there were brief intervals of tranquility. And during one of these periods, he told me that he and my mother were proud of me.

"Yep," he said. "We are. You know, despite our increased physical limitations, I'm still able to bowl in a league, and you would not believe some of the people I bowl with and the way they complain about their kids. And you know what I tell them? I say, 'Hey, before you go blaming your kids, take a good look at yourselves,' and then I tell them about you and how you're studying to become a minister."

My pleasure at hearing this was, however, brief since my father's words awakened Isaac who said, as usual, "That's not yours."

I was soon ready to head for Texas. Mother hurried out to meet me by my car. She stumbled a bit as she crossed the lawn. In her arthritically misshapen hand I could see her holding an envelope. "Ishmael," she said calling to me, "there's something I need to talk to you about. After you finish your stint in Texas, how soon before your classes start?"

"In about a week." I responded.

She handed me the envelope. "I was wondering if you could swing by this town in Missouri."

"Does this have anything to do with…?"

"Yes. Your father beat the paternity suit. In fact, they never stood a chance. But I still feel we have a moral obligation and … "

"This puts me in a rather awkward situation, Mom."

"I know. But your father won't address the issue, and I can't. Please try! Please!"

She hugged me goodbye. I started up my Falcon and began my journey to Texas.

East Texas was an enigmatic blend of rain, heat, and humidity. Furthermore, during the summer months it was a veritable nightmare for the allergy sufferer. There must have been seven different varieties of ragweed and numerous other hypersensitivity-inducing specimens guaranteed to activate the plumbing in the region of the nose and the eyes to new levels of congestion motion. It was also a haven for a wide assortment of insect life. It was considered wise not to walk in any place that was not paved: if you did, you ran the risk of being infested with ticks and chiggers.

Much of the east and central Texas terrain was undulating and monocolored, inducing in me a severe case of road hypnosis. I experienced this while traveling the outskirts of Ranger, Texas. I had to get out of the car to shake loose some of the cobwebs. It couldn't have been more than five minutes before three police cars pulled up with the result of detaining me for seven hours on suspicion of being under the influence of some illegal substance. Somehow, I don't believe they bought my story about road hypnosis, because they demanded to do a thorough search of my car before I left town. Of course, when they found out I was a divinity student, I was scrutinized even more harshly. The fact that I had let my hair grow to collar length that summer helped to convince them that I was "one o' them long-haired, dope-smoking, commie-type, pinko fags."

The next day I drove into another small rural town near the city of Tyler, home of the principle state mental health facility. It was here that for the next three months, I would do my clinical pastoral education unit, along with two other colleagues. One was a converted Hindu from New Delhi by the name of Raj Chako, who had gotten his bachelors in Religion, along with his Masters of Divinity at Oral Roberts University and was presently working on his Doctorate in Ministry at Bryte Divinity School. The third chaplain intern, Semitri Narang, who hailed from Bombay, India, was in his first year of the Masters of Divinity program at the local Missionary Baptist seminary.

The facility was a fifty-acre campus structure enclosed by a brick wall with a uniformed guard at the gate. The lower part of the sanatorium grounds housed the majority of the patient population, men and women who strolled about freely on the campus under the influence of varying degrees of medication. These patients were assigned to hospital units such as the behavior modification unit, the vocational rehab unit, the adolescent ward, the alcoholism and substance abuse rehab ward, the mental retardation unit, and the geriatric ward. Situated upon a hill on the outer perimeter of the hospital grounds was the forensic unit, which, we were soon to learn, housed the criminally insane—those who had committed crimes but were judged incompetent to stand trial.

On the first day of our training, Dr. Rafe Pacer, our chaplain supervisor, gathered the three of us into his office and mapped out our agenda.

"During the next twelve weeks I'll be acquainting you with the kinds and degrees of mental illness," he explained. "Here at the clinic, when we treat mental illness, we treat the whole person. We have social workers that take care of the sociological aspects of patient care, regular MDs who keep their physical health in check, psychologists and psychiatrists who keep tabs on their mental health, and vocational rehab specialists."

"A lot of mental illness springs from the spiritual or religious aspects of life," he went on. "In fact, ninety percent of what sends people to places like this are issues pertaining to religion and sex. As you get to know the patients here in this facility, you'll find a number of them who believe they're either Jesus, John the Baptist, Mary Magdalene, or even God Himself. And you'll be surprised at the number of sexual issues these folks have encountered. Now the people we get here at the hospital are not necessarily the sickest, but, for the most part, they are the weakest. You'll find folks outside these hospital walls who are just as much in need of psychiatric treatment as the people who reside within this facility. Perhaps, some even more so. The only difference between those out there and those who reside in here is, those in here do not possess the smarts or the emotional and material wherewithal to sustain themselves on the outside."

He went on to stipulate that on our off hours, he wanted us to look around outside the hospital walls and observe the population of this and of neighboring communities. In doing so, he was willing to wager that we would find only a small margin of difference in sanity levels among the people on the outside and the people on the inside. He further challenged us to look at ourselves and examine our own mental health. He said he could almost guarantee we'd be shocked at what we'd find. Then he encouraged us to allow ourselves a little R&R.

"In a ministry such as this," he went on to state, "you have to master the art of taking short vacations, even if they consist of just taking in a movie, going bowling, shooting a game of pool, or reading a comic book … whatever may relax you and restore your rationality. Remember… and I cannot stress this strongly enough … if you work around insanity long enough you will go insane! And you'll encounter insanity in your churches just as surely as you'll encounter it in an environment such as this. The only difference is it won't be presented to you in so blatant a fashion, and that's what will make its presence even more insidious. So, the important thing is that you recognize insanity and see it for what it is, whether the madness be in a patient, a parishioner, or yourself… and I place particular emphasis on yourself.

You'll be discovering more about this dynamic as we advance in the program, particularly the aspect known as *interpersonal relations*. This will be present in the form of the verbatims you turn in to me by way of interviews and counseling sessions you have with patients on the various wards, the sermons you deliver, and even your communal observations."

"And on that note, I believe we are ready to begin by each of us taking the Minnesota Multiphasic Personality Inventory test." He concluded.

"I've taken this test before." I told him.

"Well," he replied with a shrug, "you'll be taking it again."

Great, I thought. Guess we'll see how the Mellaril has worked.

The three-month hiatus at the psychiatric lockup facility was more harrowing than a roller-coaster ride. I cannot remember any time in my life when I watched so many movies. It didn't matter what the movies were, as long as they provided me with a modicum of escape from the stark reality unfolding before me. The first harsh reality was my test results from the Minnesota Multiphasic Personality Inventory. I always looked upon myself as being a fairly liberal-minded person. The test revealed me to be ultraconservative.

Another disturbing revelation (which would receive an even greater degree of substantiation as time passed), was the fact that I harbored strong passive dependent tendencies—meaning I was an individual who was sadly lacking personal autonomy and was in a constant quest for affirmation and nurturance. That was traumatic for me since people like Hitler suffered from passive dependence.

Next came my observations of the facility population and my examination of the surrounding community. I met several patients who thought they were Jesus. I met a lady who went insane when her husband left her, and a man who stated that upon his release from the facility he was to be ordained as a minister within the Assembly of God denomination, which I later found to be absolutely true. And this was only the beginning.

I ran into a man on the alcoholism ward affiliated with the Church of Christ who told me in all earnestness, point-blank, that I was going to Hell. A homosexual serial killer, judged incompetent to stand trial in the forensics division, fell in love with me. In the geriatrics division, I encountered an eighty-three year old woman who wanted me to sit on her lap, and when, thinking she wanted to lavish some grandmotherly affection on me, I did precisely that when she began to stroke my manhood and make obscene suggestions. But I witnessed the most bizarre behavior in the adolescent ward, where I became familiar with a thirteen-year-old nymphomaniac, a schizophrenic who didn't know whether he was a man or a woman, and perhaps the most tragic case of all, a ten-year-old girl whose father had mutilated her.

Many of my colleagues were unusual, as well. One evening, a man named Ian told me that, although he only had a seventh grade education, he had been ordained as a minister of a Southern Baptist church.

Life within the confines of those three communities lent a lively credence to one of Mark Twain's satirical maxims: "A Southerner will vote dry as long as he can stagger to the polls." That summer all three communities had wet/dry elections. During the period leading up to the election, bumper stickers were flying all over the place with the caption that read, "For the sake of my family, I'll vote dry." Another sign posed the question, "Would you rather have this?" And it showed a picture of a man with two children bouncing on his knees. Above the "Or this?" caption it showed a picture of a man with two booze bottles on his knees. Being a bachelor, my inclination was to go with the latter. But growing discernment on my part dictated that I remain silent on the matter.

Other curious examples of religious neurosis abounded. There were rumors of Bible burnings taking place in various parts of the state. The *Good News For Modern Man*, which many believers deemed as "the Bible that sprang right out of the pit of Hell," was one of the targets for burning. This was supported by the seminarians at the Missionary Baptist seminary where I resided who justified its burning with "solid evidence."

Revivals, which Dr. Pacer likened to forms of "spiritual pep rallies" and a time for certain religious traditions to "return to their roots," were also common. The Missionary Baptist denomination was quite affluent and could afford lavishly built churches supplied with central heating and air-conditioning. However, during the time of these revivals, in keeping with the biblical "tent of meeting" tradition, the use of these buildings was discarded in favor of huge tents that often created a greenhouse effect, as emotions ran wild and enthusiasm peaked, leading to many members of the congregation fainting from heat prostration.

I went to a Missionary Baptist tent of meeting rally

one hot, humid East Texas summer night. Crickets chirped loudly, while lightning bugs buzzed about in the bushes and trees, and the place was packed with worshippers. One girl couldn't have been more than eighteen. extended her arms in the air and, hyperventilating, gasped, "Oh! Oh! Thank you, Jesus!" giving me cause to remember what Dr. Pacer had noted that sex and religion were often closely related when it came to psychotic problems.

The Reverends Chako and Narang were occupied pastoring churches and attending seminary classes, so I was able to preach practically every Sunday during the unit, if not at the facility, then on certain pulpit fill-in tasks at churches in the neighboring communities. Dr. Pacer worked with me on my preaching style, my mode of presentation, and my delivery. I also received the benefit of congregational feedback, particularly during services held at the mental health facility. For instance, one Sunday, as I was delivering my sermon, a black lady stood up amid the patient/worshippers and yelled, "Help him Jesus! Oh Lord, Lord, please help him Jesus!" Dr. Pacer afterwards disclosed to me that in her tradition, that was their way of saying that my preaching really stunk. For this and for my attempts at counseling and interpersonal interaction, Dr. Pacer rendered frequent and in-depth feedback and counsel on matters that he felt needed tending to and refining.

His guidance was less abrasive and direct than was that of the Reverends Jones and Conklin. He often would tell me that my sermons were very well-prepared, but the problem rested with my presentation

"You lack passion and conviction in your delivery," he told me. "If I were part of your parish, I'd probably find it hard to take you seriously. You can't stand at the pulpit and just talk. You have to get up there and preach. And I mean really preach! Put some urgency in your voice, like it was a life and death situation because, for those out there in the congregation, it is life and death, and that message needs to be driven home time and again! That's what's expected! It's kind of like there's a football game going on and you're the lead cheerleader! Enthusiasm! That's the ticket! Emotion is what you need to exude! It's like advertising. Should you use a rational and logical approach or an emotional approach? I can guarantee the emotional approach will win hands down!"

Because of Dr. Pacer, this experience was a real eye opener. There was much to absorb, work on, and take back to the seminary community in the fall. But before I could do that, a certain side-trip needed to be made — to a little town in Missouri.

It was an exhausting sixteen-hour drive to the Missouri town of my destination. The journey left me feeling very drained, and it was too late at night to call on the people in question—Mother called them the Judsons. I checked into one of the motels, watched some TV, and then sunk into a heavy, dreamless sleep.

Next morning, after breakfast, I asked the desk clerk for directions to the street where the Judsons lived.

Upon my arrival, a sixty-year-old lady with grayish brown hair answered the door. "What did you say your name was?" she asked me, and when I told her, she invited me in and called her husband.

The Call 325

"It's someone who calls himself Ishmael O'Donnell. He came with an envelope his mom sent." She said, handing the check to her husband. "Here's a check for three thousand dollars."

"Did you say your name was Ishmael O'Donnell?" her husband demanded. "You wouldn't be any relation to that low life piece of scum that …"

"I'm afraid I am," I told him "He's my father, otherwise known as Lt. Colonel Abe O'Donnell, now retired."

"Let me tell you something, boy … if he were here I'd be takin' the shotgun to him!"

"I understand how you must feel, sir."

"And why's your mother sendin' us this child support?"

"Somebody has to be responsible. I assume she believes there's a moral obligation to be met here."

He threw the check down on the table in a fit of rage. "Does she think a lousy three thousand dollars is gonna make everything right?"

"It's a start." I replied. "How's your daughter?"

"She died less than a year after her son was born from complications brought about by childbirth … and probably a broken heart. I don't know. Her ma and me are doin' our best to raise our grandson, but we're kinda old for parentin'. We get some help from neighbors an' kin but … say, ain't you got nothing to say about what I called yer pa?"

"I said I understood. May I see the child?"

"I guess so." And he walked to the room occupied by the child. "This is Isaac," he said, pointing him out to me.

"Isaac?" I exclaimed. "Why'd she name him Isaac?"

"I dunno. I guess she just figured that's what she wanted to name him," he told me.

I fixed my eyes on the child innocently coloring his book, and instantly heard Isaac's maniacal laughter. My face turned pale as sweat poured profusely from my brow. Hurrying to the kitchen, I splashed cold water on my face.

"Hey, feller," the man said as he stepped into the kitchen, "you startin' to fester or something?"

"I'm fine," I told him, wiping my face with a paper towel.

"You sure don't look it," he said. "You're all pale an' you were sweatin' like a boar hog. Listen. I got nothing against you personally. But the point is you come from the same family as that bastard colonel who did dirty by my daughter, an' I've always been of the notion that bad blood runs in a family."

The laughter grew louder, making it impossible to concentrate on what anyone was saying. "Look," I said, trying to feign a look of composure. "I need to be going. But before I do, let me give you my number. I'll be at this address for at least the next year and a half, and I can't send you much, but maybe I'll be able to help out with a little child support. After that, hopefully more so, I don't know. All I can promise is I'll do what I can."

"So why are you so willing?" He asked.

"Well," I replied, "Isaac is my brother."

On the way back to idle, Isaac's laughter grew so loud that I pulled off the road and shouted, "Go away, Isaac! You're dead, you son of a bitch!" Quiet ensued. It was then that I was certain I needed help.

The third year of seminary got off to its usual start with our annual beginning-of-the-year retreat that had become, for me, a ritual to be endured. I resumed my job at City Hall and engaged in counseling, this time telling the therapist about Isaac and how close to the brink of insanity he was driving me. I also told him about my bipolar condition, coupled with having a schizoid personality, and characteristics that bordered on multiple personalities. I was prescribed antidepressants and mood regulators, along with an antipsychotic drug, meds that took the place of Mellaril, and affected me almost instantaneously with feelings of emotional balance, tranquility, and inner peace.

Brian Wilson again endorsed me as a candidate for the various church positions he had available through the field office, and I was able to attend many interviews as a candidate for level one and level two positions. The only difference was that this time, with a unit of basic Clinical Pastoral Training as part of my background, I was more assertive during the interviews. In fact, a member on one of the hiring committees asked, "Who's interviewing who?" Despite this, I learned later that my assertiveness was well received, even though I ended up as their third choice. In a few other interviews, I came in second. There was one position where I was told, flat out, "We feel God is leading you in another direction than just being a pal to the kids." That was God talk for "we don't want you."

Another great thing that happened to me that fall semester was that, at last, I fell in love. It happened late one evening as I was getting off work. A deluge of rain was pouring down, and I needed to make a stop at the grocery store before heading home. That was when I saw a dog, a dachshund mix, trotting across the parking lot toward the store, seeking shelter from the rain. Instantly I felt drawn to her as if she were a missing part of me. Going into a nearby store, I bought some dry dog food and, coming out, whistled for her. Tail wagging, she got into the car and, after eating the food, which I poured into an old Frisbee, began to shiver until I wrapped her in my father's old army fatigue jacket.

Before she went to sleep that night, I examined her for a collar, but there was no sign of who she might belong to. I placed a notice in the paper the next day before taking her to the vet who issued me a dog license and a vaccination tag

Over the span of the next few weeks, I received a number of calls in response to my ad. None of them matched the description. Meantime, Dog and I grew closer and closer. I took her everywhere with me. We'd frolic nightly in the park, go for drives in the country, and share many a tranquil night together. When I was engrossed in my studies, she would climb on my bed, crawl on top of me, and nudge my hand with her nose as a signal for me to pet her. They say a great cure for high blood pressure is the stroking of an animal's fur. All I can say in response is that she was such a calming influence that a number of people mentioned the change in me. After all, Dog is God spelled backwards—perhaps one of the simplest yet most profound theological truths I had encountered.

Professor Flowers was perhaps the toughest and

most thorough of anyone in the seminary on the subject of the Old Testament. Considering his reputation, many of us held off taking his course until the latter part of our seminary studies. Once in the class, it was usually considered wise for students to form outside study groups, outline the study material, and map out what topical content might be covered on the periodic exams. Ben Parson, Markem McClusky, and I were one such study group. Ben and I had to pretty much carry Markem, and Ben's availability remained questionable: he was heading up the chapel service steering committee that semester, which demanded a good part of his time. Having attended chapel services while in the seminary choir, I had since figured I had my fill and stopped going after I had ceased pursuing the free half-unit credit choir membership offered.

One Thursday morning, the three of us were studying in my apartment for an exam to be given the following Monday. It had been so long since I had attended a chapel service, I had all but forgotten that they were scheduled for every Thursday morning at eleven. At about ten minutes before the hour, Ben and Markem said they had to be going.

"Okay," I replied. "I'll see you guys later."

"Hey!" Ben said, stopping in the doorway and facing me, "What are you doing now?"

"Well," I replied, "this studying has left me pretty drained, so I was planning on taking a nap or maybe spending some quality time with my dog."

"God damn it!" Ben shouted. "You will come and support your chapel!"

"Are we having chapel services now?" I asked.

"Get out here!" Ben shouted. "I work my ass off on that fucking chapel steering committee, and I have to put up with shit heads like you who don't even know when the fucking chapel service is! I swear, it's enough to make me wanna cuss!"

And so, I went with them. Alice Masters offered the invocation, opening prayers, and scriptural readings. Then came the main speaker—the master streaker himself—Elmo Piggins.

"Oh, gross!" I whispered to Ben. "You dragged me here for this?"

"Shut up and listen to the fuckin' sermon!" Ben whispered back.

For the span of a half hour Elmo tore into the congregation with his hellfire and brimstone antics, reminding us all of the fires of Hell and the upcoming Rapture over and over again, admonishing us to "repent for the day of the Lord's judgment is at hand."

"Here's a healthy bit of feedback for you." I told Ben after the service. "If you keep scheduling chapel services like that, you're going to have to reinforce the ruling of mandatory chapel attendance to maintain an audience."

"That was really bad, wasn't it?" He responded. "But you should go, whether the services are bad or not!"

"Why?" I asked him

"Because it's your fuckin' chapel service, it's part of the Perkins's tradition, and tradition needs to be maintained! And that's it in a nutshell!"

Jerry and Linda had reached the final phases of their

research project pertaining to religion and mental health, and Jerry was busy putting it together and arranging for its publication, while Linda was becoming more involved in her studies and the peripheral tasks required of her presence within the seminary.

"Good news!" Jerry announced one day. "I met the other day with a representative of the American Psychiatric Institute and he was impressed by our study, so much that he agreed to recommend that the institute sponsor publication of our completed work! Now, can you beat that? All our efforts have paid off, and success is inevitable! I tell you, this will be the most widely read ethnography since the Lynd's *Middletown!*"

"I don't think we should have that thing published." Linda told him.

"*Thing?*" Jerry shouted. "What do you mean 'thing'? This is our work, our baby, and the reason why we've endured three stinkin' years in this sanctimonious nuthouse! And what do you mean we shouldn't have it published? It's thorough, it's complete, it's well researched, there's not a lie in it …!"

"It's also not very nice."

"Nice? What the hell does 'nice' have to do with it? We both agreed to work on this endeavor for the sake of advancing the cause of mental health and …"

"But not at the risk of tearing at something sacred. You see I've been feeling a sort of pull lately … an awakening of sorts, I believe it's what you might call *a call.*

"And!"

"I've been talking to Professor Wilson, and he's put

me in touch with the denominational conference."

"And …"

"Do I have to spell it out for you? At the end of the school term I'm going to be ordained."

"So where does that leave us?" Jerry demanded.

"Well, I was hoping you'd see the light, too, and convert to Christianity." She told him.

"What!?"

"After having been here for the past three years I would think that surely you've seen a glimmer of light in the teachings we've been exposed to."

"Well, I haven't," he assured her angrily. "Once I'm out of here, I plan to return to psychiatric social work and I expect our work to be published."

"Jerry, I can't allow you to do that."

"Allow me? You presume much! You're the one who got us into this! The compilation of this work was yours at its inception! And as far as I know, I put my very soul in peril just by being here! The work gets published!"

This was, they both knew, a breaking point, one with which they might not be able to deal.

The fall semester of my third year brought with it a number of disheartening events, including the resignation of the undergrad dean because of ill health, and Samuel Church's failure to meet the rigid academic standards, which resulted in his departure from the seminary.

Otherwise activity on the campus went about its usual routine of freshman hazing, the call for campus-wide fasting, fraternity and sorority initiations, seminary coffee klatches, and the marriage announcements. Having seen it all in the past two years I had little desire to live it again. Instead I opted to limit my world to work and classes. My near brush with madness just prior to the fall semester left me more than moderately shaken with a far greater respect for what a powerful force Isaac truly was. At his inception, he was my twin, but at his death, the two of us became inexorably joined. He was me and I was him, yet there remained, in this union, an insidious spirit of separatism based on rivalry. I could only suspect that no medication in the world could hold back his wrath. Yet I continued ingesting my meds, attending my counseling sessions, with the result that I felt more in control of my life. But was I? No, Dog was my real source of peace.

Near the semester's end, I received a call from my father. He wanted me to come home for the holidays. I told him I would if I could bring my dog with me. He refused, admonishing me, accusing me of using my dog for a crutch, insisting that I did not need a crutch. He also brought up the matter of my career as an Army chaplain. I hung up the phone in the midst of his tirade. The phone rang again but I didn't answer There was nothing to be gained by further discussion. It was clearer to me now than ever that my dear father played an integral part in my once tenuous hold on sanity. I also instinctively knew that the laughter of Isaac would be rekindled in Dog's absence were I to visit my folks during the holidays.

I remained in Idle over the holidays and put in solid forty-hour workweeks during the semester break. Dog and I were in each other's company almost constantly. She went with me to the Idle Christmas parade and I was able to sneak her into a Christmas Eve church service.

I found the time spent with Dog to be the most restful, fulfilling, and affirming time I had ever spent in my life. In a world that had been filled with an endless series of harsh demands, unrealistic expectations, and severe conditions, the unconditional acceptance Dog doled out so freely was like a healing balm to injuries that ran deep into my soul.

She was a lot like the dog we had during my childhood; the one I looked to for consistency at a time when everything was in a state of flux. Dog fulfilled these needs, as well, enhancing my new found sense of well-being. But there was something more to this dog than the dog of my childhood—something almost mystical by her nature that I could not readily identify yet could sense by her presence. As we progressed in our time together, I could perceive an enhancement in my comfort, a quieting of my fears, and a growing degree of inner calm. Isaac became only a distant memory, and I inclined myself to let go.

Around the latter part of February, the in-care committees of the regional conferences of certain select denominations started to make their appearances on campus. This year's presence held particular significance for those of us who would soon be completing the Masters of Divinity program and seeking ordination, which, in many instances, would come before graduation, a prospect that held so much promise for me.

These prospects, however, were unmercifully dashed when Dr. Hennessey called me to his office and told me that I should not expect to be ordained. And when, stunned, I asked why, he explained that when Dean Marco had found out about my mental health issues, he

The Call

had forwarded the details surrounding my case, along with a written advisory, to the regional conference. "All that personal data on me was released?" I shouted, jumping to my feet. "That is a breach of privacy! I'll sue!"

"Ishmael," Hennessey replied, holding up his hands defensively, "try to understand. We can't have someone with your case history ministering to people. Ministry is a high stress occupation that calls for stability on the part of its practitioners. We can't have someone who's prone to hearing voices … "

"But I haven't heard any voices in months!!"

"That's good. But Dean Marco's recommendation is that you continue to submit to therapy for at least another four years before … "

"Four years?" I shouted.

"Look," Dr. Hennessey replied, placing his hand on my shoulder, "I know this is a bitter pill for you to swallow. I don't think I'd be taking it so well either if it were me. But this does not preclude you from ordination at a later date."

"Yeah, in another four years, if they let me! What am I suppose to do in the mean time?"

"Look, you've almost finished your course of study. You'll at least have that under your belt. And when you're ready for the ministry, I can assure you, it will be ready for you."

Our conference didn't last too much longer. As I left his office, anger persisted at enveloping me and I could hear, after a reprieve of many months, the muted laughter of Isaac, and through his laughter he continually bolted out the words, "That's not yours! That's not yours! I told you, that's not yours!"

As I exited the seminary building, Dog met me wagging her tail. At that instant my rage dissipated and Isaac's voice disappeared.

During the spring semester I continued my therapy, although I found it hard to persist in doing so and mask the feelings of betrayal I experienced at the hands of Dean Marco. What he had done comprised a clear violation of my confidentiality, and time and again I felt like confronting him on the matter and perhaps threatening him with legal sanctions. Yet, I didn't. Over the past few years I had more than ample opportunities to observe how he functioned. Confronting him, for me, would be like confronting a stone wall. He was the sort of man, solid and condescending, whose judgment was final. I figured I had little chance of going toe-to-toe with him and winning, even if I was in the right. I also knew I didn't have the resources to take any legal measures.

So, as the semester progressed, I watched, with a repressed degree of envy and bitterness, my colleagues, one by one, achieve ordination. Laurie and Sharon were among the first to obtain their calling cards. Ben was next, and to enhance his opportunity, he invited the ordination committee over to his apartment for a soup and sandwich luncheon. It was a gesture he referred to as *greasing the wheel.*

Kathleen, on the other hand, during her ordination interview, became very nervous and tongue-tied. She received a provisional ordination.

I believe it was the meds that kept the bitterness

from festering too much. Isaac needed to be kept at bay. I knew he would spring up in all his jubilant splendor were I not to keep certain emotions under control. Even when I could not hear his laughter, I sensed his presence. But despite this, I took comfort in Dr. Hennessey's opinion that, with therapy, I could hope to one day be ordained. But it was Dog who was my primary source of serenity. The evenings would find me lying on my bed reading my texts with Dog lying beside me insistent upon me continuously stroking her. When I would stop she would vigorously nudge her nose and head under my hand and force me to continue my stroking. So, between Dog and the meds, I felt more peaceful than ever.

One evening, I took Dog with me to pay a visit to a friend in the men's dorm, and overheard some guys exchanging gossip in the lobby.

"Hey," one of them exclaimed, "didja hear what happened with ol' Sam Baker?"

Recognizing the name, my ears perked up.

"No," the other replied. "What happened?"

"Well, after four years of married life he decided to have himself a little extra- marital fling. Sort o' like being tired of filet mignon and deciding to binge at McDonald's. Anyway, his wife kicked him out."

"Really?"

"Yeah. He's livin' at the Y now! Looks like she'll be takin' him for most of his goods."

"The dumb shit."

Realizing that Becky was free again revived so many memories and awakened such a tumult that Isaac arose in his full fury. His malevolent words and laughter thundered in my brain. "THAT'S NOT YOURS! THAT'S NOT YOURS! STAY AWAY! HA HA HA HA HA HA HA HA HA HA HA HA HA HA HA HA HA HA HA HA HA HA! I TOLD YOU BEFORE, IT'S NOT YOURS! HA HA HA HA HA HA HA HA!"

His violent, verbal onslaught made me shriek with terror. Grasping my head, I ran out into the night, followed by Dog. "Ahhhhhhhhhhhhhhhh!" I screamed. "Please go away, Isaac!" I cried, collapsing under a tree in a wooded area three-hundred yards from the campus. Tears of abject agony and terror poured from my eyes while beads of perspiration discharged through every pore of my body. Dog, as though she could hear Isaac's voice, began to growl, whine, and lick my face as I lay on the ground convulsing like someone in the throes of a seizure.

Dog placed her paws upon my shoulders, looked upward, and began to bark and howl. I glanced up at her growling and barking fiercely. She can hear the laughter! I thought. She continued to bark and snarl ferocious growls at my demon twin and I could feel the laughter disperse in my brain. Isaac's taunts were starting to fade into nothingness. I lay there on the ground, still sobbing and hyperventilating as my dog whined and licked my face. He was gone. Isaac had left. I reached to embrace Dog and spoke through my tears, "Dog really is God spelled backwards!" I gave Dog another hug.

For perhaps the first time in my conscious memory I felt clean inside. The purification I had sought since before my arrival in Idle had become a reality. But this sanitization came with a price. I had gained an enhanced awareness of my reality, and that brought with it the realization that everything Isaac told me over the years

The Call

was true—that Becky Sutton, my ministerial quest, what Father had insisted was my legacy, my seminary studies—none of it was truly mine; I had sought them as an usurper, much to brother Isaac's displeasure. When souls merge as did mine and Isaac's, it's inevitable that the one who bears the souls will be the recipient of mixed signals. Now, with Isaac gone, I was free to seek my own providence, whatever that may be. I wasn't sure where it was, but I was certain it was not in Idle. I was not an actor. I could not assume the role of being all things to all people. I remembered a quote from Shakespeare's *Hamlet*, "Above all things to thine own self be true." For myself the truth was painfully evident: Even without interference from Isaac, I was not made to pursue the ministry. As for Becky, she belonged to a different place and time—a time and place when we both felt we belonged together, but we could never have that feeling again. No doubt she would have been Isaac's had he lived. The same held true of my time spent in seminary; it would have been Isaac's, as well. All those years, I thought, and nothing to show for it—years of my life, wasted.

Then I saw Dog, welcoming me with her eyes, and I heard the same voice I had heard years ago by the riverside as I stood ready to take my own life, and this voice said, "Come my child, you've dared to wander, just to see what you could find. And on the way, we found each other, so wasn't the journey worth the time?"

Tears came to my eyes as I extended my arms out to Dog, and she ran to me, leaping into my arms and smothering my face with licks — and my voice rang out with a jubilant, "Yes! Yes! My God, yes!"

EPILOGUE

I had often said that I had not come all this distance to be a secretary. Yet, while in Idle, working for City Hall, I did gain the reputation of office worker extraordinaire. In fact, before tendering my resignation, I was offered a full-time secretarial position and a glowing letter of recommendation from my immediate supervisor. It wasn't exactly the prize I had set out to acquire, but given my surrounding circumstances I decided to settle for whatever I seemed best suited for.

And so it was that, after graduation, still feeling a profound sense of fatigue, I headed back to California to resume my standing in civil service. But life had not dealt me its last blow. During my journey, Dog became ill and was diagnosed as having distemper.

My heart sank in my chest. *God has to die again,* I thought. But can God truly last long on this plane?

After burying her, I read a few words of scripture over her grave, said a prayer on her behalf, and sang a hymn. As I turned from her resting place I recounted how our time together had tallied just over a year, and I wondered how so short an expanse of time could render such a profound impact. Then I remembered an old Buddhist adage about how the soul does not measure time—only growth.

Saying one last good-bye to my erstwhile companion, I got up to leave. It was then I felt slight tremors in the area about me and beheld a thin, translucent haze rise over where Dog was buried. A familiar, gentle voice echoed in my brain as the haze vanished into the sun saying, *I'll always be with you.* At the hearing of these words, I could feel my spirit soar.

Most of my colleagues were granted ordination. Even Markem McClusky, who was unable to meet with the seminary's academic standards, was coaxed along because of his dynamic style of preaching. Everybody who knew him claimed he had an oratorical style that rivaled Billy Sunday, and when you couple that with alligator-wrestling prowess, you got yourself a real firehouse of a witness for the Gospel.

T. J. Whizzer never even aspired to ordination, having flunked out during his first year of seminary. However, he remained with the university's music department until the university closed down during the mid-eighties.

Jerry Cantrell also never aspired to ordination. He just wanted to get his research project published then return to psychiatric social work. Linda, however, did go for ordination and entered the ministry, succumbing to the demands of her new career, thereby allowing Jerry the opportunity to publish the work exclusively under his name. They eventually wound up divorcing and going their separate ways.

As for Reginald Dexter, he assumed the role of Pastor at the Unitarian Church in Norman. His ministry thrived as did his marriage.

Elmo Piggins finished his undergraduate degree in three years and started seminary just after I left. I subsequently heard that his ministry thrived. Ironically enough, his father left the ministry and became a truck driver.

Leonard DeWilde had not yet completed his seminary course work at the time of my departure, but he did attain a full-time engineering position with the City of Idle and was, when I last heard, pastoring a Sunday-only church somewhere in rural Oklahoma. He and Lonnie appeared to be happier than any couple should ever be allowed to be. Rumor had it, upon my departure, that they were expecting their first child sometime in January.

Jack Logan, too, succeeded in his ministry. For a city-bred Californian, he inclined himself to rural ministry like a native. Carla, too, made the adjustment to life in the country and found contentment and camaraderie among the farmers' wives in the area. Rumor had it that she even took to smoking a corncob pipe.

Jason Tyler's ministry was also a success. Being the authoritative and choleric individual that he was, Jason appeared bound to lead in any endeavor of his choosing. Only in this instance, and through his own insistence, it was the Almighty who chose him to lead, and lead he would in whatever fashion the Almighty had ordained.

Finally, there was Norman Decantor, our resident virtuoso performer. All of us figured that because of his resounding vocal prowess, he would most likely find his niche in the music ministry. Yet, perhaps by a divinely sanctioned turn of events, Norman became a missionary. Within a year of his graduation, he found himself somewhere in Africa serving at a mission, working diligently as part of a team effort to translate the Bible into the language of the natives until he and the others were driven out by rebel insurgents. However, despite the danger, he returned to Africa, and was ultimately killed, his body dumped in the river.

Many would say this was the end of Norman's story. But it's also said that the Lord moves in mysterious ways, and in so doing, He does not waste His resources. After being adrift for a few days, Norman's corpse washed up on the shore where an isolated tribe dwelt. It was the custom of this tribe to hear the words of any who washed up on their shores, and unbeknownst to the rebel insurgents who deposited Norman's body in the river, Norman had a copy of a Bible that had been written in the language of the natives wrapped in Biscayne wrap. The natives read that Bible, and shortly thereafter, an entire tribe had converted over to Christianity.

Once back in California, I assumed my place back behind the keyboard. I have acquired many other credentials since then, but providence is still inclined to dictate my presence remain steadfast behind the boundaries of a partition with a computer and a pile of paperwork as my constant companions.

My half-brother Isaac Judson, as he approached manhood, inclined himself almost intuitively toward the legacy my father had so intently insisted on for me. At the age of eighteen, he was granted a congressional appointment to West Point. It was there he attended four years and graduated near the top of his class. Although his association with my father was minimal, he showed up at his funeral flawlessly adorned in his military apparel with shoes shined so immaculately as to blind any onlooker positioned at the angle reflecting the rays of the sun at their most intense incline. As the procession passed by Abe's casket, young Isaac assumed his place in line. When it came his time to view the lifeless husk that once was the proud Colonel Abe O'Donnell, Lieutenant Isaac Judson snapped to attention, squared his shoulders, and rendered a sharp salute. All I could do upon taking in the spectacle was to shake my head in amazement. And for the first time since Dog's exorcism, I could once more hear the muffled laughter of my dual soul. At first a chill took hold of me, but I was quick to counter it with my own inward laughter. That laughter was triggered by my own idiosyncratic realization that God does sporadically intercede in human affairs, but the devil will always be around to mock us.

I lost touch with my fellow seminarians, but there were plenty of examples in the media to remind me of Brian Wilson's contention, that the pulpit is a stage and those who mount it are actors, although not all the "stars" lived up to their so-called promise. Some of religion's stars failed to uphold the image and fulfill the role. Shortly after my return to California, devastating news came from out of South America about a mass suicide staged by way of the urgings of some nefarious preacher who, as I was later to discover, had been ordained by the same denominational convention that considered me categorically unfit for service. I also discovered his credentials to be somewhat lacking as well ... one year of Bible College. It was said that the denomination received ample warnings of what was coming and how psychologically out of sync the man was, yet the denominational heads maintained that they could do nothing about it due to their policy of congregational autonomy.

On a less dramatic note, I discovered that Bill Jones, the minister who accorded me the opportunity to preach at his church that one Sunday during the Christmas break, caught a classic case of midlife, left his wife of twenty years to run off with a woman twenty-five years his junior. The head pastor of my own church was caught carrying on an affair with the church secretary, and a few years later, another one of our pastors publicly confessed that he was addicted to pornography.

Next came the scandals involving two prominent married television evangelists, followed closely by a money-raising tirade promoted by a well-known Tulsa evangelist. And, of course, there was the bisexual sex scandal of a prominent Christian academician. I also heard of a specific civil rights worker who wore the title of "Reverend" shaking down corporations for money and fathering a child out of wedlock. The public met both incidents with a "no big deal" attitude. And presently, I can't even pass by a newsstand without seeing headlines announcing some scandal involving a certain prominent church and their priests' involvement with pedophilia or pederasty.

So, there you have it, the story behind a play, behind the people who are called forth to the stage in the role of performers. The wise recognize the lessons found in secular events that affirm the true nature of a ministerial calling. A few years ago I remember hearing of a man who was hired by the Disneyland theme park to wear the Goofy costume. While wearing the Goofy costume, the man had to do the Goofy walk and perform the Goofy mannerisms until he was out of the public eye. One day a child saw the man remove the Goofy mask and step out of character. The child was devastated by the revelation. The parents, hearing of the incident, filed suit against the Disney Corporation for spoiling their child's fantasy. The parents won the suit and walked away with a tidy sum of money.

People want illusion. It's illusion that aids us in keeping our lives in check, and it certainly keeps us in our place. Heaven help us if we dare step out of character and reveal our true selves. After all, do we really even want to show our true selves? Our true selves might be ugly and sinister. If illusion was to fade, we might find reality to be an immeasurably hollow entity that is vastly incapable of sustaining the human spirit. Or, as my erstwhile colleague Dr. Dexter often times put it, "It's a lot of hot air." Thus, for most of us it's much better if we simply continue to wear the mask and cling tenaciously to the illusion.

So, as I sit here, my fingers flying over the keyboard, I incline myself, at first, to anger. Then I allow that anger to recede as I unite with my dual soul in our maniacal laughter, free of the mask that burdens the actors who shamelessly perform their ongoing playhouse extravaganza.